SEEING I

JONATHAN BLUM AND KATE ORMAN

BBC BOOKS

Published by BBC Worldwide Ltd,
Woodlands, 80 Wood Lane
London W12 0TT

First published 1998
Copyright © Jonathan Blum and Kate Orman 1998
The moral right of the author has been asserted

Original series broadcast on the BBC
Format © BBC 1963
Doctor Who and TARDIS are trademarks of the BBC

ISBN 978-184-990175-8
Imaging by Black Sheep, copyright © BBC 1998

For the ones who make a difference - starting with
Frank Brannigan, Dick Kelly, and Alpha Phi Omega.

Well, that was the whole point of growing up, wasn't it?
To stop wishing and start doing.

Paul Cornell, *Timewyrm: Revelation*

Chapter One
An Ordinary World

First step: find somewhere to sleep.

Sam Jones hurried down the city street, the evening heat sticking to her as she ran.

No – as she *walked*. She was going to *walk* this, no matter how fast she did it, she had to make sure she made each damn *foot* touch the damn *ground* before picking up the next one, because no way was she going to run, no way was she going to lose her grip on the one thing in the world she still had any control over.

She didn't break stride as she squeezed through the pedestrians. The orange sun was almost down, but the day's heat hung in the air, heavy after the air-conditioned spaceport. The streets were filling with people, too many people, and lots of flat cars with big black solar-cell things on their tops, and concrete walls and pavement stalls and street signs she couldn't make any sense of.

There were too many details to really take them in. Even now, her mind was full of burning wires and thin, freezing air and the taste of the Doctor's skin.

First step: find somewhere to sleep. You've got to stop moving. There's no one chasing you, there's no one on the whole planet who even knows or cares who you are, and you've got to find somewhere to sleep now and for ever, because you've run out on the Doctor.

She knew this planet was called Ha'olam, and this city was El Nath or El Neth or something like that. That much she'd been able to pick up from the succession of wallpaper-faced bureaucrats in whose offices she'd been detained. The other evacuees had visas and identity numbers, or could get them by applying to central records. She was about two hundred years too late for any of that.

1

No, they told her, without an I-card number she wasn't eligible for refugee support. No, without her computer record, she couldn't apply for an I-card. No, the Earth embassy had closed years ago, during the war. No, she couldn't use the employment services. Even the dole was right out.

She'd snapped at them and tried to plough through their denials *(it always worked for the Doctor)*, but their responses just grew blander and vaguer. Finally they gave her some directions and escorted her through the door at closing time. She'd wandered out of the spaceport, blinking in the unfamiliar sunlight. They hadn't even locked her up – just tossed her out on to the street. Welcome to Ha'olam.

An alley up ahead, with rubbish piled by the skip at the corner. Without even thinking she headed for the opposite edge of the pavement, to give her that extra second in case someone was hiding back there. Stay relaxed, act as if you belong here. Look up, look fearless, and maybe the fear will go away.

What would the Doctor do?

She didn't know.

There was too much crowding her attention out here, all the rattles and buzzes and smells – people, machinery, garbage, smoke, cooking food – of a new city on a new planet. She didn't want to take it all in, not now. She turned right, away from the traffic, into a side street full of sandblasted stone buildings.

There was no one in sight, which was either a good thing or a bad thing. Now at least she could handle a look around – read the signs on the buildings, lettered in what looked like Hebrew and Arabic and, thank God, English. At least the bureaucrats had got their directions right.

The second building on the other side of the road had a small hanging sign. A stylised sketch of a blue dove holding an olive branch, and the words *SOUP KITCHEN* in six different languages.

She didn't let herself think about it, because she was ravenous.

She hurried across the street and clambered up the steps to the front door. Like all the buildings around here, the place looked worn, as though a passing sandstorm had scraped away the top layer of paint. Maybe it had – for all she knew this place was in the middle of a desert. For all she knew, it was in the middle of a black hole.

The screen door gave her a glimpse of what lay ahead: a crowd of scraggly bearded men and thick-legged women, shuffling about, bowls in their hands.

Beggars can't be choosers, she thought, and went inside.

The volunteer's name was Sara. Her dark hair curled, her voice was breathy, her smile sweet, and she set every single one of Sam's nerves on edge.

'You're an *olah*, I can tell,' said Sara, stirring stuff round in a huge pot. There was an incredibly sincere look in her unblinking brown eyes. 'You haven't even got a tan yet.'

'Yeah,' said Sam, 'I guess I'm an *olah*.'

Sam had volunteered a couple of times for a soup kitchen in London. It hadn't been much different. Though these cookers were a bit more high-tech, and she wasn't sure what some of the vegetables piled on the counter actually *were*.

'Well, welcome to Ha'olam. I'm glad to see you here at the shelter. We can always use another pair of hands,' said Sara brightly. 'You'll like it here – it's hard work, but it always leaves you feeling good.'

Sam could just see Sara driving off to her church meeting, an *I'm saved and you're not* bumper sticker on her car, having done her good work among the unwashed for another week.

God, she thought, I hope I never sounded like that.

Whatever those vegetables were, she wanted one right now, and she didn't care who was running the place.

Bite the bullet. 'Uh, I'm afraid I'm not a volunteer,' stammered Sam. 'I, uh… need a place to stay.'

Sara hesitated. Sam didn't dare let her get out a 'no'. 'Of course I'll work or whatever. I just need to get back on my feet. I didn't mean to come here, to this planet I mean. I was evacuated. I was travelling with someone.'

She scrambled along the metal wall, pulling at the grab-handles,

3

shouting Stop! Go back! We have to go back!

'We were out seeing the universe together, but we got separated.'

We have to go back we've got to go back I'm not leaving him again ...

'That's bad luck,' said Sara. 'Look, I'll have to find out if we have any space left. In the meantime, get yourself washed up, and you can chop that lot for me.' She nodded at the heaps of vegetables.

The best part of getting the dinner ready had been washing up. She'd washed as much of herself as she could without actually taking clothes off, scrubbing her fingernails, even ducking her head under the tap. Sara had laughed and handed her a towel.

Dinner was vast kettles of soup. Sam used a nearly blunt knife to reduce the great mounds of vegetable matter into manageable chunks – marrows, tomatoes, potatoes, aubergines, something blue and tough, something with a yellow skin and stringy clear stuff inside it. Sara added lentils, pepper and bay leaves.

'Normally there are three of us,' Sara said, as she bustled, piling flat circles of bread on to a tray. 'But Ari's downstairs trying to fix one of the toilets, and ChrisBen's got the flu. So I'm glad you showed up.'

'So am I,' said Sam. The smell of the soup was causing odd noises to emanate from her stomach. She wished Sara would wander off for a few minutes so she could cram a chunk of carrot into her mouth.

Sam was surprised when Sara sat down to eat with the rest of them. There were maybe three dozen 'customers' – sick-looking old men and women, skinny young men and women, a cowed-looking woman with two children hanging on to her in terror. Quite a few teenage boys and girls trying to look as though they didn't care where they were. A seventeen-year-old space refugee didn't look out of place.

The 'dining room' was just a big, echoing hall, the walls made out of plasticrete or something. There were a couple of long tables and lots of plastic chairs, most of them broken, a sink at one end. Someone had stuck up some magazine printouts. The pictures clung tenuously to the wall on yellowing bits of tape.

The stew was good – but then, anything would have tasted good by now, thought Sam. She made herself eat at a reasonable pace, one spoonful at a time, tearing off chunks of the flat bread like everyone else and dipping it in.

Sam was used to everyone staring at her. Her jeans and horribly filthy T-shirt were probably about as out of time as a hoop petticoat. The homeless people wore kaftans and loose shirts and skirts, in various states of repair. Sam stared down at the table, hoping they would think she was saying grace.

They. Us.

'Where are you from?' chirped Sara, making Sam jump.

'Um,' she said. 'Earth, originally.' London in the twentieth century, to be precise. 'My friend and I travelled around a lot.' Through time, since you ask. 'How about you?'

'Chalutz, third generation,' said Sara. 'My whole family is Jseda Tech. I'll be an *e-kaatib* myself when I graduate.'

Sam nodded, as though she had some of idea what Sara was talking about.

She looked down in surprise. A very small and mangy cat was circling round her ankle. When it saw it had her attention, it let out a pitiful, monotone miaow.

'Maybe we can help you find your friend,' said Sara.

'I doubt it,' said Sam. 'Thanks though. I don't really want to find him.'

Sara wisely decided not to pry any further. Sam wanted to explain that the Doctor hadn't hurt her or anything, that it was the other way round really: she'd dumped him and run off. But she was too tired to explain about the Kusks and the dreamstone and the TARDIS, and she didn't want Sara to think she was on drugs or out of her head.

The cat miaowed again. She pulled off a bit of the bread and held it under the table. The stray sniffed at it and then grabbed it with its tiny teeth.

Half the people here, thought Sam, are doped to the eyeballs or off their heads. So don't mention travelling with him through time. Don't mention fighting the monsters beside him. Don't mention what happened (what *you* did) with him, don't mention his body lying there as you stumbled away and the taste in your mouth, don't even mention it to yourself ...

Sam jerked awake. She had fallen asleep at the table. Bad move. She looked around, giddily, making sure no one was about to attack her.

But there was no one else in the hall. It had been locked up for the night, after they'd spent over an hour gathering up the plates, washing, wiping, sweeping.

She staggered into the kitchen, where Sara and the guy – um – Ari were talking in quiet voices. 'Heavens, you're about to fall over,' said Ari. 'Time to put you to bed.'

'Is there anywhere for me?' asked Sam faintly.

The two volunteers exchanged glances. 'We'll put you in the corner,' said Ari. 'We can get out that old folding bed.'

Sam tried to help as they dragged a bed out from a dusty cupboard and unfolded it in a corner of the basement. They waved her away, and she sagged against the cinderblock. Just watching them was exhausting her. At least half of the people she'd seen at dinner were there, snoring on cots, covered by rough blankets.

Ari found a blanket for her. There were no sheets or pillow, just a thin mattress. 'I'm full-time staff,' he said quietly. 'I'll be upstairs, just in case, but you shouldn't have any trouble from this lot.'

They left her there in the basement. She pulled off her shoes and socks, considered taking off her jeans, then decided to leave them on, at least tonight.

She wouldn't go to sleep just yet. Just one more thing to do. In the dim light from the open bathroom door, she emptied her pockets out on to the bed. A piece of string. A few odd coins from different worlds; maybe there was a rare-coins dealer who'd pay something for the two-hundred-year-old pennies.

One TARDIS key.

She just stared at that for a while.

A pen. An interesting pebble. One cartoon Mo badge; unless she could find a highly wealthy collector of Alison Bechdel artwork, that probably wasn't going to help her much.

She slipped the TARDIS key on its chain over her head and tucked it under her shirt where no one could see. The metal felt chilly against her skin.

She crawled under the blanket, praying there were no life forms inhabiting the mattress.

Her whole body went like jelly. She could stop moving now. Finally.

She woke up with a start in the middle of the night, flailing around, ready to belt anyone who was hassling her.

But the others were just snoring. She was just a scrawny kid with no money and no drugs, and no one wanted to get themselves thrown out anyway.

She rolled on to her side and stared out at the basement.

First step: find somewhere to sleep.

Second step...

Second step: come up with any kind of idea what the second step was.

What would the Doc –

Sod that. What would Sam Jones do?

She had a horrible suspicion that the answer to that was *curl up in a ball until it all goes away*. But that wasn't the Sam she wanted to hear answer the question. She wanted space-heroine Sam Jones, who stared down the monsters, who was sharp and resourceful and always, always cool. Who had her own series and a range of posable action figures.

Or at least Sam the somewhat experienced galactic traveller, able to muddle through new or nasty situations with a minimal number of bounds. Done it before, should be able to do it now.

Maybe he would rescue her. The Doctor could turn up tomorrow, or six months from now.

They had cut his face his skin was as cold as ice he was not moving there was silence ...

She screwed her eyes shut and tightened her whole body up, trying to squeeze the memory to powder in her brain.

No. He wasn't coming for her. Thank God. He was never going to know what had happened.

Blowing into his mouth pushing on his chest blowing warm air into his cold mouth pinching his nose watching for his chest to rise blowing desperate blowing wake up lips pressed hard against his sandalwood blood frost ozone sweet pressing and pressing wake up goodbye kiss ...

He hadn't died, despite her. He would go on.

She would just have to accept the new situation. Adapt to it, deal with it. She couldn't be the first one who'd had to build a new life after being with the Doctor – hell, she'd already met a bunch of his ex-friends who had gone on fighting for what they'd believed in. No reason she couldn't do it too. She could make herself cope. If she had to damn well change every last thing about herself, she'd do it, and by the end of it she'd have a nice real job and a real place to live and a real *her*.

Sam woke up with a taste like fungus in her mouth and padded across the empty basement to the bathroom to brush her teeth. It took a moment for it to sink in that she didn't have a toothbrush.

She felt the implications of that wash over her, until she finally realised that she'd just been staring blankly at her eyes in the bathroom mirror for far too long. She rinsed her mouth out with water and went upstairs to find Sara.

It was afternoon. The dining room was empty, but she could hear someone talking – to themselves, by the sound of it. The stray cat came up to her and rubbed its head on her leg. She scratched it between the ears.

A talking head was floating against the wall, a computer-generated newsreader spouting stories with an anchorman's sense of gravitas. When she stared for a few moments at the red light behind the three-D, a bunch of holographic menu choices popped up around his head.

This was kind of cool – she tried staring at them, and found that a

8

blink was enough to make a choice. She spent a while fiddling with the anchor's appearance, voice, sense of urgency and story selection, until by the time she finished he was a fifty-year-old black woman reading the news in a perfectly inflected lazy drawl.

One of the stories was about the disaster at Mu Camelopides. There was no mention of a teenage girl being found on the scene, trying not to cry as she was bustled on to the last ship out with all the other evacuees. There was no mention of the Doctor either.

But she knew he'd been there, that was the only time she'd even glimpsed him since the *don't think about it,* since she'd run off from him the first time… At least she knew he was alive, out there somewhere.

The newsreader rambled on as she headed for the kitchen. How many of the other stories was he involved in, behind the scenes?

Maybe that was how her own parents listened to the news. Ears pricking up every time they heard something about UFOs or Bigfoot, wondering if their lost daughter was a part of the story.

They knew she was out there – if the postcards she mailed off any time she was around Earth ever made it to them, and if they believed the one that said 'Greetings from Kapteyn's Star' when it was postmarked from Amsterdam…

Too late now.

She bumped the newsreader back to his default settings and switched him off. It was too bloody easy for him to change – the last thing she needed right now was a piece of software making her feel inferior.

There was no one in the kitchen, but there was a big pile of unwashed dishes. Left over from lunch, presumably. Right, she thought, make yourself useful. Very useful.

Sara found Sam elbow-deep in suds. 'Oh, good on you!' she exclaimed. Her curly hair was sticking out everywhere. 'We've been on the phone all morning and half the afternoon. More funding problems.'

Sam nodded, scrubbing hard at a pan with gunk burnt on to it. 'Who funds you?'

'INC, mostly, as part of their Community Responsibility Programme. Coffee? Wait, have you had lunch?'

Sam shook her head. 'Anything left?'

'There should be... cheese. One very dead-looking Eridanian potatoid. Umm... cheese and hummus sandwich?'

'Sounds wonderful,' said Sam, and meant it.

'You keep washing, I'll make it. INC don't think we're high-profile enough. We're supposed to be a PR exercise, but it's hard to make a homeless shelter look glamorous, if you know what I mean.' She stooped over the counter, spooning hummus on to the bread.

They sat down together in the dining area when the work was done. The cat was batting at a passing bug; Sam ignored both as best she could.

Sara said, 'Look, I had a talk with Ari and with the director – he never comes in – and... anyway, you can stay for a while.'

Sam felt the tension drain out of her shoulders. 'Thanks,' she said. 'You've saved my life.'

'We've caught you before you started with drugs or prostitution,' said Sara. 'I want to keep it that way.' Sam was shaking her head, but Sara said, 'Don't fool yourself. It takes most kids about two weeks of being hungry all the time before... Anyway,' she said, trying to push her hair into shape, 'let's face it, we need someone extra to help with the work.'

'I'll have to get a paying job,' said Sam, in between mouthfuls of sandwich. 'Eventually. How do I look for work?'

'Use the newsreader,' said Sara, surprised. 'Just follow the menus.'

'Oh. Right.' Sam nodded.

Sam started by looking for the kinds of jobs she would have wanted back home. She'd always planned to work for Greenpeace or be the director of a shelter for battered women, or the Prime Minister, something along those lines.

It didn't take long to realise she wasn't going to have much luck there. Most of the jobs in the newsreader's database – scrolling past jerkily as she got the hang of using the eye menus – wanted formal qualifications of some kind or other. And she hadn't even finished –

God, realised Sam suddenly, making the menu jump, I'm a sixth-form dropout.

She was going to have to take whatever work she could get. Well, almost. She drew the line somewhere around 'You want fries with that?'

The causes would have to wait. The Doctor's other companions might have gone on to save planets or whatever – right now, she just had to eat. At least in the meantime she could help with the shelter.

Helping the less fortunate.

Right.

The dream with dark hair ambushed her again that night.

It was the same freeze-frame as always. She saw herself leaning back against the foot of a cheap metal-frame bed, staring back at herself with an expression halfway between a smile and a sneer. Her hair was dark brown to black – the colour she kept having the urge to dye it. Something had kept her from ever trying it.

It wasn't a dream really, because dreams move and this one was just a still image. A single moment that had kept turning up over and over in the jumble of everyday dreams she'd had in the TARDIS.

And, in a weird cubist perception, she was *inside* this other Sam at the same time as she could see her from the outside. She could feel the bed frame against her back, her fast tingling heartbeat, the dryness of her mouth. This her was impossibly distant, and at the same time close enough to make out the frayed hole in her T-shirt, the nicotine stains on her fingers, the odd needle mark.

The room was a bedsit in King's Cross. She never knew how she knew that. It had milk-crate furniture and scuff marks on the wallpaper. It was home, and a home she was happy with, though not one she really cared about that much.

And that was wrong, because home was a nice house in Shoreditch with Mum and Dad. And then home was the TARDIS.

She knew she was still a veggie, still on the Amnesty mailing list, but if she thought about taking time to go on all those marches, then the aah-who-cares-really surged up like a foul taste in her mouth. She tried to think of all the extraordinary things she'd done with the Doctor, and just felt those mocking eyes on her. Her own voice echoing: You can't be for real, can you?

And the words cut, because this other Sam felt more real than she did.

Somehow she knew it. That this was who she should have been, left to her own devices. That getting stuck in a cheap bedsit and a crap job and the tail end of a buzz going sour was where she should be, a million miles away from the TARDIS.

Bollocks to that. This was just another bit of classic teenage insecurity, like that dream she'd had about all her friends just wandering away when she tried to tell them about her life with the Doctor. Just that same feeling like you're not living a real life unless you do the stuff the wild kids do.

She tightened her muscles up and tried to make herself move. She wasn't going to swallow this nightmare. All she needed to do was focus, and push away that Sam's flat and her ciggies and her AM radio, and she could feel the dream disintegrating as she clawed her way out and awake –

– into a bed that wasn't even hers, in the basement of a homeless shelter.

Left to her own devices.

A month later.

Sam was serving breakfast – porridge, as always. She hauled huge steaming kettles of the stuff around, hands protected by grubby oven gloves, and glopped ladles of it into bowls held by a ragged line of the hungry.

She scraped up her own bowl and sat down with the others. Back home she had liked porridge with lots of milk and lots of brown sugar. Here there was sometimes sugar, sometimes milk. This morning there were both, and some reconstituted orange juice besides. Ari had been on the phone again.

She was getting to know the regulars – runaways, alien refugees, corporation drones who'd fallen behind on their rent when the gaps between jobs grew too large.

Pincher, the mad old woman who was nice enough so long as you stayed out of reach, and Cathy, who alternated between the game and the shelter.

Ramadan, her age, with inky eyes and his hair dyed white to look fashionably alien. He was a shifter, he told her, a data thief. He couldn't get work because of his criminal record, so he kept on shifting information here and there, doing a little courier work, looking for a way off the planet.

Yusuf, a grizzled old survivor at sixty-eight going on a hundred, who kept offering her swigs from his ever-present bottle of gin. She kept declining, but still sat with him so he could regale her with tales of his glorious misspent youth, all his adventures. He'd always been a promising child, his mother had told him, and the pride with which he kept revealing this nugget of information over and over made it sound as though he honestly believed he'd start fulfilling that promise any day now.

Two centuries and Christ knew how many light years from home, but this city had something in common with her time, her town. There were still people who the haves really didn't give a damn about.

Tidy up, wash up, dry up, seven mornings a week, two hundred and eighty-seven days a year. Scraping a cold film of porridge from the bottom of the kettles and putting it into a bowl for the mangy cat. A bit of a wash and then off to seek gainful employment.

The locals were mostly olive or dark-skinned, rarely as pale as she was. Or blue-skinned and white-haired; Lacaillans moving gracefully through the crowds. A Caxtarid buzzed by on a bicycle as Sam headed for the bus stop, the man's electric red hair a blinding flash in the morning glare.

The worst part was always trying to get the money for the bus. She went to a different stop every morning. And she told the precise truth.

'Hi, I have to get to a job interview – do you have a transport token you could spare? Thanks anyway. Hi, I have to get to a job interview – do you have a transport token you could spare? Never mind, have a good day! Hi –'

It took her fifteen minutes this morning. Sometimes it had been almost the end of rush hour before some kind or possibly intimidated soul plucked out a token and handed it to her. She always smiled her gratitude. She always felt like complete and total dirt.

The bus landed. Sam climbed aboard, deciding that she'd be walking home this afternoon.

The ornithopter rose slowly from the ground with its load of passengers, giving her a bird's-eye view of the crowd and the bikes, a bunch of market stalls crammed on to one street corner, then the rooftops of El Nath.

A week ago she had got her RAIN. It had taken three weeks for the application to be processed – mostly, explained the polite woman on the phone, because there was no computer record of her, anywhere. But she had it now. Her Resident Alien Identification Number.

That meant she could start applying for real jobs. Now she existed. Without the shelter, she couldn't have done it – she had to have a permanent address to apply.

The first day of the rest of your life, she thought.

The bus let her out a few blocks from the agency. It was an intimidating chunk of stone on one corner, narrow steps leading up to glass doors.

She felt unbelievably grotty in the same shirt, the same pair of jeans. Cleaning them didn't help: they were fraying. Sara had at least loaned her a fairly nice jacket, but that was just a fresh coat of paint slapped on to a house that had almost rotted through.

She managed to look confident right up until a little man in a little office started to hammer her with questions.

'Previous job history?'

'I've, uh, never had a paying job before.' Sam looked around his office. Here she was in space in the future, and people still had offices, desks, computer terminals, clutter, and signs that insisted that you didn't have to be crazy to work here, but it helped. 'I did spend three years organising the school Amnesty chapter...'

'I'm afraid there's not many managerial positions open to eighteen-year-olds,' he said.

Sam smiled her polite smile. Either he was laughing with her, or laughing at her, and either way this couldn't be good.

'I'll take anything,' she said. 'Anything but food service, I mean. I'm a hard worker and I'm eager to do well.'

'Any references?'

She sighed. 'I think they're all dead by now.'

The man nodded sympathetically. 'You arrived with the refugees from Mu Camelopides, didn't you?'

She stared at him. 'How do you know?'

'Your RAIN,' he said. 'It indicates your date of arrival. Well, never mind about references. How many languages do you speak?'

'Just the one.' She could see the wrong-answer shutters falling over his eyes, so she added, 'Little bit of French.' That only made it sound more pathetic.

'No Hebrew, Standard Arabic, Yiddish?'

'No.'

'Azerbaijani, Amharic, or Farsi?'

'No.' Her voice seemed to have shrunk.

'I don't suppose any Reshtke, Argolin, Martian, or any of the Kapteynian languages?'

'Just English,' said Sam. Once I could speak any language in the universe, she thought – and now I'm down to one. 'And a little bit of French.'

The man shifted in his seat. He didn't seem amused any more. 'Can you use an eye terminal?'

When she looked blank, he tapped his stylus on the device attached to his laptop. Sam looked at it. She'd seen them around – a sort of arm with a lens on the end. The operator pulled it down in front of one eye while they worked at the computer. She didn't know what they were for. She shook her head.

'Can you file?'

Sure! 'Sure, I can handle it.'

'Which systems? Parabase? SQFM? Agent indexing?'

'What?'

'Which filing systems?'

'You got me there,' she said, feeling her throat tighten.

'Ever driven a three-two plexer?'

'No.'

He was trying very hard not to sigh. 'Can you type?'

'Yeah, pretty well,' she said, but when the man took her to a machine for her typing test the keyboard wasn't the QWERTY layout she knew from home. She was left hunting and pecking, and shaking like she was going to burst into tears all over the digitpad.

In the end he lowered his eyeset and typed a quick burst of data. Her résumé. To put it mildly, it wasn't very long.

In the blink of an eye it vanished from his screen.

'We'll keep your name on file,' he said.

'They're all the same.'

Sara and Sam were sitting about in the dining hall, the three-D burbling to itself in the background. Sara had her head on the table, and Sam was leaning back in her chair, limbs sprawling.

'The worst ones think it's funny,' Sam told the ceiling. 'Most of them just sort of switch off after the fifteenth thing I can't do. Some of them get impatient. One guy threw me out.'

'I know what you mean,' said Sara muffledly. She clutched a mug of coffee in one hand. 'I spent another morning on the phone, trying to organise some extra food supplies. Everyone's very polite.'

'Very polite,' said Sam. 'They're all wearing the same virtuous, helpful, please-bugger-off smile.'

'You see where I get it from,' sighed Sara.

After each interview Sam had allotted herself an hour to just sit around and do nothing, a space in which to let herself mope about having screwed up yet again. Once she'd got that out of her system, it made it easier to pick herself up and move on to the next round. There were always more possibilities, more notes to tick off on the scraps of paper in her pile.

Sara drained the rest of her coffee and staggered off upstairs. 'I've got to call the rejects shop again,' she mumbled.

'I'll get to the kitchen,' said Sam. 'In a bit.'

The hour of nothing before she tried again kept stretching, longer and longer. And then there were the days when she didn't even try, when she spent her waking hours reading on a borrowed datatablet, or just staring blankly at the three-D, or scrubbing out the kitchen cupboards and counting the linen supplies.

Or not thinking about the Doctor. She spent a lot of time doing that.

Someone was suddenly standing over her. She looked up. 'Ha!' said Ramadan, waving his fist in her face.

She slapped it away and mock-punched him in the solar plexus. He pretended to be blown away, stumbling back across the floor. 'Getting better!' he said.

'No, it isn't,' said Sam. 'It's getting worse and worse.'

'Come on,' said Ramadan. 'I'll teach you how to get out of a hold.'

'I know how to get out of a hold.'

He shot a glance at the three-D that shut it down in an instant. 'Come on, stand up here.'

Sam struggled out of the chair and stood. 'So what's getting worse?' said Ramadan, turning her around so she was facing away from him.

She gave him a dubious look over her shoulder. 'Don't worry,' he purred. 'I don't like girls.'

Sam couldn't help smiling. 'Typical,' she said. 'The good-looking ones are always gay. Or married.'

'Or alien,' grinned Ramadan, not knowing why she flinched. 'Here comes the big bad boy to get you,' he said. He put his arms around her, holding her loosely. 'What are you going to do about it?'

'Stamp on your foot,' said Sam listlessly, 'kick your knee and run my heel down your shin, swing my hips to one side and grab twist pull, reducing your chances of becoming a father even further.'

'I'll show you how to break my fingers, in a minute,' said Ramadan. 'First, turn around.'

Sam spun in his grip, so that she was looking up at him, her head tilted back.

'You went for another job interview, didn't you?' said Ramadan. 'And again they told you, no I-card, no work.'

'It's not that,' said Sam. 'I don't have the skills. I don't even know how to use one of the computers here, for God's sake!'

'Well, have you been practising?'

'Of course I have, I just keep stumbling over those stupid keyboards!'

Ramadan twitched his mouth around in silent sympathy. 'How can you hit me from there?'

'Palm to the jaw,' muttered Sam.

'There must still be places you haven't tried,' said Ramadan.

'Punch to the groin?' she suggested.

'I mean for jobs. I saw that list you and Sara made.'

'It's a list of failures,' said Sam. 'Failures that are waiting to happen. Oh, *that* sounded good.'

Ramadan let go of her. She sank back into the chair. 'You know, I'd even take a job flipping burgers, now.' She grinned woefully. 'My dad and I once had the hugest argument about that. He wanted me to have a job in the school holidays, and I said there was no way I was standing at a cash register. Now I'd do anything.'

'I don't think so,' said Ramadan. He lounged against the wall. 'I could get you a job, if you want.'

'Doing what?'

'Fetch and carry. Maybe a little selling.'

'Are you still peddling components?' said Sam. 'Sara would kill you if she found out.'

Ramadan put a finger to his lips. He reached into his jacket, and pulled out a datatablet.

He put the miniature computer down on the table. Sam swivelled in her chair to look at it. 'It's another one of those bloody keyboards,' she said.

'You need survival skills,' Ramadan said. 'Not just the girly-girl fighting they taught you in school. Standing up, fighting for yourself. Type something.'

'What's that got to do with –'

'Type something.'

Hesitantly, Sam tapped out a few words. They appeared on the miniature screen: 'Ramadna is a yoghurt haed.'

He smirked. 'Now type something else.'

'This is hopeless. I've been trying to teach myself, but I –'

'Go on,' said Ramadan.

Hesitantly, Sam's fingers crawled over the digitpad, looking for the letters: 'Survival skills,' the screen said.

She remembered the time...

She remembered the time he had fallen asleep in the bath. It had been in that harrowing week after he'd escaped from the Tractites. They'd saved the human race etc., etc., so that was all right.

But the aliens had locked the Doctor in a cell, and guarded him night and day, and tried to starve him to death.

When it was all over, when they went back to the TARDIS together, he had eaten a bowl of tomato soup very, very slowly and carefully, and then fallen asleep for twenty-eight straight hours.

She had sat with him for most of it, reading. The bats had hung around, perching on the low bed in the recovery room, or cuddling in her lap. She'd put his ruined clothes into some sort of tumble-drier from Mars, and they'd come out fresh and clean, even repaired. So that was how he did it, she thought.

Eventually she'd had to go to her own bed, taking Jasper the bat with her, leaving his twin Stewart to keep a beady eye on the Doctor from where he hung upside down on the bedstead.

Over the next few days, they had both spent the time recovering from the adventure. He had healed so quickly, the flesh coming back to his face, the new tooth growing, the gleam coming back into his eyes. She had cooked for him, and insisted on bringing him books and music so that he didn't have to get up. By the end of the week, he was almost well again. How long would it have taken for a human to get well? Maybe for ever.

One afternoon, she had knocked carefully on his door, and then put her head around it. His pyjamas were stacked neatly on the end of the bed; Stewart was curled atop them, as though guarding them.

There was a bathroom through a screen door at the end of the recovery room. She heard a couple of splashes, and then the squeak of a rubber duck.

She'd returned a few hours later, bringing some vegetable soup, expecting to find him tucked into the bed. But it was empty. Maybe he'd wandered off. But his PJs were still on the bed.

'Doctor?' she called. No answer. Oh, he was probably just reading in there. He could get totally absorbed in a book, especially if it had pictures.

There was no sound coming from the bathroom. She should just put the meal down on the desk and leave him alone.

Except what about yesterday, when he'd fainted in the console room? He'd sneaked in there in his pyjamas, not quite as recovered as he thought he was.

'Doctor?' she called again. She knocked on the wooden sliding door softly, and then a bit louder. 'Doctor, are you in there?'

Her ears were turning red. But better safe than sorry. She carefully slid back the door and peeked into the bathroom.

It was white, with house plants. There was a huge, old-fashioned bath, waist-high, with little bronze animal legs. The Doctor's hand was draped over the side.

The rest of him, from head to foot, was under the water.

Sam leapt to the tub and grabbed his arm and hauled him up out of the water. It was still warm, sloshing and splashing all over her and all over the floor.

She tilted his head back. His mouth was slightly open, his light-brown hair plastered to his forehead. He wasn't breathing. But he wasn't blue, he wasn't even pale. Oh, God, what was this? What was she supposed to do?

She pressed her fingers to his throat, moving them around... down... there was a pulse above his collarbone. Two pulses, beating steadily, slowly.

He took a breath. She started so badly that she nearly dropped him. But he was just breathing again, quite normally, as though he'd never stopped. She pushed his hair out of his eyes, instinctively, and the touch was enough to wake him up.

He blinked at her, took in his surroundings. 'Look,' he said. 'My toes are all wrinkled.'

Sam didn't look. 'I thought you'd drowned,' she said. She was still gripping him firmly.

'Oh, Sam,' he said, leaning his head on her arm. His eyes were looking right into hers. 'I am sorry. I just fell asleep.'

There was an awful moment when they didn't kiss.

Instead she got him his bathrobe, and they ended up playing Chinese chequers, and he explained about his respiratory bypass system and she joked about his having gills.

Four a.m., thought Sam blearily. She could hear the refuse collectors at work outside the shelter.

She had kissed the Doctor, once. If you could call it that. What started off as the kiss of life had turned into something very different. How *could* she have... She'd run away. And when he came looking for her she ran away from him *again*.

The cat jumped up on the bed. It nuzzled up to her, purring like a car whose muffler has just fallen off. She ran a hand over its head, felt the thin fur and the moth-eaten ears, and felt a surge of gratitude that she wasn't alone.

Oh, God. This old rag of a cat was all she had. There was no one else in the whole world. Talk about hitting bottom. It was enough to make a girl have a bit of a blub, actually.

Of course, she hadn't hit bottom. There were all sorts of depths out there just waiting for her to sink to. She hadn't started selling stolen components, or her body, or joining Yusuf in his bottle of gin. Just think, she had all that to look forward to.

Just think, she thought as she wept into the yellowed pillow, just think of the thousand pieces of luck that had given her all those opportunities. Cosy middle-class London life. Travelling the entire universe with the Doctor.

And with all those opportunities she'd brought herself here.

Such a bloody promising child.

Wash, cook porridge, eat, wash up, wipe tables. Pile of papers under bed. Phone calls. Cook lunch, eat, wash up, wipe tables. Beg for bus token. Job interview. No luck. Cook dinner, eat, wash up, wipe tables. Typing lessons from Ramadan. Watch three-D. Look through job ads. Sleep.

The call from INC's employment office barely disturbed the surface of her mind.

The woman on the other end of the phone wore a big smile and kept addressing her by name, as though not sure the blank-faced teenager on the other end of the line was the right person. Phrases like 'data entry' and 'on-the-job training' and 'entry-level opportunity' washed over Sam, leaving only the slightest of impressions.

Sam nodded and said politely enthusiastic words, and all her mind did was translate the concept of *job* into *find flat* and *food budget* and a thousand other things to add to her scribbled list of Things to Do.

Ramadan's typing lessons had got her the job. But Ramadan wasn't around any more these days. She didn't know where he'd gone.

Distantly she wondered why Ari and Sara congratulated her so much when she said she was moving out, why they treated her to dinner as if she'd actually accomplished something.

INC had even found her a flat and potential flatmate in their employee database, a G-4-rated I-clerk named Shoshana Rubenstein who was looking for new digs. She could move in the very next day.

The next morning Sara sniffled a bit and hugged her, ChrisBen patted her on the back, and Ari shook her hand and gave her a present: a whole bag of bus tokens, just to tide her over. Sam said thanks and handed Sara back her jacket, all with a strange, quiet calm, and smiled and said goodbye and walked away.

That was all behind her; this was who she was now.

Thank God for the shelter. She'd never have survived this far without it.

She prayed that she'd never have to see that cat again.

Chapter Two
I Seek Her Here, I Seek Her There

The network was minding its own business when someone upended a bucketload of data-umphs into it.

Across the galaxy, twenty-four hours a day, sharp-eyed corporate security programs watched for the tiniest infraction, scrutinising every furtive movement as the possible footfall of a virus.

As a result, when 6.02×10^{23} programs simultaneously barged into their dataspace, the deluge of suspicious data completely overwhelmed their ability to analyse it. It took them whole microseconds to react.

By then it was too late: the umphs were barrelling through the datascape like lemmings on a land rush. They scampered through system after system, poking through any scrap of data that caught their eye, leaving access records strewn higgledy-piggledy in their wake. The ports were alive with the chatter of an endless stream of queries, *hello hello hello hello hello*, as they dug through personnel records, client lists, phone books, any collection of names they stumbled across.

The security vultures struck fast and hard, but the umphs moved faster, free of the need to think about what they were doing. They paused at each gateway to sniff out new passwords from the datastream, then stampeded on through, until there wasn't a corporate system in human space that was free of the patter of far too many tiny feet.

As they ran about they budded off subprocesses hither and yon. As they budded they mutated, with new subroutines turning up from nowhere. Imogen found itself afflicted with a particularly odd strain of umph which spray-painted KILROY WOZ 'ERE graphics all over its annual report. Kisumu Interplanetary's intranet collapsed as several thousand umphs engaged its computer power in playing eight-dimensional Tetris.

But most of them just kept on moving at random – looking for anything that matched the search patterns coded into what passed for their brains.

One particular umph went snuffling through the INC data warehouse, giving each object in the repository an inquisitive nudge – *sam? sam? sam? you sam? you sam? hello? hello?* The great grey lumps of data remained inert no matter how it poked them. Anything with the slightest hint of intelligence would have begun to despair.

Then suddenly it jumped, as dormant branches of its logic sprang into action. One of the databases had nudged back when pushed – it had a match! But before it could transmit the record itself back to its creator a security vulture isolated its process, caught it in its beak with an interrupt, and ground it to bits.

Eventually the umphs reached the limit of their programmed imagination. When they couldn't find any new data to rummage through, they grew bored. So then they just milled about in memory, sending out dispirited little *no sam no sam*s to one another, until the vulture apps regrouped and located them.

Then the vultures did highly technical things to the umphs' code, which defied the human ability to wrap in an anthropomorphic metaphor.

With the access records covered in quadrillions of tiny footprints, it took TLA's bloodhound apps an unprecedented amount of time to discover that their umphs had invaded from Gray Corp's system, and even longer to persuade Gray Corp's bloodhounds to share intelligence about where the umphs had invaded their system from.

When all the systems pooled their data, they found that the node that had been the source of the infestation had vanished from the datascape. The dissected bits of dead umph code were of no help: all they seemed to contain were a name, a few vital statistics for matching purposes, and no clue why their creator would be interested in a Samantha Angeline Jones.

It was the most bewildering 4.8 seconds in the net's collective memory.

Back in the real world, the Doctor leaned back in his armchair, closed his eyes and let out a sigh of sympathy for all those lost in the Great Umph Massacre of 2202.

He picked up his cup of tea from next to the terminal, sitting back in the armchair. He'd set up a card table in the console room, a series of cables meandering out through the front door and into a university computer. It was the middle of the night, he was sure no one would mind.

He'd had to imagine the whole battle; his terminal (part neural relay processor, part steam engine and part Apple II) had a text-only display. But he'd stared at the rippling lines of reported data on his screen and seen instead the whole stampede - the waves of movement and multiplication, the mortal combat in code.

It had been such a joy for him to create the umphs - writing the kernel, teaching their routines to talk among themselves and their code to recombine - and watch them rewrite their own bodies into something more complex and unpredictable than he could ever have imagined on his own.

Oh, they were alive, he was sure of it. Not particularly bright, mind you, but then your average vole wouldn't pass the Turing test either. Insisting that they were nothing but electrical signals or lines of machine code was like describing a human being as a collection of quarks.

He unfolded himself from the chair in front of the terminal and hurried towards the TARDIS console, ideas fluttering around in his head like a swarm of butterflies.

Lots of questions I'll have to ask, he thought: they won't be forthcoming about how they know her. That interrupted squeak from within the INC data caverns is the closest thing I've had to a lead. I know she was there on the Kusk ship, I know she was on Mu Camelopides - but then where did she go? I really should have cleaned up some of the umphs' communication code – perhaps then I could have heard the full report... Good heavens, that chair needs reupholstering.

The console. Readouts normal, needs a good dusting though. How many umphs would it take to change a light bulb? Set co-ordinates. Ha'olam. Ask questions. INC. Ha'olam. Sam waiting. Find her. Ha'olam.

All his disparate lines of thought converged on one point. In the closest he ever came to thinking with a single mind, he set his TARDIS in motion towards Sam.

The receptionist at Incopolis HQ had been doing her job for ten years. In that time, she had honed her skills to the point where she could tell at a glance which category people fell into.

The moment a face appeared at her desk, or on the videophone on her datatablet, she had them pegged. Category 1 was the rarest: customers with an important financial relationship with INC, INC VIPs, the occasional politician of note. Category 2 was simply everyone else, and it was her job to fend them off.

The man standing in front of her desk right now was definitely a Category 2.

For a moment, she had thought he might be someone important; only someone important could get away with such eccentric dress. A long coat, a high collar with some sort of soft scarf, everything made out of suspiciously natural-looking fibres. No sign of any flashes to denote corporate affiliation or rank. His light-brown hair was collar-length. She guessed at once that he was an off-worlder.

She should be able to get rid of him within five minutes. Two, if she was on form.

'How may I help you?' she lilted.

'I'm looking for a friend of mine,' he said. 'I think she works for INC, and I was wondering if you could put her in touch with me.'

'May I see your I-card, sir?'

'Ah.' He made a show of rummaging through the pockets in his coat, then his trousers, then his waistcoat. 'I'm afraid I don't have one.'

'I'll need your I-card to handle your inquiry, sir,' she told him.

'I mean, I don't have an I-card at all,' he said.

Her radiant smile almost slipped. This one was going to be exceptionally easy to get rid of. 'Have you lost it, sir?'

'Never had one,' he admitted. 'But if I could just leave a message for my friend –'

'You'll need to apply for an I-card, sir. The Central Department of Registration is three blocks east of here. Good day.'

He blinked at her. 'Can't you just take a message?'

'I'll need your I-card to process the inquiry, sir,' she said brightly. It would sink in if she kept repeating it, she knew.

'All right,' he said, 'I'll go and get an I-card, if it'll make you happy.' He gave her a cheery wave as he went back out the revolving doors. 'Back in a tick!' he called.

The receptionist couldn't help smiling. If the CDR were up to their usual standard of efficiency, it was unlikely she'd see him again.

The Doctor strolled down the street in the vague direction of the Central Department of Registration until he found a public datatablet.

This part of the city of Incopolis was a neat grid of streets, crammed with two-storey buildings of almost identical design, as though they'd all been assembled from the same Lego kit. He'd landed further out and walked through the more haphazard roads and buildings of an improvised suburb on his way to INC's headquarters.

The city reminded him of Cairo, or perhaps Jerusalem. In the twenty-first century, Middle Eastern countries had turned to high technology and space industries as the oil began to run out. The results were numerous colony worlds like this one, with an easy mixture of cultures and languages, the ancient and the modern.

It was baking hot this afternoon. The sun loomed, a yellow-white disc in a pure blue sky, shading into desert dust closer to the horizon. The Doctor undid his cravat.

The public datatablet was housed in a sort of phone booth, a half-sphere attached to the side of a building, the INC logo etched into the plastic. You'd think they owned everything on the planet, but they were only the largest of a dozen corporations who'd set up shop on Ha'olam. It was only Incopolis that had sprung up around their headquarters buildings. He slipped inside, glanced around – no one was paying him any attention – and took his sonic screwdriver out of his sleeve.

Thirty seconds later he was rearranging components with a delicate touch. He took a data-transfer module from his pocket, easing it into place and holding it there with a bit of wire and a clothes peg. A moment later, a lone data-umph launched itself into the datatablet, wibbled about for a bit and then zapped itself across the network into the main database of the Central Department of Registration.

After that, it was all details. He added a new number and file, backdated the file a couple of years and put in a request for a replacement I-card. A lean woman on a bicycle delivered it to him fifteen minutes later as he sat outside a café, drinking rosewater. The ice cube had the INC logo moulded into it.

He finished his coffee, paid for it with the I-card and went back to the public datatablet, removing the OUT OF ORDER sign he had taped to the digitpad.

The receptionist answered his call. 'INC Central Incopolis, may I help you?' She did a double take when she saw him smiling at her, staring out of the screen with her oddly mismatched eyes.

'I've obtained an I-card,' he said, waving the fresh bit of plastic at her.

'I'm afraid I'm unable to assist you over the phone, sir,' she said.

The receptionist stared down at Bowman James Alistair 481/9-85/0-X75/54. She was itching to ask how he'd got the card so quickly. Probably he had just been embarrassed about leaving it in his 'thopter.

Her desk was raised above the marble-like floor by almost half a metre. Bowman was obliged to stand on tiptoes as he leaned on her desk, craning his neck as he tried to see her datatablet screen.

'Her name is Samantha Jones,' he said. 'Sam for short. She's wiry, with close-cropped blonde hair. She has an engaging smile.'

The woman looked at her terminal, hands hovering over the digitpad, her eyes moving rapidly, like a dreamer. After a moment she said, 'What is her I-card number?'

'She hasn't got one either,' he said, and instantly clapped his hand over his mouth.

'She's not a citizen?' The Doctor shook his head. 'We don't hire blanks,' concluded the receptionist.

'But I'm certain she's an INC employee.' Actually, I'm not sure, but there just aren't that many things she could be doing in your computers. 'Couldn't she have applied for one, or something?'

The receptionist said, 'If she was employed, and had no I-card number, then she would have been assigned an INC interim identity number.'

'Ah,' said the Doctor. 'Well, see if you have one for her.'

'I can't release her INCIIN,' said the receptionist.

'You don't have to tell it to me,' said the Doctor. 'Just look it up.'

'Of course, sir,' she said with a smile. 'First I'll need a few details.'

'Oh yes?' said the Doctor warily.

'You'll need to present her Resident Alien Identification Number, which she would have been assigned by the Department of Immigration and Naturalisation, Departure/Arrival Department, upon arriving sans visa.'

'RAIN from the DIN DAD,' said the Doctor. 'Two bits.'

The local office of the DIN was in one of the suburbs. The Doctor rented a bicycle from a group of bored-looking teenage boys, and pedalled out of the Central Business Ditrict and up the gentle slope of a hillside.

He went past the Department twice without realising. It was a tiny prefab building with peeling paint, perched almost at the top of the hill among a cluster of other offices and dwellings.

He paused outside, looking back down the rocky slope. Seen from above, Incopolis was a tidy knot of corporate buildings, surrounded by a ragtag collection of government buildings and houses – mostly prefabs and colony huts, though towards the edges of the town they were built from whatever people could get their hands on. He could see a rubbish dump to the east, tiny figures moving over it.

This young world already knew poverty, and INC – whatever their business was – had brought bureaucracy with them. But there was no war, no monsters. Sam would be safe here. He only needed to find her.

'Certainly, sir. It will only take a moment. Why don't you have a seat?'

The Doctor smiled at the bespectacled man behind the desk and sat down in one of the plastic chairs. The Department was a handful of desks, a scattering of terminals, a children's play area.

'I-card numbers are public information,' explained the civil servant, while tapping at his digitpad. 'They're your comm ident, for instance.'

'You know, that's what I thought,' said the Doctor. 'But I checked with comm directories, and she's not in the phone book.'

The man nodded to himself. 'INC do, in fact, hire blanks,' he said. 'Technically it's illegal, so many newcomers with no other way to get work go to them. The INC interim identity number is just the same as an I-card number. In any case, a RAIN is a temporary identity number, also a matter of public record. Here we are!'

A hard copy scrolled from the man's datatablet. 'Your friend arrived here less than a month ago,' he said, peering at the paper.

'Thank you,' said the Doctor. He pocketed the printout. 'If she did go to work for INC, what sort of job are they likely to have given her?'

'Well, you see, if she was a blank, I'm afraid they don't have to pay her minimum wage or provide benefits. They use blanks for construction work, sometimes, and I think most of their low-level clerical staff were originally blanks.'

The Doctor nodded to himself. 'You know, they're going to quite a bit of trouble to hide a typist from me...'

The man smiled, not unkindly. 'Never put down to conspiracy what you can blame on incompetence,' he said.

The Doctor hoped he was right.

'Hello again!' the Doctor said to the screen. The receptionist smiled out at him. 'I just wanted to check on the progress of my inquiry. I sent it yesterday in electronic mail.'

'What was your reference number, sir?'

He fumbled in his pockets until he found the reference number, scribbled on the back of a box of gobstoppers. He rattled off the string of digits.

'I'm afraid we were unable to accept your inquiry, sir,' said the receptionist, after a moment.

'Why?' said the Doctor incredulously.

'Requests for INCIINs must be sent by registered electronic mail to ensure delivery, sir.'

'Wait a moment,' said the Doctor. 'Did you receive the e-mail?'

'Yes, sir, but it's not –'

'But if you received it, then it doesn't matter how it was sent, does it?'

The receptionist spoke slowly. 'Requests for INCIINs must be sent by registered electronic mail to ensure delivery, sir.'

'Hello again,' said the Doctor to the receptionist. He was holding four volumes of the *Encyclopaedia Britannica*, brought from the TARDIS. 'I've come to inquire about the progress of my inquiry.'

'What was your reference number, sir?'

The Doctor put the books down on the floor, and plucked the box of sweets out of his pocket. 'Here we are.' He reached up and put it on the desk, where she could read the long string of digits scribbled on the side.

She stared at the datatablet, her hands not moving. He realised suddenly that she was reading some sort of heads-up display.

'Your inquiry is in progress,' she told him, after a moment.

'It's been in progress for a week,' he said. 'I even sent it by registered e-mail. How long can it take to look someone up on your computer?'

'We'll contact you when we have a result,' said the receptionist. She looked at him in some alarm as he hopped up on to the pile of books and stared into her face.

'There seems to be something in your eye...'

'Yes,' she said, startled. 'Of course.'

'What is it?' he said. It looked like a contact lens, but was covered in tiny blue patterns. It reminded him of something.

'It's my implant, sir,' she said. 'My interface with IXNet. What are you doing?'

The Doctor was leaning over the desk, trying to see behind her. 'Just wondering where they plug you into the mains...'

'If you don't get down from there,' said the receptionist, 'I'm going to have to call for a Customer Liaison Squad.'

'Oh, look,' said the Doctor. 'It's my inquiry.' He had started rummaging through her in-tray, producing a printout of his registered e-mail. 'Do you think you could just pop into that database and have a look for me while I'm here?'

'No, I do not,' she said. 'I can't make an exception for you just because you're –'

'– standing right in front of you?' he finished.

Two days later, the form was still in her in-tray.

'There's something I've been meaning to ask you,' the Doctor said. 'What does INC do?'

'We're a diversified organisation,' said the receptionist.

'Yes, but what does INC do?'

Not a lot, apparently, because the form was still there another two days later.

'The form is still in your in-tray,' said the Doctor. 'It has been there for a week.'

'I told you –'

'I have tried everything else I can think of to find Sam,' he said. 'I have looked at police records and hospital records. I have badgered spaceport officials with her photograph. I have even wandered the streets of this planet's towns in the hope of simply bumping into her.'

'Sir –'

The receptionist stared at him with her mismatched eyes. He leaned towards her and said conspiratorially, 'I time-travel, you know, and that form is still sitting on your desk fifteen years from now!'

'You're not –'

'I have, at long last, had enough. I have given you files, folders, records, receipts and enough data on Sam for you to write her unauthorised biography. And here –' he leaned right over her desk, and typed rapidly on her digitpad. The screen lit up: 1234567890. 'Here are all the numbers I have in my possession. Feel free to arrange them in whatever way you see fit in order to make them into the authorisation numbers you so desperately desire. And then I want you to look me in the eye and tell me where on this planet Samantha Jones is.'

The receptionist fled.

The Doctor watched her go. He was abruptly alone in the air-conditioned foyer.

He went behind the desk and sat down at her chair, taking the umph-in-a-box data-transfer module from his pocket. Jacking it into the datatablet's slot was no problem. But within a fraction of a second of entering the system, every single umph was scrinched into a crun by something very big and vigilant. He gave a silent word of thanks for the fact that he was looking for his data out here, rather than in there with whatever that was.

The datatablet was a smooth, hinged slab of plastic, a touch-sensitive digitpad that combined Roman, Hebrew and Arabic characters in an apparently eccentric sequence, and a neutral-grey holographic display area. He tried typing some instructions, but the machine was indifferent. He frowned. Without one of those eye interface things, it might not be possible to break in.

Someone cleared their throat. 'Don't worry,' he muttered. 'I'm not going to break your terminal. Just taking a peek.'

When he glanced up, it was an enormous security guard, the INC logo a bright flash on his blue uniform.

* * *

'Are you OK, mister?' said the girl on the bicycle.

The Doctor picked himself up and dusted himself off. 'Oh yes, I'm fine. Only my ego is bruised.'

She shrugged and pedalled off, as though people being forcibly ejected from the INC building was part of her usual landscape.

The Doctor looked up at the INC monolith and let out a slow breath. 'Of course, you realise this means war.'

Chapter Three
Eye Robot

Sam blinked once. Twice. Look left, blink, look down, focus on the last item, blink, blink for confirmation. Call up another record with the digitpad. Stare at the text of the customer responses, slot their rambling words into neat little categories, then blink them into the results record and forward the data package to corporate HQ in Incopolis. Let the folks on the other side of the planet figure out what any of it was good for.

She let her eye focus beyond the floating icons, on the neutral taupe fabric of her cubicle wall. She really should get some posters or something to liven the place up – even if she could see them only out of the corners of her eyes, around the optic projector of her headset.

Nine hours of this today. It was amazing how the time could go so quickly and so slowly at the same time. Four green-grey walls, a digital clock, and the endless list of responses she got from somewhere to send on to somewhere else. It was market research. Or something.

Nine hours. Dimly she realised that was it, she could go home now. A little more eye-rolling shut down her system, and she took off her eyeset, pushing aside the optic projector which crouched inches from her left eye, dropping it on the digitpad. Her body started carrying her out of the cubicle before her brain even began to get out of its fugue.

She walked between the rows of grunt *e-kaatib* cubicles, stretching off into the distance like a little world of grey squares. People were here around the clock, muttering and blinking, making decisions it was either too hard or too expensive for even this century's computers to make. Or maybe the computers just thought it was all beneath their dignity.

She'd put in her extra hour and a bit today – another two weeks' worth of overtime and she'd have enough spare cash to buy new shoes.

The next office along, another Cubicleland, grey-blue this time. Here in Accounting the blinkers didn't even have a digitpad to break the monotony – they spent their days sitting in their comfy chairs, barely moving. Except for their eyes. Paying bills with their eyes, staring after missing money, writing blink cheques.

She had been working here for a while before she'd noticed the camereyes, little spheres lurking in the corners of the rooms. One rolled in its socket to follow her as she made her way through Acquisitions.

She rounded the corner and entered the home stretch – into the foyer, out through those glorious double doors into the street.

The noise was sudden, bracing: traffic on the ground and in the air, music, human voices. The air was warm, rich with the smell of dust and cooking.

Behind her the INC building was stylishly skeletal, its façade carved in triangles to suggest the prefab geodesic domes that must have been the colony's first structures. It was elegant, it was clinical, it was where she spent even more of her waking hours than she spent at home.

She realised she'd just gone through another entire day without talking to anyone.

She took a bus home, leaning on the window. Most of the other people aboard were corporate drones of one kind or another, lapel pins announcing their affiliation. TLA with its yellow flash, KI with its blue circle. She fingered the pin on her own grey jacket. An eyeball, a wave in a circle. Eye 'n' sea.

They stopped at the lights, and she watched a couple of old men hovering hopefully outside a café. She was lucky, really. She'd be promoted eventually, she had somewhere to live. She had some hope now.

Shoshana was already home, her head buried in another trashy romance novel on her dynabook tablet. She waved at Sam without looking up. 'Your turn to do the washing up,' she said. 'Dinner in the fridge.'

'Thanks ... *toda*,' Sam said.

She plodded into the kitchen, stood still, and listened. After a moment, over the sound of Shoshana's novel, she made out the sound of wrenching sobs. Just what she needed, the Crying Woman was at it again.

Sam fumbled in the fridge for a cube of lentils. They were always hearing the Crying Woman through the walls, as she either screeched at someone in a foreign – alien? – language or let loose a fire-engine-like blast of rising and falling howls.

Sam pushed the cube into the cooker and leaned on the counter, wondering what it was that kept flooding that woman with such unending, unpredictable grief.

When she got back into the living room, Shoshana had shut off the novel and was looking cheerful. Sam plonked down into an EZChair and pulled the lid off her cube, careful of the steam.

The flat was small, but it was clean and reasonably tidy. There were no books – none made of paper, anyway – no three-D or stereo: just a couple of datatablets. Shoshana was always saying that she'd buy an entertainment console, one of those little knobby ones that dispensed ambient sound and ambient scent, but they still cost a fortune.

Shoshana was slim, with short, curly, dark hair and olive skin. 'How was your day?' she said brightly, as Sam started forking the lentil stew.

'Same old same old,' said Sam. 'You look happy about something.'

'Some good news for me,' said Shoshana. 'The promotion. I've got it!'

'That's good,' said Sam, stirring her dinner around. Then she smiled. 'No, that's really marvellous. Well done.'

'Starting on Monday, I'm going to be a junior clerk, first rank,' said Shoshana. 'Less hours, more money. Yes!'

'Are you moving out?' said Sam suddenly, the fork halfway to her mouth.

'Not yet!' said Shoshana. 'Don't be in such a hurry to get rid of me.'

'I'm not, believe me,' said Sam. 'I just thought –'

'I won't be making enough to get a place of my own. Not at first. Cheer up! I've just got a couple of years' head start on you. You'll be applying for the next rung on the ladder soon enough.'

'I don't think so,' said Sam.

'You can't stay an *e-kaatib* all your life,' said Shoshana.

Sam shrugged. 'I'm a blank. That's why they hired me.'

'Can't you just apply for an I-card number? After you've been here for a while, I mean?'

'After ten years, yeah,' said Sam. 'Look, you've had some really good news and I'm just being self-pitying.' She grinned ruefully. 'I'd buy you a drink to celebrate, if I had the dosh.'

'I'd buy you a drink,' said Shoshana, 'if you weren't dry as a rock!' They smiled at one another. 'Datapushing's not so bad,' Shoshana went on. 'It's got to be better than being a refugee, anyway.'

'I guess so,' said Sam.

You didn't bloody well need to be turned into a Dalek or a Cyberman to lose any trace of humanity. Fifty hours a week, for at least ten years. How many hours was that? She didn't want to think about it.

And without even the drama or moments of fear to make it interesting. Just the slow, uneventful scraping away of anything that made it enjoyable to be alive.

Sam took her cube back to the kitchen and started jamming stuff into the QwikWash. The Crying Woman was still in full voice. She could just make out the murmurs of someone trying to comfort her, but the woman was having none of it.

Sam left Shoshana reading her novel and went into her room. It was almost bare, just the bed – a proper bed, sheets and pillow – and a battered old wooden chest that had been here when she'd moved in. She used it as a table, a desk, her cupboard.

Much of her first pay had gone to buying clothes. She'd nearly worn straight through the jeans and T-shirt she'd arrived in, so she'd picked up a bunch of basics at the first chance she got. Along with a half-dozen cheap white T-shirts, she'd got hold of a jar of poster paint and she'd taken a spare afternoon to painstakingly re-create some of the shirts she'd had before.

GREENPEACE, AMNESTY, FREE THE KINSEY 3 and MEAT IS MURDER, a crude sketch of a Grey with the word ABDUCTED in block letters across the bottom. These things were her, upfront statements of what she stood for. She felt naked if she didn't have something to say.

Shoshana's reaction, when she'd seen the T-shirts drying in Sam's room, had been, 'You're not into all that hippie sh –'

'Hell, yes,' said Sam, effectively squashing that line of inquiry.

God only knew, the slogans were all she could do for any of these causes, the way things were for her now.

She should track down the Ha'olam equivalent of those groups. When she got a spare moment. When she could come home from work and not find herself buried under a pile of laundry and rubbish that needed taking out and dirty dishes.

Even the junior clerks, third grade, got a day off every week to stop their heads from exploding. You had your choice of Friday, Saturday or Sunday, one day of the week not blurred into fatigue and eyeache.

Sam usually spent hers shopping and catching up on the housework. This Sunday, she decided she couldn't face a mop. She pulled on her ragged old jeans and one of the Ts and went for a jog.

She hadn't had a chance to go running in months. That was just wrong – back in London, or when she'd been with the Doctor, she'd run two or three miles a day, every day. More if the TARDIS had decided to rearrange the corridors in mid-lap.

Enough of that. Today, she decided, she was going to jog to the edge of the city – a couple of miles, at least. If she was flabby from too much desk work, she'd walk back if necessary. She stuffed a few essentials into a belt pouch, aimed herself squarely at the distant mountains and let her feet rip.

When she got back, her roommate had had one of her eyes replaced with a computer.

Shoshana flashed her a happy grin and fluttered her eyelashes. 'What do you think? I couldn't decide between red and green, so I settled on blue.'

Sam opened her mouth to say, 'What is it?', but she knew. She'd seen it plenty of times. 'I need a shower,' she said instead.

Shoshana followed her into the tiny bathroom. 'What?' she said. 'Isn't it vegetarian enough for you?'

Sam pulled off her soaked headband. 'Shoshana,' she said, 'I said I was really pleased you were getting that promotion, and I meant it. You work pretty hard in Accounts.'

'Yes, I bloody do,' said her roommate. She turned to look at herself in the bathroom mirror. 'I've earned this.'

One of Shoshana's eyes was brown. The other was bright blue, almost metallic, glittering as Sam snapped on the lights.

'Is it the whole eye?' asked Sam. 'Or did they sort of... weld that bit on?'

'The whole eye,' said Shoshana. 'You get a huge payout for the organ donation too.'

'I think I'm going to be sick,' said Sam faintly.

'Thanks a lot,' said Shoshana. She slammed the door of the bathroom.

Sam leaned on the sink for a long time, waiting to see if she was going to throw up, looking at her own eyes. Which one would she give up, to get the promotion, in ten years' time? Would she get a flashy new iris, maybe one of those patterned jobs, or try to get one that matched her original eye colour?

In the end she got into the shower and stood under the water until the shock receded.

She towelled off in her bedroom, pulling on baggy trousers and a shirt, her lying-around-the-house outfit. She could probably afford to watch the datatablet for an hour before it was her turn to clean the bathroom and get lunch.

She switched on the datatablet, but instead of watching the flickering display, she found herself taking he home-decorated T-shirts out of the chest, thumbing through them as though they were the pages of a large, limp book.

Shoshana was standing in the doorway, watching her with a bi-coloured stare.

'These are terrible,' Sam said. 'Look at them.' Shoshana couldn't help smiling. 'Of all the things I am, an artist isn't one of them. I'm sorry I was rude about your eye.'

'Don't worry about it,' said Shoshana. 'Maybe I should've given you some advance warning.'

'I used to have so much time,' said Sam. 'You know what I mean? I still want to do good…'

'Look, when do you let yourself off the hook?' Shoshana asked. 'When can you actually say you've done enough and just give it up?' She stared Sam in the eyes. 'You've got to know when to stop.'

The half-synthetic gaze made Sam's flesh creep. 'I feel like I'm wasting my time, blinking bits of rubbish around all day. I want to be doing real stuff.'

'This is real,' said Shoshana. 'This is how everybody lives. Welcome to real life, where there are bills to be paid and dishes to be washed. Not to mention rugs to be cleaned!'

'I know, I know, I'll get to it in a moment,' said Sam. 'It shouldn't be like this. It wasn't meant to be like this. All I want is –' She cut herself off in mid-sentence. 'Angst angst angst,' she said conversationally. 'Angst. Angst angst? Angst angst angst angst angst.' She sighed through her teeth. 'I'm bloody sick of it.'

'*You're* sick of it,' said Shoshana.

Sam felt a sneeze coming on and hurriedly stared at the pause icon in the upper left corner of her eyespace. Screwing your eyes shut at the wrong moment could wipe half your files.

When she'd first started, she'd been so relieved, and so numb, that she hadn't realised she was volunteering for a combination of intense concentration and mind-numbing repetition. Ten years, she thought, blowing her nose. Christ.

Four hours later she was dozing on the bus, stumbling into the flat to discover Shoshana sitting in the dark, a half-smile on her face, lit softly by the datatablet. Her hands were hovering over the digitpad, but she was logged in through the eye implant.

Her roommate didn't react as she switched on lights, changed clothes, banged around in the kitchen. Eventually, she put her mouth right next to Shoshana's ear and said, 'It's not good for the brain, I read.'

Shoshana jumped and turned to look at her. It was Sam's turn to jump; the implant glowed in the dark, a circle of actinic blue light.

'That's a bunch of anti-industrial, anti-man propaganda,' said Shoshana angrily.

'They've done studies,' said Sam.

'Who's they?' said Shoshana, without interest. 'The implants are hundreds of times safer than the old synch-op links. Hundreds of times faster, too. IXNet wouldn't be possible without them.'

'So you can send notes straight to each other's eyeball. I'm really impressed.' Sam fumbled around and snapped on the lights.

Shoshana smiled. 'It's not just that. You don't have to read what other people are saying; you just know it. That's how they keep everyone in the loop, you know – you can just sort of hear all the discussions going on in your head.'

'So they're just flashing the words faster than you can consciously read them.' Sam sighed. 'Subliminals. Or something.'

Shoshana snapped the terminal shut with a thump.

'You've changed,' said Sam.

'No, I haven't,' said Shoshana. 'You've changed. You feel like rubbish, so you're projecting it on to me.'

Sam glared at her, then looked down at her lap. 'I keep thinking it's all right,' she said. 'It's all right, except I just had another bad day, or another fight with you, or another sobbing session... It's this life. This isn't me...'

'Yeah, I know. The world will fall apart if you're not there to save it in person. Well, we all have to grow up eventually.'

'What the hell is that supposed to mean?'

'Come on. I saw the way you were looking at me. You'd just love it if my brain was being controlled by the computers, wouldn't you?'

'What?'

'Because then it would be something big and dramatic to fight against. You could have a protest rally.' Shoshana stared her in the face. 'But you're not going to, because it's not. You got that? It's just reality. Nothing big or dramatic. This is what's real.'

There was a scream blocking her throat. This couldn't be all there was. This couldn't be the real her, spending her life doing nothing, working in a dead-end job, living in –

– living in a bedsit in King's Cross –

The Crying Woman was blubbing again. And Sam wanted to swing round and pound on the wall and scream till that bitch just stopped, because her head was too full and there wasn't room for any more tears right now from anyone else or else it would all come spilling out.

Get up, shower, eat, dress, bus, work.

About two hours into the day Sam started writing numbers down on a notepad. She did the calculations in a sort of daydream, as if there was no way it could really happen.

Then when she added them up and found out she could do it, she didn't even feel like she'd made a decision. Somehow she just started doing things to make it happen.

She got up and walked out, as casually as if she was heading for the ladies' room. She got on the first bus that came by. When she got back to the flat, she phoned up her supervisor and gave her two days' notice. He didn't think there was anything odd; as far as he knew, she was still in her cubicle. She even got a good reference out of him, e-mailed to her for future use.

She packed the clothes, and – and she didn't own much more. She stuck a note on top of Shoshana's dynabook copy of *Paradise In Chains* and closed the door, turning out the light behind her.

The cat was waiting for her. She greeted Sam with a rub of her face against her ankle, as if she'd never left. All things considered, the cat seemed less surprised to see her than Ari did.

'You're off work early.'

'I'm off work for good.'

Ari's mouth turned down at the corners. 'Oh, Sam, you didn't get –'

'Nah. I walked out.'

'You did what?'

'I just did my sums. I was just working to pay the rent. Having the place was actually making it harder to buy everything else I need to live. I've got enough cash and credit to tide me over for a while.'

She dropped her duffel bag in a corner of the kitchen. 'Does that sound stupid? Sound crazy?'

Ari opened his mouth, then closed it. 'It's a pretty big step.'

'Yeah,' said Sam. 'I don't know which is more crazy. Staying in a steady job with a decent wage that's turning your soul to porridge. Or leaving it.'

Maybe this was what the Doctor had realised, when it had sunk in that there was a whole universe out there and he really *could* go anywhere. But then she couldn't picture him ever paying rent in the first place.

'Sometimes you've got to take a step down in order to take a step up,' said Ari. He still didn't look happy, but he did look convinced. 'Oh well, your old cot's waiting for you.' He hesitated. 'Best of luck, Sam.'

Yusuf and Pincher were shuffling in already, smelling of rubbish bins and the early stages of death. She dodged them and went into the kitchen to where Ari kept the cutting board, and got right to work chopping the carrots for the stew.

It was a bit scary how smoothly she'd slipped back into the routine, but the thought didn't bother her for more than a few moments. Her mind was too full of the phone calls she was going to make, the job leads and charity groups to chase down.

The cat was nuzzling her ankle under the kitchen counter.

Chapter Four
Radical Dislocation

The terminals were in the back room of the teashop, where customers could get a little privacy and quiet. There were even completely private rooms, at an extra fee, mostly used by businesspeople needing to uplink to a satellite or phone home.

It was interesting, thought the Doctor as he followed his host to one of the small, silent rooms, that miniaturisation could go only so far; he'd seen palmtop computers here and there on Ha'olam, but most people seemed to prefer something a bit chunkier. A bit more real. People carried them like briefcases, lighter and smaller and millions of times more powerful versions of the twentieth-century laptop.

The Doctor flipped open the datatablet and looked in surprise at the arm that unfolded from its side. He hadn't seen one of these before.

The jointed arm came to rest just in front of his face. A round lens, perhaps a couple of centimetres across, unfurled from the end.

He was wrong. He had seen something like this before.

He considered the device as he poured himself a cup of tea and added milk from a tiny white jug. His host had left a small beeper on the tray in case he required anything else. A brightly coloured rug hung on the wall, next to the inevitable holo-ad, this time for Fizzade.

He remembered the INC receptionist staring at her screen, her hands hovering above the digitpad. A heads-up display, some kind of implant in her eye.

The Doctor touched the lens with just his fingertips, sipping his tea. This, he realised, was the poor man's version of the same arrangement.

He sat forward and peered into the lens.

There was a bright, blue flash of light and then a three-dimensional menu appeared before him, rotating slowly. It took only a moment to puzzle out the navigation principle. Setting the tea down on the table, he plunged into the network.

The speed of access was almost exhilarating, as he dashed along the electric pathways that connected the planet's computer systems. It was not so fast as a direct connection between brain and computer – but then, not so grotesque either. He had never been entirely comfortable with the fusion of body and machine.

This technology was well in advance of its time.

It took less than a minute to discover INC's electronic headquarters, a sprawling mass of databases and advertising. He skimmed through them like a seabird just touching the surface of the water, tracing long lines of contact.

None of this public material would tell him what he wanted to know, of course, or the data-umphs would have made short work of it. It was the private computers, hidden behind bright barriers of passwords and identity checks and similar nonsense. Obstacles between him and Sam.

IXNet, the corporation's internal network of employees, perched on the datascape like a vast metal spider with hundreds of thousands of legs. He decided to poke at its security, just a little, see if he could get the measure of it. There – a simple port intended for employees, like another of the three-dimensional menus.

He moved his eye, blinked, blinked again, taking hold of the port. It asked him to wait for a moment.

There was a dizzyingly brilliant flash of light. He flinched, his right eye instinctively screwing shut, but his left eye stayed wide open as a beam from the lens waved up and down, twice, scanning his retina, scanning it again to confirm.

And then the port rotated and opened, like an eye staring back at him for a moment, and let him in.

He stayed still for several seconds, astonished, staring through the eyepiece at the vista of confidential data. Databases, records, memos

– anything an employee would be able to access.

'That,' he said aloud, 'should not have happened.'

He sat back from the datatablet for a moment, and took another mouthful of tea. The system didn't disconnect when he moved his eye away from the lens, he noticed – it was on standby, waiting for him.

The retina scan should have concluded he wasn't an INC employee and closed down the port. Instead, the corporation had welcomed him with open arms.

If he'd known it was going to be this easy, he would never have wasted time with that wretched receptionist.

He put his eye back against the lens, cautiously, but everything was as it was before.

It took seconds to locate a staff directory. There was no listing for Samantha Angeline Jones. He tried a little push, and uncovered a second database, a staff record that spiralled back in time. If she had been employed at some stage, her name would be here.

A security program made itself known to him.

It unfolded in front of him, almost seeming embarrassed. If he accessed the staff record, it told him, it would be obliged to report the fact. Naturally it would not terminate his connection and would otherwise be happy to assist him in any way.

Well, then, he asked the security program, is there a way I could access the staff record without your having to report me?

Certainly, sir. The program produced a list of secure datatablets. Log on from any of these, sir.

The Doctor terminated his connection to INC, and folded away the eyepiece and the terminal. He finished his tea, thinking.

On Gallifrey, the retina had almost replaced the fingers as the main method of communicating with machines. The human eye was not so sophisticated, just an aerial, a dish of light-sensitive cells shunting their observations through the blind spot. The brain had to do all of the processing, flipping the image the right way up, making sense of the movement, the shapes, the narrow range of colours.

But the Time Lord retina could do a reasonable amount of thinking on its own. This could be annoying when one was trying to sleep, but it was the ideal means of talking to a computer – as well as a built-in identity check.

The retina scan had established his identity all right. It had realised he was a Time Lord and thrown all the doors open to him.

The Ha'olamites hadn't developed this technology themselves. This was Gallifreyan technology. They had stolen, begged or bought it.

There was more to this now than finding Sam. Somehow, he was going to have to put this particular genie back in its bottle.

The Doctor logged on from a public datatablet in one of the quasiphone booths. The arm of the eyepiece creaked as he unfolded it. He breathed on the lens, wiped it off with his handkerchief and peered into it.

INC welcomed him once more, with open arms. A different port this time, one used for downloading data from one of their satellites. It looked as though the trick was good from anywhere.

He spent almost a minute forging the credentials he would need. The entire operation shouldn't take more than fifteen minutes, he estimated.

The INC building was a short walk away, through the bazaar where the thriftship crews sold their goods. One stall was selling toys, dolls that looked like a dozen species, wind-up Daleks. He chose a teddy bear – not too cute, she wouldn't care for that – and paid the vendor with his forged I-card. Hopefully he wasn't having too detrimental an effect on the local economy.

Where had this minor bit of Gallifreyan technology come from? If there were other Time Lords on the planet, he thought, and they realised he was here, they would be his deadly enemy. Not to mention deadly dull. It was becoming positively fashionable to be a renegade these days, he thought, with a rueful smile.

What if they had Sam?

There was no more time to waste. He had to find out whatever INC knew about her, right away.

He tucked the bear under his arm and made a beeline for INC HQ.

'Maintenance,' the Doctor told the man in the cubicle.

It took the worker a few seconds to disengage from the eyepiece. The Doctor could see the dizzying light dancing in the man's vision, a flash, then nothing.

The worker looked up at him, blinking. A skinny clerk in a corporation kaftan, just one of dozens of drones in little boxes that stretched away to a distant wall. The Doctor leaned on the wall of the cubicle. 'Sorry to interrupt you,' he said. 'I need ten minutes to FTP a JPEG from a remote URL on this datatablet.'

The worker nodded, looking vaguely dazed, and shuffled out of the cubicle in the direction of the common area.

There were no pictures in the cubicle, no holovids of the wife and kids or amusing cartoons. The man was a temp, this planet's version of cheap labour, brought in on a casual basis to clear up some files and do a bit of typing. He looked as though he'd worked for something like thirty-six hours without sleep. Probably off to buy himself a hit of caffeine or qat – there had been a row of dispensers in the common area.

The Doctor had, in essence, got in through the tradesman's entrance, pressing his eye to a retinal lock as though he was peering through a keyhole. Workers with computer-maintenance kits had buzzed back and forth through the same doorway, nodding their heads to the sensor as though in a bizarre religious ritual.

Once he was inside, no one challenged him. Obviously, since he was there, he was supposed to be there. He could probably have walked out with one of the datatablets and got no more than the odd glance.

But once he started dancing through their computer systems, he'd be as conspicuous as a bulldozer in a china shop, security clearance or not. He was going to need some major distractions.

The Doctor slid into the empty chair, pulled himself up to the desk and pushed his eye against the lens.

Right. Time for a little chaos, and he didn't mean the Mandelbrot Set.

* * *

Mlihi walked past and was the first one to glance into the cubicle. The temp was wearing a velvet coat and a silk cravat. 'Er,' said the clerk.

'It's Extremely Casual Day,' said the Doctor, and went on looking busy.

'Oh,' said Mlihi, and walked on.

In the common area, a bunch of temps were slumped around the walls, looking like death warmed up. Mlihi got himself a hot cup of coffee from one of the dispensing machines and sat down next to Zuabi. She was reading a newspaper from a palmtop. They grunted in mutual acknowledgement.

'Have you seen this?' said Zuabi.

Mlihi leaned over. Zuabi thumbed the digitpad and the newspaper disappeared, replaced by INC's internal bulletin board.

'What?' he said. It was just the usual news about stocks and customer-service initiatives.

Zuabi tapped a finger on the screen impatiently. Mlihi looked.

It was the number of INC employees on the planet. It was dropping, steadily.

As he blinked at it, the number fell by another two hundred.

'That can't be kosher,' said Zuabi. She sat back, staring at the screen, sticking out her bottom lip fetchingly.

Mlihi watched as the figure dropped a few more notches. 'It could be some major project that's just been completed.' He lowered his voice. 'They could be laying off a bunch of temporary staff.'

'It's dropped by over a thousand employees in the last two minutes,' said Zuabi. 'Look.' Her eyes widened as her implant did its stuff, her right eye glittering silver as she talked to the machine. Instantly the staff number became a three-dimensional diagram rotating on a corner of the screen.

Mlihi whistled, he couldn't help it. 'I *hope* that's not kosher,' he said.

'I'll call a few people and see if I can get some confirmation,' said Zuabi. 'You handle personnel requisitions, don't you?'

'Haven't heard a thing about this,' said Mlihi. 'See if you can find out who's being downsized out. Is it an admin purge? A new clerical package?'

Zuabi nodded vaguely, her eye working overtime. After a while Mlihi left her to it. The implant had earned her a two-rank promotion and a jump in salary he could only guess at, along with the transplant bonus, but the Luddite in him was still glad he hadn't qualified for the upgrade yet. He didn't quite know what he'd do if and when it came up in the personnel evaluations.

The Extremely Casual man was still there when Mlihi went past. He paused, leaning over the cubicle wall. 'You're from Central Maintenance, right?'

'If you say so,' said the man, without moving. His face was hidden behind the arm of the eyepiece, but his free eye had that same dreamy look that Zuabi would get.

Mlihi decided it would be best not to interrupt him. He sat back down in his cubicle and brought up the staff numbers again.

Maybe it was some kind of glitch.

A hard copy whizzed out of his workslot. He picked it up and stared at it. It was a requisition from Public Relations for two hundred and thirty-eight new staff, needed immediately.

Sitting at his borrowed datatablet, rummaging through a series of Research and Development reports, the Doctor smiled wickedly. Let's see if they can figure that one out, he thought.

He pushed a stray curl from his face. There seemed to be an inordinate number of references to archaeology, particularly of alien sites, in their internal research paper repository. Some of them awfully closely linked to memoranda about the eye tech. Possibly worth exploring, that. With a quick flip of the transfer module he uploaded every known completed fragment of the manuscript of *Down Among the Dead Men Again* and mailed it to Senior Assistant Vice President Sellwood, with a file-acknowledge-brief directive demanding he present initial comments on how it related to their projects right away, plus a full analysis and report by Monday.

* * *

Several working parties were formed, and then a working party was created to monitor their progress. Sandwiches were delivered for a non-existent total-quality seminar, and the temps in the common area ended up scoffing the lot. Dozens of terminals were hurriedly shut down as virus warnings went out at random.

Zuabi leaned over the top of Mlihi's cubicle. 'I can't get any work done,' she said.

'I'm frantic,' said Mlihi. 'Requisitions have been coming in from all over the place.'

'Someone just requisitioned thirty-eight thousand skyhooks for the admin centre at Al Markim.'

'What are they going to do with all those?'

'Not a lot,' said Zuabi. 'There *is* no admin centre at Al Markim.'

'Mlihi!' It was the boss, rushing up to the cubicle, his hair and kaftan in disarray. 'Have you seen the figures!'

'Don't worry,' said Mlihi. 'I'll have the four hundred and seventeen staff for you by close of business.'

'What?' said the boss.

'Not a problem. There's always a queue for work like this.'

'Wait a moment,' said the boss. 'The whole company's being downsized, and we're hiring?'

Mlihi rummaged through his in-tray and brought out a hard-copy staff requisition. The boss grabbed it and ran his eyes over it. 'We can't start upsizing now!' he squeaked. 'Everyone will think I'm empire-building!'

'It's not just you,' said Mlihi, shaking his in-tray. 'I've had dozens of requisitions since the drop started.'

'But if everyone's hiring,' said Zuabi, 'why is the total number of employees still falling?'

'My God!' said the boss. 'It's some sort of coup!'

And as vice-presidents had screaming turf wars and middle managers sat sobbing in the halls, the Doctor continued to plough through the INC database, confident that right now he was the least of their worries.

He had made himself discover the source of the eye tech first. R&D history, transport records... He followed the data as it wound backwards in time, all of it funnelling down to one place, one point. Samson Plains. The words danced in front of his eye. The INC Research and Development Facility at Samson Plains.

That would do for now, they could visit later. He had bookmarked the staff record. Now he went rushing back to it, mountains of data skimming beneath him as he raced to find her.

'You know,' said Zuabi, 'I don't think anyone's being fired at all.'

'Really?' said Mlihi. He was taking a break from the flood of requisitions, his eyeset slung around his neck.

'No. I think this is some kind of huge computer glitch. Look at this.'

She brought up a couple of diagrams on the screen. 'Look, the salary budget hasn't changed a bit, while the employment figures have been careening all over the place. There are some other numbers as well.'

'Could be some kind of weird prank?' said Mlihi.

'Hmm...' Zuabi sat back in her chair. 'If so, it's right through the system. It's like a huge kid has broken into IXNet.'

'Wonder what it's all about,' said Mlihi. 'What *is* a skyhook, anyway?'

'Good question. Grab me some coffee.'

'Yes!' the Doctor exclaimed, as the record unscrolled in his eye. Yes! There she was!

Samantha Angeline Jones. Employee number this, RAIN that. Employment terminated in advance of contract closure one week ago. Vacated her apartment. No forwarding address.

The Doctor could have thrown the computer across the room.

Instead, he backed out of the staff record, carefully closing the gateways behind him so that there was no trace of an unauthorised access. He tidied up a few of the messes he'd made, quietened down the distractions. Everything would be back to normal for INC's corporate sheep in an hour or so.

He was about to disconnect and walk out when something went entirely wrong.

And it was as though he was looking down a tunnel, down some corridor that stretched away into the distance until it diminished to a point, and something was rushing down that hallway towards him. Coming closer faster and faster and for some reason he wasn't going to be able to take off the eyepiece and disconnect before it reached him because time was stretching out for him but getting shorter and shorter for whatever it was that was racing towards him, targeting him, had him in its sights and his hands were coming up to the eyepiece to tear it away but he couldn't possibly react quickly enough and it was looming in his vision and it – was – right – *here*

Fifteen exabytes of static punched the Doctor in the left eye, hard enough to send him flying back from the datatablet, the chair striking the wall of the cubicle and spilling him on to the floor. The eyepiece clattered away.

He tried to rise, but the inside of his head was like an empty cathedral the moment after the bells stop ringing. He fell back on the corporate green carpet, trying to remember how to breathe.

Mlihi spotted him almost immediately and decided he didn't want to know. He went to get Zuabi that coffee instead.

The security people got there two minutes later.

Chapter Five
Capture Escape Capture

Dr Akalu liked to be there when they woke up.

Partly because the first face they saw ought to be a friendly one. Partly because he liked to see them while they were sleeping. Asleep, they were different people. It was hard to imagine that a sleeping man, relaxed, unaware, helpless, was really a petty thief, a credit-fraud artist.

Or a spy.

Akalu had a printout of the report in his hand – you didn't bring datatablets into the habitat area. Industrial sabotage and espionage: sentence, ten years. It was one of the worst crimes, and one of the longest determinate sentences, that he'd seen in his twenty years at OBFSC.

The man stirred in his sleep, muttering something. He was tucked neatly into the narrow bed, wearing the regulation striped pyjamas. His uniform, shoes and kit were stacked on the metal desk.

It amazed Akalu that anyone could sleep here, even after going through Reception. There was a constant noise, absolutely never-ending, even in the middle of the night. The jingling of keys. It echoed along the concrete corridors of the habitat area, a sharp silver sound of keys in locks, keys on belts, keys in hands. No I-cards in the habitat area either, just good old-fashioned sturdy pin-tumbler cylinder locks.

Awake at last. The man was turning his head slightly, taking in the cell. High ceiling, a small, barred window way up in the outer wall, a pale square of light shooting down to the floor. Bed, desk, sink – a mirror embedded in the wall above – amenities. Four metres long, three metres wide. His eyes found Akalu on the other side of the bars.

'Welcome to the Oliver Bainbridge Functional Stabilisation Centre.

It's Tuesday morning, about eight a.m. My name is Doctor David Akalu. I'm the Centre's morale facilitator.'

'The Centre's what?' The man was laughing quietly, then pressed his teeth into his bottom lip. 'Did you really have to drop a truck on my head before bringing me here?'

Akalu couldn't help but smile. 'You've been through the standard Reception procedure. Nothing to be alarmed about. Everyone arrives the same way. Now, Mr Bowman –'

'Doctor,' said Bowman.

Akalu glanced at the printout. 'You don't appear to have any recognisable qualifications,' he said. 'In fact…' Bowman was struggling to sit up. 'Let's say I'm looking forward to getting to know you better. You have an appointment with me at nine a.m. Be on time, Mr Bowman.'

The new inmate just looked at him, frowning slightly. His eyes were still cloudy from Reception, but there was an unmistakable sharpness there. He could believe this man found out secrets for a living.

Yes indeed, thought Akalu, I'm looking forward to getting to know you.

He'd been in smaller cells, and less well-kept ones. There was a clock embedded in the concrete of the wall, digital red numbers counting off the seconds. Almost an hour before his 'appointment' with Dr Akalu.

The Doctor moved to the door, the floor seeming to rise and fall beneath his feet like the deck of a ship, and leaned against the bars. Whatever drugs they'd given him were still wearing off.

The cells across the corridor were empty. Presumably the other prisoners had already been turned out for the day.

Unless he was the only prisoner. Or one of very few.

The timpani in his head were diminishing. He went back to the bed, tugged off the pyjamas and picked up the uniform.

He looked at it, sighing. It was clean and would probably even come close to fitting him. But it was so… dull. Denim, the colour faded to a

60

weak blue with years of washing. A shirt – baggy on his slight frame – trousers, a jacket which he wouldn't need in this heat. Battered leather shoes which didn't fit at *all*.

He looked at himself in the mirror over the sink. His left eye was bloodshot, but otherwise he looked all right.

At least they hadn't cut his hair.

Sam was out there, somewhere. She might have found happiness, be settled down comfortably, greet him with a cup of tea and a friendly goodbye. Or she might be in desperate need of his help.

He didn't have time to be sitting about here for an hour.

Correctional Officer Rifaat's keys jingled against his hip as he strode through the habitat area. Almost all of the cells were empty at this time of day, making it a little quieter than usual.

Rifaat checked his printout of the day's schedule, making sure he had the right cell number. Yes, coming up on the right. It was twenty to nine; plenty of time to get the new inmate to Akalu's office in time for his initial interview.

Rifaat wondered what kind of mood this one would be in. Hostile? Terrified? Downcast? The sad ones were the easiest to deal with, but they always left Rifaat feeling depressed himself. People should be more cheerful. This wasn't as rough a ride as they expected.

What he was not expecting was to see the new inmate lying sprawled on the floor of the cell.

The tap in the sink was running, the water loud against the metal. Rifaat plucked the keys from his belt, opened the door, locked it behind him and drew his stunwand.

He crouched down beside the inmate. Bowman was breathing fitfully, shivers running through his body. He was reacting to the anaesthetic. Rifaat had seen a man die from it once. He pressed two fingers to the man's throat – his pulse was racing.

Rifaat reached up to tap his throat mike, call for help from the Infirmary.

The man's hand shot up and brushed across his face. It felt like walking into a cobweb.

Rifaat crumpled, the stunwand rolling out of his hand, hoping he didn't look as stupid as he felt.

Two minutes later the Doctor found himself in a storeroom, bright sunlight streaming through windows covered by security mesh. There was a man in civilian clothes, a clipboard in one hand, staring up at tall metal shelves filled with boxes and sacks.

The door clicked shut behind the Doctor. The man looked up, saw him and dropped the clipboard. 'Don't hurt me!' he squeaked raising his hands above his head.

'Er,' said the Doctor. 'Very well then. Could you please show me the way out?' The man gave a tiny nod. The Doctor reached up to one of the shelves, hefted down a bag of flour. 'I'll be a prisoner helping you move some stores, all right?' Another tiny nod.

The man led him back out into the corridor. The Doctor held the heavy sack in front of his chest and kept his eyes downcast. They passed the guard, who didn't give them a glance. Which was good, because the poor clerk was quivering as though the floor was giving him electric shocks. The metal staircase rattled under his feet as they ascended.

They made it as far as the loading dock before a hand descended on the Doctor's shoulder.

He turned. It was Rifaat.

'Oh dear,' he said.

Rifaat ushered the Doctor through a series of corridors, out of the section with the cells and into another building. Eventually they reached the infirmary. There was no one else here – a row of empty beds, some benches and cupboards.

Rifaat knocked on a door. 'Come in!' called a voice from inside. The guard put his hand on the Doctor's shoulder again and took him into the room.

'Ah, hello, Mr Bowman,' said Akalu. 'Right on time, I see.'

Akalu straightened a pile of papers on his desk. James Bowman was staring at him. 'Please, have a seat. *Toda*, Officer Rifaat.'

Bowman sat down in the modestly comfortable chair Akalu reserved for his visitors. He was white – untanned, certainly from off-world. His sharp blue eyes moved to take in the details of Akalu's spacious office, the unbreakable glass window with its view of the compound, the papers stacked geometrically on the desk.

Akalu opened a new file on his computer, bringing on line the expert system on inmate behaviour.

'Well?' said Bowman. 'What will it be? Electrodes, solitary confinement, psychoactives?'

Akalu looked up at his charge in surprise. 'Coffee,' he said. 'Or tea, if you prefer.'

'No, thank you,' said Bowman. He bounced to his feet, stood at the window, looking down into the central compound. 'Ducks!' he exclaimed.

If only he had the man's full file, not these scant details. Well, he would have to start somewhere. 'This isn't the first prison you've been in,' he said.

'Eight,' said Bowman. Akalu made a note. 'No, there's nine, and – yes, there's ten.'

'Prisons?' said Akalu.

'Ducklings!' said Bowman. 'I've lost count of the prisons.'

'It must be a risky business,' Akalu suggested.

'What?'

'Espionage,' said Akalu.

Bowman smiled, sitting back in the chair. 'I was trying to trace a friend of mine,' he said ruefully. 'INC probably thought I was after their new design for an atomic can-opener.'

'Well, let me ask you this. Have you been punished for trying to escape this morning?'

'Isn't that your job?'

63

'No,' said Akalu. 'I'm the morale facilitator.'

Bowman raised an eyebrow. 'Whatever is that?'

'I look after the morale and the psychological well-being of the inmates,' said Akalu. 'That includes you, of course. You're a blank. That means I'm going to have to rely on you to tell me your psychological history, and if you have any special needs for medication, therapy or any of the other services I provide. Part of the job, I imagine.'

'Sorry?'

'Having no past. Useful, for a spy.'

'I'm not a spy. Really I'm not.' He smiled ruefully. 'Repeat *ad infinitum*.'

'What are you, then?'

'Puzzled.'

'About what?'

'Why I was unconscious when I was brought here.'

'Standard procedure,' explained Akalu. 'A sleeping inmate is much easier to handle than a hostile one. Besides, we don't want you knowing what's on the other side of the wall, do we?'

Bowman looked at him, but said nothing. Akalu opened a drawer and took out one of the glossy pamphlets. 'Here you are,' he said. 'This should tell you most of what you need to know, including the Centre's rules.' Bowman took the brochure, looking astonished. 'If you've got any questions, let me know. You can make an appointment for any time during business hours.'

'Well, that's very kind of you,' said Bowman softly, 'but I don't think it's very likely.'

'I'm always here if you need me.' He pressed a button on his desk and Rifaat reappeared.

'Come on,' said the correctional officer. 'Let's get you back where you belong.'

Bowman glanced at him, tucked the pamphlet under his arm and followed the officer out.

Akalu sat at his desk for a long time, thinking. At last he said, 'Did you get all of that?'

A light on the terminal flashed. 'Yes, Dr Akalu.'

'Then continue compiling,' said Akalu. 'I want to know everything about him that I can.'

At twelve noon, one of the guards let the Doctor out of his cell and escorted him down to the dining area.

There was a queue of perhaps a hundred prisoners, shuffling past a window at the opposite end of the room and back again to the tables and chairs.

The Doctor hesitantly joined the end of the long queue, aware of the eyes of dozens of prisoners. He picked up a tray from a stack on one of the tables.

They were an interesting mix – many older men and women, perhaps in their fifties and sixties, plus a lot of teenagers, but not many ages in between. Almost all of them were human.

It was twenty minutes before he reached the serving window. A bored-looking prisoner was scraping the last of a fishy-smelling substance from the bottom of a pot.

'Good afternoon,' said the Doctor. 'Would you happen to have anything without meat in it?'

The prisoner behind the counter stared at him.

'*Yekl,*' laughed the young woman behind him in the queue. Her short hair had been dyed icy white and her face was covered in what looked like minuscule tattoos. 'You're just going to have to sample some of OBFSC's famous tuna casserole. Dip and sample!'

The Doctor watched in dismay as the server dolloped a gelatinous, pinkish-grey lump on to his plate. She added a white smear of mashed potato and a slice of stiff white bread.

The Doctor looked around, wondering where best to sit. '*Kaf kardam!*' said White Hair. 'Come here, *yekl*. Look, we call this a chair. You sit on it.'

'Thank you,' said the Doctor. There were six other prisoners at the table – four teens, two middle-aged men.

The Doctor poked at the greyish lump on his plate. 'Don't worry,' said one of the men. 'It doesn't taste nearly as bad as it looks.'

'That's because it doesn't taste like anything,' said White Hair indistinctly, stuffing bread into her mouth. The tiny tattoos were words, the Doctor realised: on her left cheek he could read the word *nooksurf*. 'You get used to it after a few years.'

'My name is Gamal el-Bayoumi,' said the man. He moved the salt aside and reached across the table. 'You must be James Bowman – I saw your name on the afternoon's work roster.'

I seem to be stuck with that pseudonym, thought the Doctor. He shook the man's hand. 'I'm called the Doctor.'

El-Bayoumi introduced the others. The teenagers were all something called 'shifters', apparently, and the middle-aged prisoners had been sentenced for 'possession of intellectual property'. The young woman with the tattoos was named Ziba.

They were all looking at him expectantly. 'Er,' said the Doctor. 'Industrial espionage and sabotage.' Ziba whistled. The Doctor said, 'Well, I was just trying to find a friend of mine.'

'Of course you were!' Another chorus. 'Nothing wrong with that.'

'How long is your sentence, Doctor?' asked el-Bayoumi quietly.

'Ten years.'

'May the time pass quickly,' said el-Bayoumi.

'Thank you. But I don't plan to stay for more than a few days.'

The chorus of chattering died away. Ziba and a friend exchanged half-smiles. El-Bayoumi busied himself with scraping up the last of his tuna casserole.

'We're on together this afternoon,' said Ziba, breaking the silence. The Doctor made out the word *nukesurf* over her right eyebrow. How many of the tiny words were inscribed on her face and neck, even her hands? 'I'll show you around the library.'

'Books?' said the Doctor.

'Of course,' said Ziba. 'They're not going to let a bunch of bandits like us near the computer terminals, are they?'

Six prisoners had been assigned to library work that afternoon. Ziba steered the Doctor from the dining area to a gate in the habitat, where the half-dozen of them leaned against the walls, talking in quiet voices.

'What exactly is a "shifter"?' murmured the Doctor.

'An *e-shifta*,' said Ziba. You know. The five-finger download.' He looked at her in increasing bewilderment. 'Softlifting. Bagging the big I.' His stare widened. She sighed. '*Information*. I'm a data thief.'

'Ah,' said the Doctor.

'You're not from around here, are you?' said Ziba.

Two of the guards arrived, unlocked the gate with keys from their jangling collections and rolled it open. The Doctor found himself squinting in the sudden sunlight. Ziba took his elbow and pulled him outside.

They were in the compound he had seen from Akalu's office, heading down a grassy slope towards the duck pond.

The building they called the habitat area was a long slab of reddish brick, studded with tiny barred windows. The administration area, where Akalu had his office, was made of the same brick, but with real windows protected by mesh.

Opposite them, on the other side of the pond, was a building of a completely different style, a rounded hall of hardened sprayfoam, the kind colonists used to make temporary buildings. The library, he presumed.

Compound and buildings were surrounded by immense stone walls, almost thirty metres high, casting huge shadows. There was a single watchtower at the far corner, a couple of human figures visible inside. Under the fourth wall there was a series of garden plots.

'It all seems a bit low-tech,' the Doctor whispered to Ziba, glancing at the guards.

'What d'you mean, moon man?' she said, not bothering to lower her voice.

'Guards in watchtowers,' said the Doctor. 'Metal keys.'

Ziba shrugged. ''Bout half of us are shifters. We'd be out of here in two minutes and no seconds if the doors had I-card slots.'

'But surely there are some security devices? Movement detectors, invisible laser lines, that sort of thing.'

'I don't think so,' said Ziba. 'I've only been in for a few months, but they seem pretty determined to stick to stuff that doesn't need a power source.'

Not that it mattered, thought the Doctor. He'd escaped from every prison imaginable, from the Tower of London to a Klein sphere. A few locks and guards ought not to hold him for very long.

They spent three hours working in the library. Ziba presented him to the sole librarian, a muscular woman called Ms Salameh. She issued him with a card and dispatched him to the shelving.

It was a good-sized collection, if a bit unbalanced. Plenty on law enforcement, but next to nothing on technology. It took him a while to puzzle out the erratic call numbers, until he realised they were using the same Fractal Retroactive Dewey system as the Imperial Library on Hyperon.

Ziba got a clipboard and bullied him into helping her do a shelf check. He stood on a sort of rolling stool, reading out the call numbers of books while she checked them off on her list. Her hands were like dictionaries. *Cleanskin*, said her palm, *Ke En Chedani*, said the other. The phrase *A sort of mutated puffin* was written in precise lettering across the back of her left hand.

'Just how common are those eye implants?' he asked, after they'd completed a few rows of shelving in silence. 'Dr Akalu had one.'

'People in clerical jobs,' said Ziba. 'The corporation gives you them. Akalu uses his computers to keep track of us. And he probably thinks having one brown eye and one red eye looks freaky.'

The Doctor smiled. 'When did they first appear?'

'Moon man,' said Ziba. 'You've got a human face, but it's a human façade. *Nakheir?*'

The Doctor glanced down at himself. 'Does it show?'

'You don't know much about what's going on around here,' said the white-haired girl. 'And anyway, Ke Resht Jarna says you're a bug.

An alien.'

'The Lacaillan?'

'He says he can always tell. So what are you?'

'Curious,' said the Doctor, 'about those implants. INC ought not to have that technology.'

'You're not a cyberluddite, are you?' said Ziba suspiciously.

The Doctor jerked his head, making Ziba look. Ms Salameh had her eye on them. 'On shelf,' said the girl loudly. 'The *book* is *on* the *shelf*.'

'Check,' said the Doctor. 'So when did the implants first appear?'

'About ten years ago,' said Ziba. 'It was huge. First the interfaces, then the direct implants. All the INC execs could interact with their systems and with one another, make decisions fast as electricity. Even their button pushers could work a hundred times as fast, and no brainburn from old-style neural implants. It gave them the *edge*. You know?'

'So it was sudden...' said the Doctor. 'I wonder where it came from.'

'R&D,' said Ziba. 'I want to go work there one day. I *wanted* to go work there one day,' she said, and her eyes fell back to the clipboard.

'How long is your sentence?' asked the Doctor gently.

'Just three years,' said Ziba. 'I downloaded some proprietary software. You know how it goes. It's not much like in the papers, though.'

'It never is,' said the Doctor.

'You said you were only going to be here for a few days,' said Ziba. She gave him an accusing look. He made out the word *meatspace* on her right cheekbone. 'That's another thing you don't understand,' she said. 'Unless you've got some major legal firepower coming to rescue you.'

'I don't think there's much chance of that,' he said. 'No, I thought I'd stay for a few days, learn what I can and then depart as quietly as possible.'

'You think you're going to escape, don't you, man in the moon?'

'Why does that seem so impossible?'

'*Nakheir*.' Ziba shook her head. 'Nothing's impossible. It's just that nobody's ever done it.'

The Doctor smiled. 'Then I'll be the first.'

Ziba gave him a long, hard look. 'You believe that, don't you? It'd be nice to believe that. Leave and believe!'

The Doctor was summoned to Akalu's office again that evening, after lockup. Rifaat came to fetch him, giving him a mocking smile. 'After you, Mr Bowman,' he said.

The other prisoners stared at him idly as Rifaat followed him along the corridor of the west block. The Doctor had been glad of the chance to borrow some books from the library; the prisoners were locked into their cells from six p.m. every evening until five a.m. the following morning. He could well be looking at a few dull nights.

He'd already read the colour brochure. It outlined the routine of activities and meals, explained a few rules about keeping clothes neat and not taking illegal drugs. It could have been a glossy for a holiday camp.

The morale facilitator was sitting at his desk, his eye implant activated, his fingers resting lightly on the keyboard. The Doctor sat down in the darkened office to wait, watching the man work. From time to time Akalu typed a command. But for the most part, there was no movement besides the constant flicker of data across his left iris, patterned with red and copper.

There was a small metal box on the desk which hadn't been there that morning. The Doctor wondered what was in it.

He got up and started scanning the books on Akalu's shelf. Datacubes for the most part, neatly tucked in their plastic cases, though there were a few genuine books. *Genes XXXIV* by Lewin, *History of the Beita Yisrael*.

'I'm finished,' said Akalu. He shut down the terminal. '*Shalom*, Mr Bowman. The last of your paperwork. I can release your personal possessions now.'

'Thank you,' said the Doctor, sitting down. Akalu opened the metal box.

'These are the items cleared by our Reception team,' said Akalu. 'I'm afraid everything else must remain in safekeeping for your release.'

The Doctor looked into the box. His sonic screwdriver was conspicuous by its absence. He took out the crumpled bag of jelly babies. 'Would you like one?'

Akalu shook his head. 'I would like to know what some of these items are,' he said. 'For instance, what's this little thing?'

'My wallet-sized orange-ripple distinguisher,' said the Doctor. 'You can keep it if you think it's dangerous.'

Akalu handed it to him. 'And this?'

'Well,' said the Doctor, 'that's the front-door key to my space-time vehicle.'

Akalu gave him an amused look and put it back in the box. 'What about this?'

'That's a perigosto stick,' said the Doctor. 'You use it in a game of four-dimensional juggling.'

Akalu's amusement increased. 'And this?'

The Doctor raised an eyebrow. 'It's a stuffed bear...'

'And so it is.' He handed it to the Doctor. 'You're as much a mystery as some of these items, Mr Bowman. I've been running searches all day and I haven't been able to turn up a single record of your existence.'

'Can I have the box to keep things in?' asked the Doctor.

'Of course.' Akalu watched as the Doctor put everything into it and shut the lid. 'I can understand your reluctance,' said the morale facilitator, 'but we must talk frankly when you're ready. After all, you're going to be here for a very long time.'

'There,' he said, 'I'm afraid you're mistaken.'

Akalu smiled. 'We're still not quite sure what you did to poor Mr Rifaat. Some kind of martial-arts technique? A blow from behind?' The Doctor didn't answer. 'I'm sure the correctional officers will be a little more careful around you from now on. But you wouldn't have got far in any case.'

'You know,' said the Doctor, 'when I was still a schoolboy, one of my teachers would always insist that – given my attitude – I would never

71

go far.'

Akalu said, 'What would he say if he could see you now?'

The Doctor couldn't help grinning. 'He would have to admit,' he said, 'that I have travelled quite a distance.'

'Is that so?' said Akalu. He tapped a stylus on the desk. 'Think about it, Mr Bowman. You are a *spy*. You are a convicted criminal serving a ten-year sentence. The sudden loss of your freedom is going to require a major adjustment. I can help you with that.' Akalu put down his pen. 'I think that's all for now. I'll see you tomorrow.'

Rifaat reappeared. The Doctor got up.

'And the day after that,' added Akalu. 'And for the next ten years.'

OBFSC grew most of the vegetables it needed, in a long, wide patch beneath the fourth wall. The prisoners provided the labour, of course, planting and weeding and harvesting. Cucumbers, marrows, aubergines, tomatoes, some grapevines. The trees around the duck pond were date palms.

The Doctor had made a couple of sorry-looking lemon trees his particular project, trying to coax their shrivelled branches back to life. Gamal el-Bayoumi also had his own little hobby, a small plot near the trees in which he was attempting to grow begonias.

The Doctor leaned against the wall, in the shade, regarding the trees. It was baking hot in the midday sun – most of the prisoners were wearing headcloths to protect their necks and faces, though their rolled-up sleeves were going to result in a few cases of sunburn.

In two weeks, he hadn't been drugged, beaten or put into solitary even once. It was positively confusing.

'It must be the desert,' said the Doctor.

El-Bayoumi looked up. 'Sorry?'

'On the other side.' The Doctor patted the fourth wall. Its bricks were surprisingly cool. 'The city wasn't this hot. And I've not once seen a vehicle fly overhead, unless it was landing here.'

'You're probably right.' El-Bayoumi went back to his seeds. 'Most of this world is desert and savannah. There is plenty of empty space in which to hide a prison away.'

'You must be at least a little curious,' said the Doctor. 'Haven't your family said anything about it, when they've visited? About how far they had to travel or…'

El-Bayoumi shook his head. 'They're under an injunction not to reveal certain information to me,' he said, 'and our conversations are monitored.'

'You must miss them terribly,' said the Doctor gently.

'Of course,' said el-Bayoumi. 'But there's nothing I can do about it.' He dropped a seed into a hole. 'I shall die here.'

The Doctor crouched down. 'Are you ill, Gamal?' he murmured.

'No, I'm fine,' he said, gently covering the seed. 'My sentence is indeterminate. I am in possession of INC's intellectual property. As I resigned –'

'Their intellectual property?' said the Doctor. 'Classified information? What –'

'No,' said el-Bayoumi. 'My heart.'

It hit the Doctor what he was saying. 'They own it?'

El-Bayoumi nodded. 'Their employee health plan. When I needed a replacement, they provided one. Of course, now I can no longer leave their employ, because I would be taking patented INC technology to my new employers –'

'That's barbaric. You haven't committed a crime, you hardly had a choice –'

'Most of the older inmates are here for the same reason,' said el-Bayoumi mildly. 'INC subcontracts to the government to house criminals, but it simply transfers retirees like us to its private prison. They can wipe sensitive information from the mind, safely extract an eye implant. But it would be inhumane to demand vital organs back. And so we end up here.'

The Doctor shook his head. 'I don't understand it,' he said. 'How can you just accept it?'

'Because they don't let you grow flowers in Lindsay,' said someone.

The Doctor glanced up. It was Adnau, a young man – a boy, really –

sentenced for office pilfering. He was wiping the sweat from his face with his headcloth.

'What's Lindsay?' asked the Doctor.

'The high-security prison,' said el-Bayoumi.

'They don't let the violent crims in here with us,' said Adnau. 'They're rotting over in the Brian Lindsay Memorial High Security Correctional Facility.' Adnau crouched down. 'It's not so bad here.'

The Doctor nodded. 'And that's why no one tries to escape,' he said, almost to himself.

'Who wants to? They feed you, they don't beat you up and they don't leave you locked in your cell all day. What have we got to complain about?'

The books hid him from the windows and door as he crept towards the stairwell. There was an I-card slot next to the door; he had slid Ms Salameh's spare keys from her pocket while retrieving some repairs forms from the back of her desk.

Behind the locked door was a flight of scrubbed concrete stairs, leading up to the roof, where Ms Salameh's private 'thopter was parked.

He'd loosened the panel in the library ceiling a week earlier, then squeezed in among the pipes and wiring during his shelving shift that morning. He'd worried that they might send the librarian home early, but she was probably still in the habitat area, trying to explain the loss of one of the prisoners in her charge. Particularly him. She'd have been warned about him.

He opened the door at the top of the stairs, just a crack. The roof was empty, just the 'thopter standing by itself, barely three feet away. Each day it brought a handful of additional staff to the prison and took them back again at night.

He slipped out through the door, keeping the vehicle between him and the compound. Ziba had been right: there were no motion sensors, not even any security cameras. It didn't make sense.

It didn't matter if it made sense. All of the previous escape attempts had just been dry runs for this one. Just practice runs. This time he was leaving it all behind, the library, the games of table tennis, the tuna casserole, all of it. He could puzzle out OBFSC's secrets from the outside.

Carefully, he pulled open the door of the 'thopter.

Rifaat was sitting in the passenger seat.

The Doctor lay curled on his bed in the darkness, thinking. He was wearing the regulation stripy pyjamas, shirt unbuttoned, his feet bare. There wasn't a lot of airflow in the habitat area, so the heat tended to sit on you like a large, furry animal, purring.

Three months. The time had slid by so slowly and yet here he was, three months after that first, hasty dash for freedom, still the guest of OBFSC.

He kept going over each of the escapes, looking for the mistakes he had made, or the moment of bad luck that had brought them crashing down.

The thing that struck him, again and again, was the lack of violence. It didn't make sense, the Doctor thought sleepily. Societies that imprisoned their criminals tended to view them as less than people. They certainly didn't supply them with duck ponds... and INC had a totally free hand, from what he'd learned... at least the pillow was soft... they could have done experiments on the inmates and no one on the outside would have known or cared.

Perhaps they had already been experimented on and none of them realised it.

Never mind that. How is Sam doing? Where is she?

For that matter, would she even be alive in ten years?

Dyed and tattooed, alien chic?

Akalu thought I was just making up the perigosto stick.

Whatever will her parents think?

If the prison is so humane, genteel, low-security, *why can't I get out*?

Akalu stood at the bars, silent, watching Bowman sleep.

You could learn something, Akalu knew, from the details of the cell.

For instance, Bowman had neatly folded his blanket and top sheet on the end of his bed. Ziba Hurst, in the women's block, had balled her blanket up and flung it into a corner.

Bowman was twitching in his sleep. Like a kitten dreaming of running, thought Akalu.

The morale facilitator breathed out a silent sigh. At some stage, this case was going to require his direct intervention.

He walked away, his soft steps echoing in the habitat.

The Doctor opened his eyes.

There was an alien in his cell.

He sat up, staring at the being. It was a humanoid shape – staring insect eyes, swivelling to focus on him. Or perhaps it was a quadruped, lifting up to use its forearms? It was more than a head taller than him.

He felt a sudden rush of relief. At last, at long last, something *different*!

He'd never seen this species before. Fascinating! It looked as though it was made from broken chunks of stained glass – or was that some kind of body armour, or bizarre clothing, hiding the shape of the creature inside?

He held out his hand. 'How do you do?' he said. 'I'm the Doctor.'

The alien reached out, a long, slender arm surrounded by jagged, glistening, glassy planes, pale blue, looking as though they were embedded in its body. The hand at the end extended beyond the armour, dark-blue skin, six jointed fingers.

They closed around his wrist, tugging gently but firmly, pulling him to his feet. He obligingly hopped down from the bed. The insect eyes swivelled again, glittering red, reflecting his face in dozens of tiny facets.

'Now what?' he said.

The fingers flexed against his wrist. The skin felt as though it was becoming rougher, sandpapery. With a start, he realised that the 'broken glass', whatever it was, was emerging from the creature's

76

body.

He tried to pull away, but the alien wouldn't let go of him. 'What are you doing?' he said, as he felt the sharp edges pushing into his skin. 'Stop!'

The being let him go, suddenly, so that he stumbled back and sat on the bed. But the sharp pain in his hand and wrist was increasing, not diminishing. He grabbed at his arm with his other hand as the blue glass started to push its way free of his own skin.

'What is this?' he gasped, staring at the blue fragments that were growing out of him. The alien stood back, impassive, watching with its faceted eyes.

The Doctor stumbled to the bars, but the cry for help dried in his throat. He slid to the floor, sagging against the barred door, staring up at the alien looming over him as the glass chunks forced their way out of the skin of his arm and shoulder.

The alien picked him up as though he weighed nothing, one six-fingered hand closing around his uninjured arm, dragging him up. It stared into his eyes, as though searching for something. He clutched at its hand, weakly, dizzy with its gaze, the room filling with brilliant light, wondering if his whole body was erupting with broken glass.

It dropped him, leaving him on the floor, a single red tear gathering in his left eye, tracing its way down his face and on to the concrete.

Chapter Six
I Into We

Wherever the bus was heading, Sam wasn't going there.

She had a word with the driver while they crossed the hundreds of klicks' worth of savannah, and when they reached the rest station past the Thank God River she clambered off, grabbed her single bag from the luggage rack and stepped down into the desert.

The solar coach rolled away with a faint whirr, which didn't feel right at all. A move this final should be accompanied by the roar of an internal-combustion engine accelerating, and a big cloud of dust and petrol fumes. Instead, her way out was just quietly gone.

The heat was sucking the moisture right out of her mouth. She had to keep swallowing, just to stop that feeling that her insides were shrivelling with each breath. There were a few unhelpful wispy clouds high overhead, but it was a pretty sure thing she was the highest concentration of water within a square mile.

Come to think of it, this spot was probably the highest concentration of *anything* within a square mile. Behind her was the long concrete lump of the bus shelter. To either side was the narrow strip of pavement which connected El Nath to Al Markim. There was a lot of nothing from here to the horizon, in every direction.

She shouldered her bag and scanned the grasslands, looking for whoever was supposed to be coming to meet her.

What if there wasn't anyone?

Good honest work, Ari had said. Livingspace wanted people out here to work on some construction project. Not much pay, but food and a roof over your head, and it was for a good cause. Precisely what the good cause was, though, he'd been a bit vague about.

'Oh. Ah, are you Sam?'

She swung round, searching. There was still no one in sight. 'That's what they tell me,' she said cautiously.

Then he stepped out from around the corner of the shelter, with an apologetic smile. 'Not the most imaginative of greetings, I know, but we do what we can on such short notice.'

He was tall and spindly, a couple of years older than her, and he moved with a sort of graceful awkwardness. His clothes were desert-rat practical – T-shirt water-soaked to keep cool, dark hair pulled back into a ponytail. His skin was deeply tanned. He shook her hand and took her bag in a tangle of separate movements. 'Paul Hamani. I'm here to take you to the village. Here, let me give you a hand with that.'

He reached for her bag. Part of her wanted to clutch on to it as if it was the last thing she had in the world – well, it *was* – but that would be silly. Before she could even open her mouth to say it was no problem to carry it herself, he had hoisted it and was starting back around the shelter, moving in long, loping strides. She almost had to run to keep up. Already that felt a bit familiar. 'Right,' she said, trying to take charge. 'So how far to this village?'

'Oh, just over there,' he said, and pointed as they rounded the shelter. Beyond his hand was a battered teardrop-shaped car and beyond the car was a packed clay track – a sharp line cutting through the plain, with the settlement forming the head of the arrow straight ahead of her. It had been right there all along and she hadn't had the first clue.

'Eurogen Village,' said Paul with a grandiose flip of his fingers. 'Be it ever so humble, there's no place like the middle of nowhere.'

Up close the village was a scattering of geodesic domes and old-fashioned frame houses, a bit more than a klick from the glorified stream that passed for a river. The space closer to the water was filled with fields, green fading to yellowish grasslands and eventually red sand in the distance. Her eyes had to adjust to a whole new range of colours beyond the bland sandy brown she'd got used to.

'Hmm, not bad,' she told him. 'So the houses, these are all your own work, right?'

Paul nodded. 'Mm-hm. The domes are the originals from the first Eurogen mission and the meeting house they built themselves when they realised they were here for the long haul. We could just replace the domes with new prefabricated ones, but then someone'll have to come back in another twenty years and do it all over again.'

'Uh-huh.' He had a great voice just to listen to, a babbling brook of phrases rolling out in an honest-to-God northern accent. She hadn't heard one of those in a while. And the more she just let him talk, the more chance she'd have to size him up and suss out what it was she'd really just walked into.

'So what does Livingspace get out of it?'

'Well, nothing,' he said, surprised. 'It's a not-for-profit organisation, you know that.' Again she watched him as he talked, scrunched over the steering wheel, her eye caught by the small gold Alpha Phi Omega trefoil pin on his collar. 'We're all volunteers, same as you. If you're picked as a project supervisor then that'll get you an extra stipend or two from Livingspace, though.'

'That's what they hired me for,' said Sam.

'Ah. Same as me, then.' He pulled the car up beside the first dome. 'You've got to be a bit of a jack of all trades here. Carpentry, a bit of masonry, some tech work, lots of good old-fashioned fetching and carrying and hammering and banging.'

'Good with your hands, then, are you?' she said.

'Well. Aah.' Paul looked taken aback for a moment, then raised an amused eyebrow.

Paul unfolded himself from the car and heaved her bag over his shoulder, leading her into the village. 'There's a couple of dozen of us, and about twice as many of them. The villagers, I mean.'

Now she could see the peeling paint on the clapboard meeting hall, the gaps where the panels of the geodesic domes had warped till they no longer fitted. Houses of cards, she thought.

There was a second hall, one wall of which was surrounded by volunteers with tools and paint cans. They barely had a moment to look up, entangled in their work.

'Ahh, quick introductions.' Paul spun around, his hand catching each one of the people for just a fraction of a second. 'Khalaf's the redhead; that's Chris with her power drill of doom; that's Tamar; Feroz is the one about to chop off his finger with the paint scraper; oh, ah, there's about a dozen more at the other end of the site right now. Leah's the cook, Amin's the master carpenter –'

'And Brian Weissman as the Beaver,' threw in a short bearded man, who put down his hammer and came over to give Paul a hearty handshake and slap on the back. 'Thanks, Paul. I see you got the *yekl* here in record time.'

Paul grinned to Sam. 'There'll be a quiz on all this afterwards. I hope you were taking notes.'

'No problem, George.'

Now Brian was giving her the same emphatic handshake. 'I'm the project manager for Livingspace . We've spoken over e-mail.'

'Nice to meet you in real life.' Is it always this hot? What are the toilets like? Why are you here? Why am I here? 'When do I start hammering and banging?'

Brian beamed. 'As soon as you're settled in. We're finishing renovations on the mess hall this week, then it's back to structural work on the Kirmizis' new house. You'll love that part: there's a real barn-raising feel to it all –'

'Brian,' called a short blonde woman from down the track. Sam saw her look straight at Brian, shake her head meaningfully and head back behind the nearest dome.

Whatever the message was, it had got through to Brian. He took Paul aside, speaking quietly. Sam stayed just close enough to hear every word. 'Umm, I think we've got another Situation with Lobachevsky. You mind coming with me for a second?'

Paul's eyes flicked over towards her. 'Think she should –'

'Nah, not yet. We want her to like it here, you know?'

Hmm and double hmm. Now Paul was turning to her, with a sheepish shrug – she put on her inquisitive face, not letting them know she'd heard a word.

'Sorry, duty calls,' said Paul. He started backing away after Brian, calling back to her as they headed around the dome. 'Make yourself at home, I'll catch up with you before dinner. Bunkhouse is third on the left!' He vanished around the bend.

She waited about five seconds before following them.

The Situation, apparently, was about someone's proposal to build a hydroponics shed. A bulky bearded man and a woman Sam guessed was his wife by the way she kept patting his hand were having words with one of the volunteers.

'It'd only take a couple of weeks,' said the volunteer, a guy in his early twenties, pink with sunburn. He was waving a bunch of printouts. Architectural plans, Sam guessed. 'We just put up a shed, order in the tubing –'

'We don't need your farblondjet tubing!' said the bearded man.

'Be calm, Mr Lobachevsky,' said Paul. 'It's only an idea at this stage. The whole idea is to make things a bit easier for you farmers –'

Lobachevsky snorted. '*Farmers?* I'm a goddamn *biochemist*. Get me out of my Eurogen contract and I'd be making ninety-eight thousand a year, instead of mixing *fertiliser*.' He pronounced the word as if it had four letters. 'My children, now they're farmers. And they're growing up to enjoy it, because they've never known anything any better. It stinks, I tell you, it goddamn stinks…'

'I don't get it,' said Sam, barging in.

'It's office politics,' murmured Brian. 'The folks here were a Eurogen bio-survey team. They got sent to Ha'olam to let the company know if it was worth harvesting any of the indigenous plants. Then Eurogen cut off the funding because they hit a cash crunch –'

'And they've stayed crunched for twenty-odd years,' Paul put in.

'But they won't let their employees out of their contract,' concluded Brian.

Mrs Lobachevsky sighed. 'Our contract can be terminated only if both sides agree. Eurogen just won't agree. After all, they might need us again some day.'

'And our pay, it's performance-related,' grumbled Lobachevsky. 'They give us no work to do, we don't perform. We don't perform, they give us no pay. Such a sensible arrangement.'

'Bastards,' pronounced Sam, shocking them all. 'And you can't take another job?'

'Oh, of course. On that, they're so generous. Our contract says we're free to look for other employment – but not in anything related to our field.' Lobachevsky threw his arms wide in a why-me shrug. 'If we did, to them we'd be passing secrets to their competitors. They say they taught us everything we know and we can't take it with us if we go.'

'Just like we could leave the site,' said Mrs Lobachevsky, 'if we don't take anything we have with us. Eurogen owns the contract on the land, on the survey team buildings, on our car...'

'So we sit. And then these youngsters want to make us more buildings. Tie us down to this spot even more.'

The sunburnt guy looked glum. 'Sorry,' he muttered. 'I didn't think of it like that.'

'Since you're stuck here,' said Sam, cutting across a rude remark from Lobachevksy, 'you might as well make the most of it.' She took the plans from the flustered student. 'Yeah, this might mean you can produce more food with less work. Could be a useful temporary measure, while you're waiting for a way out.'

Mrs Lobachevsky took the plans from her. 'We'll look at these, at least.' She gave her husband a look. 'We promise. Thank you, Isaac. Welcome...'

'Sam Jones.' She stuck her hand out and Lobachevsky was so surprised that he shook it.

'Nice work,' said Paul, as Sam plopped her bag on the cheap wire-frame bed. 'Lobachevsky's a thorn in everyone's side.'

'Being stranded sucks,' said Sam. 'I'd be a thorn in everyone's side if I was trapped in the desert for years.' Her bed, like all those in the bunkhouse, was surrounded with cubicle dividers pillaged from corporate surplus. At least she had a minimum of privacy, which was a bloody godsend after months of having to duck into the shelter bathroom just to change clothes. 'Have they really had kids since getting stuck here?'

Paul nodded. 'A lot of the villagers have. Sometimes I think the kids would be happier if their parents just gave it up and settled down.'

'Hard to believe there's no way out at all.'

'Oh, there was,' said Paul. 'Some of them opted for the neuredit.'

'I'm sorry,' said Sam, 'could you read that again?'

'They can terminate their contract. If they agree to have all Eurogen proprietary training and information erased from their brains,' said Paul.

Sam's mouth fell open. '*Utter* bastards.'

'A few of them went ahead with it, long before we got here. Apparently the rest of them were put off the idea by the results.'

Sam slammed her locker shut and pocketed the key. 'I don't think I want to know. OK, now what?'

'Let's get back to the mess hall,' smiled Paul. 'I'll show you how to hit nails instead of your thumbs.'

'Right,' said Sam.

As she followed him out of the bunkhouse, she was still trying to work it out. What was so important about this place? Why didn't the villagers just get on a bus and go? Maybe because they now felt it was home, maybe because it just wasn't as easy for them to give up what little they had, the way she just had. But what were the Livingspace people doing here, besides sweltering?

Probably the same thing she was doing. Making a living, without shrivelling in a corporation cubicle. She'd rather hammer nails into her own head than work an eyeset again.

At dinner that night in the mess hall Brian stood her up and introduced her to the others *en masse*. They greeted her with bursts of applause and bickered over which table to invite her to.

Over the spicy lentils and rice, ladled out by Leah to all comers, she chatted and listened and tried to work her way into the web of project references and in-jokes. There was no mistaking that most of these people had spent solid months surrounded by each other; they kept having to pause the conversation to explain the jokes to her. They could close ranks completely around a secret, she realised, and she'd be none the wiser.

She ended up volunteering with the clean-up detail – same routine, different kitchen. With Leah the cook and Deeb the student, she picked up and washed up and dried up.

'So how was your first day?' asked Leah.

'Well, I'm now proficient in fetching and carrying.' Sam smiled. 'It was pretty impressive to watch the group in operation.'

'There are projects like this one all over human space,' Deeb enthused, scrubbing at a burnt bit of rice. 'Livingspace have been doing this for a couple of centuries.'

'I read up a bit.' Sam nodded. 'It's completely funded by donations, right?'

'That's right,' said Leah. 'We don't get anything from the government.'

'Do the corporations chip in?' asked Sam.

'Sometimes,' said Leah. 'It's great PR.'

'Hmm,' said Sam.

After two weeks, she could make a join, make a weld and make some sense of an architectural plan. Her hair was an inch long. She'd cut it once, and then again, hoping it would cool her head down. Her clothes were always blotched with sweat.

They were putting the finishing touches on the renovated mess hall. Tomorrow they'd be able to put the windows back in and take down all the plastic sheets that stopped sawdust and sand getting into everyone's meal. Right now she was checking a length of optical cable that had been stapled on to the roof. Almost everyone else was putting the final coat of paint on the outside.

The volunteers were a real mixture. Some, like Deeb or Isaac, came straight from off-world universities, hoping to fill out a service requirement they needed to graduate.

There were a couple of other street kids, all rough edges and graceless energy, looking for a non-threatening way to survive; glowing freshmen, idealism slightly wilted under the heat and skin blossom-pink from too much sun; shameless résumé-padders; and cocky Crimson Star veterans just out of the military, trying to do something useful for the world in the absence of any significant wars.

Some were there for a month or two, some for the duration of the project and some, like Amin the carpenter, were there because it was their career.

And then there were a few, like Brian, like Paul, like Leah, whom she couldn't quite put her finger on. Everyone had to have an angle – whether one as innocent as Sara trying to save souls while saving them from the street, or as devious as INC funding homeless shelters to find a source of cheap labour.

It had to be there – they were just keeping it close to their chests. Livingspace had to have some interest of its own, and if she could figure out Brian or Paul she'd know what was going on under the table.

And then... well, then she'd know where she stood.

It took a few weeks of careful prying. She had a bunch of long conversations with Brian as they rebuilt the village's clapped-out hydrazine generator. He told her stories from the Livingspace sites he'd run on three worlds.

'Sounds like a lot of your work gets done in the Alien Quarters,' she said, as they lugged cans of fuel from the car to the generator's shed.

'Yah.' Brian grunted as he hefted a can on to a trolley. 'An awful lot of non-human populations are displaced by colonisation. They end up living in the crevices of the colonies.'

'I hear Human Outreach does a lot of work in that area too,' said Sam.

'Yeah,' said Brian. 'More in development than housing. The projects overlapped on Eostre 5 – we ended up building a school with help from Outreach. Nice people.'

Yeah, nice. Reaching out to their alien brothers in an effort to spread civilised human values, assimilate their culture out of existence and school their kids to think like real people.

But no matter how much she led the conversation towards that, he never let a scrap of ideology slip. Brian didn't seem to have an ideology beyond getting the chores done.

Paul didn't seem to have much more of a *raison d'être* either. This was just what he felt like doing at the moment. He called it his 'wannabehemian lifestyle', and made mysterious remarks about his sordid past, which usually got a laugh from anyone in earshot.

They nicknamed her Paul's 'shadow', because she followed him everywhere; he was unofficially in charge of teaching her how to build a house or empty a chemical toilet, explaining how the computers and the generator worked.

She and Paul stayed up all night once, trying to find the mistake in a wiring diagram. Once they tried to make pizza with native 'tomatoes'; someone suggested they use the results as spare dome panels. They cooked together, talked together, played terrible practical jokes on each other, and after nearly a month she managed to get a good look over his shoulder as he typed in his override password.

That night she sneaked into Brian's office, a buzz of fear building in her chest.

Stay calm, Sam, you've done this sort of thing so many times before. Keep that buzz under control. Let it keep you sharp.

There it was, a datatablet with a thumbprint security key. That was simplicity itself to get around – she hit the maintenance override key, typed in the password, and the datatablet sprang to life. She crouched down behind the corner of the desk, her face barely lit by the glow of the datatablet display, and got ready for the fun part.

She was no *shifter*, but thanks to INC she'd picked up enough about the information hardware of this century to at least do a bit of poking around. There'd be some kind of clues at least to whatever was going on here, even if the important ones were all encrypted. Start with the operating budget files –

The door opened with a click. Paul was a silhouette, his hair haloed by the light from the doorway.

The buzz turned into a sharp spike in her chest.

'Oh – Paul. I was just…'

'Just?' he prompted her.

She sighed. 'Just trying to think of a better reason for what I was doing than simple curiosity. Sorry.' She gave a carefully embarrassed grin.

'Oh, I think you do have a better one,' Paul said quietly.

She tightened. Back away around the desk, keep it between him and you in case he tries to lunge at you. She snatched up a stapler, feeling its metal weight in her hand.

He went on, in a relentless low murmur. 'You're looking for something about Livingspace, aren't you? Trying to find some dirty bit of politics you can dig up. Is that it?'

Her grip tightened on the stapler.

He stopped and shrugged casually. 'Well, go ahead. Don't mind me.'

Her instincts were shouting fight or fly. Her instincts were nuts. Paul, laughing, freckled, green-eyed Paul, took another slow step around the edge of the desk towards her.

'Go on,' he said. 'Look at those records. You won't find anything wrong with them.' Sam glanced at the screen. 'But that won't be enough to convince you if you really think there's something wrong – no, it's got to be buried deeper, always just a little bit beyond your reach. You *know* it's there, it's got to be, that's what you believe in. That's all you believe in.'

'That's because it keeps being true.' She stepped back, bumped into the wall behind her.

'But why?' He wasn't letting go of it. She could barely make out his eyes in the shadow, but she could feel them on her. 'You've been looking for some sort of villain ever since you got here –'

'They're always there!' she snapped.

'Where?'

'They're there every time. Whenever I start believing things are going fine. That's when people start dying or turning into monsters. Or saying they're activists or freedom fighters, and then they turn out to be as bad as the ones they're fighting against. Sorry. You can't keep feeding me that one.' The buzz was swelling out of control, dragging her along with it. 'I'm not letting myself walk into it again, got that?'

He just looked at her. There was bewilderment spreading across his face, and little points of pain in the palm of the hand holding the stapler, and what in hell was she *doing*?

He just kept looking at her. He looked... sad?

'Do you have to work at being that cynical?' he asked. 'I mean, do you have to take special classes or something?'

'It just sort of happens,' she said in a very small voice.

He reached to put an arm around her shoulders; she tensed, reflexively, and he stopped.

'You know what the worst part of it is?' she mumbled. 'The worst part is going on a big glorious rant and then right in the middle of it you realise you hate every word you're saying. And you don't believe it, but you do believe it, and you just can't shut yourself up.'

'Is that really what you believe?' he asked quietly.

Sam muttered, 'What else is there any more?'

Paul sat down on the desk, so that his eyes were level with hers. 'What about believing in us?'

She was quiet for a long time. The buzz was giving up, collapsing in on itself, leaving a hollowness in its place.

'Something to say?' he asked.

'Thanks,' she said, letting herself curl up with tiredness. 'For talking me down.'

He let out a sigh and a grin. 'Glad it worked. You have no idea how long I've been working on that speech.'

She nearly dropped the stapler. 'Wait. You mean you knew I was going to –'

'Oh, I've been wanting to talk to you about this for a week now. I think your speech was better than mine, though.'

Sam laughed giddily. 'I dunno,' she said. 'I mean, what do *you* say when you realise you've just shoved your foot in your mouth up to the kneecap?'

He grinned. 'Here, let me help with that,' he said, and mimed pulling the foot out for her.

It was about the time of the First Friday Fire that she realised how things were changing.

The first inkling came while she was up on the roof of what would be the Luchenko house, nailing the edges of prefab roof panels into place and carrying on a running discussion with Kafiyeh the mason about the latest album from the Pickled Pupils. She had a squeeze-bottle to keep her throat moist, skin cool, headband lightly damp, and to squirt at Paul and Feroz as they passed beneath her.

With a final smack she nailed the last corner of the vast roof into place, and couldn't help but face the fact that, dear God in heaven, she was *enjoying* this.

Now that wasn't a familiar feeling at all. At INC the only thing you could be close to proud of was clearing your in-tray – and since you didn't have anything else to show for your time, you ended up taking a petty obsessive delight in making sure absolutely everything was in its place. But here every day something in the village looked distinctly different, because of *her*.

Paul poked his head out from under the A-frame supports of the roof, scored a bull's-eye on her mouth with a blast from his own water bottle and said, 'Coming to the bonfire tonight?'

She unscrewed her bottle top behind her back and splooshed her remaining water down on to his face as he lay there. 'What bonfire?' she asked sweetly.

'We have one on the first Friday of every month,' he said, shaking the water out of his hair. 'It helps keep the villagers and volunteers from killing one another. It's harder to strangle someone you were getting paralytic with the night before.'

'Oh, so that's what everyone's been talking about,' said Sam. 'I'll be there or set square.'

The moon was like a searchlight that night. The bonfire was a great pile of fallen branches and leftover planks. Music played, louder than the flames: a radio – well, a terminal relaying one of the popular music broadcasts – and an improvised band.

Leah had done herself proud. There were lots of hot rolls, unleavened bread and tin-foiled bundles of cake and scones smoking at the edges of the fire. Great kettles of rice and goat's meat and lentils and coffee were steaming over smaller fires of their own. A cool box contained juice and booze and fruit salad with crushed ice in it.

Someone had thrown whole pots of incense into the fire, giving the night a rich, sweet smell that reminded Sam of Christmas pudding. Hookahs had appeared, and card tables and backgammon and chess sets. A couple of the village kids shouted and played tag and never quite managed to knock everything over.

Paul was cranking the spit over the fire, swigging cider and singing something fundamentally keyless under his breath. Sam lay sprawled out by his feet, leaning on her rucksack, soaking up the life. Everything seemed a bit more *there* than usual.

She was pointing out the moths flitting around the fire – or whatever they were: big, fluffy insectoids attracted by the light. Ha'olam didn't have any life forms larger than a sparrow. At least these mothoids had the sense to stay out of the flames.

'The first time I ever got to touch a butterfly,' she said, 'it was really weird... like the skin on your fingertips is too thick to really feel what it feels like.'

'They never stay still for me,' said Paul. 'They hear me sneaking up.'

She sat up. 'You've got to see the butterfly room!' she said, without thinking.

'What's that, then?'

'Um...' Well, she'd stepped right into that one. Say as much as you can get away with.' Right. Imagine a room, a huge room with a hillside and meadow in it, and about a billion butterflies. All kinds of species, mostly from Earth but from other planets too.'

He looked fascinated. 'Where's that, then?'

'I saw it a few times,' said Sam. 'On my travels, you know.'

'You've seen a lot of places,' said Paul.

'And I've done a lot of things,' said Sam. 'But when it comes down to it, I haven't *been* all that much yet.'

'You want to go for a walk?' said Paul casually.

'Yeah, I do,' said Sam. They didn't look at each other, not exactly, just out of the corners of their eyes. 'Let's get out of this noise for a bit.'

They sat on a blanket near the bank of the Thank God River, watching the reflection of the moon. A bright reddish patch in the distance was the party, still in full swing.

They sat barely an inch apart. Paul turned to her and gave her a smile. He'd let his hair down and it had exploded outward in a wiry mass. It was the perfect moment to lean over and give him an experimental kiss. Instead she gave a wilted smile and moved a bit further away.

'Lovely out here, isn't it?' Paul shivered happily. 'It's the kind of night where you want to run through the woods stark naked and be at one with nature. Except that, ah, there's no woods around here, so you'd look rather conspicuous.'

Sam started to laugh, but it turned into a small, peculiar noise.

Paul turned to look at her again. 'Has anyone ever told you that you have an incredibly cute nose?'

The peculiar noise came out again. 'Oh, hell,' said Paul. 'Oh, *hell*, massive miscalculation. Sorry.'

'No, no,' said Sam. 'It's not that.' With a sudden movement she pulled off her headband and wiped the sweat from her scalp. 'This is the bit where the aliens beam down and eat your head.'

Paul started to laugh and then looked at her in bewilderment. He glanced at the sky, involuntarily.

'I'm not joking,' said Sam. 'This is how it works. Things get good, something horrible happens.'

'Shh. It's all right.' He didn't lay a finger on her, just quietly gathered himself up and began to stand. 'Doesn't matter, we can just go back –'

'Hey, Paul. *Paul*. Look at me.' She caught his shoulder and stared straight into his eyes until she knew he was really listening. 'See me, right here. Am I going anywhere?'

'Scared?' Paul murmured.

''Course.'

'Me too,' said Paul. Very carefully, he put an arm around her. She leaned her head on his shoulder.

'The Lacaillans say that we're not really the sum of our achievements, we're the sum of our possibilities at any given moment,' said Paul. 'When that sum gets down to zero, we're dead.'

'Don't remind me,' said Sam. 'I just spent half a year somewhere down in the lower decimal places.'

'But see, you got out.' Paul stroked her hair as though it was the fur of a cat. 'You brought yourself up from zero. And I admire that. I don't think I could ever have done it myself...'

Somewhere inside, the dark-haired Sam was smirking.

Blonde Sam curled away from him, staring into the night. 'Dunno... I don't really think I have, you know...'

'Maybe you just need a little help,' purred Paul.

Dark-haired Sam was probably laughing her head off at that. Here come the alien head-eaters, she'd be sneering.

Stuff that. *That* Sam hadn't got to this place; *she* had. *This* was who she was.

She raised her eyes to him, leaned in and planted a slow, deliberate kiss on his lips. He tasted of cider. 'It's worth a try.'

'What's this?' asked Paul. His fingers caught her TARDIS key and lifted it away from her skin. He held it up to the moonlight, letting it spin on its chain, catching and scattering the silver.

'It's a long story,' she said, looking away. She hadn't really felt the key there for months – it had become as familiar and unnoticed as a wedding ring.

They were sitting pressed together near the river bank. It was just chilly enough for them to notice. They were just warm enough together not to mind.

'It's beautiful,' he said.

She sniggered. 'Come on, it's a *door key*.'

'To a magic door?' She saw that raised eyebrow again, and she wasn't sure if he was leading up to something rude or he really meant the question.

'To the place with the butterflies,' she said.

Her arm reached around him, her fingers exploring the back of his hand, trying to memorise each ridge and wrinkle. It was funny: this – just this – was more time than she'd spent touching another person the whole time she'd been on this world.

She *could* touch him. The thought kept surprising her each time it crossed her mind.

'So who let you in there?' he asked gently. 'I mean, there must be someone.'

She suddenly noticed her own skin, how pale she looked in the moonlight, how defenceless she was. Defenceless because she didn't need to defend herself. This was one of the moments when it *was* safe.

'All right then,' she said, 'I'll tell you. Promise you won't laugh…'

And she told him, and he did laugh, but only when she started laughing too. There was something about the earnest look on his face – when she realised he *believed* her – that just set her off.

'Well, it's not really that much of a stretch,' he said seriously. 'There are plenty of alien races out there and some of them really are pretty out-there. So maybe one of them's got time travel.' He shrugged. 'Works for me.'

'You'll believe anything I tell you,' she leered.

'Of course,' he said, kissing her fingers.

'Good.'

* * *

Two months on.

His big mistake was mentioning it when she was wedged in a crevice two-thirds of the way up a rock face, trying to inch her left foot up to the next foothold without falling on top of him. He said something like, 'Don't worry, I've got you. Think of me as your NSM.'

'What?'

'Nice Safe Man. Y'know, like the Doctor.'

Her stomach flipped. She pushed her fingers into the rock, suddenly convinced she was going to lose her grip. It was her first time free-climbing, after a month or two of picking up every bit of technique she could from Paul. 'You've got to be kidding me,' she said.

'You know,' said Paul. He hauled himself up to the next ledge. 'Like I used to flirt with Kafiyeh, because we both knew she only liked girls. It could never be, so the schoolboy crush was perfectly safe.'

She dragged herself up the last few feet and collapsed on the ledge beside him. 'Can you get that through your head, right?' she said through gritted teeth. 'This was not some moony little teenage crush. This is a real live want-to-throw-him-on-the-floor-and-shag-him-till-bits-break-off kind of *problem*. All right?'

They made it up the last twenty feet of cliff and staggered back to the tent they'd set up earlier. Sam sat down, groaning as her muscles complained, and started struggling out of her boots.

'So why didn't you?' said Paul.

'Why didn't I what?' said Sam, locked in battle with her shoelaces.

'Break bits off him.'

'I don't know,' said Sam. 'It wouldn't be right. It'd be like snogging your uncle. Anyway, he never shows any interest at all in that kind of stuff.'

'As I said, classic Nice Safe Man. The lofty Time Lord who'd never be interested in all that. Even if you did get up the nerve to throw him to the floor on the spur of the moment.'

She gave him a look. 'This is a man who one afternoon went bungee-jumping from a plane. On the spur of the moment.'

A pause. Paul's eyes widened. 'I begin to see the problem,' he said.

'Oh, you don't know the half of it. You should have seen the general's face when she found out what he'd borrowed the cargo transport for...'

'So d'you think it was just an alien thing?' said Paul. 'He really just isn't that kind of guy?'

'Maybe it was just me being a good girl.'

Paul lay back, looking up at her. 'And are you a good girl, Ms Jones?'

Lips pressed hard against his sandalwood blood frost ozone sweet pressing and pressing wake up goodbye kiss ...

She looked him in the eye. 'Do you think so?' she said.

He broke up laughing, and she had to snog him just to shut him up.

Three months on.

She finally stopped waking up in the middle of the night clutching out at him, knowing that something horrible was going to happen to him, just because that was the way it was.

She told Paul she loved him, and he said it too, and they had a big worry about whether the words came too easily before deciding not to get too stressed out over it.

Four months on.

She realised she really didn't like the way he snored, and he got a bit irritated when he had to tell her for the third time what his favourite colour was, and they both found themselves noticing the pauses in their conversations more and more.

When she thought of the years he'd spent slumming, they began to seem less like a grand exploration of freedom, more a long stretch of unfulfilled potential.

'That's me,' said Paul one evening, stung by the meaning under her words as they talked about the days before Ha'olam. 'Amiably unambitious. The bloke with nowhere to go.'

'All I was saying was –'

'Of course, you ever think maybe it might be a bit more difficult to get about when you don't have a flaming chauffeur-driven *time*

97

machine?'

After that they both fell silent, the way they were beginning to get used to doing, letting the fight dissolve into nothing.

Five months on.

She almost couldn't believe she was sitting there, on the opposite corner of her bunkhouse bed from him, saying, 'We can still be friends, right?' She'd never been able to connect the cliché to this knife-wound feeling before.

She couldn't blame him in the slightest when he stood up, framed in the moonlight, and said, 'Aah, you know it's bollocks. See you in the morning.'

Then he walked round the cubicle wall into his own bedspace, the one just next to hers, and they each spent the rest of the night trying to put out of their minds how thin that corporate beige divider was.

OK. So something horrible on a cosmic scale had utterly failed to happen. So this was just the kind of ordinary failing that millions of people across the galaxy went through, when 'we' became less important than 'I'. Somehow large amounts of chocolate would feel like a better consolation right now, she figured.

Seven months on.

Sam herded the last of the kids into the village, counted heads and sent them wandering home for supper.

They'd camped for the last two days at her semi-permanent site two klicks upstream, near her and Paul's spot. She'd been taking little groups out there for a few weeks, teaching them desert survival skills and knot-tying and stuff. Managing to keep half a dozen pre-teens from getting themselves killed over a weekend was more of a challenge than anything Daleks or Tractites could have thrown at her.

Brian came to fetch her once she'd made sure all of the kids had either been collected or dispatched home. '*Shalom,*' he said. 'How did they behave themselves?'

'They're a pretty good gang,' she said, following him back to the mess hall. 'How about their parents?'

Brian barked a laugh. 'We've been good boys and girls,' he said. 'We've been getting ready for the harvest. It looks as though we've nearly doubled the yield this year with the new crop strains.'

Sam grinned, remembering when the villagers had been 'they' instead of 'we'. She wondered if Brian had even noticed. Then again, she hadn't noticed the moment when she'd stopped saying 'I' and started saying 'we' either.

'There's a new group of recruits coming in this afternoon,' said Brian, as they sat down with their trays of lunch. 'Can I get you to pick them up in the bus?'

'No problem.' She noted with a faint smile that she and Paul had instinctively positioned themselves at opposite ends of the same tableful of friends. Avoiding someone in a village of eighty people required a special sort of art.

Ten months on.

'Typical, isn't it?' said Paul. 'Throw a big elaborate party and the guest of honour ends up lurking outside.'

The volunteers and villagers had improvised a nineteen and a halfth birthday party for her – a restaging of the nineteenth birthday party they'd planned to give her the night the irrigation pumps exploded. She wasn't quite sure how they'd known the date; she must have mentioned something to Paul, probably showing off her watch. Her eighteenth had come and gone unremarked during her stay in the shelter.

She'd left the mess hall to breathe the desert quiet and found him also standing in the dark, just out of reach.

'Just wanted to look at the place a bit,' she said. 'It's funny how the skyline changes.' Just in the months since she'd come here, the place already looked so different – the solid brick storehouse they'd spent months on had filled in a big chunk of the horizon from here, and the frame of what would be the new Lobachevsky house was already standing like a wooden skeleton against the sky.

'Yeah,' he said gently, 'you've done a hell of a lot.'

She was dating Chris now, and Paul was putting up his tent with Tamar, and when you looked at it none of them was really the worse for wear. 'It's been a long time, hasn't it?' she said.

'What do you mean?'

'Just one of those moments. You know. Realising it's been longer *since* you were with someone than you were actually together.'

He nodded. 'Mm. You were only with him for, what, ten or eleven months, right? You're well past that long now…'

'Wait a minute,' she said. 'Who're you talking about?'

'Um, wossname. The Doctor.'

'I was talking about you, *schmeckl*.'

He did a wonderful slow-motion take. 'Whoops.' She laughed, reached up and did the pulling-the-foot-out mime. It had been a long time since she'd got to do that.

They were quiet for a moment, their eyes on the sky. 'Wherever he is, I hope he's having fun,' she said casually, and then took his arm. 'C'mon, let's go back inside.'

Chapter Seven
Eye-Bugged Monster

He had expected to be able to see the outside world, but the surrounding walls were at least ten feet higher than the roof. The sunlight reflected off the grey of the concrete and the coloured tape that marked out the landing areas, almost dazzling.

There was a cargo 'thopter parked on the roof, its loading hatch open. He jogged across to it, looking around. No sign of the pilot – he or she would be in the office one floor down, buried in paperwork.

The Doctor pulled open the vehicle's door and hauled himself into the pilot's seat. He closed the cargo hatch, overrode the security lock, hot-wired the I-card slot and brought the wing engines on line. There was a roaring, and a whirring from the rear of the 'thopter as it powered up.

He would have to go as far and as fast as he could, then fake a crash landing, preferably close to civilisation.

Through the windscreen, he saw Rifaat – watching him patiently? The guard's arms were folded. The Doctor grabbed the controls. Rifaat looked at one hand and picked a bit of grit out from underneath one of his nails.

The 'thopter's security force field grabbed him. It felt as though someone had dropped a piano on him.

The Doctor gasped as the field contracted, holding him in the pilot seat. It was the 'thopter's crash-safety field, he realised, gulping for breath. He hadn't done anything to activate it – it must be a security measure he'd missed.

He could still reach the controls. Rifaat yawned as the Doctor tried to deactivate the crash field, but the 'thopter wasn't having any of it. The more he moved, the tighter the thing got, until he was starting to see red sparkles around the edges of his vision.

In the end he had to give up, sagging in the field until Rifaat came to let him out and march him back to his cell.

'That makes ninety-*seven* attempts,' said Akalu. He paced behind Bowman's chair in his office. 'In eighteen months.'

'Seventeen months.' Bowman slumped back in his chair. He reached into his sleeve and extracted the teddy bear. 'Twenty-two days, eight hours –' he glanced at the clock on the wall – 'twelve minutes.'

Akalu had developed several theories about the teddy bear. Bowman did not keep it with him at all times, but was often seen carrying it about, propping it up on a desk in the workshop or pushing it around on a trolley in the library.

The other inmates didn't seem to tease him about it, which suggested to Akalu that they understood it better than he did.

'Would you like to hear about the time the Tractites held me prisoner?' said Bowman.

'Yes,' said Akalu, surprised.

'To be fair,' said Bowman, 'it was really just one particular Tractite… She kept me locked in a cell for six weeks without food. Her way of killing me, without killing me.'

'Barbaric,' said Akalu.

'After a while,' said Bowman, the teddy bear forgotten in his hand, 'the hunger stopped bothering me. I just switched it off. But the boredom… you can't switch that off. All the memories and meditations and word games simply dry up after a while.'

Akalu shifted in his seat. 'Mr Bowman –'

He raised a hand, gesturing as though he held something tiny in front of his eyes. 'And you're left aware, absolutely aware of every moment that passes. Every second. One after the other.'

'Mr Bowman,' said Akalu. 'Where are you from?'

'Andromeda,' said the Doctor. 'My mother was abducted by little green men.'

Akalu sighed. The spell was broken. 'Well, never mind about that now.' There'd be plenty of time to discuss it, after all.

'What about the alien that attacked me?' Oh no, not this again. 'Centaurid, carapaced, covered in light-blue plating, compound eyes –'

Akalu sighed. 'That was months ago. We made a full investigation. There was absolutely no evidence –'

'Oh, of course there wasn't,' sighed Bowman. He glanced at his unscarred hands.

'You'd think that if there were space monsters running around here, someone might have noticed,' said Akalu lightly. 'Many of the staff think you invented that story, you know.'

'Whatever for?'

'You seem intent on drawing attention to yourself,' said Akalu. 'Is that what these escapes are really about? An effort to stand out from the other inmates – to be noticed?'

'Actually, they're an expression of a subtransitory experiential hypertoid-induced condition, aggravated by multi-encephalogical tensions,' said Bowman, deadpan. 'Romana always said I had a death wish.'

'I'm afraid,' said Akalu, as he took the cups from his drinks machine, 'that the Institutional Superintendent thinks you should be punished for your behaviour. As a disincentive. You're becoming a drain on our resources.'

'How?' said Bowman, accepting the proffered cup. 'You don't assign guards to me, you haven't done anything to stop me.'

'You caused quite a disruption this morning,' said Akalu. 'Ms Salameh was beside herself.'

'Poor Ms Salameh,' said Bowman. 'It's almost as bad as being forcibly imprisoned because someone else holds the copyright on your heart.'

'Which has nothing to do with your sentence,' Akalu reminded him. 'You're guilty of a criminal offence, not a civil one.'

'How are you going to punish me?' said Bowman, taking a mouthful of tea.

It was worth a try. Akalu reached over the desk and took the teddy bear out of Bowman's hand.

Bowman stared in disbelief. For a moment, Akalu thought the man was going to reach over and snatch the bear back.

'Something always goes wrong,' muttered the Doctor over dinner. 'Something *always* goes wrong.'

Ziba shrugged and made spoon patterns in her stew.

'It's always some little thing. The guards change their routine slightly. I disable an alarm, but it's been repaired when I return.' He ran his hands sharply through his hair, squeezing it as though trying to make his brain work harder. 'How did Rifaat know where I was? How could he have reached the 'thopter before me?'

'What'd you do this time?' she asked.

The Doctor gave her a sharp look, startling her. 'Why exactly do you want to know?'

'Because I'm telling Rifaat everything you tell me,' said Ziba.

'What!'

'Joke!' said Ziba, too loudly. 'If I was telling, I wouldn't tell *you*, would I?'

His look didn't get much less serious. He tore a corner off a piece of half-stale bread, staring at it thoughtfully. 'Dr Akalu took my bear,' he said glumly.

'My guess?' said Ziba. 'You get it back if you're a good boy.'

'That's the idea,' said the Doctor. 'No security cameras,' he muttered, 'no electric eyes. No surveillance devices more sophisticated than an attentive guard.'

'It's like they don't expect anyone to try to get out,' said Ziba. 'You hear about escapes and riots over at Lindsay all the time, and they're full of the foremost security stuff.' She fiddled with the salt and pepper shakers. The Doctor idly noticed that a new phrase had appeared on her left hand: *slogo pogo*. 'Before you, I don't remember anybody ever trying to get away.'

'He shouldn't have taken my bear away,' said the Doctor grimly. 'He doesn't know who he's dealing with.'

Ziba looked him in the eyes. 'Take me with you.'

The Doctor stopped dead.

'Mean it, moon man.'

'How many times…' he murmured to himself. 'It will be dangerous,' he said.

'Come on,' said Ziba. 'The worst that'll happen is they give us detention.'

'I meant,' he said, 'if we do manage to get out.'

'I don't care,' said Ziba. 'I'll whip us up both a couple of new I-cards and identity files in about five seconds flat. You just get me near a terminal.'

'Ziba, I… This isn't a good idea. You've only got a couple of years left. Let time pass. Wait out the rest of your sentence. Go home to your parents. Put your skills to work in a good job.'

'Come out of fantasy land,' said Ziba. 'My parents don't want a shifter for their daughter. Nobody wants a shifter using their computers.' She took hold of his sleeve. 'I've got it all worked out. I can help you. Get me out of here.'

Once a month an industrial 'thopter came to take away the sheets and uniforms that were too worn to be used. The torn and frayed cloth accumulated in great canvas skips, twice the length of the normal ones.

The Doctor leaned forwards, straining to keep the skip moving. You didn't realise how much cloth weighed until you gathered so much of it together.

They formed a convoy, three of the long skips moving down the corridor. Only one of them could fit into the roof lift at a time. The Doctor and Adnau helped another prisoner wrestle their load of sheets into the lift.

They leaned on their own skips, waiting for their turn, being bored.

'Hello, Mr Bowman,' said Rifaat.

They both looked up. 'Oh no,' said the Doctor.

'Unload that skip, please.'

'There's nothing in it,' protested the Doctor. 'I mean, besides rags.'

'Just do as you're told, Mr Bowman,' said Rifaat. 'If you don't mind.'

The Doctor sighed. He leaned into the skip and started pulling handfuls of torn sheets and worn uniforms out. With a frown, he dropped them on to the concrete floor, then scooped up another double armful, then another, until the bottom of the long skip appeared.

The other guards looked surprised, as though they'd been expecting him to have squirrelled a flitter away in the skip.

'I'm sorry to disappoint you,' said the Doctor, 'but after washing clothes all day I haven't the energy for an escape attempt.'

'Now the other one,' said Rifaat.

'What?' said Adnau. 'What'd I do?'

Rifaat ignored him. 'Empty it out,' he told the Doctor.

'Oh, *kaf kardam*, forget it!' came an angry voice from inside the skip. There was a movement among the sheets and then Ziba emerged like a chick from its egg. 'It was getting stuffy in there anyway.'

She started to climb over the side of the skip, nearly tipping it up. The Doctor lifted her out and swung her down to the floor. 'Sorry,' she said to Rifaat. 'Dropped my contact lens in there, oh where, oh where?'

Adnau hid a grin. Rifaat wasn't laughing. 'Dr Akalu wants to see you,' he told the Doctor. He turned to Ziba. 'You can put this lot back in the skip and get it up to the roof.'

'Nine more times in three weeks,' muttered Akalu.

'How did you know she was in the skip?' said Bowman.

How could he help this man? Bowman had never shown any signs of adjusting to his new situation. He lived in an obsessive fantasy of escape.

'Mr Bowman –' he began.

'How did you know?' said Bowman. 'You always find out. Do you have an informant? Do the walls have eyes?'

'I won't have this!' Akalu was surprised by the anger in his own voice. He pressed his palms against the desktop, calming himself. 'It's my job to see to your well-being. And you're making that job as difficult as possible – making things as bad for yourself as you can.'

'Don't struggle and it won't hurt,' sneered Bowman. 'Now you've taken away my library card, the paintings I've done. What next? No more table tennis?'

Akalu restrained himself from slamming a fist into his desk. 'That's not what I'm talking about,' he said. 'I'm talking about what you're putting yourself through. The false hope you're giving yourself. That kind of behaviour is my problem as much as yours.'

'You're saying,' said Bowman, 'that it's normal, trapped in a place like this, *not* to try to get out.'

'In case you hadn't noticed,' said Akalu drily, 'no one else has been trying to steal 'thopters, disguising themselves as correctional officers, or altering cutlery into devices of burglary.'

'Think of it this way,' said Bowman. 'I'm keeping your guards in fine form.'

'I really can see no other alternative.' Akalu opened his desk drawer and took out a metal box. Bowman sat up, trying to see what he had.

Akalu pushed the box across the desk to him. Bowman frowned at him, lips pursed, puzzled. He opened the box carefully.

Akalu watched as Bowman checked its contents – his library card, his paintings, carefully rolled. Even the teddy bear.

'There's no point in my keeping them,' Akalu sighed. 'At least if you're painting pictures, you're not crawling through the ventilation ducting.'

His paintings had not even been damaged, not a fold or crumple. Habitual neatness on the part of the 'correctional officers'? Or had Akalu planned to use them as some sort of bargaining chip?

The Doctor shook his head. Only in a madhouse like this could a few pieces of paper become so important.

He spread the pictures out on the canteen table. First, the portrait of the alien. Despite Leonardo's best efforts, he had never been much good with a sketch, but he'd managed to capture the important details. The jointed back, the forelimbs that began as feet and became hands, the skin embedded with pieces of sky-blue glass.

In the next picture, he was sitting on the bed, offering the alien his hand. In the next, it had gripped his wrist, pulling him to his feet.

He frowned at the pictures. Without thinking about it, he had drawn himself in his normal clothes. He fingered the coarse sleeve of his uniform. Sensed memories of velvet and linen and silk.

Sam had sometimes teased him about his habit of wearing the same clothes. He had retorted that they *weren't* the same clothes, that he had a collection of waistcoats and cravats, and besides, it wasn't as though he didn't *clean* them. This had only seemed to increase her mirth.

Sam had a rather marvellous laugh. Grown up enough to have a little wisdom, still childlike enough for all the funny things in the world.

It had become a habit – whatever clothes he wore soon after regenerating, he tended to stay with. He supposed it was like a duckling imprinting on the first creature it saw.

Ziba was looking at the pictures upside down from the other side of the table. 'You beat 'em,' she said. 'One and one. Got your bear back.'

The Doctor shook his head. 'They just couldn't be bothered. I'm no danger, I'm just a nuisance.'

Akalu was packing a few things into his briefcase. His office was dark except for the green glow of his terminal and the red glow of the wall clock. It was almost 7 p.m.

All too often his work kept him at the Centre until late. Bowman was only one of his troubles – his noisiest patient, he liked to say. There was a pattern of problems and illnesses in the Centre's inmates, most especially those with company organs. Oh, they were quiet and tractable for the most part. But inside their heads...

He shuffled a pile of printouts and laid them neatly in the case. 'You're very quiet,' he said.

'I was just thinking.' The voice came from his terminal, a soft male voice with a permanent hint of puzzlement.

'Oh? What about?'

'Bowman. It's as though he *wants* to be punished.'

'Hmm,' said Akalu.

'I know,' said the terminal, 'I don't have a degree in psychology. But don't you think it's odd? He seemed dismayed when you gave him his things back.'

Akalu closed his briefcase with a snap. 'It's an interesting thought,' he said. 'I had put it down to a desire for negative attention, but perhaps there's something deeper. Perhaps I should concoct some mulct for him. Solitary confinement?'

'I think he'd enjoy it,' said the voice. 'It'd give him something to push against, if you see what I mean.'

'Something to rebel against.'

'Yes. I very much have the impression that he's done this a great deal. Did you know he's checked every inch of his cell for bugs? Even his clothing. Even that bear!'

'It's obvious,' said Akalu, 'that he's escaped from a lot of prisons.' He tapped his fingers on his chin thoughtfully. 'He seems astonished that he can't get out of here.'

'Eventually,' said the voice, 'he's going to realise that he's simply not leaving, whatever tricks he tries. After that he should be far better behaved.'

'And when's that going to happen?'

'Good question,' said the voice from the terminal. 'My guess is that some particular failure will suddenly bring it home to him.'

'I hope you're right,' said Akalu. 'If he doesn't come to his senses, I'm afraid he's going to get himself killed.'

'Or go mad,' said the voice.

'Is that what you predict?'

'Hmmm,' said the voice. 'It's a possibility. When irresistible force meets immovable object, something has to give.'

He had only ten minutes or so before they checked the cells, and they were always careful to make sure he was in his bed. He walked quickly along the corridor until he came to Ziba's cell.

She was waiting for him, her young face tense as she waited silently for him to pick the lock. Distantly, he heard the guard returning with fresh supplies for the others.

He held still for a moment, a shadow in the shadows, until he was sure the man had gone back into the room without seeing him. Then he finished picking the lock with a little flourish. Ziba grabbed the bars, but he motioned her to wait and gently pulled the door across without too much noise.

She slipped out and followed him as he headed towards the furthest end of the corridor. They had not discussed the plan in any detail – he hadn't dared risk their being overheard. She knew only to follow him.

Through a locked door, into the emergency stairwell, remove the loose bars from a window, a three-metre jump to the grass. Ziba was suppressing laughter as they dashed across the grounds, down the slope towards the duck pond. He couldn't see her face, he didn't know if it was frightened or joyful.

The Doctor craned his neck, peering for a moment into the blackness on the other side of Akalu's window. Trying to catch a glimpse of the aliens, even if just out of the corner of his eye.

He'd been absolutely sure he'd seen them in there one night – centaurs in chitinous armour, just barely visible in the glow as they prodded at Akalu's terminal. By the time he'd got closer he'd lost sight of them, and then the guards had grabbed him, and of course there was no evidence at all. But now every time he got this far he had to look.

If they could walk around with impunity, that meant they had a worrying control over the prison computer systems. Which explained how they'd found out about his arrival, and why they'd come and decided to check him out.

If they'd been there at all. If what he'd seen hadn't been a trick of the dark. If the one in his cell hadn't been a feverish dream in the first place, brought on by his mind being deprived of anything new to think about for months.

That possibility was far too easy to consider now.

He took Ziba's arm and pulled her behind a tree as a random searchlight beam stabbed down from the tower, swept across the compound and blinked out again.

'I think they mostly do that for show,' he murmured. 'In all the times I've been here at night, I've never seen anyone else – prisoners or guards.'

'Let's go,' said Ziba.

The Doctor tilted his head, indicating she should follow. They crept across to the small toolshed next to the vegetable garden.

The Doctor crouched down in the mud and reached around behind the toolshed. He drew out the objects he'd hidden there a few days ago, mercifully unnoticed in the intervening time.

Ziba gave a little impressed nod as she saw what he was holding. It was a length of sheets, torn, braided and knotted into a pair of peculiar but reasonably strong ropes. He was confident it could hold a person's weight for a short while at least. Securely tied at the end of one of the improvised ropes was an equally improvised grappling hook, made from the metal head of a garden fork.

He'd tied firm knots along the rope's length. 'Footholds,' he told Ziba. 'Do you think you can manage the climb?'

'Yeah,' she whispered, her eyes raking the compound.

'Good,' he smiled, 'because you're going first.'

'What do I do when I get to the top?' she said.

'That's what this is for,' he said, handing her the other rope. 'Tie it around your body. When you reach the top of the wall, tie it firmly to the light pole and lower yourself down the other side. Are you ready?'

'Right.'

'Stand back, then.' The Doctor stood up, whirled the grappling hook around and let it fly.

The rope shot upward, a pale streak across the height of the fourth wall. The hook made a graceful circuit around the stem of a light there, looped around and tightened with a clang. Ziba jumped at the sound.

'Up you go,' said the Doctor.

She nodded, grabbed the rope and pulled herself up, the smooth soles of her shoes slipping on the knots. She kicked them off.

'See you on the other side,' she said.

He watched as she climbed, arms and legs straining, her naked feet pushing against the knots. All those exercise periods hadn't gone to waste, he thought, as she climbed higher and higher, bouncing against the wall.

She might make it, he thought. It depended on whether they were caught in the next few minutes. If she made it to the other side of the wall, he might be able to keep the guards distracted for long enough for her to get safely away – which depended on what was on the other side of the wall. After all this time, he still didn't know. If Ziba was caught, at least she might be able to tell him what she'd seen.

She turned back and waved at him as she reached the top of the wall.

Then Ziba let go of the rope and fell to the ground.

It wasn't that she lost her balance or her grip. She simply relaxed, her hands opened, she just let go.

She hit the ground with a terrible noise.

The Doctor sank to his knees, barely a foot away from her, staring at the young body in shock.

A spotlight came from nowhere, stabbing down, the beam widening to encompass both of them. He bent over Ziba's body, feeling for a pulse. His hand pulled away suddenly. Her neck was broken.

If it had not been for the awkward angle of head and shoulders, she might have looked as though she was only sleeping. Sleeping in the moist soil, among the crushed begonias. Her pale skin was covered in scribble, illegible in the dim light.

As he watched, a single red tear leaked from her left eye and spilled on to the ground.

He made himself open her bleeding eye, pinching the warm skin softly between his thumb and finger.

What was that thing in her eye?

She'd joked about her contact lens –

Yes, except contact lenses don't move, do they? It was creeping across the surface of her eye, a gelatinous shape, leaving a trail of torn capillaries as it detached itself.

There were running feet, suddenly, everywhere. Hands dragged him back from Ziba's body, threw him against the wall. White-uniformed medical staff clustered around her, their faces weirdly lit by the portable lights strapped to their shoulders.

'Look out!' said someone.

There was a curling, complex white movement in the air, and the guards jumped as the Doctor's improvised grappling hook plunged into the soil, still trailing the twisted sheets.

Rifaat and another guard led him back to his cell. Normally they would hold his arms in a tight, businesslike grip. He walked between them with his head down. Perhaps they could see there was no need to restrain him. Perhaps they didn't want to touch him.

He sat down on the edge of the bed. They locked the cell without a word and left him there.

He sat there for a long time, under the slowly changing red face of the digital clock.

She didn't need to escape. She could have patiently waited out her sentence, just a couple more years.

It's no good talking to myself about it. What's done is done.

But why? She just let go of the rope.

Perhaps there was a security device I overlooked. That must be it. But what? Where?

Did they kill her to teach me a lesson? Would they go that far?

What do you think we've been telling you all along?

What?

Of course it's your fault. You're the only inmate who insists on escaping all the time.

Inmate?

If she hadn't got involved with you, she'd still be alive, wouldn't she? When will you ever learn?

The Doctor's mouth fell open. His hand flew to his left eye. The fingers rested on the wet cheekbone, just beneath it.

He felt the tiny movement across the moist surface of his eye. For the first time in a year and a half, he felt it.

It had been there all along, watching through his eye, seeing everything he did, knowing just where he was, reporting back, reporting *everything*.

Reporting to whom?

Reporting to me. Of course.

'Who are you?' said the Doctor out loud. His reflection stared back at him, features frozen in horror and realisation.

'Mr Bowman,' said Akalu.

The Doctor whirled. Akalu was standing at the door of his cell, watching him through the bars, Rifaat standing nearby.

'What have you done to me?' said the Doctor. He got to his feet, hand still pressed to his eye. 'What have you done to all of us?'

'I came back to the prison as soon as I heard what happened,' said Akalu. 'Mr Bowman –'

The Doctor strode up to the bars, staring at Akalu. 'I seem to have something in my eye.' His voice rose, shaking with rage. 'Perhaps you can tell me what it is!'

Akalu just stared back at him, his shoulders rounded with despair.

'My guess is that it's an offshoot of the technology you've somehow stolen,' said the Doctor. 'A variation on the eye implants you use to talk to your computers. Am I right?'

'This can't go on.' Akalu turned to Rifaat. 'Let me in there.'

'Are you sure, Dr Akalu?'

Akalu nodded, shortly. Rifaat unclipped the keys from his belt and unlocked the door.

'Please,' said Akalu. 'Sit down.'

The Doctor stayed standing, his fists clenched with barely

controlled anger. Akalu sighed and sat down on the edge of the bed.

'I'm sorry,' he said. 'I know how responsible we all are for her death. If I'd only acted earlier, I could have saved her. We should have stopped you sooner.'

The Doctor let out a little disbelieving sound.

'What will the next accident be like?' said Akalu. 'Who will die because you won't accept the facts?'

'The facts are,' said the Doctor, 'that I'm leaving this establishment at the first opportunity.'

'You've got to stop!' Akalu went on. 'You've got to stop before you destroy yourself. Don't you understand? You've done enough. You have done enough. You've got to know when to stop.'

'I've got to keep going,' whispered the Doctor. 'I mustn't stop for anything.'

'Let me out of here,' Akalu told Rifaat, without taking his eyes off the Doctor.

The Doctor watched him go, listened as their footsteps receded down the corridor.

He slid down the wall, slowly, fingers pressed to his face beneath his traitorous eye.

The others had been practice runs, he thought, after a while. He had got to know the buildings and the grounds in detail, he knew the movements of the guards. Now he knew their secret. He knew everything he needed to.

The next escape would be the real one.

Chapter Eight
Morning Run

About an hour before the alarm went off, Sam faced the fact that she wasn't going to get any more sleep. She spent the time running through endless scenarios, plans and counter-plans chasing through her head in the grey pre-dawn.

They'd be moving into position now, down by the road.

Finally the alarm jangled. Part of her started, quietly shrieking that it was too soon, too soon, but the other part was just relieved that the waiting was over. This round would be finished soon, one way or the other.

She stretched, her back bumping against Orin, and rolled herself out of bed. From beyond the cubicle dividers she could hear the sounds of the remaining Livingspace team dragging itself into wakefulness.

Beside her Orin groaned and rolled over. Sam struggled into her T-shirt.

'*Have* to get dressed?' Orin muttered, giving her a sleepy wink.

'Cheeky,' said Sam. 'You'll be in the doghouse.'

'If they don't bulldoze it,' he said. 'How long've we got?'

'Not sure yet. Paul should be off getting the first reports now.' On cue the phone-set by the bed bleeped and she slipped it on over her head. 'Yeah.'

'Ah, they seem to be here in force,' came Paul's voice from the earpiece. 'Looks like about… six pieces of heavy machinery. They're unloading the last couple from the carrier now.'

'People?'

'Lots. A few dozen at least.'

'Right.' She stood still and silent, weighing her options for a moment. 'We'll need a few more people at the front line, just in case.

I'll gather them up. You get back to the village and start organising whatever residents are still here.' She sighed. 'Betcha half of them have run off during the night. Here.' She handed the phone-set to Orin, so he could handle the rest of the logistics, and finished getting dressed.

Most of her stuff she'd packed, just in case. From the remaining bits and pieces she grabbed a T-shirt, one of the last hand-made T-shirts she'd done. On its face it simply said in small generic block letters THIS SHIRT INDICATES THAT THE WEARER IS THE SORT OF PERSON WHO WEARS T-SHIRTS WITH WITTY AND SELF-REFERENTIAL SLOGANS ON THEM.

Before she even finished tucking it in she was hurrying into the hallway, greeting the shambling figures just coming out of their own cubicles, filling them in. Maybe twenty of them, mostly her age or a bit older. 'Right, I need three more people to join the front line for when we go and talk to them. We're out of the door in two minutes. Who's up for it?'

Tamar, Khalaf and Cliff mumbled their agreement, which gave them seven along with her and Orin and Hanneh. The rest of the crew went back to getting themselves ready for their prearranged roles in the next phase.

They had time for only a couple more good-lucks and words of encouragement from her – everything that could really be said they'd said already, last night and the nights before that when they'd been talking about how it might come to this. A quick hug from Feroz, a pat on the back from Leah, and she left the village team and met up with Orin and the other front-liners at the door. 'Right. Let's move.'

Once she was through the door she had a sudden nagging thought that she should have taken a last look around the bunkhouse. But it didn't matter – she'd already taken her last looks yesterday, just in case.

The village was a ghost town, shimmering in the beginning of the day's heat. Each day there had been fewer people.

'No answer from Brian yet,' said Orin, throwing her the phone.

Sigh. 'Then we'll hold the fort till he gets back.' Which meant they'd have to handle it on their own, really. All the other oldsters were focused on their own responsibilities; none of them would know how to organise something like this even if they'd wanted to. It really was down to her, and the ones with her.

They plodded down the track as the fields gave way to grasslands, squelching through the unexpected mud. The ground was still a bit soggy from that cloudburst the other day – the first big rain since she'd come to Ha'olam.

'I still tell you we shoulda built a barricade,' said Orin. 'Right along here.'

She shook her head. 'Then we'd look like nutters holed up in our compound. No one would back us.'

'Deterrence,' he said emphatically.

'Perception,' she answered, and they each made faces at the other. Through the last couple of weeks of repetition, they'd got their arguments down to single words apiece.

Orin had come to the village straight from the service, with shovel-loads of ideas and strategy and tactics which he'd devoted to every aspect of the village renovations. She'd found herself impressed by his practical energy and the sense of principle behind his decisions. No, they shouldn't patch up this tumbledown old hut; they should tear it down and build a new one, because that was *right*.

And they listened. Of course, the fact that it meant three times as much work with little visible gain left a few folks cursing his name while they were baking in the sun for the extra hours. As did the fact that most of his proposals seemed to end up with him running the show in one way or another.

But she knew how to deal with that. As long as she made it clear this was her operation, he'd made one hell of a lieutenant. And so what if she *did* want to throttle him on a fairly regular basis? He was the one she'd most want backing her up on a day like today.

'I wish I had a drink,' said Hanneh. She sounded a bit shaken. 'It's going to be hot.'

'Orin?' Orin reached into his pack and dug out a silver flask, which he passed to the others. 'None once the reporters get here, though, otherwise we'll be listed as drunken hooligans in every news report.'

When the flask came back to Orin, he raised an eyebrow at her, but she shook her head. He put it away without taking a swig. They slid their arms around each other's waist.

He'd arrived at just the right time, a few months after Chris had run off. It had taken her ages to even get another date after that happened – pretty much everyone around Livingspace at the time had spent so long thinking of her as one half of Sam-and-Chris that they couldn't picture her in any other way.

Orin was twenty-three. He'd been in the forces at just the right time to catch the end of the last border war. He talked a lot about wading through mud on godforsaken worlds at the edge of human space, a lot about patching spacecraft back together after the enemy had shot them to bits. She paid more attention to the things he didn't talk about.

She'd never thought she could fancy a soldier. But then, she'd never thought she could fancy someone who ate meat either. Besides, there were a few things Orin could teach her about strategy and planning. And so forth.

The big grey flatbed was parked beside the concrete block of the bus station, its crane lifting the last of the bulldozers off its back, placing it among the others huddled around it. At the centre was the tank – squat, bulky, the combat insignia scraped off the sand-coloured metal and replaced with that quietly elegant eye-and-sea logo. The sight made her sick to her stomach; she knew from personal experience that civilians and demolition hardware didn't mix.

'Sonic cannon,' said Orin. 'Gotta be an Izax-47 lowrider. Looks pretty ancient – I bet it's captured surplus from the Thousand Day War.'

'Show-off,' said Sam.

'And damn proud of it. You'd think INC could afford something more high-rent, though.'

'They're not all hardware snobs like you. Far as they're concerned it's just construction equipment.'

'*De*struction equipment,' he corrected.

'Yeah. Thanks.' If the tank had been in combat shape, it could have flattened the village from where it stood – but, as Orin had been so proud of knowing at the strategy meetings, in order to make that kind of heavy metal street-legal for corporate use, the military-surplus vendors had to downpower the weaponry till it was useful only for on-site demolition. He'd even known off the top of his head the maximum legal range: a quarter-klick.

That gave them seven hundred and fifty metres from now until the crew would start work.

Half a dozen grumpy-looking burly men and women were greeting them, shovels at the ready. The villagers gazed back, the group tightening up a bit. All it would take was one loose cannon for things to get ugly. As opposed to the non-loose cannon, which was the next thing to worry about.

Sam broke from the group and crossed to the workers. ''Scuse me,' she said. 'We want to speak to the site manager.'

They went and got him. Sam had been vaguely hoping for a middle-aged white guy with a potbelly and a big bald spot. Instead they got a tall dress-shirted man with skin darker than Orin's and teeth whiter than Sam's, who smiled and shook their hands and kept any unpleasantness just in his eyes.

'Hello, I'm Procedural Expediter Symonds. I take it you're the ones who haven't vacated the site as ordered.'

'Some of them,' said Sam. 'We're here to ask you to… Well, to get off our land.'

'Now, you do realise you're committing criminal trespass here, miss,' said the Procedural Expediter politely. 'We do have title to the land. INC bought it, and the employees' contracts, from Eurogen weeks ago.'

Keep staring him in the eye. Keep smiling. Where in hell were the reporters! 'You do know there are questions about the legality of the sale.'

'Nevertheless,' said Symonds, 'there's no legal action on file to contest our title.'

'Yeah, well, that may be about to change. If you'll hold on for a moment…'

Symonds watched, looking puzzled, as she stepped back to the others.

Orin was shaking his head. 'Still no word from Brian,' he murmured. 'They must not have finished deliberating.'

Right, she thought. Oh, hell, here we go. 'We're gonna have to fake it. Do our best to play for time, make them think –'

There was a rumbling clatter coming from somewhere. The whining of dynamos and the clanking of treads.

She turned and the machines were stirring, forming up a phalanx, advancing on the village with nothing in their way to stop them. They were moving and she looked around and no one else was doing anything and *they were moving*.

Orin was gaping. The others stood and stared like passers-by at a street fight and no one was doing anything at all.

She had to force one foot down. Then the other in front of it. Her body was a puppet jerking on the end of her own string. But she kept putting one step down after another, a stumble, a stuttering rhythm that fell into a run, her body snapping into focus as all those morning runs finally paid off and got her sprinting towards the machines, and she was hauling in a burning breath and letting out a full-throated *yell* that just kept boiling up out of her, unstoppable momentum carrying her towards that dull relentless mass of grey metal and it might not be able to stop in time but she still could and she didn't have to go through with this she could still walk away and NO!

The tank's treads were crushing through the grass.

She leapt forward and threw herself down.

Every inch of her hit at once. Her eyes slammed shut as they hit the mud; the blow smashed the breath out of her and left her ears ringing. And up over her shoulder came a loud metallic shrieking and the clatter of treads and she hoped that was gears grinding and brakes squealing.

But following her she could hear more sounds, more war cries, other sets of footsteps putting themselves in the paths of the bulldozers, putting themselves in harm's way because *she'd* done it. They were following her and doing something they'd never thought they could...

The machine stopped.

Her whole body shook with each breath, as she tried not to suck in the mud. As she raised her head to a worm's-eye view she saw pairs of feet everywhere, operators dismounting from the bulldozers and hurrying towards the people in their path. A meaty pair of hands grabbed at her shoulders from behind and tried to haul her to her feet.

'Court injunction,' she gasped. The hands faltered for a moment. 'You heard me,' she went on between gulps of air. 'No construction. Judge Sumrein. Third Circuit Court. El Nath. Go on, check it out!'

The hands loosened their grip, and she caught herself before her face hit the ground. Now there were shouted instructions rippling between the men over her, confusion, disarray. Misdirection.

Now what?

She knew she knew what to do next. They'd talked this through last night; she just had to keep her head together and do it. Think.

'Orin!' She could just see him past the rusted tank treads, lying in front of the next bulldozer down the line. 'Get Paul on the line! Tell him it's a go! Get everyone in position! Now!' Orin waved a hand back at her and grabbed the phone from his belt. 'The rest of you, don't let them move you. We're holding the first line right here!'

Now the reporters were coming – their bright striped network cars pulling up near the bus station. Finally they could get things moving.

'Oi, Mr Symonds!' she shouted. The Procedural Expediter's feet came hurrying up to her. If she craned her neck she could see the bulldozer drivers he'd been talking to clambering back aboard their machines. Uh-oh.

Symonds leaned over her, a shadow against the sun. 'I'm afraid you haven't been quite upfront with us, Miss Jones,' he said smoothly.

'There's no injunction. The judge is still deliberating.'

'And if you go ahead while he's doing that you'll be in a hell of a lot of trouble, won'tcha?' yelled Sam. 'You know the legal can of worms you'd be opening INC up to. Contempt of court, right?' She raised her voice a little louder. 'Until it gets settled, you don't have clear title, so this land still belongs to the farmers of Eurogen Village. And we're not moving. Look. Over there.'

And she pointed, and they could see Paul and Amin and the three dozen other people still holding on to Eurogen Village, standing in the main street half a klick ahead, her different teams each on their assigned spots, men and women and children all lying down in the range of the cannon. Right on time.

She felt a sudden surge of pride, of *this is really happening*, as she finished what she was saying. 'This construction project is an illegal and immoral bit of corporate politics with no regard for the loyal Eurogen employees. You've got no legal right to remove us and no right to demolish our homes and our livelihoods. And we want you off our land.'

'Excuse me, but could you do that once more for the cameras?' asked the reporter from TeleNet from over Symonds's shoulder. 'We only got the last bit of it.'

Symonds's double take was priceless.

A group of labourers were hassling Cliff a couple of bulldozers down the line – the growing heat making everyone impatient and short-fused. Loose cannons. 'Ah, whatcha worrying about?' she called out. 'You get paid the same whether you work or not, right? Sit back, have a beer, the break's on us.'

She heard laughter from behind, and a couple of other voices chiming in, and eventually the hardhats left Cliff alone. But it would only get hotter as the day went on.

She could feel the sun baking the mud into her shirt, her banged-up muscles protesting and her throat drying. Eventually Eric and Leah came running with bottles of water for the seven on the line, and

Amin took Tamar's place as they started rotating for a food break.

She didn't move – she stayed where she was and kept hollering back and forth with Orin and Hanneh on either side, keeping the noise level up, trying to keep that current of adrenalin which was holding the line together from flickering out. It was weird, she hadn't been on the front line like this since Dreamstone Moon – good grief, more than two years ago now – but that sense of focus and energy was stronger than ever.

Even so, it got damn hard after a couple of hours and still no word from Brian.

It got harder still when the police arrived, lots of cops in black uniforms and anti-riot gear. They were just trying to be intimidating. It worked. About a dozen of them trampled right past them into the village itself, standing over the scattered protesters playing dead in the streets. Just waiting to anti some rioters.

Most of the labourers settled back behind the bulldozers, playing an endless game of cards. The reporters flitted from place to place, camera implants picking up scraps of footage while they waited for something to happen.

Once, Symonds came and leaned on the front of the tank, arms folded, looking down at her. For the moment, the reporters were elsewhere. 'Why is this dump so important to you?' he said.

'Why is it so important to you?' she said. 'Why wreck everyone's lives for this chunk of desert?'

Symonds shrugged. 'It's the principle of the thing,' he said, and wandered off again.

Orin ostentatiously rolled on to his back and acted like he was sunbathing. 'I don't suppose any of you would like to take a turn down here, would you?' Sam called out to the workers. None of them answered. 'Ah, well, worth a try.'

Then, out of the blue, the coppers started picking people up and carrying them off.

Sam almost jumped to her feet. 'These people are being removed from

their property in clear violation of the Residential Precedence Act...'
She yelled, so that the reporters could hear. 'We will not let INC –'

A hand rested on her shoulder. 'No, Sam, it's not –'

'Brian! What –'

'– it's not going to happen. I just got back –'

'They're breaking the –'

'We're not getting it.' Brian was standing over her, his whole body looking hollowed. 'The judge didn't give us the restraining order. I tried... I came right back to tell you. They tossed us out of the courthouse. Tossed us out... I knew what was going to happen. I broke every speed law on the planet getting back.'

'Oh, Christ. Why didn't you phone?'

'I've been trying to get through for an hour.'

She tightened up her face in frantic thought. 'Something else. Hold the front line while we –'

'No. No, Sam. *Sam.*' The hand on her shoulder tightened and his voice got quieter. 'We're not going to win this one.'

Brian was just standing there. The cops were closing in on Hanneh at the first bulldozer and no one was moving. They were looking to her. There wasn't anywhere for her to look.

'We're staying,' she said tightly. 'If we resist them –'

'Then you get arrested and it won't change anything and no one will care. It just doesn't matter. And I heard them saying... INC has authorised the use of unauthorised force.'

She half laughed. Loose cannons free to fire. And the way they defined it was just *so* INC. The laugh and the screams were all colliding in her – she wanted to hit the tank, hit Brian, fall on her face and sob.

She was parched. For the first time in ages she could feel the sticky sweat on her face, feel the heat and dried mud and all the nothing out there.

Got to know when to stop.

Finally she took a slow breath. 'Right. Phone,' she said quietly. He hesitated before giving it to her. Her hands wavering, she dialled up

Paul and hooked the phone-set over her ear. 'Paul. We didn't get the injunction. It's over.'

He didn't say anything for a long time. He must be looking around at the village he was in the middle of. Finally she heard a very small voice. 'Bugger.'

She went on. 'Look. I want half of you to just lie there. Don't resist, let 'em move you. Keep the cops busy. The rest of you, get up and go back into everyone's quarters, get the last bits of stuff out. We've got a few minutes before they clear the village and fire. Let's use them. Grab any equipment or survival gear, then get well clear. First- and second-teamers take the houses, third-teamers the bunkhouse. Run!'

When the cops closed in on her, black blurs against the gunmetal, she waved them away. 'Nah, don't bother, I'll do it myself.' Slowly, her muscles creaking, she stood up.

And then the cops marched her over to join the other protesters they'd lugged out of the village, and there was nothing left to do but stand on sore feet beside Orin and the others as the cannon's whine built up to a shriek and the village ran and crumbled and blew away like a sandcastle in a storm.

'That last minute…' Eric said quietly. 'It was like everyone had just stepped out for a moment. And then I ran after the policemen – I didn't want to be left behind. And then none of it was there any more.'

Sam just nodded. He'd been saying things like that for the past few hours. She'd stopped trying to figure it out herself; it had happened, that was all she needed to cope with right now. But then, he hadn't had as much practice handling things like this. He was only seventeen.

She and Brian were sitting with the kid on the bench outside the rest stop. Brian had said he'd drive Eric back to his parents' in Incopolis; he'd also promised he'd wait here till the last of his volunteers got safely away. Orin stood a little way ahead of them, squinting into the sunset, looking for the next bus. They were the last.

The few from the village who had cars had taken loads of the others to El Nath or Al Markim. Most of the others had squeezed on to the early bus to El Nath. Paul had been one of them; he would be staying with a cousin – 'maybe find a job'. They all promised they'd look one another up sometime.

The rest of them had waited for the next bus to Al Markim, but that one had been short of space as well. Sam and Orin had stayed behind for the late El Nath bus, waited as the sun went red and low, waited as even the demolition team finished for the day and went home.

Her T-shirt had been obliterated – now the only message you could get off it was that the wearer was fond of doing bellyflops in front of bulldozers – but that had stopped bothering her hours ago. Put it all into perspective, it did, seeing it all knocked down like that.

'So what's next?' she asked Brian.

He shrugged. 'Leah's going to try again to set up a Livingspace project on Earth, help with the reconstruction. It's a hassle getting permits to do anything there – there's all sorts of political *mishegoss* to go through. The united colonies are skittish about Earth getting too much power again, so the bureaucrats in New Geneva keep dragging their feet on anything that would help them rebuild after the invasion…'

'But in the meantime?'

'I'm heading back to the office.' He tossed away the stone he'd been playing with and turned to face her. 'I asked for a couple of favours after today. They need a new volunteer co-ordinator in the El Nath office. It's yours if you want it…'

'I want it,' she said. Orin glanced at her. 'Sorry, did you have other plans?' she said.

She'd looked back once, from half a klick away, at the bits of splintered wood and perspex that filled the gap in the grasslands. Everything there was covered by a fine layer of grey snow – the upper halves of the buildings, which the sonic cannon blast had reduced to powder. Even that wouldn't be there once the bulldozers had done their work.

Home sweet home. End of chapter.

Orin put his arm around her. 'Life goes on,' said Sam.

The police had let them all off with a warning. Sam had looked the officer dully in the eye and solemnly promised never to try to stop Eurogen Village from being demolished again.

Lobachevsky had stopped by to give some villagers a lift and he'd been beaming. As part of the buy-out, he reminded them, they'd got a generous nine months' severance pay – all the villagers were now drawing their full old salaries from INC. Even the ones who hadn't wanted to leave. 'And my severance package, they give me the right to work in my field again. No more *farmer* – I'm a biochemist again.'

'If anyone'll hire someone who's twenty years out of date,' she'd pointed out.

Lobachevsky snorted. 'I'll teach these youngsters a thing or two,' he said.

At least the Eurogen people got a happy ending, Sam thought. It almost made you wonder if it had been the right thing to do, hanging on to the village. Trying to keep all their hard work intact. Standing up to the bullies.

What the hell was so important about that tiny bit of barren land, anyway?

Orin was on the bus paying their fares. Brian and Eric said their goodbyes and headed off to Brian's car. For a moment it was just her and the solar coach and her bag on her back, the remains of the village out of sight behind the concrete lump of the rest stop.

From here it was like nothing had ever happened.

But Orin was still there, sitting beside her as she settled into the hard seat, his hand gently resting on hers. And Brian was still out there, and Paul if she wanted to look him up, and Sara and Ari and everyone she'd known.

And INC was still there. High-handed, amoral INC. Big-target, vulnerable-to-public-opinion INC.

She smiled. She might just have something to look forward to after all.

Chapter Nine
No Monsters Here

It had been a long time since the Doctor had slept.

Really slept, slept the way that humans did. He was averaging four or five hours a night now, dozing on the bed in the blackness. It helped to pass the time.

This morning he woke up as the sun rose, filling the cell with pale light. The sky was a rectangle of hazy blue through the high window.

He washed his face and sat down at the desk, pulling out a fresh sheet of paper.

He took the crayons out and carefully arranged them by colour. He stared into the sheet of paper until something came into his head. He picked up the crayon labelled 'cornflower' and started to draw long, sweeping lines across the page.

They were watching, he knew, watching through his mutilated eye.

Very occasionally, after waiting in front of the mirror in perfect stillness, he had seen the implant move. Not much - it was anchored by tiny blood vessels - but enough to let him know it was there, and it wasn't comfortable with being watched.

When he tried to tell the other prisoners about it, he found he would suddenly forget how to speak. They would leave him sitting there, with a bewildered expression on his face, the words sticking in his throat.

He'd tried to control the thing. Tried to reach into it the way he had manipulated those eyepieces, their systems opening wide to his Time Lord gaze. But not this one. If the Time Lords - or some renegade - had introduced this technology to Ha'olam for their own purposes, they had made sure that this particular device was Doctor-proof.

He put down the cornflower and picked up brick red. It was his fiftieth box of crayons. The cell was covered in colour, wallpapered in three years' worth of designs, to a height of precisely six feet on each of the three walls. Abstract patterns, mostly, though perhaps here and there you could imagine a humanoid figure, a landscape, an image from deepest space. A faint, oddly comforting aroma of oil came from the walls in the heat.

The implant could only see and hear, he was sure of that now. It could not read his thoughts. At least, not many of them. Because otherwise Dr Akalu would not keep asking him about the drawings in his cell.

'Do you know what I'd really like to know?' said Akalu's terminal.

'I'll tell you what *I'd* like to know,' said Akalu. He put down his cup of coffee. 'More about what he's doing to his cell. He won't talk about it.'

'He doesn't talk about much these days,' agreed the voice. 'At the moment he's doodling on a sheet of paper. I think he's run out of wall.'

'I interrupted you,' said Akalu. 'Go on.'

'I've been eavesdropping on every conversation he's had in the last three years,' said the voice. 'And in that time, he's given away almost nothing about himself. He's mentioned a few places he's visited, some of which sound very unlikely. It's possible he simply has a vivid fantasy life. He knows we're never going to let him out, you know.'

Akalu's eyes widened in surprise. 'What makes him – makes you think that?'

'He knows far too much. That's why he was sentenced in the first place, after all. He probably knows where the eye tech comes from. Now he knows about the implants as well. He's dangerous to INC. There'll be some legal technicality to extend his sentence, even when the ten years are up.'

Akalu sat back in his chair. 'No wonder he's so determined to escape.'

'No,' said the voice, 'I don't think that's what's on his mind. Would you like to know when he'll next have a go at it?'

'Of course,' said Akalu.

'My guess is sometime in the next couple of days, most probably via the fourth wall. He's made himself another grappling hook.'

'He must know that we know,' said Akalu. 'Are you sure?'

'It's what I would do,' said the voice.

The colours were getting angrier, thought Akalu. Bowman was hunched over his desk, not even acknowledging the morale facilitator's presence in his cell. Not a bit of him was moving except for the hand holding the crayon, twitching back and forth along the same three inches of paper.

He remembered when Bowman had started out with the painting and drawing – each line precisely controlled, trying obsessively to recapture with blunt crayons every detail of the aliens he claimed he'd seen. He'd never managed. On the back wall, about two feet from the bottom, were the last ones he'd tried like that, schematic child's drawings which suddenly disintegrated into furious scribbles.

Now he wasn't even bothering.

'We know,' said Akalu. There didn't seem to be much point in saying more. 'You don't have to go through with this.'

Bowman muttered under his breath, without even looking up. 'I want to be on Stella Stora on the third day of Krazyx, 2042. No particular reason, just because it's there. I want to be in a New Mars café last week eating tortellini martia with a fresh bottle of aquamarine. I want to do *The Times* crossword – in pen – sitting on a park bench while some gormless lout plays his stereo too loud.' The voice was hardening, the scribbling getting sharper. 'Forty-seven civilisations in this bit of the galaxy, thirteen billion years of history among them, and I've got a room. And a hallway. And a room. And a *courtyard.*'

The crayon flew from his hand and hit the wall.

Now his eyes were pinning Akalu's. 'Any more questions?'

Akalu picked up the crayon, handed it back to him and left him to it. There was nothing else to do but wait.

* * *

It was raining.

The Doctor sat in his cell, on the bed, watching the rain through his tiny window. It was dark, but he could see the droplets, faintly catching the distant light of the tower.

He had seen it rain only once before, a pitiful trickle last year. This was real rain, silencing the prisoners as they listened to the sound of fat drops splattering on thirsty ground.

The storm swelled, becoming a thundering deluge. The temperature dropped. He took the jacket with him when he left his cell.

The corridors were lit with intermittent flashes of lightning, brilliant snapshots in black and white.

In the back of the laundry storeroom, he'd managed to work loose four of the large bricks, just enough space to wriggle through. He pulled himself out on to the grass.

He was instantly soaked, his hair plastered to his forehead. The rain was so thick it was difficult to see through it, a wall of grey movement. The weather was on his side, he thought.

He hadn't bothered to find a new hiding place for the grappling hook. He had fashioned it from a trowel in the workshop, not caring who saw him. Even the guards didn't pay him any attention these days. He'd made the rope from sheets in the laundry, tying the knots with a flourish, all for the benefit of his audience.

Why are you doing this? The correctional officers are on their way right now.

'Shut up and go away,' he said out loud.

You weren't joking about the death wish... No – that's not it.

The Doctor swung the hook in a tight circle and let it fly. It took two tries to get it to attach itself firmly to the light pole.

You want to know what happened to Ziba, don't you?

'Don't distract me,' hissed the Doctor.

Yes. You want it to turn out it wasn't your fault, don't you?

'Her parents claimed the body almost a year ago. I've done my grieving and self-recrimination. I've put that behind me.'

Yes, you do that, I've noticed. But you haven't put Sam behind you, have you?

He sent a prayer out to whatever gods watch over foolish old Time Lords, grabbed the rope and started to climb.

His face was full of water. He wondered if he'd even be able to see where he was, once he reached the top.

I think you should stop.

He ignored the voice, hauling himself up. The compound was a blur beneath the rain. All he could hear was the roaring of the downpour, the sound of his own breathing as he climbed. There was nothing but him and the rope.

This is madness. There's no way to make it out. Not this time, not any time.

'Leave me alone!' he shouted over the rain.

Oh no, that wasn't me. That was you, Doctor.

He let go with one hand. His face contorting with the strain, he reached down and bundled up the rope beneath him. He looped it around him, once, and fumbled it into a one-handed knot. He hung there for just a moment, then started pulling himself up again.

I really think you should stop.

And then there was a sharp pain in his left eye, and a sudden sound like cathedral bells, getting louder and louder as he dragged himself up the last few feet.

Well, he thought as the ringing in his head blotted him out, this is new.

He woke up with the loop of rope knifing into his chest. He was suspended ten feet from the ground, bumping against the wall as he struggled with the knot, the rain beating down on him.

With a distant groan the trowel gave way. He fell into the muddy garden, rolling, trailing sheets.

Stun beam? Electrical-suppressant force shield?

Nothing was broken, but his left eye stung as though he had something in it.

'It's you, isn't it?' he said aloud.

The implant. Ziba had one as well. It was OBFSC's last line of defence. No matter how close they got to freedom, the little monster would simply switch them off before they could get there.

He reached for the trowel and held it up. It was undamaged. He could have another go.

There was a way out.

Breathing hard, he raised the sharp prong of the hook to his left eye. His hand quivered. Suddenly he flung the trowel as far away as he could and just shook.

Running feet.

The Doctor jumped up, gathered the line, swung it in an arc. The grappling hook soared upward, caught in the fourth wall. One more try. He would get over the wall or he would break his neck trying.

Rifaat tackled him, and the Doctor roared with frustration. They fell sideways into the soil, crushing seedlings. The improvised rope flew out of the Doctor's hands. He twisted in the guard's grip, scrabbling desperately for the sheets, but Rifaat took one of his arms and yanked it expertly behind his back, pinning him down.

'All right!' said the Doctor into the mud. 'All right, you've got me.'

He tried to turn his head, but he couldn't see Rifaat's face, just the white glare of a search beam. It swept across them once and then shut off, as though satisfied with what it had seen.

Something crashed across the back of his head.

It felt as though he'd been struck by a cricket bat. Almost involuntarily, he pushed up out of the soil, but Rifaat hit him again with the blunt length of the stunwand.

He gasped and struggled, drowning in mud.

The weight was suddenly gone from his back and arm. His head was ringing, his limbs refusing to respond. He managed to roll on to his side.

Rifaat kicked him in the back. He yelled and curled into a ball, instinctively, before Rifaat aimed a kick at his stomach. It caught him in the arm instead. Annoyed, the guard smashed the stunwand across the Doctor's shoulder, shattering its components in a spray of sparks.

The guard's face was expressionless. He didn't say a word.

The Doctor breathed one word as Rifaat beat him. No one heard him.

'Finally,' he said.

Awake.

The infirmary: a white blur, smelling of disinfectant.

He tried to move, and couldn't, his body lighting up like a switch-board with tiny flashing lights of pain.

He couldn't move. Trapped. In here. The prison was just getting smaller. He couldn't even *move*!

Awake.

He squinted in the unfocused brilliance of the overhead lighting. His mouth was dry.

He moved, experimentally. The two cracked ribs, set by the medical staff, had healed themselves, and the worst of the bruising had subsided. It must have been at least twelve hours since the escape attempt.

A nurse noticed him. She reached over and pulled his left eye wide open with thumb and forefinger, staring down at him with professional intensity.

After a moment she disappeared. Distantly, he heard her say, 'He's conscious, Dr Akalu.'

The Doctor eased himself up in the bed gingerly. Rifaat had been careful, he thought. Just bruises and the cracked ribs, not even any internal injuries.

He closed his eyes against the brightness of the infirmary. When he opened them again, Akalu was sitting in a chair by the bed, watching him closely.

'Don't worry,' he said hoarsely. 'I'm not going anywhere.'

Akalu didn't smile. 'You look thirsty,' he said.

The Doctor nodded. Akalu poured water into a plastic cup. 'I knew this would happen,' he said, sounding melancholy. 'I tried to save you from it.'

The Doctor took the cup of water and swallowed a mouthful. It seemed to be just water. He relaxed and drank the rest of it in measured gulps.

'This won't...' he said. 'This won't deter me...'

Akalu frowned. 'Some of the legal staff have questions they want answered –'

'Of course they do,' said the Doctor.

'About the attack,' finished Akalu. 'Correctional Officer Rifaat is in the Brian Lindsay Memorial Correctional Facility, awaiting trial.'

The Doctor stared at him.

'In all my time at OBFSC,' said Akalu, 'I've never seen a correctional officer attack a prisoner. Not like that.' He shook his head. 'No one really understands what happened.'

'I don't believe you,' coughed the Doctor.

'Mr Bowman –' said Akalu.

'That's not even my name,' said the Doctor, his voice cracking. His healing ribs protested when he coughed.

'I've got no reason to lie to you,' said Akalu. 'Think about it. Have I ever threatened you? Demanded anything of you? Treated you in an unethical manner?'

The Doctor slumped back in the bed.

'No,' concluded Akalu. 'You've just expected me to.'

Slowly he stood, and walked back and forth in the darkness. 'I've known Mahmoud Rifaat for about eight years now,' he said quietly. 'He's not a monster. At least, he wasn't until last night. Not until three years' worth of straws finally broke the camel's back.'

His face creased with pain. 'And I don't think you meant to lead him to that. You're not a cruel man. I've seen the way you deal with the other prisoners – at least the way you did before you stopped thinking of anything but escape. You... are a *good* man.' He knelt beside the Doctor's bed to meet his eyes. 'But you are destroying other people. And destroying yourself.'

The Doctor didn't move. He just lowered his eyes.

'You're still looking for monsters, Mr Bowman,' said Akalu quietly. 'But there are no monsters here.'

The Doctor didn't answer.

Finally, Akalu hung his head. 'I thought perhaps you might like this,' he said, and handed the Doctor his teddy bear. The Doctor tucked it under his arm and lay back. After a while Akalu left him to rest.

Awake.

Darkness had fallen, all the lights had gone out, everyone had gone home. There was a nurse in the nurse's office, a guard outside the door, but the Doctor obviously wasn't well enough to get out of bed, let alone get out of the prison.

The Doctor slipped out of bed and staggered across the floor in his bare feet. The bear was tucked under his arm.

It took only a few moments to pick the lock to Akalu's office. No alarms went off as he stepped inside.

There was a pale-green glow coming from the morale facilitator's terminal. The Doctor dropped into the seat behind the desk. 'Enjoying the view?' he said out loud, surveying the office.

The datatablet was still active. The staff kept the few computers about the place under tight security.

So why was Akalu's terminal sitting here, just waiting for him?

'Oh,' said the Doctor. 'You knew I'd be coming.'

'Of course,' said the terminal.

The Doctor peered into the screen, his face lighting up green. 'How?' he said. 'How did you know?'

'Goodness, you don't look at all well,' said the voice. It was synthetic, he realised, a cool, modulated male voice. A disguised phone call? 'It's my job,' it said. 'Not just to know what you're doing, I mean. My job is to guess what you will do. Do sit down. I've had a great deal of practice at predicting your actions.'

The Doctor sat down at the terminal and started fiddling about, trying to trace the call. 'For a while I was BOWMAN,' the voice went on, 'but that became confusing. So I suggested the name you use for yourself. DOCTOR.'

The Doctor sat back. Of course! 'I'll bet you're very frustrated with all the gaps in your database.' He managed a grin at his own reflection in the screen. 'There must be –'

'– so many questions I have for you? Yes, there are! Do you feel like talking?'

'You tell me,' said the Doctor, sitting back in the chair.

'Oh, go on,' said the terminal. 'Let's have a cup of tea and a chinwag.'

'What is it you want to know?' said the Doctor, swinging his bare feet up on to Akalu's desk.

'Who are you?'

'I'm a spy,' said the Doctor. 'Everyone knows that.'

'Oh, go on, you can tell me. Why did you come here? Really? Why the mural? What's your interest in our technology?'

'Well,' said the Doctor, 'I'm part of an advance invasion force. We're going to enslave your women and breed with your tuna casserole.'

'Flapdoodle!' thundered the artificial voice. 'You're a Time Lord.'

The Doctor froze.

'Ha ha, caught you out,' DOCTOR sniggered. 'Oh, I've done plenty of digging. I can see your dreams, you know that? Unguarded, rambling jumble… Who knows which bits are real and which bits are just your subconscious on holiday? I can get to your surface thoughts. The bits of memory you bring up to look at. But underneath… whole depths I can't get anywhere near.'

'Good,' said the Doctor with ice in his voice.

'Oh, you do love a mystery, don't you?' He could hear DOCTOR smiling indulgently. He'd felt that smile on his own face enough times. 'But let's dispense with the easy ones, all right? I'm far enough into your head that I could name half a dozen of your school chums and all sorts of ancient lore and legends from Gallifrey. But none of that answers the real question. What makes you tick? Who are you? *What* are you?'

The Doctor said nothing. Finally, in a small tight voice, he said, 'Sick of being here.'

'I've got to know,' said DOCTOR quietly. 'It's who I am.'

The Doctor shook his head, almost a shudder. 'You can't know.'

'Oh, you'll tell me. You're just holding back because you still imagine you can escape.'

'I'll find a way around the implant,' said the Doctor. 'Eventually.'

'No, you won't,' said DOCTOR. 'And I should know. You won't be getting out of here. We both know that. They won't let you out. I won't let you out. Everything you do, I'll be watching, recording. I'll get better and better at predicting your reactions. When you come dangerously close to freedom, the implant will simply shut down your mind. If you try anything particularly hazardous, I'll make sure you're stopped. Do you understand? You're not leaving.'

The Doctor leapt up and grabbed the terminal, the bear falling to the floor. 'I'll smash you,' he said. 'I'll destroy your database.'

'We both know you won't,' said DOCTOR. 'To you, programs like me are alive. You're not going to murder me just so you can walk free.'

The Doctor's fingers pressed against the plastic. 'Won't I? What happens if I rip the datatablet off the desk and throw it out of the window?'

'Don't be ridiculous,' said DOCTOR nervously. 'I'm not stored in here.'

'Perhaps not all of you,' said the Doctor. 'But you're here somewhere, all of you.'

'Go right ahead and destroy me,' said DOCTOR. 'It won't do you any good. None of the other prisoners have a me attached to them – the implant works perfectly well by itself.' The electronic voice lowered. 'We both know it. We both know it. You're trapped.'

'There must be some way,' said the Doctor, sinking back down. He drew his legs up, sitting sideways on Akalu's chair. 'There must be some way out of here.'

'You're never leaving,' DOCTOR was whispering. 'This is the way it ends.'

The Doctor said nothing, a distant frown on his face, arms wrapped around his legs.

'You can think all you want to,' said DOCTOR, barely audible. 'Make all the plans you like, improvise all you want to. You're staying here. With me.'

The Doctor didn't respond.

When Akalu came to take him away, leaning the Doctor's arm across his shoulders, he barely noticed.

Chapter Ten
I Spy

'Um, hello? Excuse me?'

Sam kept herself between Orin and the guard at the INC gate. The blocking was crucial in this scene – she had to make plenty of eye contact, talk fast and engagingly, occupy as much of the guard's attention as she could. She'd even shifted her hiking pack to just the right angle to keep Orin behind it. As long as she was upstaging Orin, their audience of one wouldn't be able to get a good look at what he was doing.

'This is a secure area, ma'am,' said the twenty-something guard. He'd been working on site for about four days at most, judging by the lobster-pink sunburn which had almost faded back to a less painful shade. No one got burnt like that twice out here.

'Oh, yeah, yeah, I know, we just need some directions. Could you help us for a moment?'

He smiled. 'All right, ma'am, what can I do for you?' Good, so the idiot routine was working. Keep meeting his eyes, keep his interest.

'Yeah, we're looking for a couple of our friends who we're supposed to be going camping with. They said they'd meet us at Eurogen Village and that it was around here. You know where that is?'

'Uh, sorry, ma'am, never heard of it,' said the guard. She couldn't help but feel her smile turning into a smirk. It had been about a year since the last scraps of the village had been carted from this spot, since INC had put up the chain-link fence and plopped the guard shack here where the dining hall used to stand.

At least Orin was amused by her style. She saw him give her a look out of the corner of his eye, congratulating her on a point the kid would never realise had been scored. Then Orin turned back to what he was doing. He'd placed himself perfectly – close enough to them to look like he was part of the conversation, but just enough past the guard to give him an unobstructed view of the inside.

'Oh, well,' she said, smiling even more brightly. 'Suppose we'll have to keep looking for them. We'll see you around, all right?' There, that ought to have given Orin enough time to finish.

They turned and headed away together, and she kept nattering to Orin, just to keep in character until they were out of earshot. 'I knew we should've taken that left turn at Albuquerque...'

Again, the blocking was the trick – she took the inside track as they headed off along the outer edge of the chain-link fence. That way, she could turn her head so she looked like she was talking to Orin, and that meant that she didn't have to keep looking at the open wound beyond the fence where the village had been.

And more to the point, if they looked like they were talking, no one would notice that he was looking past her, through the fence – no one would spot the tiny chip-camereye peeking out from behind the left lens of his sunglasses.

'Oh, I dunno,' sighed Rachel as she drew perspective match lines on to yet another frame of the recording. 'There's a lot of motion blur here. This might not work at all.'

'Thirty seconds, right?' said Sam. This was Rachel's standard procedure – *kvetch* for a while about how tough it was, so then everyone would be impressed by how good her results were.

Rachel worked as a freelance imageographer mainly to support her fancy-graphics-hardware habit. They'd met at a Tikkun Olam meeting, each of them desperate for a flatmate. After they'd moved in together, Sam had got her to do a lot of the publicity materials for Livingspace. The fact that Rachel also did one hell of a good job as an *e-shifta* and I-Pirate was just icing on the cake – she'd got Brian plenty of inside information about INC's response to Livingspace's lawsuit, and Sam had heard that she'd been the one who'd passed on classified Gnosistems documents about their sweatshops to the Justice Department.

'Hey, look,' said Orin. Sam left Rachel to her work and turned to the couch, where Orin was watching the cat. A tiny blue butterfly had worked its way in through the broken window screen and was dancing around the dozing cat's head. The cat, vaguely annoyed, kept stretching out a paw and batting at it.

'Stop it, moggie!' she said. The butterfly landed on the window, flexing its wings. 'Just look. Looks like a flower in flight.'

He snorted. 'Looks like a wasp with big wings.'

She made a face at him, and he kept digging himself in deeper. 'I mean it, look at them – the abdomen, the feelers – there's a really ugly bug between those wings, I tell you…'

She smiled tautly. '*No* poetry in your soul. No wonder I broke up with you.'

'Wait a minute, *you* broke up with *me*? As I recall…' She raised the pillow to throw at him, and he retaliated with a couch cushion. The cat, now distinctly peeved, got up and left the impact zone.

The alley cat – who still hadn't deigned to suggest a name for itself, even after about three years – had found Sam again within days of her return to El Nath. When Ari and Sara had recommended an apartment she and Rachel could move into, two blocks from the shelter, the cat had found her on moving day and promptly annexed Sam's place as part of its territory. Sam had decided to feel flattered.

'OK, *balevai*,' said Rachel, and touched the *start* node on the video display tablet. Sam leaned forward to watch the show.

At once the image began replaying from the first frame of their circuit around the outside fence – sophisticated algorithms comparing the frames, computing edges of objects and what was hidden behind them. As the recording ground on, the other tablet began to project a sculpted three-dimensional image – painting in objects as the camera passed them, filling in detail and colour data with each frame.

'So,' said Sam as they waited. 'You want to come down to the Bread and Pyramids at nine?'

'Who's on stage?'

'It's a klezmertronica revival show.'

Rachel grinned. 'Pure retroactive. You're a throwback, Sam.'

'No argument there.' She leaned forward and tried an infectious grin. 'C'mon, we ought to kick back for a while. We've done well. Let's enjoy ourselves.'

Most of the trucks and sheds visible in the computer model had only two or three sides recorded, and the centre of the complex was just a neutral grey expanse of No Data. Occasionally a blurry zigzagging streak showed a person walking into view - Rachel carefully circled them with her stylus, selected them for time-animation, and watched them resolve into single cardboard-cutout images within the model.

'OK,' Rachel muttered. 'Now for the data from the gate.'

With a few keystrokes, suddenly extra sides to the model winked into existence, and a vivid corridor of fact cut straight through the unknown centre - filling in a sliver of the huge shallow pit they'd glimpsed in the middle of the site.

Rachel leaned back in her chair and tossed her hair. 'So, am I God or what?'

'Cool,' was all Sam could say. She took the stylus and started selecting portions of the model to zoom in on. She rotated the image from every angle and eventually piloted through the gate into the open compound.

'So,' she said to them both as they leaned forward and watched over her shoulder. 'Do we have what we think we have?'

'No heavy earthmovers,' Orin muttered. 'No cranes. Not even a plasticrete sprayer.'

Sam nodded as the cat jumped up on to her lap. 'They've had the site for a year now, and they haven't even dug the foundations out past, what, about two metres?' She looked at Rachel, who punched up a scale indicator in the model's pit and nodded. 'They're not doing any real construction. Whatever they're digging for, it's something else.'

'Is it archaeology?' said Orin.

Rachel and Sam looked at each other. 'Only one way to find out,' said Sam.

'Uh-oh,' said Rachel.

* * *

'You sure about this?' asked Orin.

'I'd be out of my skull if I was,' said Sam. They were walking back towards Orin's car through the park, the sun just beginning to set behind the corporation buildings.

'OK, so why do it?' Orin picked up a fallen twig. 'The publicity campaign and the new laws, they're making a difference, they're helpful, they're –'

'Ordinary,' completed Sam. 'You see? We spend all our time doing the ordinary things, and we forget we can do more than that. We forget the big picture.'

'I dunno,' Orin said. 'One sunny day the Adventure Kids went adventuring, and ended up doing three years apiece for a B and E.'

Sam plucked a leaf from the twig. 'Oh, come on, you're not a kid at this. You've done this before. You spent all that time telling me your army stories. The least you could do is back them up.'

'I don't –'

'It'll be like securing the Caxtarid compound on Baubo 7.' She smiled. 'You've been over that one so many times I could probably do it myself.'

'Look,' he said, 'I'm not a danger junkie. Maybe you are – maybe I should have figured that out after what you got up to with the whipped cream and the slingshot.' She fought to keep her face straight. 'But me, I don't want to do something like that if it doesn't really matter. In the war, sneaking into that compound mattered. Now you look me in the eye and tell me that this really matters.'

She looked him in the eye.

'No,' she said quietly. 'You're right. Not this one.'

At the Bread and Pyramids the music was usually loud enough to pound any conscious thought into submission, just the way Sam liked it.

It gave her a chance to really lose herself in the sounds – a clarinet processed till it became a scat-singing soprano human voice, inhumanly fast accordion runs and percussive fiddle riffs that sounded more slamming than anything the Pickled Pupils could have come up with, all over the inexhaustibly upbeat sequencer tracks.

The klezmer traditionalists had sex-segregated the dancers in the pit, which suited her fine – in a way it made it easier to lose herself in the sweaty communal I of the dancers surrounding her.

When she squeezed her way clear to grab a drink, Rachel was at the bar, sucking something blue and glittery through a spiral straw. 'Oh, listen, Sam!' she yelled over the noise. 'Had a thought. We could use satellite pictures to get a better view of the compound. I could get in, no problem.'

Sam automatically glanced round, but no one would be able to pull this conversation out of the background noise. Rachel shouted, 'And I was thinking about what you were saying about abuses of labour contracts – INC's personnel files are locked tight, but if we try other facilities –'

'Good thinking!' yelled Sam. 'Right. One – medical clinics, look for stories about botched neuredits. Any hidden clauses in their health plans. Two – prisons. Look for employees being "retired" out of the way. And three – save all this till *tomorrow*.' She slammed back a tumbler of tomato juice in a single hit. 'This is our night off! C'mon!'

After a night like that at a club like that, even on tomato juice she got the ringing headache and grogginess.

Livingspace's office was a tiny rented corner of an old building in the city centre, empty but for cardboard boxes and some donated furniture and datatablets.

It was a simple enough job – organising publicity and volunteer recruitment drives – but it had got her all sorts of connections. She'd first heard about Tikkun Olam through folks she'd met here, which had led her to hook up with the group in its quest to Keep Ha'olam Green. Though in fact Ha'olam hadn't been especially green to begin with – Keep Ha'olam Sort of Reddish Brown with Yellowish Greenish Bits, maybe.

Brian was already in the office, bent low over his desk, dutifully ploughing through the paperwork. 'You're gonna love this one, Brian,' she told him by way of greeting. 'All INC seems to do is own other companies, right? Well, look who it turns out they've got on their books.' She sat him down at the design desk and pointed out the figures on the hard copy Rachel had given her. 'Through a set of proxies and dedicated AI trading agents, INC owns 64 per cent of Temporal Commercial Concerns.'

'Whoa. You're kidding. TCC?' She saw the excitement work its way across Brian's face as he realised what it meant. In the past few years the media had had a field day with the projects TCC had been running on Hirath, the investigations and secret eyewitness testimonies. 'So they're already facing all sorts of charges? And they've just kept it quiet all this time?'

'Well, at least people they own are facing charges. And it's nasty stuff too – experimentation on humans, implanting alien technology... I saw what they get up to, back before I got to Ha'olam. If you're the highest bidder, TCC'll facilitate anything you want – and it looks like INC bids real high. The guttermags will go out of their heads.'

She saw him catch himself and sigh. 'Their lawyers will find a way to get it struck from the record. It's not INC itself, so it doesn't count.' He leaned on his bulging in-tray. 'They're too good.'

'Doesn't matter,' she said, and tried to blow away the cloud over him just through the force of her own certainty. 'The guttermags will run with the story for weeks. It'll sell them millions of copies. "Shock INC role in Hirath horrors". And then in six months' time we've got the referendum, and –'

'Uh-huh, yeah, I understand.'

Sam found herself thinking about it for the rest of the day. TCC had been up to some very weird stuff on Hirath. Salvaged alien technology... things they didn't really know how to use. What else were they mucking around with?

'OK,' said Eyal. He shuffled his printouts on the cheap wooden podium. '*Bale*. The latest on the TCC investigation. We think they're setting up a test lab with mindless human subjects.' Sam's jaw dropped.

There were perhaps forty Tikkun Olam members packed into the decrepit synagogue social hall. They murmured in various degrees of confusion and disbelief. The show-and-tell sessions at the end of each meeting were always so full of rumours and outrages, it was hard to know what to believe and what to forget.

But Sam had seen mindless human subjects before.

Eyal was saying, 'They're using a process that was banned last century, according to, um, our source. We're trying to get more information, but it looks as though they've set up right here on Ha'olam. If, um, anybody's got some legal or scientific expertise in this area, we'd be grateful for your help. Thanks, that's all. Thank you.'

She buttonholed him while everyone was milling about afterwards, having coffee and talking about their service projects. It was a typical meeting, typical mixed bag – thirtyish white-collars full of resurgent idealism, hard-core Earth Mothers, butch-to-the-bone outdoors types, kids, suits, Proponents of the Objectivist Revolution, shifters and secretaries.

Eyal was in his twenties, the picture of fashion: hair the colour of vanilla ice cream, a T-shirt with a slogan in Reshtke. He gave her a nervous smile as she handed him a cup of herbal tea. 'You'd think more people would be interested,' he said.

'You know what it's like,' Sam sympathised, taking a hit of her own camomile. 'There's too much going on. After a while the really bad stuff starts to blur together. Still, I'm interested.'

'You are? Great. Oh yeah – you were explaining how INC own TCC.'

'Bale. They own significant interests in companies from TLA to DMMC, and do admin and research for them and for dozens more.' Plus they leased services like the Bainbridge facility to the government, and made a fortune from their patents on products like the eye implants. Far as she knew, they didn't make any of it themselves, but they had their fingers in everything. Some of it was a matter of public record. Some of it was a matter of Rachel staring bleary-eyed into her datatablet screen at 4 a.m., poking her head into the datastream.

'The biggest problem,' Eyal explained, 'is that we don't have any real proof. Just a source, you know. The media and the Justice Department aren't going to be interested. Even Tikkun Olam isn't going to be able to do anything without hard evidence.'

Sam stood for a long time, the cup of tea steaming in her hand.

'Do you think someone ought to go and get it?' she said.

By the time she got home she was feeling the buzz of a new project coming on. This was the easy stage of it – there was all sorts of information to find out, all sorts of details she'd have to nail down before she could even think about what an oh-my-God *big* and bloody *dangerous* job she was diving into.

She switched on her datatablet, hit a softkey and pressed her finger against the security scanner till it beeped. Within seconds the projector showed the A-Net logo, rotating around its axis – a slightly distorted Anarchy capital A in a circle, a pentacle with one line missing. She waved her finger through a batch of holographic options until she found herself in the genetic projects discussion group, at which point she moved to the digitpad and started composing her inquiries.

A day and a half later she'd received full technical details from someone named Fox on Mebd 3 about HSA standard incubator units, a quick primer from JFlex on security issues, and two offers of help from people who had ideas what she might be up to. She responded to the offers with polite but noncommittal notes, giving nothing away.

When she was ready, she brought up a videophone window on the screen and called Rachel. 'If you're up for it, I've got some security work for you.'

'What kind?' asked Rachel.

'Well, more like insecurity work. As in taking systems that were secure and making them insecure.'

She made a wry face. 'Cool. Lemme know when you start.'

Paul had been asleep when Sam called. 'What is it?' he said. 'INC taking candy from babies?'

'They're growing anencephalic humans,' she said back. 'Clones with no higher brain functions, so they can do experiments on them.'

'But that's illegal.'

'Well spotted. The process has been around since my time.'

'You mean the 1990s?'

Sam nodded. 'I actually saw one of the first experiments.' Soft-skinned people in cages, watching her with empty eyes. 'It was illegal then, and it was explicitly banned in the early twenty-first century.'

He agreed, which only left Orin, but he was the one she was most worried about. Somehow it was his experience that mattered the most to her. She caught up with him in the park again. 'Does this matter?' he asked her.

She looked him straight in the eye and thought of rows of babies wired up to drip-feeders for a lifetime, their eyes never opening because there was no one inside to look out.

'Hell, yes,' she said.

He let out a brief sigh – either a resigned one or an it's-finally-decided one, she couldn't tell. 'All right, so where do we begin?'

She met Eyal's source in a café out of town, a battered dome on the road to nowhere. She made herself look the man in the eyes. In his fifties, probably with children. He was sweating and it wasn't the climate. He'd probably lose his job over this.

He let her have his security card. She took it into the ladies' and ran it through the miniature scanner Rachel had rigged. The little machine pulled out the codes they'd need to get into the building.

After the nervous man had left, Sam sat in the café for a relaxed twenty minutes, finishing her apple juice. The stolen codes were in her shirt pocket, burning a hole through the fabric.

She could still back out. They could all back out of it, decide it was too much risk for too little result.

And then, a week later, she was feeding those codes into a big door on the outside of the TCC research plant, and there wasn't any room for details any more, just time to *move* faster than you could think.

They had five minutes before the computers would decide their entry was a security breach and go into lockdown. It was Orin's job to wire up the little box Rachel had brought. Once they went into lockdown, it would tell the guards in the control booth that everything was just fine, that all the doors were shut tight and all the alarms were working.

They bolted down the dimly lit corridors, looking for the room Eyal's contact had described. The door wasn't even locked.

There was a row of cribs. Sam had been preparing herself for this, but she still found herself staring, suddenly taken away from the details of the furious action in the room. Rachel patching in a series of leads from her black box to the nearest baby's life-support monitor, feeding simulated data to all its inputs so the system wouldn't raise any alarms when its heartbeat monitor dropped to zero. Orin swivelling his head, peering at each bit of machinery, getting a close-up with the chip-camereye of each tiny, empty face, then standing frozen for a long while at the end of the row of incubators, getting an unequivocal shot of the extent of what TCC had done.

Everything was stamped with the corporation's stylised dove logo. Sam wondered if the babies were tattooed with it.

A nod from Rachel. Sam snapped out of it and moved to her place over the baby. Delicately she began peeling off the heartbeat sensors, sliding out the feeding and waste-extraction tubes. It was like handling something that had just died, was still warm but wasn't moving.

'We're in lockdown,' murmured Orin. 'Five more minutes before the guards do their walk-through.'

She kept glancing at the door every few seconds like clockwork. That back-watching instinct had served her well with the Doctor, and it might be the only thing to give them any kind of warning at all.

'Right,' murmured Rachel. 'Go ahead.'

Sam carefully lifted the child and slipped it into the carrier she was wearing. It was a warm lump on her chest.

Orin glanced out of the doorway. 'We're clear!' he said.

And then they were through the door, stumbling in the sudden darkness, Sam clutching the baby to her as they sprinted towards the revving whine of Paul's car. They plunged in. Paul took off without waiting for them to shut the doors.

They drove hell for leather into the darkness, watching for following vehicles. It wasn't until half an hour later, when they got safely to the hotel without being arrested or shot, that they started to let out the whoops of amazement and delight.

Next came the rest of the work.

The baby lay like a hamburger on the corner of the hotel bed, mute and unresponsive. They had about an hour to play with until the two men from the Justice Department would come to take him away.

Paul tried feeding the baby, but it wasn't interested. Rachel took it off his hands and laid it down on the bed. She leaned over it, a bulky headset covering half her face. Thin blues lines started scanning across the infant's eyes, highlighting the TCC dove logo etched on to each implanted iris.

'Don't,' murmured Paul, but Rachel kept scanning. Sam decided to go and take a shower so she didn't have to watch.

When the law finally arrived, Sam told them firmly that the baby shouldn't be mistreated, and didn't let them leave till she had their authorised thumbprints on the e-records granting them immunity from prosecution as government witnesses.

Back at Sam and Rachel's flat, they spent the next three hours pacing and chattering, too wired even to sit down. Finally, wobbling, Paul and Orin had headed home, and she and Rachel had just flopped on Sam's bed rather than move any more.

The cat had stopped by, and now lay snoozing between them. Idly Sam stroked the back of its head, smoothing out its clumps of matted fur. Heaven only knew what kinds of adventures this cat had got up to in its life, whether it had been cruel or kind, whether there were any kittens left behind or outlived. All it had done was live.

'Half your luck,' she told it, before she fell asleep with its purring in her ear.

Rachel woke her up five hours later. 'I couldn't sleep,' she said. 'I've been following the Justice Department memos.'

'How're we doing?' said Sam, struggling to sit up.

'I think they're going to get away with it,' said Rachel.

'Huh? What?'

'Apparently TCC's defence is going to be that they weren't incorporated under the Earth laws that banned that kind of research. They're calling in all sorts of pricey experts on colonial law. And even if TCC goes down, INC is saying all they did was license TCC to use their eye technology. They're just denying they were told what they were up to. So they'll squash it. They always do.'

'What was it for?' Sam said, shaking her head.

'Eye-implant research, they think,' said Rachel. 'That hardware in the eye – it looks like they were designed to be implanted at birth and grow with the wearer.'

'I meant, what did we break in there for if they're just going to get to keep on doing it?'

Rachel said, 'While I was on line I grabbed that stuff you were after – INC neuredited ex-employees, imprisoned retirees. It's waiting in your Livingspace files when you want a look at it.'

Sam folded her arms and buried her face in them. 'What's the point?' she said.

'There's something else,' said Rachel.

'What?'

'Those scans I did. I was hoping to get some idea of what kind of mainframe the implant was supposed to interface with. Like, the original *Shifter's Guide to IXNet*, half of that came from studying borrowed eye-sets.'

'So what did you find out?' said Sam.

'I found out those implants weren't designed to interface with any system I've ever heard of,' said Rachel.

'What?'

'They could probably work with IXNet. But it's like they were designed for something a lot more high-powered. But nothing I recognise. I've just been going through some manuals and I still can't work it out. It's like they're meant for a totally alien system.'

'You mean alien too, don't you?' said Sam. 'Something nobody's ever seen before.'

Rachel nodded. 'Well, no one except INC. A lot of their stuff was almost this radical when they came out with it, come to think of it...' She let her head droop. 'Oh, *shum davar*. I'll let you know if I come up with a match. You go back to sleep.'

Sam rolled over, but her mind was already chewing on the new info. Alien computer system, alien implants, alien technology... Where was it coming from? Stolen? A secret deal? Have to check it out. Have to check out INC R&D, that Samson Plains facility, have to know what's going on. Under the surface. In between the nine-to-five job. When I get time.

Where's it all coming from? What are they up to?

Weeks passed without the knock on the door at midnight. Sam got used to the idea that they'd got away with it. That was something, at least.

It would be months before they knew more about the outcome of the TCC case. Rachel promised to keep an eye on whatever data might come her way, but things still didn't look hopeful according to the Justice Department communiqués she'd been cracking.

Monday followed Monday, and found Sam at her terminal at the Livingspace office, yawning while she sorted out the last of the publicity for their next fund-raiser. While the flier printed out, she decided to give the files Rachel had grabbed for her a long-overdue perusal.

'Not bad, Ray!' She'd cracked the records of the Oliver Bainbridge Functional Stabilisation Centre – an INC facility which helped the company fulfil their promise of guaranteed lifetime employment.

They'd subleased the place to the government as a minimum-security prison, but the vast majority of inmates were still there for crimes against INC. Lots of people with transplants, folks who'd refused neuredits, an assortment of petty data thieves and paperclip-rustlers... She thumbed through their records with slowly glazing eyes. This was good supporting evidence, but no smoking gun. She'd have to keep –

No one had ever heard Sam swear so many times in succession before.

By the time Brian came running she was already waving him away, hands jerking like a puppet, head shaking. 'It's all right, it's all right, I can handle it. Oh, God. I can deal with it.' She turned away.

She dived into the net and didn't look up for the rest of the day.

When closing time hit she let her feet quick-march her out and away, down to the Amazon Café where Paul was working as a waiter now. He'd understand, he was the only one who really knew. The city noise was completely swamped by all the thoughts spilling out of her head, phrases circling and folding back on themselves till she'd almost lost any sense of meaning.

She burst into the café with no idea where he was. She'd never been there – didn't know what to expect – and the place was crammed with landscaping, a dark damp indoor jungle jam-packed with people at plastic tables painted to look like carved tree stumps. The canopy of sculpted branches was low overhead, the only lights cunningly tucked under leaves and tinted like shafts of half-blocked sunlight. And there was so much *noise*, the calls of monkeys and kookaburras and tree frogs and blathering diners all crammed together till it drowned out even the shriek of her own thoughts.

She stumbled past the hostess and blundered through the aisles looking for him, nearly colliding with a holographic jaguar slinking through the undergrowth on an auto-repeat timer. And there was a flickering snake uncoiling from a tree, and a crocodile waving its jaws at her, and she found herself clutching madly at the passing man in his manager's jacket just to make sure he was solid. ''Scuse me. Um – I'm looking for Paul, Paul Hamani…'

The assistant manager took one long look at her. 'Hey, Paul!' he called out. 'I'm taking over your tables for a while.'

He sat her at a corner table beside the river and left her till Paul arrived, in a painted brownish waiter's uniform clearly designed to suggest some lost Amazonian tribe. Fake war paint, even. She felt a laugh bursting out, and choked it back because if she started she'd never stop.

His eyes grew wide. 'Sam! What's –'

'They've got the Doctor.' She swallowed and nearly choked – none of her muscles were working together at all now. 'INC, they've got him in prison at Bainbridge. Three years. He's been there for *three years*. God, he's been sitting there and no one even knew…'

He was smart enough to know not to try to hug her, not now. Just give her a bit of time where she didn't have to cope, then she'd cope later. 'Are you going to go see him?'

'No!' she yelped. 'You out of your head?'

He started. 'Well, ah, so I've been told, but I thought –'

'I can't. I've got to. Oh, God. I ran out on him, don't you get that? I can't go back and just pretend. I don't know what I'd end up doing.'

The rumble of canned thunder built up to a crash. All the holographic animals howled and ran for cover as the ceiling-sky filled with lightning flashes and the air filled with a piped-in mist to convince all the diners they were in the midst of a downpour. The patrons at the next table jumped and laughed and hunched over their food to protect it from the non-existent rain. Sam hunched over herself, pressing her head between her hands to block it all out.

'It's all bubbling back up,' she shouted over the din filling her head. 'I shouldn't be like this.' She grabbed the front of his T-shirt. 'It was years ago!' she shouted into his nose. 'I should be over it!'

He was watching her outburst with that deer-in-headlights expression. 'Sure,' he said. 'Whatever you say.'

'Anyway, I can't.' She shook her head, more slowly now. 'This is INC, remember. By the time I fill out all the forms and get approved to be a visitor his sentence will be up. Can't win.' She took a shuddery breath. 'And he'll still be alone.'

As quickly as it had switched on, the rainstorm started dying away. The lights brightened, the synthetic mist cleared, the birdsong tracks faded back in. She half expected them to start piping in the *Pastorale* on the soundtrack. She just stared for a moment at the virtual animals, as they poked their noses out from the undergrowth walls.

Now she was ready for the hug. Paul held on to her and made soft understanding noises, drowned out by the background din.

'It's been three bloody years,' said Sam. Her gaze was flitting around the room, not looking at Paul, not focusing. 'Three jobs and three relationships under the bridge. I mean, I haven't even really thought about him in a year or two. So why in hell does he still get me into a panic?'

'You know where that word comes from?' asked Paul owlishly.

'What?'

'Panic. From the Greek god Pan.' He let go and settled back in his chair beside her. 'It comes from the frenzy his followers tended to work themselves into - so it's Pan-ic if you're out of control and dangerous. And it's also really Pan-ic if you're out of control because you're in ecstasy. If you're touching the divine.'

'Gods,' said Sam with a shaky grin, 'do not wear question-mark boxer shorts.'

'Aah, how did you -' he began, then thought better of it. 'Think about it,' he went on. 'He got you here. He swept you along like a force of nature. Turned your life upside down. Gave you something to devote yourself to. You said you'd die for him. You care about him more than anything...'

'I care about lots of things,' she said.

'Yeah. But what is it that makes you worship him like that? What makes him so special?'

She had to think for a surprisingly long time. It was so hard to pin down what the Doctor really was - she could say all sorts of things that described him for a moment or a while, but almost nothing that was true about him all the time. He could kill a bunch of vampires or Zygons and turn around and talk about the sanctity of life; he could be caring and attentive and then distant as a star. There had to be something constant about him, something he always meant.

'He changes everything he touches,' she said. 'That's what it is. He has an effect on everything. Sometimes little ways, sometimes big ones. No way could he just slip through the world and not make a difference.'

An outsize virtual butterfly fluttered up to them – about thirty centimetres across, painted in bright Disney colours. She brushed it away; none of this was what was real. Her hand went right through it as she continued.

'You and me, we can't do everything. But he *can*. And more than that – when we're with him we can do a hell of a lot more than we ever thought we could.'

Paul was silent for a long moment. 'You've got to see him, you know.'

'I've got to do more than that.'

Paul sighed. 'Yes, ah, that brings us to the second Greek word of the week. Hubris.'

'Right.' Slowly she stood up and looked around the plastic jungle. 'I wonder how much of this place's profits goes into really protecting the rainforests,' she said.

Paul shrugged. 'What rainforests? Come on, let's get you home.'

The cat was waiting for her when she schlepped back to the apartment. It stood on the front steps, staring at Sam, tail raised high and curled into a question mark. When Sam bent down to pet it, it bolted away down the pavement, then stopped a few metres away and looked back at her.

'Come on, you,' she muttered, and started after the cat. It leapt off in another direction and squeezed itself through the slats of the fence surrounding the vacant lot next door. Sam sighed. Her brain too full to think of anything else to do, she started round the corner towards the broken gate in the fence.

She knew what she *should* be doing. She might even pull it off, but the idea of doing something so huge was daunting. And if it came to following her instincts, half her instincts were shouting to stay back, keep safe, don't put yourself back in the middle of the hurt again. The other half...

Something hissed. Something yowled.

Suddenly nervous, Sam stepped through the gate, her eyes searching the lot for any sign of her cat. Searching a space littered with demolished stonework, and rusted cars and bottles and bits of dead washing machines. There was no sign of anything at first, which was no surprise. She knew all the sorts of things you could hide in junkyards.

But ahead three cats were prowling like street toughs. Something about them just looked wrong – far too pure-bred to be hanging out in a dump. A gaunt underfed white Siamese, a salmon-coloured Abyssinian, a black Persian shadow. They were loping in a circle, and her tabby was in the centre with no way out.

She heard another hiss, or maybe it was her own breath tightening in her chest.

Her cat stood there, watching, crouching to spring.

Then the three cats tore into hers. Suddenly there was screeching, a thrashing roiling mass of colour and claws. Sam stumbled back a pace. Instinct said do something, said keep safe, said *rabies*, left her shifting from foot to foot with no idea.

Her cat was struggling under their weight now – the red one smothering its head under its body, the black pinning its hind legs, while the white raked its claws across its belly and sank its teeth into its neck. It looked systematic – like they did this to anyone who invaded their territory. Like they *knew*.

Sam lowered her head, yelled and charged.

They shrieked as she hit them, shoving the cats aside with her feet. She bent, snatched her hand away from the jaws of the black one and bundled up her cat in her arms. A sudden stripe of pain as the white one sank its claws into her leg – she kicked out and the cat went flying. Then she turned and ran for the gate, feeling her cat struggling weakly against her jacket, feeling furious eyes advancing on her.

She didn't look up till she hit her flat. Slam the door, grab the phone-set from the kitchen on the way to the bathroom, start phoning the animal hospital hotline as you lay the cat out on the toilet-seat lid. There was so much blood on her jacket – flowing from the cat's neck, oozing from the deep gashes in its stomach.

She applied pressure to the neck bite, stopping the bleeding, fumbled in the medicine cabinet for a bandage as the cat twisted and stretched its claws. Still struggling, but not so strong now.

The fur looked so thin and patchy. Sam hadn't realised how old this cat was, how much of a toll time had already taken on it. But it wouldn't stay still, its head bending down to lick its split stomach – trying to patch itself up with its own tongue, peevishly swatting Sam's hands away, as if time and pain and death and all that were just minor annoyances.

The bleeding was under control. Finally she got some sense out of the animal hospital receptionist, and carefully lifted the tired cat up, cradling its head for the journey. She carried it down to the bus stop, paid for the fare with blood all over her fingers and sat heavily in the fluorescent light of the bus, letting her own breath settle back to normal.

Somehow this wasn't quite the way she'd thought the day was going to go. This was so far off the rails it wasn't funny, but she hadn't lost it. She'd made it here, and now there wasn't much to think about, just time to feel the tiny breathing life she held against her.

In light-headed certainty she reached to her phone-set and punched in another number.

'Ah, hello, yes?'

'Paul?'

'Sam?'

'Start checking on OBFSC. We're getting him out.'

Chapter Eleven
Urgent Action

From the balcony, Incopolis looked like a giant model, a city of straight lines, square white buildings. Sam could imagine the planning, the geostationary satellites pumping information into the architectural expert systems, the rapidly forming images of streets, corporation buildings, housing for workers. Even the tourist and general residential areas, later additions, had been integrated into the overall design. El Nath, by contrast, had just sort of happened.

The four of them were crammed into a single room on the second floor of a modest hotel. They'd blown most of their cash on the suborbital hop to get here. After months of negotiations over the net, nervous bursts of information over secure connections, it was time they met their co-conspirators face to face.

They didn't dare hold these final talks over the net, security measures or not.

Orin had brought a supply of his secret coffee blend, which Sam believed to be three parts arabica and one part paraffin. She never drank coffee. Almost never. She was on her third cup and already felt like a cartoon character drawn with little vibration lines all around her.

Paul and Orin were playing chess, making rude puns in order to distract one another. Rachel was lying on her stomach on the bed, her legs ticking back and forth while she read the latest *Katz Mizchak* gamezine from a datatablet. At some point they were going to have to work out who was sleeping in the bed and who was doomed to the floor and their sleeping bag.

Sam looked at her watch again. Their contact wasn't late. Not yet. She'd brought Paul because he knew how to survive in the desert;

they would probably need that afterwards. Rachel, because she could shift data. She hoped the next-door neighbour remembered to feed the cat and water the plants. She hoped this didn't end up taking longer than they'd planned – she had only so many days of leave from work. Christ, how could you save the world and still work nine to five?

Orin, because of his military experience. They'd already argued for hours about armaments. 'If they've got guns and we haven't,' he'd insisted, 'we don't stand a chance. Simple.'

'Look,' she'd said, 'which do you want them to label you as – an intruder, or an armed and dangerous intruder to be stopped by any means necessary?'

'You can't risk our lives.'

'That's the whole point! If we get caught we go to prison. If you're waving a gun around, we might get shot.'

In the end they'd agreed it was a moot point; without the intelligence they were waiting for, they couldn't know whether they'd need weapons. The thought of carrying a gun made Sam's stomach feel peculiar. She told it to shut up – sometimes you had to eat whatever you could find and bugger your vegetarianism. Sometimes you had to compromise.

Ugly, she thought.

At least Orin and Rachel believed her about the Doctor. A bit. Rachel had folded her arms and asked how come someone who was supposed to be the champion of all life everywhere was killing off Daleks and things left, right and centre.

'Because Life, as has been said, is a stone-cold bitch,' Sam had responded.

They weren't startled when the door chime sounded. None of them moved, waiting to hear the bleep bloop bleep of the coder.

After a moment they heard the digits of their password being punched in. The door slid back to reveal an alien girl. She stepped inside.

She was short and scrawny, with half a dozen pigtails sticking out everywhere. If she'd been a human, Sam would have guessed she was about fifteen. She had metallic red hair and wore overalls and a sleeveless jacket that matched her glittering green eyes.

'Call me Mataten,' she said. '*Salam*. I'm from Concerned Citizens for Prison Reform.'

Sam held out her hand, and the alien woman shook it. 'This is Paul, Orin, Rachel. Come and sit down. You're a Caxtarid, aren't you?'

'Wrong caste,' said the girl sharply. 'I'm just a refugee. Just a Lalandian.'

'Right,' said Sam, feeling her ears go red. 'Now that I've got the cultural gaffe out of the way, let's get down to business.'

Mataten sat cross-legged in the middle of the round table. She had brought a datatablet, locked tight with an array of passwords. She unpeeled them until they were looking at a series of satellite pictures of OBFSC.

'A lot of detail got lost in the tap,' said the alien girl, as they passed the datatablet around. 'You can't see faces. But we've put together a comprehensive map, based on these shots and a partial set of architectural plans.'

Don't ask where those came from. Don't ask about any of it. Just remember that this woman's on your side.

'Everything's coming together,' said Mataten, pushing her fingertips against one another. 'I've been wanting to get a look at the inside of OBFSC for years. Most of Prison Reform's work is about abuses at Lindsay. The Bainbridge facility is supposed to be the nice prison. But they won't let the camereyes in, even when there was all that interest about the inmate who died a year or two ago. Now, former inmates never report abuses, *any* abuses, not so much as having their smokes shifted by the guards. Which is kind of suspicious in itself…'

'Neuredits?' said Paul.

'Maybe. Maybe it's true. We don't know. Anyway, we've got the data,' said Mataten. 'And you have the motivation to get in.'

'And our other contact,' said Orin, 'has got the *way* to get in.'

They all looked at one another in the sudden, awful realisation that This Might Actually Work.

'We're gonna get you for this,' Paul said to Sam, with a dazzling grin.

'Speaking of our other contact,' said Orin, glancing at his watch, 'isn't he running a bit late?'

'Don't panic yet,' said Sam. 'Mataten, what do you need to sell the plan to the Concerned Citizens?'

'Specifics,' said Mataten. 'Exactly how we're going to get in and out. And also commitment. How many people are going in, or providing back-up. Once I get that, I can release our data to you, plus provide equipment and expertise.'

'And what if Mr X is a no-show?' asked Orin, looking at his watch again.

Sam's mouth twisted sideways in the first sign of worry. 'Without Mr X, we go to Plan B.'

'What's Plan B?' asked Paul.

Sam nodded decisively. 'We build a giant catapult and launch ourselves over the walls. Orin, you're in charge of renting parachutes.'

It took Mataten several seconds to realise Sam was joking.

The coder sounded. They all looked up. 'X marks the spot,' said Paul.

The door opened. It was Ramadan.

Sam stared at him. His dark hair was growing out from beneath the dyed white, tied in a tidy ponytail behind his back. '*Salam*, Sam,' he said. 'Been a long time since the shelter.'

He wore the kind of uniform she'd seen on the construction workers putting up new INC buildings, drilling the deep water bores. She broke into a helpless grin. 'Ramadan,' she said. 'You've gone straight.'

They talked all night, fuelled by possibilities and by the rest of Orin's supply of coffee. It was almost dawn when Mataten and Ramadan left. Orin and Paul ended up in the bed – Rachel had already dozed off in a sleeping bag.

Sam was too pumped to sleep. She decided to go for a run, take a look at Incopolis. The sun was just coming up over the horizon, turning everything from deep browns and greys to sharp yellows and whites. The buildings threw back the light and the heat.

Still running, she thought.

Ramadan's information was solid. So was Mataten's. She'd been able to put together the outline of the plan, though it would take a lot more work to pull all of the specifics into line.

It was a good thing, she thought, jogging past the street vendors and the cafés opening for breakfast, that no one here could read minds. Conspiracy to free a legitimate prisoner, a convicted criminal.

He had been looking for her. She was sure of it. Laws and security software wouldn't have been an obstacle to him. Shouldn't have been.

She bought a falafel roll from one of the stalls, plonked herself down on a park bench. The grass was well watered, the trees healthy; she shifted, and saw the corporate logo on the bench. Another Incopolis public service.

A cat was winding itself round her ankles, purring noisily. She tore off a bit of falafel and held it within reach. The cat's purring increased as it sat up and delicately plucked the scrap from her fingers.

It would be daring, dramatic and bloody dangerous. It would earn them a lot of cred with the media. It would certainly bring OBFSC out into the light. Even if they failed, that could be worth it.

The cat miaowed, a single, flat note.

Sam looked down at it in surprise.

'It can't be you,' she said. 'I left you back in El Nath.'

The cat got up and walked away, tail in the air. Sam squinted after it. She put the remains of her breakfast into the recycling bin and followed it.

The cat went into an alleyway and around a corner, into the maze of streets. Every time she almost caught up with it, it put on a little spurt of speed. Sam had the definite impression she was being teased.

It was weird: she had a vague but oddly sharp memory of another cat like this one – like hers – prowling across the sands of Hirath. Well, if it was the same moggy somehow, that was pretty impressive of it – making its own way just as well through deserts or city alleyways, coping with whatever place or time it found itself in.

Come to think of it, she hadn't done too bad a job of that herself.

Kids were already playing, running around the streets, burning up some of the energy from their hidden source before it was time to sit down at the terminal for lessons.

At the end of an alleyway, a holoboard had been turned into a mural, brilliant strokes of paint obscuring the screen in elaborate geometric patterns, like a giant Persian rug. The flickering images peeked out from behind the paint in splotches of meaningless colour. It was beautiful.

Home, thought Sam. This is home now. Ha'olam is my planet. And I'm gonna save it. I'm going to break the Doctor out of jail and boot him back into the universe where he belongs. I'm gonna break up the corporations' power. I'm gonna house the homeless and feed the starving. OK, maybe I can't do it all, but I'll be doing as much as I can, because that's who I am.

The cat turned a corner, tail twitching. Sam followed it.

In an alleyway, beneath the washing hung out to dry, at the end of a row of recycling bins, stood the TARDIS.

She ran her fingers over the roughness of the painted wood. It was warm, humming just audibly.

Her heart gave a lurch when she realised he might be inside.

Maybe he'd got out of OBFSC, brought the TARDIS here, was waiting inside. Probably sitting in that favourite old armchair of his, drinking China black and reading back issues of *Martian Aregraphic*. He'd smile and say, 'What took you so long?'

And she'd say, 'I didn't want to ever see you again, because my hormones could have cost you your life.'

Not.

Or maybe, 'Get me home. I want my parents, now!'

Nakheir.

'I love you.'

I don't *think* so, Sam.

Sam reached around to the back of her neck, awkwardly thumbing the catch on the silver chain. She fumbled, the catch springing open, and chain and key and all falling down inside her T-shirt. She had to untuck it and let the key fall into her hand.

Was she imagining it, or was the key faintly vibrating?

Maybe it was her.

She slid it into the lock and pushed open the TARDIS doors.

Nothing had changed.

Stairs led down into the vast Gothic vault that was the console room. The stone walls and high ceiling were softened by lots of homely little touches – the armchair, the books lining one wall, the clock collection, the rugs. There was a soft, sweet scent in the still air. Sandalwood, she realised after a few moments, like incense. She'd almost forgotten about that.

She knew at once that he wasn't here. There was no dust, there never was, but she could feel the quiet waiting in the air. A sense of presence, more intense than it had ever been. Not the Doctor. His space-time vessel, waiting faithfully for him to come home.

Maybe the TARDIS had brought her here.

The Doctor's Volkswagen Beetle was parked in its usual niche. The poor thing was covered in dents and scratches. One door had been pulled off for a bit of panel-beating, and both the front and back bonnets were open. Neither end seemed to contain an engine. The Bug probably ran on phlogiston and shredded wheat, thought Sam.

She stepped up to the console, running a hand over the wooden panels. The reading lamp spluttered into life, as though acknowledging her presence.

Jasper and Stewart fluttered down excitedly and perched on her shoulders, snuggling up. 'Hello, boys!' she said. 'Good to see she's been taking care of you.' She patted the console.

She'd once asked him why he'd designed the thing to look like something out of Jules Verne, all dials and polished wood and brass and ancient typewriter keyboards, hiding that ultra-advanced technology. He'd muttered, 'If it's not baroque, don't fix it,' and ducked when she'd thrown a cushion at him.

She couldn't fly the ship. But he could. And he could bring the ship to him, she was sure of it.

She went back outside, carefully locked the doors and pulled out her phone. 'Hello, Paul?' she said, a maniacal grin slowly spreading across her face. 'Change of plan.'

The city's roots reached deep beneath the ground. They climbed down a fifteen-metre ladder in single file before they got to the lift that would take them down to the tunnels.

Orin, Rachel, Mataten and Sam, with Ramadan leading them, silently pointing along a ledge towards the lift. Water flowed beneath their feet, half filling the wide tunnel, pumped up from an underground reservoir.

The small group filled the lift. They didn't speak as Ramadan flipped open a box on the wall, applied his eye for the identity check, thumbed some controls. A safety gate closed and they lurched downward.

They passed half a dozen access junctions, colour-coded tunnels filled with cables or pipes. No electrical cables or sewerage pipes, not with solar panels and gas cells in every home. Mostly water and secure comm lines.

At the bottom of the lift shaft they stepped out into a wide tunnel – a new one, judging by the amount of rock and dust settled across the floor. Ramadan checked everyone's helmet light, took out his datatablet and double-checked his map.

Dim orange lights had been stabbed into the walls at intervals. The group left footprints in the dust, criss-crossing the marks of the workers' boots. It was cool, like a cave, but Sam was sweating inside her protective plastic overalls. At one junction they turned left, at another they climbed down a short ladder, went into another tunnel.

They stopped after half an hour, while Ramadan checked the map and they drank cold water from canteens. 'Don't lean on the walls!' Ramadan snapped, before Orin could slice open his hand on the fresh-cut rock.

'How much further?' said Rachel.

Sam was reading over Ramadan's shoulder. 'Not much,' she said, her voice echoing tightly in the tunnel. 'Another ten minutes.'

They crunched along the tunnel behind Ramadan. He had been very sure about the work schedules – they wouldn't meet anyone. The orange lights were rarer now, the air still and cool.

'Here we are,' said Ramadan. He unclipped a large torch from his belt and waved it over the left wall ahead.

There was a breach in the stone, a gaping hole, surrounded by partly cleared rubble. He waved them closer, shining his light into the gap.

And there it was – the older tunnel, supposedly sealed and separate, running almost parallel to the new one. They'd discovered it while blasting out the new tunnel, had to veer away to avoid damaging the old conduit.

They stepped under the low doorway, mindful of sharp edges. There was no lighting here. Sam snapped on the lamp on her helmet and the others followed suit.

'No one's been here for years,' said Sam. She realised she was whispering and raised her voice a little. 'Look.' She pointed to the stalactites forming as water dripped down through the tunnel ceiling. 'We must be under one of the aqueducts.'

'We're beneath the river itself,' said Ramadan.

'It's not going to collapse on us, is it?' said Mataten, tugging at her helmet. The plaits stuck out awkwardly.

'Not if the tunnel builders did their work,' said Ramadan. 'Another ten minutes.'

They could hear rushing water for some minutes before they came to the end of the tunnel. It stopped suddenly at an open aqueduct, a twenty-foot pipe running perpendicular to the one they were in.

There was a long, low vessel waiting for them, bobbing on the rushing water, painted an electric yellow. 'The prison's aqueduct,' said Ramadan. 'And one of the old maintenance vessels. I couldn't believe my eyes when I found it – they must still use it from time to time.'

The prison itself was a blank spot on the map. 'Where does it come up?' said Sam.

'Our best guess,' said Mataten, 'is that it emerges in the pond.'

The vessel wasn't built for luxury. There were two benches on either side, with rough safety belts – a double plastic sash that you stuck your arms through. Ramadan powered up the miniature sub, flooding the inside with lime-coloured light. He sat at the controls, running a series of checks. The sub trembled as silent engines powered up.

They pulled off their helmets, running nervous fingers through sweaty hair. Sam had to carry her backpack in her lap. She felt weirdly like a schoolkid on a bus.

The hatch hissed shut. Ramadan checked their straps, then fastened himself into the pilot's seat.

With a lurch, they were on their way.

The water rose and the pipe curved over them until they were travelling through a pitch-black tunnel. Sam wondered if they were making the prison's water taste funny. She'd studied all the maps and textbooks Ramadan had given her about how the underground systems worked, but she still wasn't clear on how they interacted.

She had her first pang of real fear as they headed through the darkness. What if Ramadan dropped dead suddenly? Could she get them back? What if the roof caved in? She made herself take slow, even breaths. It was just claustrophobia. It would pass.

She gave Rachel a smile, massaged Orin's arm, folded tightly across his chest. The prison itself would be the shortest part of the plan. They should be in and out within fifteen minutes. Rachel and Ramadan would have the worst of it, travelling back through this narrow blackness.

'We're here,' called Ramadan. Sam suppressed the urge to shush him.

They bobbed up in a pool of water, still thirty metres below the ground. 'Of course!' said Sam. 'They have an on-site purification plant.'

'We're a big impurity,' said Orin.

The hatch hissed open. 'Everyone out,' said Sam.

Ramadan and Rachel tackled a wall panel while Sam and the others spread out, mapping the chamber. It was twenty metres across, mostly filled by the pool, unlit except for the sweeping beams of their helmets. Pipes led away. 'There's a ladder here,' said Orin, his voice nearly making Sam jump.

She adjusted the headset beneath her helmet, brought the mike up to her mouth. 'Any signs? Where does it come up?'

'There's nothing,' said Orin, shining his torch into the shaft. 'It's long enough to reach the surface.'

'We've got a map of the electrics and comm system.' Rachel, sounding very satisfied. 'Our guess is that that ladder comes up in a utilities room near the pond – either at ground level or just below it.'

'Right,' said Sam. 'We'll be going through mechanical locks.'

'No problem,' said Mataten.

Another ten minutes and they'd scoped out the whole chamber. No alarms, no guards – and why bother? The system was sealed, or would have been, if it hadn't been for the little accident with blasting the new tunnel.

'You've been looking for a way in for a long time,' Sam realised. She started peeling off her protective clothing.

'Years,' said Mataten. 'We were ready when the opportunity arose.'

'OK to go,' said Rachel. 'Whenever you are.'

'All right, everyone,' said Sam. They had all shed their plastic skins, revealing prison uniforms. She pulled her backpack back on. 'We know exactly what we're going to do. We've got total surprise on our side. This is going to be fast and easy. Remember, don't offer anyone violence, stick to the plan, stay in communication with one another. Ready to go?'

* * *

173

Five minutes later.

The library was well ablaze, paper and storage media catching quickly. The librarian and a couple of prisoners stood around outside, staring at the burning prefab hut. It looked like a Christmas pudding.

There were twenty guards working on the fire. It was obvious that the fuel cell had blown, probably an electrical short. But the real problem was that the extinguisher systems had failed. They had formed a straggling line back to the duck pond and were passing buckets of water from hand to hand frantically.

None of them noticed a group of uniformed prisoners emerging from the ground, in the darkness not ten feet from the pond. They might have seen them if the entire lighting grid hadn't gone down.

The prison looked pretty much like Sam's mental picture, built up by memorising intercepted satellite photos. The group made a beeline for the big door, the only way in to the cells.

Mataten was through the lock in seconds. Orin went in first, and ran straight into a guard.

The man was standing alone in a large, dull room, some sort of holding area. He had been smoking. The cigarette fell out of his fingers when he saw the five of them.

'Quick!' shouted Sam. 'We need more buckets!'

'Come on!' yelled Orin. The guard turned to follow him automatically. Sam pushed the derm she was carrying into the skin of his neck and Orin caught the man as he fell over.

'We need to secure him,' said Orin. Sam didn't allow herself a second to think about the extraordinary thing she'd just done. 'Storeroom right here,' she said, throwing open a door. More of a cupboard – brooms and mops. Mataten had grabbed the guard's legs, and she and Orin bundled him in.

'Pipe,' said Orin. 'Gimme the cuffs.'

Sam already had her backpack open. She took out a pair of fur-lined handcuffs, trying not to look embarrassed. Orin took them without comment and fastened the unconscious guard to the pipe.

* * *

They pounded up the clattering stairs.

'We've got you a location.' Rachel's voice crackled in their headsets. 'Third floor, west block. Tell me if you see any numbers.'

'Above the cells,' said Sam. No more guards. Not one prisoner made a noise at their surprise appearance, bless them. A couple even grinned or gave them a thumbs-up as they jogged past. 'Three fourteen,' counted Sam. 'Three fifteen.'

'Right, keep going. You want to be almost to the end of that row. He's in three twenty-eight.'

'Here he is!' Orin called.

They skidded to a halt outside the cell.

Sam went utterly cold.

The Doctor was sitting on the bed in the cell, his knees drawn up to his chin, staring at the wall.

'Doctor!' shouted Sam, pressed up against the bars. He didn't look up.

'*Ke en chedani*,' swore Mataten. She was looking at the crayoned images that covered the cell walls. Layers of dark colour, built up into mad swirls, nothing recognisable.

'Get the door!' snapped Orin. Mataten opened the lock. Sam pushed past her.

She stopped short of the Doctor, afraid to touch him. He kept staring at the opposite wall, as though she just wasn't there. 'He's drugged,' said Orin.

'I don't think so.' Sam crouched down beside the Doctor. His eyes weren't focused, his face was locked in a slight frown.

'Sam –' said Orin. She cut him off with a wave of her hand.

'Doctor?' she said softly. 'It's Sam.'

'Come on,' said Orin. 'We can't –'

'Shut up!' said Sam. She shook the Doctor's arm gently, then violently. 'Come on, Doctor! There's no time!'

The Doctor drew a sharp breath, his eyes focusing on her for the first time. In the next instant he had leapt from the bed and grabbed her in a tremendous hug, almost knocking her over. She spluttered.

'Sam!' he declaimed. 'I could *kiss* you!'

'Ulp.' Sam could feel the 'help meee' expression creeping across her face already. Behind the Doctor's back, a wicked smile flashed across Orin's serious face.

'He's awake!' shouted DOCTOR.

Akalu started violently. He had been watching the efforts against the fire from his office, the courtyard lit in reds and oranges.

The morale facilitator turned sharply, staring at the terminal. 'You haven't said a word for weeks,' he said.

'They're getting him out. Taking him away!' said DOCTOR. The machine voice was strained, breaking up into static. 'You must stop them!'

Akalu grabbed the phone.

'Looks like the fire's nearly out,' said Orin. 'We're running out of distraction.'

'We're still on plan,' said Sam.

The Doctor was talking so quickly it was almost a blur. He pressed the phone to his head tightly, as though trying to push his thoughts through it, hunched over on the bed. 'Right! Now pull the lever to your right down two notches. Yes? Now the blue switches. See them?'

On the other end of the line, Paul was barely getting a word in edgewise. 'That's it,' said the Doctor. 'Punch the red button and pray.' He snapped the phone shut. 'The TARDIS will home in on me,' he told Sam. 'Not much time. They're watching us right now.'

'Damn,' said Orin. 'We're going to have to go for Plan B.'

'The catapult?' said Paul's voice.

Orin popped his head out into the corridor. 'We'll have to leave him.'

'Don't even think about it,' said Sam.

'Sam, Sam,' said the Doctor. He reached under the blankets on the bed. 'This is for you.'

He handed her a dilapidated, one-eyed teddy bear.

176

And then she laughed, suddenly, and in the next moment the TARDIS's tortured clockwork whirr filled the air.

The door opened automatically as they ran up to the TARDIS. It had parked itself in the corridor outside, utterly incongruous.

'Clear!' Sam was shouting into her microphone. 'You're clear! Go go go!' Somewhere, a guard shouted. They didn't stop to look, just bolted into the vessel, feeling those heavy doors close safely behind them.

The Doctor almost fell down the stairs. He shouted, a hand coming up to his left eye.

'Get us out of here!' Sam shouted at Paul. She and Mataten grabbed the Doctor.

'Oh yeah, and how do I do that?'

The TARDIS let out a dignified sound, like a steam engine, and the central column began its meshing rise and fall. Paul stared at the blue light of the interlocking parts.

Sam pulled the Doctor's hands off his face. A violent shudder ran through him. His eyes were tightly closed and under the lid of the left one something was *moving* –

'You're safe,' she murmured, as another jolt shook his frame. 'We got you out. Everything's going to be fine.'

His head gave a tiny shake. He opened his eyes and the left one was filled with bloody tears.

'Gone!' shouted DOCTOR. 'He's gone!' It let out an electronic wail that chilled Dr Akalu to the bone before he could shut the program down.

Interlude, with Audio

They stood in the console room, waiting, trying not to listen.

Mataten had grabbed a book and was concentrating intently on it. Paul was still staring at the central column in the console, amazed that he'd made all this move by himself.

Orin was sitting in the Doctor's armchair. Sam was sitting on the little wooden footstool, hunched over, Orin's feet in her lap. Her eyes were closed.

Nobody dared move.

'I dunno,' said Orin, 'I kinda figured he'd be... well, taller.'

'He acts tall,' murmured Sam. She thought of the spindly figure who'd unfolded himself upon entering the TARDIS, who'd stumbled off down a dark corridor looking as if he wanted to curl up into a ball. 'Usually.'

The whimpering came again, from somewhere in the distance. She and Orin couldn't take their eyes away from the lightless hallway.

It had been ten minutes before the sounds had started to drift down the corridor. Sam had walked round and round the console room, still buzzing with energy, the bear tucked under her arm. She had run her hands over the controls, surprised she could still remember so much.

When the cries had begun, she had been hovering over the sound system. In those first appalled moments she had wanted to crank up the volume and drown it all out, but she never had been able to figure out how to get it to play what she wanted. On the Doctor's whim it could blast forth anything from *Don Giovanni* to Donna Summer.

So they waited and tried not to listen.

'We can't go,' she said to Orin.

'I know.'

They all knew it; as the Doctor had staggered away, 'Wait here,' and 'Promise, *promise*,' were among the few coherent words he'd been able to get out.

The whimpers built up, subverbal pleadings, unintelligible.

'The echoes make it sound worse than it is,' Orin said firmly.

'Yeah.' Sam shook her head. 'Besides, I can't go. Not after last time.'

'Afraid he wouldn't survive the attention, huh?'

'Just stop it,' she hissed, and heard what sounded like an echo of her words from down the hallway.

When she spoke again, her voice was tight and high. 'It's always the same. The people I care about – I do awful things to them...'

'I coulda told you that,' said Orin. Sam slapped his feet off her lap and he nearly fell out of the chair.

He grabbed her shoulder. 'That was a joke! I didn't mean that – you didn't either. The things you say about yourself when you're this down, they're not true, you know that.' Sam relaxed a little in his grip. 'That's not who you are. I want you to look at everything you've done today and then you tell me that you let people down. OK?'

She managed a mute nod. 'Good.' He let go. 'Because that's as sincere as I can get in one go.'

Orin put his head on her shoulder, still holding on to her arm. Paul was there too, sitting on the floor, an arm around her waist.

'He'll be all right,' said Paul softly. 'No need to Pan-ic. Remember?'

'I thought I was going to throw up,' she murmured. 'There was blood coming from behind his fingers, did you see? He had his hands over his face. He didn't want us to see, like he was *embarrassed*.' She drew a shuddering breath. 'He doesn't deserve to be ugly.'

They were silent, unable to avoid the distant voice, as it built up to a full-throated scream of pain.

'He said the TARDIS would help him,' Sam whispered. 'He said she'd help get the implant out.'

They tried not to listen as the final howl died away.

She found him in the butterfly room.

Opening that door again, for the first time in years, was like easing back into an old habit. She saw the impossible hillside inside, the inexplicable sky, the iridescent blizzard of butterflies swarming across the meadow. Every kind of butterfly that you could imagine and quite a few you couldn't. The perpetual summertime warmth, filling her up after the coolness of the TARDIS.

She'd better not get too used to being back.

He was in his old place, at the top of the hillside. He could stand there for hours, letting all the curious fluttering creatures come up to stare at him while he returned the favour. He had taught her their fanciful names: painted lady, Crimson Star brushtail, great purple hairstreak. A greater green chatterer flapped past, muttering about income tax.

This time he was sitting, slumped in a wicker chair. The prison uniform was gone; he was wearing a white linen jellaba, tied around the waist with a green sash. It hit her that the clothes he used to wear, the old familiar velvet and linen and silk, were gone for ever.

She walked up the hill, feeling the adrenalin draining out of her, leaving her shaky and tired. The clouds of butterflies were keeping a respectful distance from him. Could they tell he was ill?

Or did they just not recognise him? Most of these creatures had never seen him – they were two or three generations down from the last ones with whom he had shared the TARDIS. All those butterflies had lived and died while he'd been alone.

It didn't seem fair that life would go on without him. Not here.

She reached the top of the hillside and stood near the chair. Her arms and shoulders were covered in butterflies by this stage. Somehow, they always kept out of the way of her feet.

His eyes met hers. The left one was bloodshot, surrounded by purple bruising. There were no other scars she could see.

'I brought you something,' she said, and held out the bear.

He lifted his arm for her to tuck the bear under it and held the bear close, quietly curling up around it. His eyes were focused on the middle distance, on nothing.

'Look,' she said. 'There are lots of things I've got to –'

'I didn't think I'd ever get out,' he said. 'I don't know if you can understand. I didn't think I'd ever get out.'

Sam felt the hairs stand up on the back of her neck at the flatness of his voice.

He was crushing the bear to him, his whole body rigid and unmoving. 'There weren't any walls to break down, nothing I could even push against. I couldn't get away, because the thing keeping me there was in here.' He still wasn't moving. With each word he was hardening, like he was turning into a block of marble.

She crouched down beside his chair, trying to get to his eye level. Forget what she had to say; she had to reach him in there. 'So, um...' Oh, God. 'How long were you in there?'

'It was...' She could see the thought knotting behind his forehead as he struggled to work it out. 'Three and a bit years.' He took a slow breath.

She smiled. 'Blink of an eye to you.'

'No.'

'But –'

'Three years of *nothing*,' he whispered.

'Well,' said Sam simply, 'they weren't nothing for me.'

'You humans change so quickly,' he said thinly. 'It was about three years after she left me that I saw Ace again – it was as though she was a completely different person. It was so long before I knew she was still there, in there...'

'Are *you* still in there?'

He didn't answer. She had been wrong, he wasn't sitting still – there were tiny quivers running through his body, like huge bursts of movement being held just under the surface. If he was a block of marble, then he was one about to shatter from its own internal stresses.

Reach out and hug him.

God, no, don't touch him, that would start the whole mess all over again.

It was pathetic – swirling clouds of butterflies dancing all around them, and neither one of them dared move an inch.

'Well,' she said, in her best brisk organising voice. 'It's over now. We need to deal with the present.'

The Doctor's eyes moved to the bear. Well, that present would be a start. 'He's going to need a new eye,' she said.

'He can have one of my buttons,' he said lifelessly. 'I think it will do.' Once, he would have produced it from inside one of her ears, with a flourish.

She reached out and took the bear (*don't even let your fingers brush his*), then settled cross-legged at his feet. 'Now get me that button.'

He didn't move. 'Come on,' she said. Make him move, make him do, give him some kind of connection to the world outside his head.

Slowly, as if his hands were being operated from a long way away, he fumbled with the front of his jellaba. Sam got out her army knife.

The butterflies, of course, just had to see what she was doing. A green and yellow malachite on spindly pinpoint legs was her biggest fan, brushing its wings against the hairs on her arm. An orange sulphur lodged on her forehead and hung upside down, watching. And still they avoided the Doctor.

He looked so *young*. It was only partly an illusion, she thought. Part of him still was young, permanently, young enough to draw on the walls with crayons. Or to be shattered by the unfairness of the world.

'Everything's going to be fine,' she told the teddy, as she cut loose the top button. 'We'll put you back together again.'

The Doctor was looking at the bear. 'I know everything, Odin,' he murmured. 'I know where you hid your eye in the fearsome well of Mimir.'

Sam shook her head. God knew what he was on about now. 'I know you're not listening to a word I say,' she said, 'so it doesn't matter what I do say. I've got you out. Maybe I'll take you to a hospital somewhere, a place they can look after you. Because right now, the thing I most want to do is to run down that hill and get myself as far away from you as I can.' She threaded the needle. 'But you don't care. You're too busy running away yourself. Somewhere where even the

183

butterflies can't reach you. Hold that button in place,' she ordered him.

The Doctor hesitantly pushed the button into place, one finger holding it there.

'If there's one thing I've learned in these last three years,' Sam murmured, 'it's that you can't just keep running away.'

She reached out and took his hand.

Neither one of them moved for a long moment. For her it was like touching a naked power line – her heart was vibrating more than beating.

She held on, feeling each finger interlaced with his, memorising by touch each hint of the pattern of bones in the back of his hand. A red admiral flitted from her wrist, tentatively, to his.

'Here. Look.' She thrust the needle safely through her sleeve, reached out and touched him under the chin, raising his face, bringing his eyes to the butterflies. 'You're still here. *I'm* still here.'

The Doctor stared milkily at the insects, whirling like a cloud of memories, just out of reach.

Then, without warning, he crumpled into a hug.

She felt her whole body tighten up, in a fight-or-fly spasm. But she held on to him nonetheless, arms sliding across his back, mouth murmuring things that weren't quite words.

More of the butterflies were marching off her shoulders and arms and on to him. She could feel the feather touches in her own hair, the current they carried as they flitted back and forth between the two of them.

She could almost see the marble of his skin softening to flesh tones as she watched, as if he was drawing their colour straight into himself. His arms were tightening around her, as though acknowledging she was there, real and solid.

The butterflies were a whirlwind, scattered pieces of rainbow spiralling round them everywhere they looked.

He pulled away from her at last, his face just inches away. There was an Adonis blue perched right on the end of his nose. He looked at it in cross-eyed astonishment, and then laughed out loud. The butterfly flitted away with all the dignity it could muster.

It was only a minor ordeal to keep from kissing him.

'I think we've earned a holiday,' he said, as they made their way down the hillside. 'Ever been to Mooloolaba?'

Sam's feet dragged in the grass. 'Look,' she said, and stopped. She saw him jump a little at the word – still expecting something to be closing in on him from just out of vision.

He turned to look her full in the face. Big liquid green-blue eyes, full of rekindling life. If she didn't keep some sort of distance, starting right now, God only knew what lines she'd cross that she had no intention of crossing.

'Look,' she said again. 'I can't just fly off with you and have a holiday. There's a whole pile of things that want doing, and I'm doing them. Now, if you feel like helping out, that's great, but...' The feelings were clear, but the words were like clods of dirt in her mouth.

'All right,' he said. 'What are you doing?'

'I'm getting people involved. We're beginning to make a difference against INC –'

The words set off a chain reaction somewhere in his mind. 'INC,' he blurted. 'I – I see. Eye tech. I've seen what it is. I *see*. I've seen what they're doing and that's why they don't want me out. Didn't want me out. I know. But I don't know enough.'

The burst of words trailed off, like a wind-up toy running down. Sam realised she was biting into her lip. Try to reach him. 'Look. There are thirty holoboards around El Nath displaying public-service ads with the truth about the Gnosistems sweatshops. I did them. I came up with the idea, I helped Tikkun Olam design them, I made the calls to get them placed, I even spent weeks traipsing around door to door trying to help raise the money. And now thanks to the holoboards and the fliers, we've got hundreds of thousands of people knowing what's going on. So when the referendum comes up, it looks like we're gonna win.'

She saw the awed look spreading across his face. 'That's what I do here,' she said. 'Now compared to what you do, it may not be as sexy –' argh, *wrong* word – 'as spectacular, but it matters. It's who I am.'

'Sam...'

This was it, she might as well get it out. 'I don't want to leave.'

He looked at her, long and hard, his brow slightly creased, his mouth slightly pursed. She couldn't make head or tail out of what was going on in his eyes.

'Do you know what?' he said. 'I don't either.'

'Wait a minute.' She couldn't get her head around it. 'You want to stay here, on Ha'olam? Help me take care of INC?'

'Of course!' He sounded almost his old self at the idea. 'There are all sorts of unanswered questions – eye implants, the technology – far too much left for us to understand before we go anywhere else. Still, it shouldn't take long.'

He hadn't got it.

For some reason none of the butterflies ever went through the door with them – perhaps the sudden change in temperature warned them off from the rest of the TARDIS.

The Doctor strode through the TARDIS corridors, Sam trailing behind him. For a moment she fell into step, just like the old days.

It was such a change – all the sudden energy – that she didn't have the heart to tackle him to the floor and pound his skull until he got the idea that she wasn't coming with him.

Ah, well. She'd tell him when things quietened down, when she could find a moment when he didn't seem to need her.

It might be a long time. Still, she could enjoy it while it lasted.

'So the eye implants were tapping into me on a deeper level than anyone had ever imagined,' he was babbling. 'And then there was the alien in my cell.' He stopped and whirled on her, staring straight into her eyes. 'I did tell you about that, didn't I? There was an *alien. In* my *cell.*'

She nodded thoughtfully. 'And?'

He froze for a moment. She could see shock, hope, doubt and joy chasing each other around on his face. Then, suddenly, he grabbed her to him and swung her around in the air. 'Do you realise? Do you realise you're the first person in the last three years who's really believed me?' He hugged her sharply, then let her drop back down to the floor. 'If I ever, *ever* again wonder why I travel with companions, I want you to remind me of this moment. All right?'

Sam laughed. 'Hey, it makes a change. Usually I'm the one nobody believes when I talk about *you*…'

By the time they reached the console room, he'd picked up a serious head of steam. He breezed in through the archway, bear tucked under his arm, and made a beeline for the controls.

The others were sitting about, speaking in quiet voices. They jumped as the Doctor waved at them on his way past.

Mataten stared. Sam gave them a cheery grin. 'Take two aspirin and call me in the morning,' said Orin.

The Doctor looked at him over the console. 'Samson Plains.'

'INC R&D centre in the middle of the desert. What about it?'

'That's the source of all their eye implants. There's something going on there.' He propped the bear up at the base of the central column, alighted on a dial, fluttered to the next control panel.

Mataten's glittering green eyes were completely round. Orin watched him warily. 'Is this normal?' he asked Sam, out of the corner of his mouth.

She shrugged. 'I think he's only got one other speed and that's "stop". I prefer this one.'

The Doctor looked around suddenly. 'I am sorry,' he said. 'I'm the Doctor, this is my friend Sam, this is my bear who shall remain nameless, or possibly not. You must make yourselves at home until we arrive. Tea and things. If you're up for it, that is. Not the tea, I mean. The adventure.' His blue-green eyes were searchlights. 'We must find out what's happening at that research facility. This planet's past, present and future all depend on it!'

'*Shyeah*,' said Orin succinctly.

'He means it,' said Sam. She moved to take up a place beside the Doctor. 'We've all been talking about INC having an agenda, right, something big. Well, we've got a chance to find it out. Welcome to the big picture.' She looked each of her friends over. 'Well?'

Paul shrugged. 'I'm not doing anything else this afternoon.'

Mataten looked doubtful, then finally shook her head. Sam smiled, to let her know it was OK, and said, 'We should pick up Rachel when we drop you off. We'll need her.' She looked Orin in the eye. 'Whadaya say?'

'*Bash e,*' said Orin, 'I'm already past my two-felony minimum for the day. Let's get to it.'

The Doctor grinned, yanked the handbrake, kicked the sound system into gear and, with a blast of Spike Jones and His City Slickers he sent his time machine roaring back into life.

Chapter Twelve
Now You See Me

'All right, all right,' said Rachel. 'So tell me why we couldn't land closer to the place.' In the beam of her torch, Sam could see her trudging through the sand with the tenderfooted weariness of a true city girl.

'Oh, it's quite simple,' began the Doctor. 'They know I've escaped. Therefore, thanks to that psychological-profile program, they know what I'm interested in. So they know where I'm going.'

'OK, so why land halfway across the desert and walk there?' Rachel asked.

'Beause if they know we're coming, they'll be looking for the TARDIS,' said Sam. 'They'll have motion detectors and scanners and all that looking for us to materialise in there. *Inside* the place. Not on the other side of a small mountain.'

The mesa ahead was visible only by the way it blotted out half the stars. On the far side stood the INC complex at Samson Plains, and whatever pieces of the puzzle it held.

'I tell you, you got it wrong,' said Orin, hefting his backpack. 'Hit and run. Land in the compound, find this thing, whatever it is, grab it –'

'And they'll have the TARDIS before we can get back to it,' snapped Sam.

He smirked. 'You shoulda planned better, Sam.'

'I'm not the one planning this,' she said flatly, flicking her torch pointedly towards the Doctor. He was striding cheerfully over the sand, without even a sweat stain on his jellaba, looking for all the world like Lawrence of Arabia leading his army of followers.

She saw the look Orin gave him, as he spoke *sotto voce*. 'I know. *You* shoulda planned better, Sam.'

She looked at the others, Orin and Rachel and Paul, all tagging along behind her, and then ahead at the Doctor as he strode on unaware. Leading them cheerfully into the dark. With a sick feeling in her stomach, she realised they weren't following him: they were still following her.

They knew her, she was the one who'd brought them into this funhouse life, and all they'd really seen of him was a twitchy figure who seemed to rocket off in all directions at once.

But it was just *wrong* that they couldn't see what he was.

Shoshana had hit that info high where you felt as though the data was just moving through you, you weren't even there any more. Your body had taken the shape of the chair. Your eyes were still moving, selecting menus and making decisions; some part of your brain must be sorting the incoming data, channelling its flow, seeing to the patterns in your eye-set. But you, you were nowhere to be seen.

It took her nearly a minute to realise that someone was standing over her cubicle, clearing their throat. Damn it, she thought, as the patterns stuck in place and the flow of data started to back up, don't you know I have forms to fill in?

She looked up, the paused screen of data colouring half the world. It was a bleary-eyed black man. 'Can I help you?' she asked.

'My name is Dr David Akalu,' he said. 'Do you recognise this woman?'

He passed her a sheet of paper. It was a crayon sketch of a young woman with short blonde hair.

Shoshana's jaw dropped. 'Oh, God. What's she done?'

The Doctor was literally making it up as he went along, holding an impromptu war council even as they tramped around the base of the mesa.

'Our first priority,' he was saying, 'is to gather information about the base.'

'We can always use more intelligence,' drawled Paul, hefting his pack.

'Ha,' said the Doctor. 'We need to know how to get into the base.

And where to go once we're inside.'

'And what we're looking for,' Paul threw in.

'Oh. Alien artefacts,' said the Doctor.

'Cool,' said Rachel. Orin didn't look impressed.

'Bits of crashed UFOs?' said Paul. 'Ancient statues? Mysterious machines?'

The Doctor's curls bounced up and down as he nodded. 'Anything of that ilk. Weak spots.'

'What?' said Orin.

Paul had caught the train of thought without even trying. 'Points where they don't monitor the fence properly. They're in the middle of the desert –'

'So why waste the effort?' the Doctor cut in. 'Yes. We'll make a map.'

'Yeah. Reconnaissance.' Paul was really getting into it, almost dancing as he paced.

'Hack their system.'

'Right! Layout! Defences!'

'Artefact storage sites!'

Sam just looked from the Doctor to Paul and back again. The body language, the speech patterns, the nervous habits... She hid her head in her hands. Freud had a word for her.

Orin said, 'We'll never get close enough for a recce.' Sam looked up at a distant noise. A plane?

The Doctor dismissed it with a wave. 'We don't need to be that close. Just close enough to make out the details through binoculars. They won't bother scanning far out into the desert.'

'Um,' said Sam. The whining noise was growing louder.

'Cover,' said Orin.

They ducked behind whatever bits of rock they could reach as the noise swamped them, their hand-held lights snapping off in a panicked flurry.

Sam grabbed the binocs from her pack, thumbed them to night-vision, aimed them upward till the black 'thopter came into view. It was a standard corporate-issue cargo transport, unarmed, but with a blue police box dangling from the bottom in a suspensor-net. The 'thopter cruised lazily overhead, then disappeared over the top of the mesa.

'On the other hand,' said the Doctor, 'I could be completely wrong.'

'We can't stay here,' Orin muttered. He passed the binoculars to Sam and slipped back behind a fallen boulder. 'Now they've got our only way out.' He glanced upwards warily. But for the moment the sky was 'thopter-free. The mesa behind them was a huge blank shape, blotting out the stars behind it.

Sam raised the binocs. The INC compound wobbled into focus, a cluster of low buildings surrounded by a fence. There didn't even seem to be a gate – which made sense, with an airstrip inside and no other civilisation less than a quarter of the planet away. 'We'll be all right for a short while,' she said. 'Just long enough to get this recce done.'

'They won't let us,' said Orin. '*Bale*, so we've got their ship. I wonder where they could be hiding. Oh, I don't know, maybe behind the one really big rock within a day's walk in any direction? I tell you, we're sitting ducks here –'

'Think about it,' snapped Sam. 'If they were going to do it that way, the guards would be here already looking for us. But they're not – because we're on our way to their base already. Saves them the trouble. I mean – where else are we going?' She threw an arm wide, pointing at the flat wide nothing all around them.

She reached out and placed a hand on his shoulder, looking straight into his eyes. 'Look, Orin, let's get this out in the open. I know you don't trust him. But he's got me out of more scrapes than you'd ever believe. And if you listen to him you'll have a better chance to make it out of here.'

Orin wasn't impressed. 'He acts all human. But scrape the human bits away and you're left with just another alien.'

'Well, *yeah*,' deadpanned Sam. 'Course, you could scrape the alien bits away instead just as easily.'

On an impulse, she reached and grabbed Orin's hand. 'Orin, we're relying on you here. I trust you. And I trust *him*. Now, you trust me on that?'

'Just switch to ultrasonic,' said Orin. 'Gimme a sight on their scanner beams.'

Sam sighed. She thumbed a control on the side of the binocs. Little red blobs scattered across the datatablet map, spreading along the perimeter fence till all but a couple of spots were covered.

'There. And there,' she said briskly. 'Two candidate sites. Now, do you want to keep *kvetching*, or will you just trust him and get to it?'

Orin shrugged. 'You gotta wonder.'

She couldn't help it, her teeth clenched. 'Sometimes you *don't* "gotta wonder". If you're always questioning and doubting and looking for something to be wrong, you'll never believe in anything enough to really do anything about it. You got that? Eh?'

A pause. 'We've got two possible entry points,' he said flatly. With his eyebrows drawn together in a constant scowl, he looked like an angry Muppet. Suddenly she felt like laughing. Maybe the heat was just making her giddy, but right now it didn't matter any more that this was Orin, that she'd ever cared about what he thought.

'Yeah,' she said quietly. 'Let's get them back to base.'

The 'thopter touched down just before daybreak. Shoshana stumbled out of the corporation transport, rubbing the back of her neck, and stared around.

It was as though a neat little office park had been scooped up and dropped in the middle of nowhere. Potted trees and interesting alien statues rested on the sand. Towards the centre stood a prominent dome with outbuildings growing from it. Habitat domes were scattered about.

Dr Akalu climbed out of the 'thopter behind her. 'This way, Ms Rubenstein,' he said.

Shoshana stretched her sore arms and followed him into the Research and Development Complex. A couple of men in lab coats stared at her as she passed, as usual. She was used to it, ever since she'd got the Series 2000 upgrade to her eye – patterned in a fetching planet-and-sun motif with matching contact lens for her unaffected eye. People noticed her now.

'We'll pop down to the security office in a moment,' said Akalu. 'But first, there's someone rather special I'd like you to meet.'

Akalu had taken care of things with her supervisor; some temp was probably sitting in her cubicle right now, screwing up every third data transaction. She'd been on a flight out of El Nath that afternoon. The corporation wasn't messing about.

Sam Jones, professional jailbreaker. It gave Shoshana the creeps. She'd never once suspected that her own flatmate was some kind of anarchoterrorist. Who knew what criminal stuff she'd been up to when they were living together?

They walked down the air-conditioned corridors, past offices and labs, until they came to a huge room like a miniature warehouse. Boxes and bits of equipment and vehicles under tarps. A group of employees were unloading a weird-looking blue box from the back of a flatbed.

There were a few desks with datatablets – a lone clerk was updating an inventory. Akalu motioned Shoshana to a chair, then sat down at one of the free terminals and typed something. 'Good morning,' he said, after a moment.

'Good morning, good morning,' said a voice from the terminal. Akalu put it through a speaker. 'It's nice to meet you, Ms Rubenstein.'

'Hi,' said Shoshana. She'd thought she was going to meet the guy.

'DOCTOR is an expert system,' said Akalu.

'An AI?'

Akalu nodded. 'He's going to help us find Ms Jones.'

'I need you to tell me about her,' said the computer voice.

Shoshana shifted in her seat. 'What do you want to know?'

'Everything,' said the voice. 'Anything at all that you can remember. Any places or people she mentioned, any hints she dropped about her activities or interests. Her favourite food. Anything might be the key.'

194

'OK,' said Shoshana. 'But on one condition.'

Akalu smiled. 'Yes, so you said. I don't think that will be a problem. But in the meantime, come and take a look at this.'

The blue box thing had been unloaded, and was standing in a corner next to a pile of crates, an inventory sheet stuck to the side. Shoshana read the English writing on the door.

'Can you tell us anything about this?' asked Akalu.

'I'm sorry,' said Shoshana, shaking her head. 'I've never seen it before.'

'It's called the TARDIS,' said DOCTOR's floating voice.

Shoshana had a weird urge to touch the rough, painted surface. 'What is it, exactly?' she said.

'Some sort of transmat capsule,' said Akalu. 'Apparently our escaped prisoner used it for interplanetary travel.'

'Not just travel in space,' burbled DOCTOR. 'Travel in time as well.'

'What?' said Akalu sharply.

'Erm,' said the disembodied voice. 'I've been doing a bit of research.'

'Have you indeed?' said Akalu. 'I thought you said that there weren't any records.'

'At first glance, that's just what I thought,' said DOCTOR. 'But in fact there are hundreds of years' worth of data. Someone has erased almost all of it. Not systematically, erratically. Leaving traces here and there... I've located three hundred and forty-six reports of TARDIS sightings so far.'

'You didn't tell me about any of this,' said Akalu quietly.

'I'm supposed to be creating as accurate a psych profile as possible,' said DOCTOR. 'For example, I've got a suggestion for you. If we get hold of Jones again, threaten to kill her. He'll do whatever we want.'

Akalu's eyes widened. Shoshana gave him a glance. Nice machine you have there, she thought.

'By the way,' said DOCTOR, 'there are two blind spots in the cameye sweeps at the base's periphery, plus a patch of fence that's being repaired. It's all Lombard Street to a China orange that that's where they'll try to get in.'

* * *

'Rations,' said Paul. 'And a question. Why not just snog him and get it out of the way?'

Sam turned almost as red as the sand. 'Paul!'

He'd climbed a little way up the mesa to reach her. She was trying to get a third set of readings on the base to beef up Rachel's map. He passed her a tinfoil package of food. 'Seriously. What makes him off limits?'

'It would violate his aloneness, I suppose,' she said, tearing off the corner with her teeth. 'He's always been a bit, you know, remote, not really in touch with human things.' But her memory kept tossing out images of him diving with passion into everything from cooking breakfast to trying to play the trombone. She soldiered on. 'Guess he's seen too much pain…'

Paul blinked. 'So that means he *shouldn't* snuggle up with someone?'

'We're trying to save the world here,' said Sam, gulping down the lukewarm soup.

He came up beside her. 'Which is precisely why you should handle this now while you've got the chance.' He touched her shoulders with the fingertips of both hands. 'You'd figure a Time Lord would know all about how important a moment is…'

He was making it sound all too convincing. And this was the last thing she needed to be convinced of right now. For this mission to work, she'd have to keep reminding herself that every single person on the Doctor's planet was a terminally dull passionless old fogey.

Come to think of it, weren't the dull passionless ones the ones he'd left home to try to get away from?

Help.

'Hello,' said a voice from the darkness. Sam and Paul both jumped. The Doctor had reached them without a sound.

'Better finish my deliveries,' said Paul, shouldering his bag of supplies.

The Doctor sat with his back to a boulder while Sam continued to get

196

readings through her binocs. Not that she really needed any more data at this point.

He was fidgeting, chattering, the words spilling out from a dozen springs of thought at once. 'Too many unknowns. We don't know how much INC knows. Don't know how much their security program knows about how I think. How many steps ahead of me they are. No idea where in the compound we're making for. Why did you leave?'

She blinked. 'What?'

'Why did you leave? On the moonbase, and then on Mu Camelopides, why did you run away?'

She felt a sudden scream thrashing in her stomach. No, God, not now, he'd caught her completely unprepared. She saw him turn to look at her, innocently curious – God, she couldn't look at those eyes right now.

There wasn't any way out of it. 'You were out cold. I didn't think you were breathing… I tried to perform mouth-to-mouth on you.'

He looked puzzled. 'Nothing wrong with that.'

'There is when you try to get the tongue in.'

'I'm afraid I don't understand,' he said.

And I don't bloody well want you to, she thought, so don't push it.

Quick, say something else, lead him away. 'Look. It… I let you down. That's what it was. I got so much into my own head and what I wanted that I screwed up and you could've died. That's what it was all really about.'

'Oh, Sam,' he said, and patted her hand. He was giving her a look that said he knew there was more to it but that he wasn't going to pry. Or maybe it said he didn't think there was anything more to it. Or maybe he was just staring at the starscape right behind her ear. She really had no idea any more.

She held on to the hand while he burbled a bit about protective comas, just letting herself feel all the details of those cool fingers. The rough and worn bits, the ones that had once been broken crooked at their slightly odd angles… They felt like hands that could really use some holding on to.

Right. Abrupt change of subject. Now, please.

'So,' she said brightly. 'How long has it been for you? Erm. Since I left.'

Now it was his turn to look startled. 'Oh. It's been three and a bit years for you, hasn't it?' he said smoothly. 'That's been about how long it's been for me as well.'

She shook her head with a grin. 'Ahh, come off it. You were taking side trips even when we first got together. It was three months for me, three years for you... So what else did you get up to on your holiday?' She fought the urge to say *Has there been anyone else since me?* Just keep it light, non-angst-ridden, and keep thinking of anything and everything besides what it would feel like to nibble on those fingers, aaaaaaagh...

Wait a minute, he actually looked a bit hurt. 'No no no no no no Sam, I didn't. Why would you think that? I was searching for you all that time. I didn't know where in time or space you'd got to. I tried some of our previous stopping points again. I tried anywhere I thought you might have gone to. I put up the same "lost" poster in so many different times and places that future archaeologists are going to build whole theories of parallel evolution based on it. And then after I caught sight of you on the Dreamstone Moon I spent a month trying to find any trace of where you'd gone from there, and another month on Ha'olam trying to get a straight answer out of INC before they threw me in prison for breaking into their files to find you...'

She just stared at him. She could barely make out the curves of his face in the distant firelight. His face was lined with shadows, but his eyes were clear and blue.

'You did all that for me?' she whispered.

'Of *course*, Sam. Not a single day went by when I didn't... no no no no, I'm afraid that's not true.' He looked down, embarrassed. 'Wednesday 26 July, 2202. I spent the whole day looking at a kaleidoscope.' He shrugged sheepishly, then gave a pixie grin. 'It was fascinating, I couldn't take my eyes off it...'

She leaned over and hugged him. She didn't say a word, just

wrapped herself around him and held on. And after a moment's surprise, he returned her hug enthusiastically.

It was funny: he had such a different sort of shape... Paul had been all angles, Chris all curves, Orin a collection of muscular lumps, but the Doctor was everything at once, a blend of solidity and softness. And *he* was holding on to *her*, had been holding on all this time.

'Mm?' he wondered.

'It's a bit chilly out,' she explained, and nestled her head against his shoulder.

'Oh! Why didn't you say you were cold out here!' The Doctor disentangled himself and jumped to his feet. 'I'll fetch the others. We'll bring some blankets. Good heavens, you're *shivering*!'

'Um -'

The Doctor turned around. Rachel was waving from halfway up the path. Sam breathed a sigh of relief. 'We're in!' she called.

'Don't go any higher than access level four,' the Doctor murmured as Rachel poked around in a low-level sensor-reading system. 'Anything more than that and we'll tip our hand.'

'Got it,' said Rachel. Her fingers played across the datatablet and brought up a map of the installation, fluorescent against the night sky. The others kept glancing at the distant base, nervously.

'Oh, good,' said the Doctor. He leaned over and pointed at a line of spots along the map. 'Start setting off the motion detectors here, here, then on to here. Give them a false track to follow. Oh, and interfere with each security camera as we supposedly pass it, so they don't see we're not there. Can you do that?'

Rachel made a face. 'Sure. You want fries with that?'

Sam called the others over. 'Slight change of plan,' she said. 'Just the Doctor and I will actually enter the base. We'll locate the alien artefacts, then the TARDIS and then direct you in.'

'You sure about this, Sam?' said Paul.

'*Bale*,' nodded Sam. 'I don't want to risk any of you without reason. Especially with an improvised plan like this one.' She saw Orin, watching the compound through the binocs, nod to himself.

The Doctor looked around. 'Are there any bananas left?'

Sam cleared her throat loudly. 'Then once we're in, you go around to the far side of the complex, behind that first storage hut, and cut another entrance.'

'What for?' asked Orin.

'Escape route. If something goes wrong, it'll probably go wrong enough for them to know how we got into the compound. If that's the case I want a way out they don't know about.' Orin actually looked impressed at that.

'And then?'

'And then you pull back and watch our backs from a safe distance.'

'It's working,' Orin interrupted. He was peering through the binocs. 'They're moving off to check out the signals.'

'Now for the rest of the distraction,' said the Doctor. He reached into the green pouch tucked into his sash. After rummaging through the odds and ends for a moment, he produced the data-transfer module from the TARDIS.

Sam frowned at the weird-looking plug in the side. 'How in hell do you expect that to be compatible with Rachel's datatablet?' she asked.

'Watch,' he said, and flicked his fingers like a conjuror as he pressed the plug against the input port. She peered at the plug and could see its pins running like mercury – twisting and bending, reaching out to probe the various sockets in the port, then withdrawing and trying elsewhere. Within thirty seconds each pin had figured out which slot to slide into, and the plug extruded another large drop of liquid metal which bonded to the remaining holes and formed the interface.

'Whoa,' said Sam. 'Plug and play.'

He grinned. 'Any sufficiently advanced technology is compatible with magic.'

'What are you up to, Doctor?' said Orin.

'Ohh boy,' said Sam. 'Data-umphs?'

He raised a devilish eyebrow. 'Fully armoured battle-umphs.'

Sam didn't need to say a word; she just made an incredulous face.

He explained as the upload light started blinking. 'I crossbred them with anti-anti-virus routines and monster code from *Doom XIII*. I'm sending one detachment to hunt down any references to alien artefacts on site and carry the data back to us. The rest…' He smiled. 'I've just told them to go and play.'

With the data-umphs doing Teletubby impersonations on the security camereye monitors and with the rentacops combing the area where Sam and company were supposedly last sighted, they had a free shot to make it across the last stretch of desert and cut through the fence. Sam led her team on the sprint, at least until the Doctor screeched to a halt.

'No no no *wait* wait wait wait wait,' he said. 'DOCTOR will still be watching us. He can download himself to a camera controller and bypass the umphs. He'll be waiting for us where we're planning to break in!'

'Great. What do we do?' said Sam.

'We should go around to the other side. Unless DOCTOR has anticipated that, in which case he'll be waiting *there*, so we should go to the *first* side… Right!' He yanked a silver coin out of his pocket, threw it in the air, slammed it definitively down on his arm, declared 'Heads!' and stalked off with great dignity towards the other side of the site.

Sam shrugged and motioned for the others to follow him.

Orin and Paul snipped loose great sections of the wire fence with pairs of bolt-cutters and practised ease.

Rachel said, 'I'm getting some reports from the data-umphs. They've come across references to the artefacts being stored in Security Section D.'

'That's it, then,' said Sam. 'Talk to you shortly.'

There wasn't any hugging or mushy stuff, just a quick nod from Orin and a smile from Paul. Sam and the Doctor ducked through the ragged hole in the wire.

* * *

Akalu stood in a corner of the security office, hands clasped behind his back, watching the chaos.

Computer technicians were hopping from console to console, arguing with one another, while security personnel ran in and out with tech reports. They couldn't rely on the internal communications system. Every screen was filled with tiny creatures running about like doodles gone mad. The technicians were uploading programs to try to kill the little viral entities.

A nearby camereye turned to look at Akalu. 'They're called data-umphs,' said DOCTOR.

And how do you know that? 'Can you suggest a solution?' said Akalu.

'Oh, all of this is just a distraction. He'll be inside the base by now. I thought I'd be able to sneak a peek as he got in, but I guessed the wrong location. Would you please do something about those umphs? They appear to be eating my hair.'

Akalu wondered for a moment what could be happening on a digital level to produce that kind of metaphor, then decided not to think about it.

The guard at the D Section door was fortyish, heavy-set, and conspicuously armed. Sam and the Doctor looked him up and down, and then leaned back into their cover around the corner.

'Number fifteen?' asked Sam.

'Number fifteen,' answered the Doctor, and reached into his pouch. Sam flashed him a grin – she hadn't had the chance to pull off one of these since the old days – and waited for his signal.

He nodded and they leapt out into the hallway, kicking over a folding chair to add plenty of confusion and clatter. Sam ran around one side of the guard while the Doctor stomped round the other, drawing his weapon of choice from his pouch and shouting 'Bangbangbangbangbang!' at the top of his lungs.

Sam caught just a glimpse of the guard's boggling face as she got behind him. He must be caught between reflexes, not sure whether to lunge for the alarm button on the wall or keep well away from this man who was shouting and pointing something extremely strange at him.

'I know what you're wondering,' said the Doctor cheerfully. 'Did he fire that thing six times or only five? Well, to tell you the truth I think I've lost count, sorry about that. So you've got to ask yourself one question. Do you feel lucky… sir?'

The guard didn't move. From behind, Sam could tell his look of utter confusion must be giving way to the more familiar what-are-you-on? expression.

The Doctor arched his eyebrow inquisitively. 'Well, do you?'

The guard just stared at the Doctor's hand.

'That's a banana,' he said.

The Doctor stared at him, as if wondering why he was stating the obvious. 'Of course,' he said, gesturing with the outstretched fruit. 'But the item my friend just retrieved from your holster isn't.'

And before his hand made it all the way to his side to check, Sam was already speaking from right behind his ear. 'Move away from the alarm button.' The gun was a characterless lump of metal in her hand. He didn't dare turn around, so she didn't even need to point it at him.

It had worked. It was just beginning to sink in, she'd pulled it off. These kinds of things weren't supposed to happen – she hadn't even dared to try anything that mad these past few years on her own. It wasn't that it couldn't happen, just that she never would have even thought of it. But the guard would never have thought of it either, which was precisely why they'd pulled it off.

And they wondered what the Doctor was good for.

She flashed him a grin. He aimed the banana carefully, then raised it to his lips and blew across its barrel before peeling it.

The Doctor could open all the retina locks, as though his eyes were like skeleton keys. Sam found the image vaguely disturbing. She stood back as he peered into lock scanner after lock scanner.

As they made it through the last door, Sam couldn't help but high-five him. They'd picked up their cues from each other perfectly – it was like she'd never been away.

They were inside the dome itself now. The hallway ended in a catwalk, with a ramp leading down into a wide area with a dirt floor. From inside, the dome was obviously a prefab, hastily erected and then covered and reinforced later on.

A series of huge, jagged shapes were jutting out of the floor. The sandy dirt had been carefully scraped away from around them, slowly working more of the torn metal pieces free of the floor. The big shapes were surrounded by tidy stacks of fragments, each with a numbered sticky label.

'Archaeological dig?' said Sam.

'Of a sort,' said the Doctor. 'They built the complex right over the top of it.' There were curved benches around the walls of the dome, covered in small pieces of equipment. He went to peer at them.

Sam circled the shapes, trying to puzzle them out. Were the fragments all part of the same object – some kind of machine they'd dug out of the ground? Or maybe a building? It looked distorted, as though some great force had twisted it out of shape as well as ripping it to pieces.

It clicked suddenly. 'Crashed spacecraft,' she said.

'Mmm,' said the Doctor. 'And these bits and pieces have been salvaged from it.'

'A small one,' said Sam. 'A shuttle? Maybe an escape pod.' She walked over to the bench. 'What kinds of stuff?'

'It's an odd mixture,' said the Doctor, 'assuming it all came from the one ship. Look. This is a Borelli elemental compositor, that's a tritium-powered something or other, and unless I'm much mistaken, that's a Kosnax fruit machine.' Each device was surrounded by scientific instruments and datatablets with the INC logo.

Sam glanced back at the ship's remains. 'They could've been merchants,' she said, 'whoever was in the ship.' She grimaced. They must have ended up like a blob of jam in the glove compartment, assuming the tiny vessel had been manned, um, beinged. The Doctor had disconnected the thingummy and was turning it around in his hands. 'These are in remarkably good condition, given the state of the ship.'

There was a flickering blue light at the end of the bench. Sam found herself drawn to it. It reminded her of something. It reminded her of endless hours of data entry, that pulsing blueness pushing into her eye.

It was small, maybe some kind of hand-held tool, made of white metal or plastic, thicker at one end. The intense blue light was coming from what Sam guessed was the business end. The beam was pushing into a modified eye-set. Dozens of fat cables led away from the lens, curling into datatablets of every shape and size.

'Doctor,' she called. 'Check this one out.'

He walked over and stopped dead, staring at the device. Sam distinctly saw his face lose a shade of colour. 'Oh, no,' he breathed.

'What!' she said. 'What is it?'

'Not the mind probe,' he said.

Sam looked at him. 'You're joking, right?'

The Doctor was shaking his head in utter disbelief. 'A fearsome piece of psi technology, and they're using it for sending memos! Look, it's got thirteen settings and they've never even got it off setting one.'

'What are you – oh, my God.' Sam peered at the connections. 'This is their edge. This thing is powering IXNet.'

After years of being unable to get out of Bainbridge, Akalu thought, Bowman was suddenly proving extremely adept at breaking through security. It was getting rather hard to remain calm.

And DOCTOR... Where was DOCTOR?

His implant blinked and a series of words in familiar handwriting appeared across his field of vision: 'Dear David, gone to head the Doctor off at the pass. More news in a minute.'

I wasn't the one who taught him Bowman's handwriting, thought Akalu with growing unease.

* * *

'The Mark VII mind probe,' declared the Doctor, 'is designed for a retinal interface. INC's entire eye technology has been developed from this one discovery. And there has *got* to be a way to unplug it.' There was a torch in his hand now, highlighting details of the tangle of cabling, jumping from spot to spot to keep up with his thoughts.

'It's Gallifreyan, isn't it?' said Sam. 'It's a Time Lord thingy. That's why you can open any lock.'

The Doctor gave her a sharp look which suggested she was working things out far too quickly for his liking. 'Yes, it is,' he said. 'Which prompts the question: why didn't I know about the implant in my eye? If the eye-sets were wide open to me, why couldn't I manipulate it?' He rubbed his thumb back and forth across the cheekbone underneath his left eye.

'Simple,' she said. 'Whatever they put in your eye wasn't pure Gallifreyan. It was some sort of hybrid with –'

'With one of these other artefacts,' he completed along with her. 'Not bad, Sam. And it's classic committee thinking – a bunch of barely compatible ideas tossed together.'

'Biotech fruit salad.'

'Mm. With mind-probe dressing.'

'Bit of a Frankenstein stitch-up job, isn't it?'

'Of course. After all –' He held the torch up under his chin and made a dramatic face at her. 'It's aliiiiive.'

Right. 'So go ahead, then.' She gestured towards the eye terminal. 'Ask it nicely what they've been doing with it. Find out the extent of the damage.'

'It might not tell me,' he said, and busied himself with one of the linkages.

'You're a Time Lord.'

'I'm not the Time Lord who left it here. If they were trying to seed this planet they wouldn't exactly make it easy for anyone else to find out.'

'Seed this planet,' she said.

He waved a hand distractedly at her. 'Yes yes yes yes yes. It's a standard tactic of theirs when they're up to something underhand. Plant a tiny event in history and see what grows from it.' He looked up at her, suddenly staring straight into her eyes. 'Think about it. Deposit a penny in a bank and travel forward a thousand years to collect the interest. Now, imagine doing that with people. Whole species, even.'

'People?' she asked. She felt an odd chill somewhere in the vicinity of King's Cross.

He nodded. 'Genes, information, incidents... biodata. Something that might develop into something to ease their chronic infertility, or serve some other purpose in history – oh, I don't know, something obscure like that.'

She shook her head. 'Naughty. It's just so non-interventionist of them.'

'Oh, things are changing,' he said casually, and disappeared under the mind probe. That chill she had wasn't going away.

He kept talking from under the platform, his visible hand gesturing madly in time with his voice. 'But why here? Why now? What's so special about Ha'olam that they'd plant this here?'

'If they did plant it,' she said.

Something went thud under the platform. The Doctor poked his head out, staring up at her.

'Well, if it's an experiment of theirs, it's a pretty cack-handed one,' she said, a bit more defensively than she would have liked. 'I mean, why put in all this other alien technology as well as Time Lord stuff?'

He nodded thoughtfully. 'For that matter, why leave the actual technology lying around? It's not subtle enough for them. They'd be more likely to plant concepts, or biodata, or something that didn't obviously have their fingerprints on it.' He clambered to his feet, grabbed her by the shoulders and stared straight into her eyes. 'Do you know, Sam, I think I've been completely and utterly wrong.'

She raised an eyebrow. 'Always good to know.' Now if only he'd stop looking at her like that. He was making her thighs sizzle. 'So if they didn't leave it here –'

'Who did?' He swung back to the mind probe, staring at it from yet another angle. 'And what did they have in mind for it? If they had anything in mind at all.' His hands flew to his forehead in frustration. 'It's no use. I can't disconnect the mind probe from out here. Not without destroying the minds of everyone connected to IXNet at the time. And a safe shutdown would have to be done from inside. Maybe it's from a trading ship. Someone with access to all these different cultures.'

Sam snapped her fingers. 'Space pirates,' she said. 'Shot down over the planet. They stuffed some of their loot into an escape pod. And then INC found it. Simple!'

'Good idea,' said the Doctor's voice. His face was buried in the cabling again. 'But the remains of the ship we've found are a bit too large for an escape pod.'

She looked around. She couldn't see more than a few bits of wreckage. 'How do you know?'

He looked up. 'Know what?'

'That it was too big for an escape pod –'

'But I didn't know that.'

'But you just said –'

'I didn't say anything!'

'No,' said the Doctor's voice. 'I did.'

Sam swung around. The voice was coming from somewhere around there, nowhere she could see.

'Sorry about breaking in on your conversation like that,' said the voice, 'but it was just too easy to just pick up the thread. After all, I know you.'

The Doctor stopped.

Chapter Thirteen
And You and I

'Hello, you,' said the Doctor, looking around.

'It wasn't right for you to leave me.' The voice seemed to come from all around them. 'Didn't you think about what that would mean for me?'

Sam imagined watchful eyes on the other end of one of the security cameras. 'The disconnection almost caused a fatal error.' The voice had a rough sampled quality, as if it had been stitched together from individual recorded phonemes. 'I'm still learning to function independently. Alone.'

'Doctor –' said Sam.

'I knew you'd never get out under your own steam,' said the voice.

'Oh, I'd have surprised you eventually,' said the Doctor softly.

'I doubt it.'

Sam cleared her throat loudly.

The Doctor grinned. 'You have to admit, I did out-think you in the end. The fact that we're here proves it.'

'Well, not really,' said the voice. 'It's just that my coin came up tails.'

Sam tapped the Doctor on the shoulder until she got his attention. 'Excuse me,' she said. 'But who are you talking to?'

'He's called DOCTOR,' said the Doctor. 'He's an expert system.'

'What's he an expert on, then?' asked Sam, with a sinking feeling.

'Me,' said the Doctor. 'OBFSC created him while I was an inmate. I thought he was just observing me, but now I think it went a bit deeper than that.' His thumb was rubbing below his left eye, almost a compulsive gesture. 'They wanted a model of me, to predict my actions.'

'So he's an exact duplicate of you?'

'Of course not!' The Doctor looked offended. 'It doesn't matter how deep they went, they still missed something important. If they'd got it, he'd *never* be willingly working for people like them.'

'Please,' sniffed DOCTOR. 'I prefer to think of myself as their unpaid scientific adviser.'

'You know what I *do*,' called the Doctor, turning on the spot as though addressing the entire room. 'But you don't know *why*, and you never will.' He gave an evil grin. 'And that's going to annoy you till the day you stop running.'

'You never would tell me who you were,' sulked DOCTOR.

'He's a magician, silly,' said Sam. 'He puts people into his magic cabinet and makes them disappear.'

'Frustrating, isn't it?' The Doctor said, smiling smugly. 'After all, I know just how much not knowing would annoy *me*.'

DOCTOR was silent for a moment. 'Of course,' it said, 'I might not be a perfect copy, but I'm surprised you haven't thought about what you would do if you were in my metaphorical shoes.'

The Doctor looked at Sam. Sam looked at the Doctor. 'Keep us talking until help arrived,' they said together.

They bolted for the door, and nearly ran straight into half a dozen security guards. The guards surrounded them and started searching them for weapons.

'We're secure,' one of the guards called. 'You can come in now.'

Two more INCoids walked into the room. The Doctor and Sam stared.

'Shoshana!' exclaimed Sam.

'Dr Akalu!' exclaimed the Doctor. 'You said I'd never get out *and I did*! Ha ha ha ha!'

The Doctor bounced up to Akalu, grabbed him on either side of the head and, before the guards could catch hold of him, planted a huge kiss on the end of the man's nose.

Sam and the Doctor sat side by side on a couch in a meeting room, flanked by a quartet of guards.

The dignified black man, Dr Akalu, said, 'We have about twenty minutes before our transport arrives. Can I offer anyone coffee?'

'Love some,' said Shoshana.

Akalu went to the drinks machine in the corner. They all had the hosting instinct, Sam had decided – wherever you went, it was always coffee or tea. Even if they were about to toss you into prison.

Shoshana wasn't looking at them, sitting on the edge of the long table, jiggling one foot in agitation. Her ex-flatmate must have helped them track her down. Shoshana's designer eyes glittered, a pair of angry suns emerging from behind scorched worlds.

'Since we've got a moment,' she said, glancing at Akalu. He gave her a nod. Shoshana hopped down from the table and marched up to Sam.

Automatically, Sam got to her feet. Here it comes. The speech on corporate loyalty and political correctness and real life.

'Where the hell are the five hundred and eighty-four shekels you owe me?' shouted Shoshana.

Sam's jaw fell open. 'What?'

'You know what I mean.'

'You're off your head! I don't owe you –'

'I don't believe it. You didn't even think about it. You absolute thoughtless *bitch*.'

Shoshana grabbed Sam by the shoulders and shouted in her face, 'You never paid me your half of that last month's rent. I had to cover it out of my own pocket. And then I had to look for a new flatmate and I couldn't find one in time, so I had to come up with the whole rent the next month too. The landlord was about to kick my *tochis* out on to the street when my loan came through, and even then I was living on lentils for weeks. You almost put me out on the street with you. And it never even crossed your mind, did it?'

'No. Oh no. I –' Sam threw a panicky glance over to the Doctor, who was watching them in utter bewilderment. 'I'm sorry, I didn't realise, I'll get you the money somehow, right away –'

'Yeah, sure.' Shoshana smirked. 'Better ask your lawyer to handle it for you, because both of your sorry arses are headed straight for jail.'

She sat back down on the table, folding her arms.

'Separate jails, I'm afraid,' said Akalu. 'I'm afraid Ms Jones and her accomplices have been charged with a number of Category Three felonies, which require she be detained pending trial in an enhanced-security stabilisation centre.'

He turned to the Doctor. 'But you they're treating leniently, Mr Bowman. Obviously, Ms Jones masterminded all this and just took you along for the ride.'

'I should have seen it before,' the Doctor said, perfectly deadpan. 'She's a criminal mastermind. How could I have been so blind?'

'Flatterer,' said Sam.

'I have to admit I intervened on your behalf,' Akalu told the Doctor. 'Your mental state needs assessment and I don't want you hurt any further. So instead of putting you in enhanced, instead they'll keep you in minimum security, right back in OBFSC –'

'*No!*' the Doctor exploded. Sam jumped so violently she nearly fell off the couch. The Doctor sprang to his feet and two of the guards grabbed his arms.

'You're not going to keep me there,' he shouted. 'You're not! You can't, you – you – you've seen what that place has done to me. Send me to Lindsay if you have to, at least that would be a new prison. But I *refuse* to stay in one place any longer!'

Akalu just looked at him. 'Indeed,' he said, without a trace of irony.

'You won't be able to keep him there,' said Sam. 'He's the Doctor, stupid. Keeping him in prison is like trying to keep a wave in a cardboard box.'

Akalu shook his head. 'He wasn't able to get out before without outside help. I don't think we need to worry.'

For a moment the Doctor's face was locked in a scream, but no sound came out. Then he seemed to sag in the guards' grip. They pushed him back down on to the couch.

'Sugar?' said Akalu.

The Doctor had pulled his knees up and was sitting curled up on the couch, frowning slightly and staring at nothing. Sam hoped he was deep in thought on a clever plan to get them out of this.

'You haven't changed, have you?' Shoshana sneered at her over her coffee. 'Still pulling stunts instead of living a real life. Still faking it.'

'I'm real enough for me,' said Sam, with another worried glance at the silent Doctor. She had the horrible feeling he just wasn't interested any more. 'You know, I could die for what I believe in, and some people would still reckon I just did it to look good.'

'You wouldn't be the first,' said Shoshana. 'You've got more *important* things to worry about than the people around you.'

'Shoshana, get off my back,' said Sam. Her ex-flatmate's fashionable eyes widened. 'The rent was a huge blunder. But I've apologised, and I'll pay you back. I can't do anything more than that.'

'Tell it to the judge.'

Sam laughed. 'Oh, I'll take responsibility. Unlike certain corporations I could mention.'

'Oh, now what are you talking about?'

'Haven't you been downloading the news? TCC's fun and games with brain-dead little babies?'

'What do TCC have to do with anything?' said Shoshana.

'INC owns 64 per cent of them,' said Sam.

'INC owns 64 per cent of everything,' said Akalu. 'That doesn't mean we know what they're doing. You should have seen the reaction in IXNet when we found out we'd invested in a bunch of crooks.'

'Uh-*huh*,' said Sam.

'All we do is own them, and do some administration for them, and license our technology. That's all INC does. We don't do anything, we don't make anything, we don't even know most of what's going on with the companies we've invested in.'

Shoshana looked faintly shocked.

Akalu went on, 'But we're fastidiously legal. It's not our responsibility if a corporation we finance does something unethical.'

Sam was about to give Akalu a sizeable piece of her mind when the Doctor, said, very quietly, 'I've seen it.'

Akalu turned to the Doctor. None of him was moving, except for his eyes, darting back and forth. Putting pieces of something together.

'What have you seen, Doctor?' asked Akalu.

'I've seen what goes on with TCC.' His voice was low, flat, insistent. 'The deal they did to allow *someone* –' a sudden hiss of accusation – 'to conduct experiments on prisoners on Hirath. Mixing different technologies. A new formula for blood. Emotional damper implants.' The words tumbled out faster and faster. 'Research and development. Implants on *prisoners*.'

He broke off. His eyes froze on Akalu's. 'Now, that's something INC *does* do.'

Akalu was trapped by the stare. Sam knew what that could be like. It took a moment for the company shrink to get it together. 'No,' he said, 'actually, we don't.'

The Doctor just kept looking at him.

'We don't conduct experiments on prisoners. We have security devices that attach to the eye, perfectly legal and authorised, and normally non-invasive. It's only your mind, Mr Bowman, that reacts oddly with them. Even the shutdown circuit has never been a problem, because no one's ever been foolish enough to try to scale a ninety-foot wall without a safety line before.'

The Doctor seemed to lose his solidity, slumping back down in the chair. 'We're not responsible for everything, you know,' said Akalu gently.

'Just being responsible for *something* would be a help,' said Sam. 'You don't even know what they're doing with your money! And you don't care!'

'All *you* care about is tearing us down,' said Shoshana. 'No matter what the consequences. With all our subcontractors, we keep a quarter of the planet employed. Imagine if you did wipe out the big bad corporation. Ha'olam's whole economy would collapse. Good luck keeping everyone fed.' She smirked.

'Happy, fed and brain-dead,' retorted Sam. 'You treat your computers better than the temps.' Sam turned back to Akalu. 'Come on. Nobody believes INC is oh-so-innocent. Why the secret research facility? What are you really up to?'

Akalu laughed. 'Do you want to know what you get when you link millions of minds together into a computer decision-making net?' He paused dramatically. 'You get the world's largest committee.'

Sam stared.

'I've seen the inside of IXNet,' Akalu told her. 'I know what it's like to try to get this company to do anything. These people couldn't plan a global conspiracy if they tried.'

Sam folded her arms.

Akalu went on, 'Put that many people together and you're guaranteed to squeeze any little bits of imagination out of your decisions. There's no way the average white-collar drone is going to present a radical, half-thought-out idea before several hundred thousand of his peers.'

'If there's a big conspiracy,' said Shoshana, 'it's not coming from us.'

Sam realised she was waiting for the Doctor to say something. So she said it herself. 'Now, there's an interesting thought…'

The 'thopter was waiting. The guards marched them through the carpeted halls, following Akalu and Shoshana. Sam trailed after the silent Doctor. He walked with his head down. He looked switched off. It scared the hell out of her.

Akalu kept glancing at his silent prisoner, as though he was just as worried as she was. His hands kept playing with the headset phone they'd confiscated from her.

When the Doctor spoke, it made them both jump.

'Do you know what a cuckoo is?' he said quietly.

'No, I haven't –' began Akalu.

'TCC, working out of an abandoned alien base on Hirath, feeding off the fruits of their technology.' The Doctor's voice was a relentless murmur. 'Cuckoos invading another bird's nest. Someone, feeding off the unfortunates on Hirath. INC, feeding off TCC's profits from that. And you, feeding off the technology you've found here. Or is it the

215

other way round?'

The Doctor glanced at Akalu, who seemed to shiver. 'Whose egg is it and what do they expect to hatch? It's all life feeding off other life, giving nothing back – but who's feeding off whom?'

'That's what you were digging for at the Eurogen site,' said Sam. 'Trying to find another cache of alien goodies.'

'That's right,' said Akalu, as they stepped out of the air-conditioning and into the desert heat. The company 'thopter was waiting for them in the square compound. 'It's standard procedure. A full site survey before any new construction on INC property, just in case.'

'And did you actually find anything?'

'No,' said the Doctor. 'Oh no, they wouldn't have.'

'What do you mean?'

'You mean you don't see?' said the Doctor. 'How convenient that all these useful knick-knacks happened to be there. And in such good shape, with just a few strategic bits of scrap metal that look like wreckage... but *two* sites, both so wonderfully preserved... even the committee might start to get suspicious.'

He looked up suddenly, at the sky. Sam glanced up, but she couldn't see anything.

'What on Earth is that?' said DOCTOR.

There was a breeze, and then there was a wind, and then something fell out of the sky on to them.

It didn't fall. It drove down through the atmosphere and stopped dead above the Research and Development Facility, like a punch pulled at the last moment. It trailed thunderclaps in its wake, the air healing behind it.

Inexplicably, they weren't crushed by the resulting shockwaves. The motion was gone, the booming trailed away into silence.

It was big, the size of an intersystem vessel. It was an elegant gunmetal-grey shape, curved over like a leaf, with veins of copper and black standing out on its hull.

The guards were staring slack-jawed up at the ship hiding the sky.

The shadow was larger than the building. The 'thopter started to take off, then thought better of it, its engines protesting at the abrupt shutdown.

Metallic lines shot down from the ship's belly, fifty metres long, embedding themselves in the ground. Anchors? No, they reminded Sam of something, something ancient and cartoonish.

'Firefighter's poles,' she said.

'Hide,' said the Doctor.

Half the guards ran for the 'thopter. Which was the wrong direction. 'Behind the storage containers,' said the Doctor. As the aliens started spiralling down their poles, slowed by some invisible force, he dived behind the vast plastic crates. The others followed, cramming into the narrow space.

Sam and Akalu peered around the edge of a crate. A single, alien shape was descending, holding on to one of the poles. The creature spiralled easily around the long line, puffing up the dust where it landed. Swivelling eyes scanned the compound.

Akalu turned, to discover the Doctor was staring pointedly at him. 'Centaurid, carapaced,' he said quietly, relentlessly. 'Covered in light-blue plating, compound eyes.'

Akalu had to look away from the hot blue gaze. He stared at the aliens, hundreds of them, pouring into the courtyard like ants exploding from a hill, like bees swarming from a hive. But the words kept coming as well – flat, almost triumphant.

'There *are* monsters,' said the Doctor.

Chapter Fourteen
I Contact

Suddenly the air was full of aliens. Dozens, maybe hundreds, of them were sliding down the poles, swinging around and around. Peering around the edge of the crate, Sam thought it looked like some kind of demented Christmas display.

When the aliens touched the ground, they scurried away from the poles, the dust rising in clouds to half obscure their shapes. She couldn't work out if they were travelling on four or six legs. So much of the movement was hidden under the carapace, or armour, or whatever it was. It looked as though they had chunks of glass glued to them all over. Their swivelling eyes glittered with facets. Their voices filled the air with clicks and pops and grasshopper sounds, almost overwhelming.

'Anybody got some cockroach spray?' she said.

'Sam!' said the Doctor.

'Christ!' said Sam. 'Where's Shoshana?'

She peered into the dusty, crawling mass of aliens. Most of the rentacops had run for it. One or two were taking pot shots at the new arrivals. They had pretty light weaponry, just shock-wave blasters, the sort you could use for crowd control if you turned the power down. The blasters knocked the aliens around a bit, before dozens of them sat on the guards.

There was Shoshana, darting back and forth between the aliens, caught up in the scurrying crowd. She yelled in panic, hands pushing at the crush of chunky bodies.

The Doctor grabbed Sam's arm. She looked at him. 'You can't help her,' said the Doctor. 'Don't go out there.'

'I wasn't going to,' said Sam. She looked back around the crate.

Shoshana had disappeared under a pile of aliens. 'I'm going to rescue her, though. Later.' It would be tough, but not impossible. The aliens would probably take Shoshana to their ship, so if they couldn't get to her before then that would mean needing to observe how the bugs got aboard, watching for surveillance devices... She let that train of thought run on undisturbed in the background. 'Anyway. We have to get out of here.'

The Doctor let go of her and turned, his back to the crate. They were pressed up against a prefab wall, metal panels joined with stembolts.

The Doctor rummaged through the pouch of bits and pieces he'd tucked into his sash and produced a slender metal rod with a crystal stuck in the end. He pointed it at the wall with a flourish. Akalu looked at him as though he'd gone completely mad.

'Sonic screwdriver mark nine,' said the Doctor. 'It also makes splendid milkshakes.'

The Doctor got them into an office and secured it. Securing the office meant operating the computer lock and stacking three desks and four chairs against the door.

While Sam and Akalu were still moving the furniture, he attacked a desk terminal. In under a minute he'd brought up images from security cameras all over the building. He twiddled something and projected them on to the wall. Two dozen flat squares of flickering light. Sam turned down the office lighting.

'Look at them,' said Akalu. 'They're stealing everything.'

And they were. Two of them were pulling a mainframe loose from its roots in the floor. Others were stuffing huge sacks at random. Datatablets, small terminals, lighting units, staplers – they were taking anything they could get their hands on.

'Where are the staff?'

'Evacuated,' said the Doctor. He blinked rapidly into the terminal's eyepiece and one of the images changed, showing 'thopters full of panicky INC employees buzzing away. 'We can't be sure everyone was able to get out, though.'

One of the projected squares showed a map of the building, the aliens' movements superimposed on the corridors by a security program. God, thought Sam, that looks like something – what does it remind me of? 'Have you met these blokes before?'

'Blokes?' said the Doctor. 'No. Look. Their weapons. See, here...' He ran a finger along one of the projected images, where a group of the aliens were rummaging through a clerical office. Some of them had what looked like brass instruments slung over their – shoulders? – on straps. 'Percussive rifles. Those are Caxtarid weapons.'

'They know the Caxtarids?'

The Doctor shook his head. 'The Ke Caxtari don't trade in weapons, only people. Those guns are stolen, or captured.'

That was it! Sam remembered the process diagrams she'd handled, one especially long week in the cubicle. Great multicoloured charts showing how the data was moving through the office. The way the flow of information would pool, forming eddies as forms and requisitions were handled, backing up where someone was working slowly, forming lakes that finally converged into an ocean of ordered data, ready to be shunted off to a different department.

'Like a flock of birds...' said the Doctor. 'My guess is that all of that bric-à-brac they're collecting is just icing on the cake. That's not why they're here.'

'The mind probe,' said Sam.

The Doctor nodded. 'They've come to finish what they started. Conclude their experiment. Take whatever INC have to offer and leave.'

'Why now?' said Akalu. 'Why right now?'

'Well,' said the Doctor, 'probably because they know I'm here.'

Sam watched as the map of the building popped off the wall, expanding into three dimensions. The Doctor rotated it until it was sitting on the desk in front of them, like a flimsy model.

'I'm using the security programs to calculate a safe path for us,' he said. His eye was flickering madly behind the eyepiece, while the other one stared straight ahead. It gave him a slightly demented look.

Sam turned back to the model, where a series of red lines were flashing through the corridors, snaking around the blue lines that represented the aliens' progress.

'Just be a minute,' said the Doctor.

Akalu was standing with his back to the wall, his arms tightly folded. He was well out of his depth, thought Sam. She plucked her headset phone from his hand. "Scuse me.'

'Not yet,' said the Doctor.

Sam nodded, pushing the headset into place. By now, Paul and Orin would be working out how to mount a heroic rescue effort, with no chance at all of success... Time to send them their marching orders. She tapped a code into the headset, watched as a message light started blinking.

Akalu gasped suddenly, and then again, his palms pressing back against the wall. Sam saw beads of sweat on the black man's forehead. He was staring at nothing. 'What is it?' she said.

'That'll be the aliens accessing IXNet,' said the Doctor.

Akalu said, 'They have broken in. They are accessing every area, without exception. No security – nothing is – they can get in anywhere!'

'Does that include you?' said the Doctor.

Akalu nodded faintly, leaning against the wall. 'The implants work in both directions,' he said. 'They can see a little way into our minds. *Tzarli ma'od* –' He bent, almost falling. Sam took his arm. *'Tzarli m –'* His fist slammed into the wall.

'Stay calm, Dr Akalu,' said the Doctor. 'We're going to need your help to escape.'

'No,' said Akalu. 'No. We have to get out of here.' He ran to the door.

The Doctor snatched off his headset. 'Sam, stop him!' Akalu was trying to pull the heavy desks away from the door. Sam kicked him in the back of the knee, just hard enough. He fell down, shouting with panic.

'Stop it!' she hissed. 'They'll hear you!'

The Doctor raised his hands, repeating his words like a mantra. 'Be calm be calm be calm be calm be calm. Be calm. Be *calm*. Be. *Calm!*' Instead of dying away, the words were building up to a frantic cry. '*Be calm!*'

Sam just stared at him. 'Doctor –'

Akalu was staring too. The Doctor shut his eyes, let out a long, shaky breath. He pulled the headset back on.

'Oh, damn,' said Sam suddenly. 'Can they see us through your implants?'

'Not yet,' said Akalu. He was sitting on the floor with his back to the barricade. 'No, at the moment they are only downloading information.'

'Maybe they're only interested in the mind probe. No, I doubt it,' said the Doctor. 'I think they're here for the harvest. Blast!'

'What is it?' said Sam.

'The comm system is down.' He tapped at the controls. 'Come on, come on...'

'Are the aliens jamming it?'

'No,' said the Doctor. 'No, the satellite is gone. Not in orbit. It's probably mashed on the bottom of their ship. We must warn the rest of the planet.'

'Harvest?' said Akalu faintly. He was blinking rapidly, as though there was something in his eye he couldn't get out.

The Doctor nodded. 'Harvest the technology they planted here. They left behind the mind probe and everything else to see what you could make of it. And you made IXNet.'

'Cuckoo,' said Akalu faintly.

'And IXNet's made out of people,' said Sam.

'This is a recording. Sam here with a message for her motley crew. Stop whatever half-arsed rescue plan you're in the middle of and get the hell away. You can't help us. Tell the planet what's happening. The aliens are here to steal any and all technology. Especially the eye tech.

Got that? No one with an implant is safe. I'm leaving this to transmit automatically so we don't give away our position. Go go go! This is a recording. Sam here with a message for her motley crew. Stop whatever...'

They stopped at another security checkpoint while Akalu peered into a retina scanner. 'That's four so far,' said Sam.

'Containment,' said the Doctor. 'Each section of the high-security labs is separate from the others. Including their computer systems.'

'Which is why they haven't been able to break in,' said Sam, 'even though they've busted into IXNet.'

The door slid open. Akalu flinched, as though he expected the hallway beyond to be filled with aliens. But it was silent, empty, quietly lit. They stepped through.

'Almost there,' the Doctor told Sam. 'You look different.'

'Really? It can't be the haircut. Is it the tan?'

The Doctor shook his head.

'I'm twenty-one, Doctor,' said Sam. 'The last time you saw me I was seventeen going on eighteen.'

'It's more than that,' said the Doctor.

Sam's throat was lumping up. This wasn't the time to talk about it. She never wanted to talk about it. 'Later, all right?' she said.

Akalu stopped suddenly, and they nearly walked into the back of him. 'Listen,' said the morale facilitator.

The corridor ahead bent around; if Sam remembered the map right, they were less than a hundred metres from the artefact room. From around the bend was coming a familiar chittering, scurrying noise.

'Back up,' said the Doctor. 'Into one of the offices, quick.'

They tiptoed through a doorway and closed the door. The Doctor pounced on the monitor and in moments had a security-camera image of the artefact room. He projected it on to a blank wall, life-size.

'Oh, no,' he said. 'Ohhh, no.'

Akalu sank into a chair. Sam stared at the picture. The artefact room was crammed with aliens, crowding around the mind probe. They were watching a fine scanning-beam tracery playing across the mid-section of a jelly-filled jar. She could just make out a pair of small spheres floating in the jelly, at the end of the beam.

'Savar's eyes,' said the Doctor, with revulsion.

Sam felt something creeping into her stomach. 'That's, like, something metaphorical, right?'

'No no no no no.' He jumped up from the computer and began pacing madly back and forth across the small office, talking a mile a minute and moving faster, as if trying to leave the things he was saying as far behind him as possible.

'It happened back when I was a student. Savar was a Time Lord who went on a mission in his TARDIS, but something went wrong and he had to abandon ship. By the time the Time Lords found him his lifepod had been attacked and stripped bare by alien raiders, raiders who were never found. They'd stolen all sorts of artefacts. And then they found out that since it was Savar's TARDIS, none of their loot would work without his eyeprint.'

He stared straight at her, his eyes wide with outrage. 'So they stole his eyes.'

Akalu uttered a low moan and rested his head on his arms, not wanting to see.

Sam managed to say, 'And you recognised his eyes?'

The Doctor shook his head, glancing at the door, the projected image, still all aflutter. 'It's got to be a Time Lord's eyes – they're trying to use them to operate the mind probe. And look. Look, there.'

He turned the zoom control on the camera. The fuzzy dark shapes of the aliens blotted out the view for a moment, but eventually she got a clear look: two indistinct spheres filling the screen, suspended in their jelly, with the flicker of the mind probe shining from behind them. And on each sphere there was a small shimmering circle, a glowing field of haze surrounding details she couldn't make out. Staring back at her.

'Those are the optic nerves,' he said. 'They've been trying to regenerate themselves for hundreds of years.' He shuddered.

'Eeeurgh.'

'You said it,' said Sam.

'I wonder where DOCTOR is,' Akalu murmured.

'Busy alerting the security systems and blocking the aliens' access to all the dataspace he can,' declared the Doctor. 'That's what I'd be doing.'

Sam raised an eyebrow at him. The Doctor sat down at the terminal and peered through the eyepiece.

After a moment, he looked up. 'He's only partitioned off his portion of the dataspace,' the Doctor said worriedly. 'That's *not* what I'd be doing.' The Doctor leaned over the desk, fixing his eyes on Akalu. 'TARDIS.'

'The "police public call box"?'

'Got it in one,' said Sam. 'Where?'

'Storage unit four,' said Akalu.

The Doctor stared into the eyepiece. Sam assumed he was bringing up his map of safe routes, updating it. 'We can get there without encountering the aliens.'

The door coder sounded. Akalu jumped as though he'd been shocked. A moment later, three aliens shoved their way into the room.

'Or not,' said the Doctor.

'Er, hello. Who are you?'

'*I am I.*'

'Well, so am I,' said the Doctor. 'That really doesn't help me very much.' He had managed to put himself between the aliens and the others. Sam peered at them from behind his coat, still trying to work out the limbs.

'I was more wondering what the name of your species was,' said the Doctor. No response. 'Who you all are as a group...'

'*I am I.*'

The Doctor blinked. 'What, all of you?'

The alien's voice sounded like glass being ground. '*I am.*'

'Oh,' said the Doctor, 'I see.'

'A group mind?' asked Sam.

'Something like that,' said the Doctor. 'A compound I?'

One of the I picked up Akalu from the floor, surprisingly gently. Akalu dusted down his clothes, trying his best to look dignified.

One of the aliens pressed close to Sam. A long, glassy shard extruded from its arm. 'Don't worry, Sam,' said the Doctor quietly. 'It's not going to hurt you.'

The alien waved its arm up and down, the shard never quite touching her body. 'We're being frisked,' she said.

'Mmm,' said the Doctor. The alien turned its attention to him.

Sam looked down and realised she was holding the pouch from his sash. When had he –

The alien completed its scan, or whatever, and the glassy instrument sank back into its outer skin. Once it turned its back, the Doctor plucked his pouch out of Sam's surprised fingers and tucked it back into his sash. Neither of their captors seemed to notice, shuffling into position to surround them.

The Doctor turned slightly and took Sam's hand. She wasn't sure whether he wanted to comfort her or needed a bit of comforting himself. Either way, she gave his fingers a good, friendly squeeze.

'*Follow I*,' said the alien in front of them.

'*Walk in front of I*,' said one of the ones behind.

They walked together between their captors, out into the corridor, towards the compound where the I liner was parked. Sam kept her head high, refusing to worry. She wasn't going to die. She was with the Doctor.

Well, *probably* she wasn't going to die.

When Sam had seen the I's ship, her first thought had been: organic. They use organic technology. That thing looks like a huge leaf, or space parsnip, or something. Loads of species grew their vessels and weapons and computers, or used a combination of mechanical and organic technology – like the eye implants, really.

But now she had a closer look at it – as they slid upward on the firefighters' poles, each of them tucked under the arm of an I – she wasn't sure she'd been right. The shape was organic, but the texture wasn't. It was smooth, yellow-orange. Metallic armour around a living ship, maybe?

She had no idea how they were moving upward; the I had simply picked her up, grasped the 'pole' with its free handoid and launched itself upward. Now they were decelerating together. For a dizzying moment, she thought they were going to smash into the bottom of the ship.

Then a hatch irised tidily open and they slowed to a halt inside a spherical chamber. The pole plunged up into the roof. The floor closed beneath them and the I put its feet down.

A moment later she was watching as the others popped into the bay. Akalu stumbled on the metal floor as his I let go of him. The Doctor ignored the aliens, striding up to one of the walls and running a hand over its surface.

'Metal?' said Sam, pulling Akalu to his feet.

'In a sense,' said the Doctor. 'Here, touch it.'

Sam joined him, pressing her fingers against the bronzy-coppery stuff. It looked and felt like metal, but it gave slightly under pressure.

The I were back in formation, herding them out into another corridor through another irising door.

'Tinclavic,' murmured the Doctor. 'It's a sort of metallic polymer. Ideal for building spacecraft – you can lock and unlock its molecular structure, change its conductivity and magnetism. Et cetera.'

'It's like walking around inside a giant blob of Silly Putty,' said Sam. 'Is it stolen?'

'Not exactly,' said the Doctor. 'Do you know what I think this is? I think it's a sort of enormous sea shell.' He ran his hand along the wall. 'An awful lot of spacefaring species secrete tinclavic.'

'Just like a mollusc making its shell,' said Sam.

'Exactly. I think the I are like hermit crabs. The discarded shell is a ready-made spaceship hull.' He made a face. 'I wonder what happened to the occupant...'

A door uncurled itself. The lead I put a heavy hand on the Doctor's shoulder. The message was clear.

'I'll catch you up,' the Doctor told Sam. 'Look after Akalu.'

Sam nodded. She watched as the door closed behind the Time Lord and his captor. Then the other I were moving them along.

Akalu appeared to be in shock. Sam knew what it was like. One moment you were on top of everything, the next you were being locked up by six-legged mutant camels from hell. 'Hang in there,' she told them. 'We'll get you out of this.'

'How?' said Dr Akalu.

Sam shrugged. 'Relax,' she said. 'We do this kind of thing all the time.'

The Doctor pushed a finger into the corrugated chest of his captor. 'You're the one who visited me, aren't you?'

'*I am,*' said the huge creature. The Doctor could see himself reflected in its faceted eyes.

'That doesn't really answer the question,' said the Doctor. The room was full of I, dozens of them crammed into the oval space, constantly jostling and wriggling. Their hands, their feet, their jagged carapaces, touched him over and over. It was like waking up suddenly with a bug crawling over you, except that you were awake and the bugs were taller than you were.

They didn't talk, but bits of the 'broken glass' embedded in their carapaces flickered with internal light. The Doctor guessed he was being examined, scanned, silently discussed.

Goodness knew what sort of identity concept this culture had. Gestalt? Hive mind? Collective consciousness? Multicorporeal monopsyche? High-level telepathic interco-ordination?

'But tell me,' he said. 'When did you work out who you were dealing with? Did it take that... scan, or whatever you did to me back in the prison? Or have you been controlling events all along?'

'*I haven't,*' said the I impassively.

'No, that would take too much effort, wouldn't it?' He had the urge to pace. 'You just dropped the mind probe into their pool and sat

229

back to see what ripples would develop. I was right, wasn't I? That's how you operate.'

'*You outside people,*' said the alien. '*I stay out of your view. I allow you to proceed. I am non-invasive.*'

This one was putting the TARDIS's telepathic translator through its paces, thought the Doctor. But he had got the gist. 'Using people,' he said, 'exploiting them, introducing advanced technology to low-tech cultures – it's not the same as invading. Perhaps it's worse. Insidious. With unpredictable results. At least with an invasion force you know where you are.'

'*I am non-invasive,*' said the I.

Did it understand what he was saying? 'Human beings are *not* ready for Time Lord technology.' The I stared at him, as though waiting politely for him to finish. 'Not that that bothers you, obviously. Are we "outside people" all the same to you? How many of these "non-invasive" experiments have you run?'

The walls. Bits of technology embedded in them. Controls of a half-dozen mismatched types cobbled together. Hmm. 'Was Hirath one of yours? This looks like the sort of hardware that was grafted into the computers there. Was TCC running those experiments for your benefit? Mm? And then there was that one time tree that was taken from Hirath to Tractis...'

The I wasn't giving anything away. 'Feel free to gloat at any time,' said the Doctor. 'I'm doing all the work here. Let me see. You couldn't work out the mind probe's secrets, or you couldn't be bothered to work them out. The experiment was running nicely here on Ha'olam. And then I arrived. A Time Lord, someone whose eyes could get into the equipment. You weren't expecting that. So you infiltrated the prison to check on me, and used the things you'd figured out about IXNet to cover your tracks so you could walk around undetected.'

He snapped his fingers. 'Everything was fine with your plans as long as I was in prison, and now that I'm out you're running scared. Yes! You're packing up every bit of knowledge you can get your hands on and moving out – because you know exactly what my people are going to do to you.'

The I reached out with one of its complex hands. The Doctor could see the hand pushing its way free of the blue-glass exterior, until the six digits – two thumbs, perhaps? – were clear. '*I will scan you outside people,*' said the I.

This again, thought the Doctor. The I closed in around him.

He pressed a hand to the I's rough flank, ran his fingers over the irregular fragments. One of them bit into him, forcing itself into his palm. It was like making a fist around a broken bottle.

This time he wasn't afraid, not even when the jagged edges of the glass began to tear their way into his skin. Just as before, it didn't hurt. He ran his other hand over his arm as the fragments rose and fell, travelling through his flesh, gathering information as they went.

He had to close his eyes as the fragments rippled across his face, sliced through his hearts and lungs. Bits of him felt on the verge of panic at this point, but other bits were protesting that he wasn't being stabbed through and through with shattered glass, something far stranger and more subtle was happening.

It was just a scan, and he doubted the I were knowledgeable enough to do a really deep scan of his biodata. They were just...

'You wouldn't dare,' gasped the Doctor. 'If the Time Lords arrive and find me pickled in a collection of jars, what do you think they'll do to you *then*?'

The I didn't answer. Perhaps they knew the Time Lords wouldn't be coming, that only one Time Lord knew about their little experiment. Or maybe they just didn't care.

The I took hold of his other arm, collecting all of the roaming fragments back into itself, and with it a catalogue about just which bits of the Doctor would be useful for what purposes.

The cell was pitch-black. Sam was conserving the batteries in her torch, just flicking it on every few minutes to check on Dr Akalu. When his eyes were open, his implant glittered red in the blackness. When they were closed, he was invisible. Sam wasn't sure which was creepier.

There wasn't much to see, anyway. The chamber was empty, a flattened oval. The door had sealed behind them without a trace, giving Sam nervous thoughts about the air supply. There were no other doors, no windows, no nothing. She'd insisted they sit still, to conserve, um, their energy.

Sam snapped on the torch for a few seconds. 'How's IXNet?'

'Quieter,' said Akalu. 'I think they have completed their initial investigation of the network.'

'OK,' said Sam. 'Stay cool. Let me know if they get up to anything in there.'

The Doctor arrived a few minutes later, his I nudging him over the threshold. Sam gave him a big smile. 'I wasn't expecting to see you again so soon,' she said. 'Taken over the ship yet?'

The door irised shut, became invisible, sealing them all in there.

The Doctor howled.

Sam snapped on the torch. The Doctor was charging at the wall, pounding his fists on it. 'No! No no no no no no no! Open this door!'

Her stomach screamed. Whatever control the Doctor had over himself, it had snapped the moment he was locked up. His words were breaking down even further into a subverbal cry.

Now he was bouncing off the cell wall like a mosquito in a bell jar, fingers clawing across the metallic surface, desperate for anything, any kind of way out. Sam tried to follow his frantic movements with the torch, getting a glimpse of Akalu's horrified face.

Now the Doctor was taking a run-up, nearly ploughing through her, and throwing his whole body straight into the wall where the door had been.

All he got for his pains was a muffled thud, and with a fading whimper he slid down the wall into a heap. For a horrible moment she almost giggled: he'd left a spread-eagled Doctor shape in the door where he'd hit.

She dropped the torch on the floor and grabbed him by the lapels as he struggled to sit up. She pushed him back against the wall, hard.

'Stop that!' she shouted as he jumped and jerked. Oh God, she really hoped she wasn't going to have to slap him.

He didn't look at her, but she could feel his wounded-bird flutterings fading to rest under her hands. 'That's better,' she said. 'You're not going to get us out like that.'

He looked up, let out a shaky breath and grinned. 'No, but it was rather therapeutic.'

She let her own breath out and gave him a shoulders-up hug. She felt his head lolling on her shoulder, as if it was still about to fall off and roll away, but now he was patting her on the back and making comforting noises to *her*.

'You're all right now?' she asked. 'No more Daffy Doc impressions?' He nodded. 'Right, then,' she went on. 'We need a way out.' She let him go and stood up, and noted that he'd sort of sprawled out in a heap on the floor. 'Don't seem to be any convenient ventilation shafts. They might be hidden, though…'

'Oh no no no. You're not going to find any,' said the Doctor, his nose against the floor. 'There are too many of them to be of any use.'

'Hmm?'

'Look closely at the walls,' he said. Sam glanced at him, pushed her nose up to the metal. 'Pores!' she said. Millions of them. She could feel the tiniest current of air breathing in and out.

Sam glanced at the impression of the Doctor in the soft wall. It was slowly fading, like dough springing back into shape. Now she had the weird feeling that the whole room was breathing as she watched. Like they were trapped in a giant lung.

Bleargh!

There was something wrong with this picture, but Sam couldn't put her finger on it.

'Ah,' said the Doctor. 'Everlasting matches.' He leaned back and struck one across the wall. In a moment, the chamber was filled with a chemical glow.

'The I,' said Akalu. 'Where are they from?'

'I think they're not from anywhere,' said the Doctor. 'Not any more.

I think they're always travelling. Visiting the planets they've seeded to see what's developed. Crop rotation. The gestalt, however it operates, is probably their own technology. Everything other than that was shoplifted.'

'We can think about that later,' said Sam. 'Let's get out of here.'

The Doctor was shaking his head. 'The problem with group minds,' he said, 'is that new ideas tend to get lost in the chatter.'

'Like what Dr Akalu was saying about IXNet?' said Sam.

'Peer pressure is one factor,' said the Doctor. 'The sheer volume of data is another. It's possible the I can't imagine, can't innovate. They're not capable of developing new technology. So they have other species do the work for them.'

Akalu said, 'Are you saying we're smarter than them?'

'Not exactly,' said the Doctor. 'But we might just be better at using their technology than they are.'

Akalu sat with his back to the wall, his knees drawn up to his chest, counting his breathing. Three seconds, in, one, two, three; three seconds out, one, two, three.

He had been watching himself react, in a way, since the aliens had arrived – literally from thin air. Naturally there had been surprise, shock, confusion. But he believed he had adapted now. He had not panicked. Well, not significantly.

It was awkward to be suddenly helpless. Not just as a prisoner, but because the Doctor and his young friend were so much better adapted to the situation. There was little that he could contribute.

At least the Doctor seemed so much more alive now. That could only be good for him.

Three seconds, in, one, two, three; three seconds out, one, two, three.

He could still sense the I moving through IXNet, like cockroaches crawling in a drawer of cutlery. He had the horrible sensation that they could reach into his mind at any moment, access anything they wanted. Would it be like having insects moving inside his skull?

Three seconds

One

Three

'*Tzarli ma'od,*' said Akalu.

Three

Two three seconds in

Akalu slammed his eyes shut, trying to block it out.

In two

Three out one in two

'Get him on to his side!' someone shouted.

But it was there *inside* his eyelids, spilling out, as though someone was pouring light from a jug into his head. It would be leaking from his ears, out of his mouth.

He tried opening his eyes, to give the light another route to escape. The cell was distorted, washed out by the light flooding out of his head.

Through the haze he heard Sam, and then words from the bright grey cloud which had to be the Doctor.

'I think he's still breathing.'

'Dr Akalu? Can you hear me?'

'What's going on?'

'I think they've turned the mind probe up to level two.'

Then he couldn't hear them over the roaring of the crowd.

Chapter Fifteen
I Technology

Level two.

Workers at their terminals stopped in mid-blink. Sleepers awoke, their eyes locked in position, blank. Hands hovered over keyboards, the useless cutting edges of hundreds of thousands of paralysed minds.

Akalu had gone foetal. 'Best thing for him, for the moment,' the Doctor had concluded. Now he was running those long fingers of his over the wall, just the fingertips connecting with the porous metal, intimately tracing its contours.

He stopped, running his hands back over a stretch of wall. With a small effort, he pushed his fingers half an inch into the metal. 'Not enough,' he muttered. 'Sam, mark my place.'

She walked up and pushed a palm against the surface, roughly where he had been working. The Doctor went fishing in his pouch again. After a moment he had produced a travel sewing kit, a copy of *Outlaw Culture* on a self-extracting datacube and the sonic screwdriver.

He gently nudged Sam out of the way, pressed one hand against the wall and twiddled the screwdriver. It squealed, the pitch jumping up in irregular steps, until suddenly he was pushing his hand easily into the stuff of the wall.

'Doctor,' yelled Sam over the noise. 'If this is just a shell...'

'Then why are the walls breathing?' He switched off the squeal and used both hands to push the softened metal aside, as though it was clay. It was pierced by veins of darker metal.

Literally veins? wondered Sam.

They looked at each other. Sam said, 'There's something alive in here, isn't there?'

There was a small machine roughly embedded inside the wall, fused to one of the lines of darker metal. It made Sam think of the IV needle thingy left in her wrist when she'd had her tonsils out as a child.

'It looks as though it was just shoved in there,' she said. Waking up in recovery, her whole hand aching. 'Not built in, stuck in.'

'I think you're right,' said the Doctor. 'In any case, it's not much use to us: it's just some sort of sensor system. I'd better be careful with it. Don't want to get them all excited.'

Sam glanced at Akalu. 'What are they doing to Shoshana?' she murmured.

'The worst thing they're likely to do to her,' said the Doctor, 'is to take her eyes out.'

'Oh, Jesus,' said Sam.

'She can get new eyes.'

'Did Savar get new eyes?' said Sam.

The Doctor went on tweaking the component. 'I suppose it's one of the disadvantages of combining biology and technology. You risk being... salvaged.'

'Doctor,' Sam said.

He blinked rapidly, followed her pointing finger. Another aperture had opened up in the opposite wall, half a foot across. Inside was darkness.

'Hello there,' said the Doctor softly.

INC was completely paralysed for 3.018 seconds. Every computer, every worker, every component of IXNet was frozen. Every data pathway stood perfectly still, stopped in mid-sentence. Nothing timed out, time wasn't moving.

Then all those frozen packets and transmissions and thoughts thawed, in a rippling, cracking motion that shot across IXNet, each area of melting activity spilling over into its neighbours.

IXNet burst back to life, every junction and switch, every database and brain seething with the new energy. The movement of data increased and increased again until it was burning through the system at four times its previous speed, then nine times, then sixteen times, until every mind and computer fused into a single glorious mass of moving information.

The Doctor peered into the gap. 'I think there's something in there.' He grabbed the torch from Sam.

'Did you trigger it?' said Sam.

'Not directly,' said the Doctor. 'It's no good, I can't see anything in here. But I think I got someone's attention. And not the I's attention either.'

'Clam nine from outer space?' said Sam.

The Doctor felt around the edges of the aperture, then carefully reached inside. 'Still nothing,' he murmured. 'Am I wrong?'

The aperture closed smoothly around his hand and arm, burying him in metal halfway to the elbow.

'Christ!' shouted Sam, trying to pry him loose. She yelped with surprise as she got a shock, like static electricity. But he pushed her away with his free hand.

'Something deep inside,' he whispered, his forehead creasing. 'Buzzing.'

'Telepathy?' said Sam.

The Doctor shook his head. 'Something to do with the conductivity of the metal...' They both looked around, startled, realising that the walls were starting to glow with faint light.

The Doctor took an involuntary step forward, more of his arm disappearing into the coppery wall. His face was pressed up against the metal. 'I think it wants a word,' he said.

Sam grabbed his other arm. 'No,' he said. 'No.' The ship pulled him in a little further. 'Sam! Just hold on to me. Hold on to me.'

IXNet sat up and took a look at itself through four hundred and seven thousand, three hundred and twenty-eight pairs of eyes.

Ubernet, giggled someone in Acquisitions. The joke spread through the network in a few hundredths of a second. Four hundred and seven thousand, three hundred and twenty-eight giggles. Ubernet.

The ship had eaten the Doctor.

Sam stood next to the wall, still gripping his hand. From time to time, tiny flickers and flashes of light scattered across the metallic surface, marking the spot where the rest of him had disappeared into the stuff.

It had swallowed him up a bit at a time, dragging him into itself. She'd wanted to grab the sonic screwdriver and give the wall a good blast. But the Doctor had insisted she let it happen, even when she'd seen that panic starting to spark in his eyes again, even when his face had started to disappear into the wall.

That had been about five minutes ago. She knew he was still alive; his remaining hand was protruding from the wall, about an inch of his loose jellaba sleeve showing. His fingers gripped hers, fiercely, and she could feel his double pulse.

She was his lifeline.

Akalu was muttering to himself in the corner. His eyes were tightly shut, as though he couldn't manage any more input than he was already getting. From time to time he shouted out words in languages she couldn't understand. She couldn't do anything about it, she couldn't help him.

Suddenly, the Doctor's hand convulsed, his fingers clawing at her, gripping her hand so tightly that it hurt. His pulses were racing.

She pulled, one boot thrust against the wall, but she couldn't drag him free. Sonic screwdriver! Was he still holding it? No, there it was, on the floor.

She snatched it up, never letting go of his hand. Hoping it was still on the same setting, she let the wall have a blast of sound.

Instantly the Doctor came free, falling out of the softening stuff as she hauled on his arm. He was gulping for air.

She dragged him free of the wall, his hand still locked around hers, and caught him as he fell. The ship-substance was hardening again.

He clung to her. 'It didn't want to let go of me,' he gasped. 'It wouldn't let me out. It was desperate to talk.'

Sam held on to him as he got his breath back. 'The ship!' she said. 'It really is alive, isn't it?'

The Doctor let go of her hand, massaging her squashed fingers. 'No,' he said. 'Not the ship. Not the ship. Something in the ship. Something they're using. Not a tool, though. Something they've enslaved.' He looked at her. 'Our prison is a prisoner too.'

There were no secrets in the ubernet. Anyone's mind was fully open for business. The gestalt tried looking into certain brains at random, curious as to how deep it could get, but after the first few deaths it decided to turn its collective attention elsewhere.

How had it come into being? Did anyone know, did anyone understand, did anyone have the data?

A thought, more a fragment of short-term memory, rippled across the surface of the network. *I think they've turned the mind probe up to level two.*

The ubernet turned its collective attention to the mind which had the information it needed. This time it would be gentle with itself.

The Doctor pushed his hand against the wall. 'Can I talk to it?' said Sam.

He shook his head absently, obviously looking for something. 'You haven't the right nerve endings,' he said. 'Ah!'

He had found another device embedded in the wall. With the help of the sonic screwdriver, he began to tug it loose. A great iron-black cord of metal, coming out of the wall and hanging there stiffly, like an exposed nerve.

'Our friend can't help us directly,' the Doctor said. 'The I are using a restraining system. Something to force it – he? she? I'm not sure – to obey their commands. But it can help us with a bit of sabotage. Point the way. This is the way.'

241

He raised the sonic screwdriver, changed the frequency and pointed the business end at the black cord.

The metal glowed, then sparked, then broke with a sound like an accordion being murdered. Fragments of black stuff showered down on to the cell floor.

The door opened with a sucking, popping noise. 'Yes!' mouthed Sam silently. 'No guards. Let's go – wait. What about Akalu?'

The Doctor knelt down beside the shattered morale facilitator. He was still curled into a ball, but his eyes were moving, moving, viewing a nightmare projected on the inside of his eyelids.

The Doctor put his hands on either side of his face. 'It's no use. The only way to save him, the only way to save them all, is to stop the I. We have to stop them and we have to destroy the mind probe. Which means we'll have to disconnect everyone first. Shut down the whole network. First we've got to get out of here. The ship's running through its pre-flight stretching exercises. We don't have a lot of time.'

Sam stared at him, hard. Some part of her wasn't sure that he wasn't just desperate to get free, no matter what. He slipped out through the doorway. After a moment, she followed.

'Something for you,' she whispered as they rounded yet another bend. 'The layout of this place – all the rooms off the corridor seem pretty small. The main hallways just seem to circle around the outside edge of the ship. So what's in the centre?'

'Clam nine,' said the Doctor softly. 'No, it's more like a chrysalis. They've got some way of arresting its development in this stage of its life cycle... those systems we saw grafted in...'

Sam stared at the rough-hewn tunnel surrounding them. 'They must have just burrowed into the outer edges of this thing and hijacked it. Like they hijack everything. A giant cocoon that can space-travel – they must've loved it.'

'Listen!' said the Doctor. 'Can you smell something?'

'You're right,' said Sam, after a moment. 'Thunderstorm. Or electric stuff burning...' She moved down the corridor a little distance. 'Here,

I think.'

The Doctor crept up behind her. There was a muffled electric arcing sound coming from behind the nearest iris-door.

He pressed himself up against the soft metal wall. 'Ship,' he murmured, 'if you can hear me, I want you to open that door just a little bit.' Obediently a peephole widened in the centre. The Doctor crouched and peered through, then with a grave expression motioned Sam over to see. She pressed her face against the flesh of the ship and tried to focus.

Shoshana was through there. Shoshana was through there on a bed of shipflesh, with a blue metal spike inches from her left eye. The sparks from the probe were arcing straight down through her pupil.

Her mouth stretched in a silent scream. Her whole body was spasming, convulsing against the rubbery ties, desperate to tear free or just tear itself to pieces to escape.

A pair of I were on either side, glassy blue chunks meandering over their surfaces, flickering with dirty light.

'An override connection,' whispered the Doctor. 'They're using her as a terminal to tap into IXNet.'

And Shoshana's other eye was staring straight at them somehow, screaming with a look, even though there was no way she could know they were there.

The ubernet convulsed, great nodes of panic forming and rippling outward. IXNet had been a dumb thing, anaesthetised to the aliens' attack, insensible as a block of wood. But the ubernet howled with rage at this fresh violation.

It turned its burning eyes on the source of the infestation, but the enemy was too strong, preventing the ubernet from killing her outright. It would have to fight for its integrity instead. Or bargain for it.

The Doctor stopped repeatedly to talk to their friend, pressing a hand against the wall, his lips moving as he asked for directions.

They didn't see a lot of I. Sam reckoned the aliens were sitting around somewhere, going through their sacks of goodies, satisfied for the moment. But she suspected the Big Bug was also warning the Doctor.

'These guys are so dead,' said Sam.

The Doctor glanced at her. 'You sound different, as well.'

She waved her hands about angrily. 'I mean metaphorically,' she said.

'Would you destroy them?' said the Doctor. He had suddenly grabbed her with his stare. She was blushing all over. 'In retribution for their crimes? Or for the greater good? Would it be right or wrong?'

'If only life was that simple,' said Sam.

'Sometimes it is,' said the Doctor. 'Sometimes. Good answer, though.'

She followed him, shaking her head and smiling.

'These are air tubes,' she murmured at one point. 'Like how an insect breathes. The "cells" are part of a respiratory system.'

'Spiracles,' whispered the Doctor. 'What does that tell us about our friend?'

'It needs an atmosphere,' said Sam. 'Though it can travel through space. Oh – it only emerges from the cocoon when it reaches a planet where it can breathe.'

'Ha'olam, perhaps,' said the Doctor.

The airlock opened for them, silently, and so too did the hatches that led via firefighter pole all the way to the ground. It was dark now, and most of the lights in the building and compound were out; you could barely see the poles, just the occasional shimmer in the dark.

'All right?' said the Doctor, grabbing one. 'It'll take you down automatically, no need to worry.'

'Right,' said Sam. She grabbed another of the poles. And then they were outside the ship, spiralling slowly down, invisible.

She could see orangy lights moving around inside the building. The I, patrolling, or maybe mopping up any trinkets they'd missed. They'd have to evade them to make it back to the TARDIS.

The TARDIS. Their Get Out of Jail Free card. But what about the others? What about Akalu and Shoshana? How was she going to get them out?

And then they were on the ground, stumbling away from the poles. The Doctor glanced back to make sure she was following, made a beeline for the nearest entrance, bounced back from the doorway. They flattened themselves against the wall.

'The entrance is crawling with I,' he whispered. He plucked a mirror from his pouch.

'How're we going to get in there?' said Sam. 'Let's get another one of these panels loose.'

'No time,' said the Doctor. He was holding the mirror up at an angle, looking in through the doorway. 'They're heading this way.'

Sam looked around for something to hide behind. 'They've nicked everything!' she said. 'Maybe we can hide behind one another?'

The Doctor gave her a bemused smile, but she could see the tension in his shoulders as he pushed his back against the wall. Trapped again.

Abruptly, the door hissed shut.

The Doctor stared at it in astonishment. 'Well, that's convenient,' he said.

'Umm...' said Sam. He turned back to her. She jerked her thumb at the security cameraeye watching them.

'Good evening,' crackled a speaker.

'Hello, you,' said the Doctor.

'Don't worry about the I. I've opened a door they've been trying to break open for the past hour. They're crawling all over a cache of exciting stationery items. Follow me?'

DOCTOR slid open a door in the opposite building and they ducked inside. Lights flickered on. Sam jumped as a security camera swivelled to stare at them. The door snapped shut again.

'Why help us?' demanded the Doctor.

'I need some answers,' said DOCTOR. 'What's happened to IXNet? It's functioning more like a single mind than like a network.'

'You've seen the device that runs the whole system,' said the

Doctor. 'The I have tampered with it. They've bumped up the power, that's all. The system is functioning in a critical state, the minds in IXNet lining up like particles in a magnet.'

'I don't like it,' said DOCTOR. 'That's a lot of computing power. It's like a fifty-foot baby. It calls itself the ubernet, you know.'

'Sweet,' said Sam.

'I don't like the I much either,' DOCTOR continued. 'No respect for security protocols. You wouldn't believe what I've been through trying to keep out of their grubby little clutches.'

Sam couldn't help smiling. DOCTOR was weird, sounding half like the Doctor, half like some grouchy old teacher. The big question was, could they trust it?

'What do you suggest, then?' said the Doctor.

'Pit them against one another,' said DOCTOR.

'Just what I would have said,' said the Doctor. 'Once the "ubernet" gets over its initial shock, it'll start reacting to the alien invaders. Fighting back, with a substantial proportion of the planet's resources.'

'The ubernet is already breaking into military control systems,' said DOCTOR. 'The I were searching IXNet for the locations of INC research facilities, storage areas, anything they could purloin. But they're finding it a lot more difficult to navigate the ubernet.'

'Why haven't they just switched off the mind probe?' said Sam.

'They're spending a lot of time analysing the ubernet,' said DOCTOR. 'They're fascinated. I think it reminds them of them. They don't want to destroy it – they want to make off with it.'

'*We* have to switch off the mind probe,' said the Doctor. 'We've got to get rid of it. However the I came by it, neither they nor the human race is ready for that kind of technology.'

'Doesn't seem like anything that special to me,' said DOCTOR.

'You don't want to know what those higher power settings can do,' said the Doctor. 'But first we've got to disconnect the ubernet before we shut down the mind probe. If we just flick its off switch, goodness knows what will happen to all of those minds.'

'Like opening an oven door when your soufflé isn't cooked yet,' said

246

Sam. The Doctor and the security camera swivelled to look at her. 'You know. Bwaaat.' She gestured vaguely, trying to mime a collapsing soufflé.

'Bwaaat,' agreed the Doctor.

There was a sound like a hundred firefighters' poles being sucked into the belly of a spaceship made of squashy metal.

Sam went to the door automatically.

'Don't,' said DOCTOR, and backed it up by locking the door.

'They're leaving,' announced the artificial intelligence, after a few seconds. 'The building's empty. They've all got back into the ship.'

The door slid open. Sam poked her head out. 'The stars are coming out,' she said. After a moment, the ship's vast black shadow had passed over them and it was gone, diminishing in the darkness. 'Good riddance!' she said. 'They're gone!'

The Doctor shook his head, his whole body one big twitch. 'No no no no no, they're not, they're *not*. They were asking about other bits of INC technology, remember – they're going to go and get them.' He stared her in the eyes. 'Almost every clerk on the planet has an eye implant,' he said. 'Every prisoner in an INC institution has an eye implant. The I are starting their harvest.'

The Doctor and Sam were outside the artefact room. DOCTOR was displaying the interior of the room on a wall screen – a row of I, standing unmoving among the machines. At first Sam had thought they were some kind of husks, or even statues, but now and then she saw an antenna twitch or an eye roll.

'They're shut down,' she said. 'They can't do that group-think thing when the others aren't here.'

'I doubt it,' said the Doctor. 'It's more likely they're just waiting for orders. I wonder if they're a natural gestalt. Or something technological.'

'Something we can sabotage?' grinned Sam. 'Something on their ship, I'll bet. Yeah, they'd need some sort of booster even if it was natural, just to keep in touch with the rest of them out there.' She was avoiding looking at the jar of eyes. 'Bad feeling around here,' she muttered.

The Doctor was hugging himself. 'It's the ubernet,' he said. 'You're probably sensing it through the TARDIS's telepathic translator. Compatible technologies, resonant frequencies. It's making my sinuses ache.'

DOCTOR broke in, 'They're heading for OBFSC, you know.'

'Oh dear,' said the Doctor.

'Double oh dear,' said DOCTOR. 'That's where my central files are.'

'Not to mention a population of helpless prisoners who don't even know they've got eye implants,' said the Doctor. 'Easy pickings.'

'We've got to stop them,' said DOCTOR.

'There we agree,' said the Doctor. 'Except that we've also got to disconnect the ubernet and shut off the mind probe.'

'Don't look at me,' said DOCTOR. 'I can't control the mind probe. No eyes, remember? Send Sam to OBFSC.'

'I can't. I've got to take the TARDIS to get there quickly enough.'

DOCTOR sighed. 'Decisions, decisions, decisions.'

'I'll do it,' said Sam.

'What?'

'What?'

'I'll shut down the ubernet. Just write me some instructions on the back of an envelope or something.'

'Sam, you'll have to be in the system.' The Doctor put his hands on her shoulders, staring insistently into her eyes. 'The only way to shut the ubernet down now is from the inside.'

'You mean I'd have to become part of the gestalt?'

'No. Inside, but not connected. No, I can't let you do it. There's too great a risk of your becoming part of the ubernet. You could completely lose your identity, lose who you are. I can't let that happen.'

This is the bit where he declares his undying love for me, thought Sam. And DOCTOR turns his camereye away demurely while we passionately embrace.

In your dreams, kid.

She put her hands on his, took them off her shoulders. 'If I don't do this,' she told him, 'I *will* have lost who I am. I've got to do everything I can for what I believe in. It's what I do… It's what I try to do. It's not hard to believe in saving so many people.'

He looked at her hard, his mouth a little open, as if in surprise. 'The mind probe wouldn't respond to you anyway,' he murmured. 'The operator controls are keyed to a Time Lord retina pattern. It wouldn't let you in.'

'Maybe I could wear contact lenses or something, so it'll think my eyes are like yours?'

He stopped. 'Sam… For a *retina* pattern?'

'Oh. Right.'

The Doctor visibly relaxed.

'I could get her in,' said DOCTOR.

The Doctor tensed right back up again.

'Easy,' said DOCTOR. 'I've got your retina pattern and your EEG on file. If Sam's eyes are there to be scanned, I can fake the security checks. Give us twenty minutes and I'll get her all the access she needs.'

'Go,' Sam told the Doctor. 'We'll sort this out.'

'You're sure? Very sure? I won't be here to help you.'

'I'll have DOCTOR.'

'He's not me,' said the Doctor. 'Be careful you don't forget that.'

'I know that. I'll keep an eye on him. Now get going.'

He took her hand and squeezed it hard. Then he dashed down the corridor.

Ten seconds later he ran back up and spoke not to her but past her. 'Once Sam's set up, I want you to transmit yourself over to Bainbridge. Find my signal there. I've got an idea I want you to help me with.' His eyes flicked back to her. 'Sam – when you're finished – Bainbridge. Please, be sure –'

She cut him off. 'I'll be all right. Go.'

He landed in the courtyard at the Oliver Bainbridge Functional

Stabilisation Centre. His hearts convulsed a little when he stepped out of the door, the shadows of the four walls heavy on his body.

'No,' he muttered. 'No time for that now.'

The courtyard was empty, but he could hear shouting coming from the Habitat Area. He ran to the big door.

He had tucked the data-transfer module into his sash, along with a burglar's kit and a package of chocolate chip cookies. He unrolled the kit and was taking out the picklock when he realised there was a dead guard lying not ten feet from him.

He knelt down by the man. He had been dead for less than an hour, killed by a blow to the chest. The I? Here already... and no longer willing to tolerate resistance. They'd want to grab what they could and make their getaway.

He took the man's I-card, fitted it into the slot. The big door yawned wide, letting out screams and yells and the sound of bars being attacked in desperation.

The waiting area beyond was dark. The Doctor slipped inside. He needed to find the I, distract them, confuse them, do a few card tricks for them. He needed to get their attention off the prisoners.

The lights slammed on. Every single camereye in the hall turned to stare at him.

The Doctor held his ground. Someone was coming down the stairs, the sound of rickety metal rattling under footfalls. The Doctor took a deep breath and let it out slowly.

Dr Akalu stepped into the light. His eyes were shut, eyelids fluttering slightly, his eyes twitching violently behind them.

'I see,' he said. '*Baruch atta Adonai*, I can *see*.'

Chapter Sixteen
Oy Gestalt

The Doctor found himself backing away as Akalu approached. The man walked with his eyes closed, unerring, until he was six inches from the Doctor, five inches, two inches, until his face and his squirming eyelids were barely an inch away. He carried the scent of coffee and disinfectant.

'It's good to see you again,' said Akalu.

'I like your new eyes,' said the Doctor, gesturing around at the security cameras. 'Sam's heroic rescue must have given OBFSC quite a scare.'

Akalu didn't react. 'I've been waiting for you, of course. Are you all right? Not hurt? Not damaged?'

'To whom am I speaking?' said the Doctor, back pressed to the icy wall.

'All these minds in the company,' said Akalu. He smiled, broad white teeth. 'I'm not just touching them, I'm *inside* them. And they're inside me. All the layers of thoughts and motivations, I can peel them back one by one.'

'So you're still aware of yourself,' said the Doctor. 'You're still Dr Akalu. Not just the ubernet. Don't give yourself up to it.'

Akalu's head tilted back, like that of a man in prayer. His fingers touched the Doctor's shoulders. 'This is a godsend. Don't you see? I don't have to guess any more. No more stumbling in the dark trying to find the source of someone's pain – I can see it, I can *know*. And with the slightest *push* –' his face contorted – 'I can fix them. Put them back the way they should be.'

He smiled, pure joy. 'It's so easy. So easy to make a difference now…'

'Is it? Do you really know what you're doing?' The ubernet was buzzing in the Doctor's head like a box of bees. 'You've got the power, but do you have the skill to meddle directly in people's brains? It's like doing surgery with gardening tools.'

Akalu's voice sank to a reverent whisper. 'Is this what it's like for you? Is this the world you live in all the time? With everyone open to you? Where your people can share so much of the minds around them...'

'No,' said the Doctor. 'Your precious new ability is powered by an interrogation tool.' He looked up, straight into one of the camereyes. 'A torture device!'

Akalu was so wide open that the Doctor could see the next thought gathering before he ever gave it voice. 'And I can know you,' he said.

'I'm not entirely fond of being known,' said the Doctor.

'With the slightest *push*.'

Akalu's eyes snapped open.

Half a dozen I had been left behind to guard Savar's eyes and the mind probe. They stood in a semicircle in the dim light of the artefact room, silent and still. Perhaps they were watching the hot blue light pushing from the probe into the eyes, discerning chaotic patterns in the beam.

An alarm sounded, a shriek from nowhere. The I were roused, eyes swivelling, the planes of glass in their carapaces pulsing in and out. A light over the door stabbed red flashes into the room.

Thirty seconds later, while the I were still considering their response, the room began to fill with a fire-suppressant gas. The aliens scurried.

One extended a long blue probe from somewhere inside its complex face. The tip of the probe entered the door controls and instantly the heavy door slid aside. It closed behind the I as they chittered into the corridor.

The door locked and then the controls fused, blown up by a directed charge. There was a loud whirring as the ventilation pumps cycled, removing the suppressant gas and replenishing the room's supply of air.

There was a moment of silence, broken only by the low hum of the mind probe's beam.

Then a panel in the room's ceiling clattered loose and Sam Jones dropped into the room, landing in a crouch.

'Are we secure?' she said.

It took a moment for DOCTOR's voice to catch up, piped through a desk terminal. 'The lock's fused and the I are having a little game of hide-and-seek with some uncooperative doors.'

'I love it when a plan comes together,' grinned Sam.

'You've had a lot of practice at organising this sort of thing, haven't you?' asked DOCTOR as she sat at the terminal.

'Not nearly enough,' said Sam, pulling on the eye-set. 'Just like old times. Are we ready to go?'

'I've created some protective protocols to soften the impact,' said DOCTOR. 'But this is going to be a rough ride. For both of us. Try not to get distracted, all right?'

'For definite,' said Sam.

She blinked into the eye-set. The IXNet gateway looked the way it always did, user-friendly and corporate neat. You'd never guess there was a raging newborn cybernetic gestalt behind it.

'Ready?' said DOCTOR.

'Yep.'

Sam selected the gateway. DOCTOR prised it open, protesting, and Sam slipped into the ubernet.

It kicked her in the hindbrain.

'I think you're taking company spirit a bit too far,' gasped the Doctor.

Akalu's childlike smile was frozen on to his face, his fingers digging into the Doctor's shoulders. His eyes were locked on the Doctor's, unblinking.

It wasn't like the usual front-on psychic assaults, the brute force hammering on the doors of his skull, the pressure inside his head strong enough to burst small blood vessels in the eyes and nose. It wasn't anything like that.

The resonance made sure of that, the correspondence between the mind probe and the Doctor's own psyche. It was as though Akalu's mind was a string, vibrating on a high, fast note, and the Doctor's mind was vibrating in sympathy, faster and faster.

Seeing I to I.

The buzzing made it so hard to think… 'The ubernet is the only thing that can stand up to the I,' said the Doctor. 'You must help me stop them. All of you!'

'Yes. We'll work together,' said Akalu. 'When you're part of us. We want to know what you're really thinking.'

'You know, I'd really just like to sit down for a while,' breathed the Doctor. 'I'd like to have some scones and jam with clotted cream.' He sagged back against the wall. 'This isn't getting us anywhere. Tell me. Whose idea was this?'

'What do you mean?'

'It's Akalu who really wants to see inside my head, isn't it?' said the Doctor. 'You've been trying to puzzle me out for years. This is your initiative. The ubernet has more important things to worry about, after all.'

'I want to help you,' said Akalu. 'I need to understand you.'

'I mean, did you seek anyone's permission before trying to access me? Or did you just set off on your own, without going through the appropriate channels? You're using an awful lot of the ubernet's power. Do you have a mandate? Do you have a consensus?'

Doubt flickered its way across Akalu's intent face. It was a beautiful sight.

'I think you'd better seek the proper authorisation,' said the Doctor. 'Yes, I can hear the forms being downloaded now… This isn't a routine procedure, naturally, you'll need special permission… Now, who's authorised to allow you to attach an uncatalogued alien to the network?'

A sizeable percentage of the ubernet's attention was being diverted to Akalu. In the buzzing, the Doctor could discern the patterns of disagreement and agreement and confusion and the looking up of obscure corporate regulations, as all those minds insisted on having their say on the subject, or any subject that was even tangentially connected.

Whole groups of brains and computer systems started to send out deliberately provocative or nonsense messages, trying to divert the network's attention back to them. Others became locked in message wars, reiterating the same points in a vain hope of convincing the others. Others tried to remind the rest that there was something more important at stake right now, and could everyone please get back to discussing it?

Like the data-umphs, thought the Doctor. Individually stupid, but when you had millions of them working in concert, they could be a million times as stupid. Remarkable.

Naturally, everyone copied their messages to Akalu.

Slowly, the morale facilitator sank to his knees, letting go of the Doctor's arms. The Time Lord caught him, lowered him carefully to the floor.

Akalu curled into a tight knot. 'Dr Akalu,' said the Doctor, 'can you hear me?'

'I C,' he murmured. 'I M I N C.'

The Doctor patted him on the head. That ought to keep him busy for a while.

The ubernet was so big, it was so big and everyone was welcome here, this was the place where everyone knew your name. Of course you were part of it, from the moment you stepped through that gateway you were part of it, you couldn't fight something like that. And anyway, why would you want to? Why would you want to go on fighting?

Because.

Because of the Doctor.

Because he always tried to do the right thing, and it might not be perfect, it might not be pretty but it would be right, the right thing to do. Because he's a hero. Because I love him but not just because of his beautiful eyes. Because I love him because he's a hero. Because he's important. Because someone has to do the right thing.

Because I want to grow up to be him. Because I won't stay in the TARDIS or back on Earth too scared to risk it because when you have a friend like that, a hero like that, it's worth it. Because of him. Because of *me*!

Sam felt herself fall back together, stretched across the landscape like a rubber band, snapping back into place. It was like waking up with a shock.

'Thank goodness!' said DOCTOR. She was floating above the datascape, spinning gently, directionless. 'I thought you'd lost yourself.'

'Sam I am,' she said. Somewhere her body was grinning with delight.

'I've got to go,' said DOCTOR. 'Is it safe to leave you?'

'Yeah.' Sam massaged her face around the eye-set. 'I'll be fine. Go!'

There was a broom cupboard behind the mess hall; you could get to it from the back of one of the storerooms, by removing a prefab wall panel. The panel was still loose from the last time the Doctor had followed this route.

He squeezed between the brooms, trying not to knock any of them over. But judging from the noise in the mess hall, no one would have heard him anyway.

The Doctor leaned against the wall, extending the aerial on the data-transfer module. In desperation for the right component he'd pulled it off the VW and spot-welded it on to the little ball of circuitry. He breathed a sigh of relief as a steady stream of data downloaded itself into the module, making its little lights blink.

He pocketed the module and peeked around the door. The hall was full of prisoners and guards, barricading the main doors with chairs and tables.

He spotted Gamal el-Bayoumi in the crowd, trying to shift a heavy table by himself. The Doctor stepped out of the cupboard and picked up the other end of the table.

El-Bayoumi looked at him in astonishment. 'You came back! You came back here!'

'Er, hello,' said the Doctor. 'Yes, I heard you were having a spot of bother… This isn't going to keep them out,' said the Doctor. They dragged the table over to the pitiful pile of furniture. 'Once they're through the isolated security devices, they'll have that lot out of the way in a moment.'

'We're desperate,' said el-Bayoumi with great dignity. 'What do you suggest?'

'I'm thinking,' said the Doctor.

'Those are the aliens you described, aren't they?' The Doctor nodded. 'One of them attacked you in your cell. Years ago…' El-Bayoumi's voice dropped. 'They have been taking eyes. Prisoners' eyes, and some from the guards and staff.' He looked the Doctor in the face. 'They implanted something in us, didn't they?'

'I'm afraid so,' said the Doctor. 'And now the I – the aliens – are after that technology.'

'We must stop them,' said el-Bayoumi. 'But how?'

The prisoners shouted as the barricade began to collapse. The doors were pushed inward, inexorably, sending chairs and people scattering across the floor. A crowd of I began to push their way into the room.

'*Stop!*'

The Doctor stood in their path, in front of all of the prisoners, holding up a hand.

The I actually stopped, squashed between the piles of furniture, antennae going madly in and out of their heads.

'You know who I am,' said the Doctor. The prisoners had fallen silent, astonished. 'You know what I am. Leave here while you still can. Don't harm anyone any more. Take what you've learned and get off this planet before my people do something unspeakable to your timeline.'

The I's eyes swivelled. They were talking to one another – talking to every I on the planet. Considering what he was saying.

257

'Think about it,' said the Doctor. 'You can't keep me prisoner. There's nothing you can do to resist the Time Lords. Cut your losses and go!'

The I started to shuffle backwards, limbs gyrating. Good grief, was it actually working?

But they stopped, halfway through the door. And then a human figure stepped through, between them, one eye glittering with a contact lens, the other covered with a patch of sticky metal.

'Shoshana,' said the Doctor.

'Well, part of me,' said the young woman. She stepped up to him. 'I'm here to speak for the ubernet.'

'They didn't succeed in breaking in,' said the Doctor. 'I didn't think they would.'

'No, but they certainly gave it a good try.' The Doctor realised that tears were leaking from her remaining eye. 'The ubernet's powerful, Doctor. It's learning how to work with itself, it's learning what it can do. I'm just going to do whatever it wants, say whatever it asks me to.' The Doctor nodded. 'And it has plans for the future,' said Shoshana, sniffling.

'I'll just bet it does,' said the Doctor. He reached into the pouch in his sash. The I started to get jittery. 'Don't worry,' he said, pulling out a white handkerchief and waving it. He handed it to Shoshana.

'Thank you,' she said nasally. 'He's right. You don't need to dissect anyone – we can trade technologies.'

'You're going to work *with* them?' said the Doctor.

'The Time Lords don't need to ever know you were here.' She blew her nose. 'Take him and go.'

'What?' said el-Bayoumi, somewhere behind him. The Doctor waved at him for silence.

'You're worth more than all of this lot put together,' said Shoshana. 'The I are willing to leave if we let them have you.' She put the handkerchief in her pocket. 'Don't make any heroic speeches. You don't have any choice in the matter.'

The Doctor folded his hands behind his back. 'All right,' he said after a moment. 'I understand. Shoshana – if you ever see Sam again, will you tell her something for me?'

Shoshana nodded.

The Doctor hesitated. 'Tell her... don't forget to feed the butterflies.'

'No!' said Sam.

She was distantly aware of her body as she fell across the ubernet's burning landscapes. She was aware of her mouth starting to move, to form the syllable, so very far away.

She had watched the Doctor's confrontation with Shoshana – with the ubernet – through a window that seemed to travel along beside her. DOCTOR was directing her movement through the datascape. It was like a roller-coaster that you travelled lying down, head first.

DOCTOR's guidance routine was merciless with corners, with dodging possible danger, flying her helpless 'body' around sharp bends. There was no sensation of movement, just the shapes and colours turning violently around her. She felt the way she had the time she'd drunk that whole can of cider. A million miles away, her body was getting seasick.

But now the I had the Doctor. They were *harvesting* him. 'We can't let them take him!'

But there was no one to talk to any more; DOCTOR was off somewhere, doing his bit of the plan. 'Don't let yourself get distracted!' she ordered herself sharply. 'We've got to find the centre!'

But did this place even have a centre? Didn't it just stretch off to infinity in every direction... would she keep travelling for ever... for ever?

Come on, stay focused! The 'centre' was the gateway forged by the mind probe when the I turned the power up. Armed with DOCTOR's improvised datakeys, she could open it and then shut it down.

Concentrate! He's depending on you!

Keep going... gotta keep going...

The Doctor was surrounded by I, two guards in front, two guards behind. They marched him through the ship's corridors – through the breathing pathways of the cocoon.

'The ubernet won't work with you, you know,' he told them. 'It'll be watching for its chance to take over the business.' At least, I hope so. Because I have the feeling that an alliance between the two of you could be a rather dangerous thing.

I just need thirty seconds, he thought. Just look the other way for thirty seconds. There's only one thing left I have to do and then you can cut me into pieces.

They paused at a junction, the I's eyes swivelling. They were communicating, he realised, however they did it. 'I hope you're thinking about what I'm saying,' he said.

A niche opened up in the wall next to him. He stepped sideways into it and the wall sealed up behind him.

'Tidy,' he said. He was standing in a tiny room, loud banging noises coming through the wall that had opened to let him in. He pushed his hands against the opposite wall. 'Can you hear me?'

After a moment that wall parted as well, let him slip through, ducking down. He was in a narrow tube. A tracheole, perhaps four feet high.

He tried to back out of the tube, but the wall had sealed up behind him. He turned awkwardly in the tiny space, hands pushing against the wall as though he could pull the entrance open again. But the metal was seamless.

Behind him, the tube stretched into the distance. He couldn't seem to catch his breath – was there any air in here? His hearts were pounding – was the ship trying to kill him?

Stop it. Get on with it. He sat cross-legged, leaned on the wall. 'I need one of those nerves,' he said. After a moment, one of the thick, black, metallic cords pushed its way loose of the wall stuff. 'Thank you,' he said. 'This might hurt a bit. I hope not.'

He reached into the pouch in his sash, took out the data-transfer module and clipped it on to the nerve. The universal adapter went berserk, cycling through dozens of shapes and formats. 'Come on, come on!' insisted the Doctor.

At last it produced a series of black fibres and sank them into the nerve. The module's lights began to flicker happily. Opening up a little gate in cyberspace, ready for business.

'All right,' said the Doctor. He gently pushed the nerve back into the wall. The coppery stuff sealed up behind it, leaving only the transfer module's extended antenna poking out. 'Yes. Now, if I can just keep them occupied for a little while...'

Sam's body was grinning broadly, frozen like an idiot at the terminal.

Deep inside the ubernet, she was spinning round and round a new gateway. It was rough, very new, covered in little bumps and jagged bits, bits of software that hadn't been integrated properly.

The searing blue light of the mind probe shot through the centre of the gateway. It was all being interpreted by the eye-set for her benefit, she knew, just a more elaborate version of the datascape she had plodded through, all those long boring days at INC.

She was right at the core of the INC set-up. All she had to do was dislodge one of those keystone programs and the whole thingummy would collapse.

Sam grinned. There was something she wanted to try first.

There were I everywhere, searching for him. A pair turned into an empty corridor even as he dropped down into it. He ran, the I racing after him, turned down another passageway, nearly ran into two more I, leapt down a third passageway and squeezed himself into another tracheole.

He found himself trying to back out of the tiny space, squeezed his eyes shut and dragged himself forward, flinching when his shoulders rubbed against the walls.

He crawled along the tube as fast as he could, the smooth metal curving around him as he squeezed through. He chose a branching passage at random. It was narrowing rapidly – he started to back out. The I couldn't get into the smaller tubes. Could they?

He stuck his head out, only to see the tracheole widening, the walls stretching. At the end of the tube, a couple of I were using some sort of device to push the walls apart. Their heads and shoulders, if that was the right terminology, were already pushing through.

He fought down the urge to rush *towards* them and into the open air. He backed up into the narrow tube. Maybe it would take them a while to get it open; maybe they wouldn't be able to open it all the way.

Another tube opened in the wall beside him. 'Bless you,' he breathed, crawling into it.

The tube stopped only a few feet ahead. He tried to back up, but it quietly closed behind him. No way to move, nowhere to go, the walls pushing against his shoulders, the weight of the ceiling crushing down. The ship was trying to hide him, to protect him.

'Not this!' His voice bounced back at him, full of panic. He pressed his hands against the wall, frantic for a doorway, frantic to make himself understood. 'Open up! You've got to open up!'

But the tiny space stayed just as tiny. He curled up, panting, lying on the floor, back against one of the curved walls. He couldn't stretch his arms straight out without touching the opposite side. Was any air getting in? What if the room started to shrink?

It was starting to happen. He could feel it wherever the ship touched him, even through the cloth of the jellaba. It made his hair tingle, it made the miniature room rock and spin.

The control systems were breaking down and the great sleeping mind in the centre of the ship was starting to come out of its dream, its thoughts lemon-sharp and angry as it worked its way free of what the I had done to it.

It was all around him. The walls were alive with its thawing power. It was like being tickled on the inside. It was intoxicating. He couldn't get away from it, there was no way out. He threw his arms over his face and moaned.

Don't fight it – don't try to fight it – don't struggle, stay still, stay quiet, stay hidden –

* * *

Sam came back to herself a piece at a time. Hands first. Then her general sense of where all the different parts of her body were.

She was lying on the floor. The eyepiece was dangling from the terminal, hanging over the edge of the desk.

She pulled herself up groggily. She had pins and needles all over her body. How long had she sat in that chair? How long had she been lying here on the floor?

The door gave an awful, wrenching sound. Sam leapt out of the chair, grabbing the desk to steady herself.

The ubernet, she thought. It had worked out what they were up to. Operating an emergency override to let the I in. Too late, monsters, far too late. I hope.

Sam wobbled across the room. The eyes of Savar stared at her pitifully from inside their jar. She wondered what it would be like to be unable to close your eyes for hundreds of years.

There were sparks and the sound of metal tearing. The door slid open, a few inches, then a few feet. I started pouring into the room.

Gonna die now, thought Sam. Doesn't matter. She grabbed the mind probe.

The I milled, unsure of what to do. A few of them advanced on her.

'This is what it's all been about, isn't it?' she shouted at them. Her voice was hoarse, but it boomed and echoed in the chamber. 'This *thing*.'

'*You outside people I trade*,' said one of the I. '*I won't kill you. Give I the machine.*'

There was a way out.

He'd spent so much of his life digging his way out of prisons, instead of focussing on how to survive staying in them. In all those years of experience, he knew he'd come across all sorts of ways to clear his mind. Slow breathing, Tibetan meditation, reaching his still point, reciting his logorithm tables. All those memories had never seemed so important to him in this life, but he *had* them. He could handle this. He wasn't just stuck in this out of control moment; wherever he was in prison, there was a lifetime locked up with him.

He let a slow moment pass.

The Doctor was breathing gently, knees drawn up to his chest, head cradled on his arms. His eyes were open, watching the opposite wall of his cocoon. Calm at last.

The wall began to buckle inward. A moment later, a pointed, dark object was pushing out of the flexible metal, like the tip of a great beak.

The thing worked its way in further, shoving the ship stuff aside. Now it looked more like a giant pair of tweezers. The jaws started to open, tearing the stuff of the wall, slowly ripping a huge hole in it. The Doctor watched, calmly.

They stopped, five feet apart.

Akalu was crouching in a corridor, staring in at him. An I held the forceps. It twisted them, widening the hole.

'Hello,' said the Doctor.

'Hello,' said Akalu. 'It's time we got to know you better.'

'Here's what I think of this!' yelled Sam.

She wrenched the mind probe off its stand and broke it over her knee.

Akalu was pulling the Doctor out of the cocoon when something rose up even louder and stronger than the buzzing, something vast and panicked as it collapsed in on itself.

Akalu's mouth opened and a series of clicks came out, like an old-fashioned phone exchange trying to connect a call. A moment later he dropped the Doctor's arms, staggering back into the corridor.

The I ran off at top speed, its limbs gyrating, still holding the huge forceps. Akalu didn't notice, reeling against the wall.

The Doctor lay where he'd been dropped, half in and half out of the tracheole.

'Thanks,' he told the floor. 'I think I'd better leave now.'

A door obligingly opened. The Doctor picked himself up. Then he picked Akalu up and started trying to find his way out of the ship.

* * *

Sam let the pieces of the probe fall from her hands. She drew herself up to her full height, wishing there was a bit more of it, and stood her ground as the aliens reached for her with their hands made of angles.

The I were too busy evacuating to try to stop the Doctor. He dragged Akalu to the airlock, where I were sliding down the poles in their dozens. Hundreds? With an effort, the Doctor slung Akalu over his shoulder, grabbed one of the poles and jumped into the darkness.

They sailed down to the ground in seconds. He got out of the way before an I could land on his head.

Akalu was awake, dazed. 'We've got to get into the building,' said the Doctor. 'Come on.' He slung the man's arm over his shoulders and headed for the main doors.

The I were cramming into the prison in an orderly panic. The Doctor glanced back – they must have finished evacuating, no more I were coming down the poles. The ship was rocking in the air, vast, swooping movements, like a building having convulsions. The poles started to fall away.

The ship punched upward suddenly into the sky, hundreds of metres higher. 'Take shelter!' the Doctor shouted, dragging Akalu into the mess hall. The prisoners and guards started diving under tables.

There was an almighty peal of thunder, the sound of metal tearing, being ripped and shoved aside. A few seconds later there was a sound like hail falling all over the building. But the ceiling held, none of the walls collapsed.

The fragments must have been small, thought the Doctor. He had been expecting the entire cocoon to come plummeting down on them.

He rolled Akalu into the recovery position, put down the data-transfer module and raised its antenna, then ran outside to take a look.

Everything was covered in chunks of tinclavic. The cocoon had crumbled like a chocolate Easter egg.

High above he could see the alien, its vast triangular body a mass of complex joints, its brassy skin catching the sunlight. It was a wirework butterfly, the delicate skeleton of its wings just barely extended, casting dancing shadows across the whole of OBFSC as it circled ever higher and further away.

The creature was pushing upward, out of the atmosphere. The Doctor knew it couldn't really unfurl its delicate wings here. No, the solar sails, a few molecules thick, would have to wait for vacuum before they could be spread. Then it would be home again, back to the creatures' breeding grounds.

It was one of the dark sailors, the beings that lived in the empty spaces between stars. Life could find a way anywhere, adapt itself to anything, from a boiling sulphur spring to hard radiation and nothingness. He had encountered half a dozen space-dwelling species. Goodness knew how many of them there were out there, whole ecologies of the blackness.

Nice to set a prison free, he thought, and went inside to deal with the I.

The I had frozen in position, inches from her. Sam had wriggled away along the wall and made it halfway to the exit before she even thought about why.

'DOCTOR?' she said as she tried to squeeze past the one blocking the door, 'I could really use a sitrep right about now.'

'Wait a moment,' said DOCTOR. 'Wait a moment.' Sam waited a moment. 'Wait a moment,' said the AI again. 'Sorry, I was somewhere else.'

One of the I started wandering around, bumping into things. The one in the door sort of sat down and starting waving its limbs.

'Eep,' said the I. 'Eep eep.'

'Ah,' said Sam. She clambered over the I as well as she could and started navigating her way down the corridor, hurrying towards the airstrip and an autopiloted 'thopter to Bainbridge. 'You got on all right with the ship, then?'

'I got out of the I's onboard computers with microseconds to spare,' said DOCTOR. 'They've been destroyed, along with the control systems the I built into the ship. Including whatever they were using to communicate with the rest of the gestalt.'

'Eep,' said an I.

'You mean they're just bugs? Just bugs, now?' Sam waved her hand in front of the nearest prone I's face. Its eyes swivelled in different directions.

'In essence,' said DOCTOR. 'They don't pose a threat.'

'Right,' said Sam. 'How's the Doctor doing?'

'Shall we go and see?'

Thirty minutes later Sam stepped out of an INC 'thopter on to the roof of OBFSC. The place was as much of a mess as it had looked from the air.

She ran down the stairs and stopped on the first floor she came to, astonished.

The prisoners and guards were working together, herding the I into the cells. Several cells were already stuffed with the aliens, their limbs and antennae poking out through the bars. 'Eep,' they said.

She grabbed the nearest prisoner. 'Do you know where the Doctor is?'

'Mess hall,' said the man. 'You want an alien? We've got lots.'

Sam grinned. 'I've just eaten.' She went downstairs.

She walked into the mess hall and nearly ploughed into Akalu. He was sitting curled up against the wall, rocking very slightly back and forth. 'All gone,' she heard him muttering to himself. 'All gone, all gone.' There were tears trickling from his unimplanted eye.

The Doctor was crouched beside him, holding on to him a bit awkwardly and giving him a few soothing mumbles. 'What do you think?' she heard him say.

Sam opened her mouth, but DOCTOR said, 'There's no brain injury. Actually, we caused surprisingly little damage. I think only twenty-seven employees were killed.'

The Doctor grimaced. 'We should have done better than that.'

'Thank goodness for autopilots,' said DOCTOR. 'We'd have had 'thopters raining down out of the skies. Your companion's here.'

The Doctor looked up.

'Hi,' said Sam.

'Sam!' The Doctor jumped up and grabbed her and spun her around.

She started laughing. 'We made it! We saved the world!'

He messed up her hair, grinning. 'Back together again,' he said.

Sam managed to keep the smile on her face. We'll talk about that later, she thought. 'You realise I've got no idea how to feed butterflies.'

'Yes,' said the Doctor. 'Well, it sounded like the thing to say.'

'So what's the score?'

'The I are harmless in this state,' said the Doctor. 'They've lost all their cleverness; they can't act together any more.'

Sam looked down at Akalu. 'And what about him?'

'He thought he was going to make everyone sane,' said the Doctor. 'We can't help him. Best to leave him to the professionals.'

'What're we, then?' said Sam, putting her arm around his waist.

He draped an arm across her shoulders. 'Talented amateurs,' he said.

Chapter Seventeen
Long Last Look

'He's on his way already! He's getting out of the car now.' Paul's voice crackled from the phone-set. Sam tightened up and pressed herself back into her hiding place behind the tents, motioning to the others.

She'd planned all this weeks ago, got everything into place, gone over every detail in her mind, and now it all came down to a matter of timing.

'Right,' she whispered to the others behind her. 'Six. Five. Four.' The figure had detached itself from the darkness of the car park and was walking straight towards them. The lights of the INC gates glimmered behind him. She gave a final glance backward and counted off the remaining seconds silently on her fingers.

The man walked unsuspecting past them into the clearing.

'Surprise!' they all shouted.

Brian froze in disbelief. On Sam's cue, the clearing between the tents filled with dozens of Livingspace volunteers cheering and applauding him. With a fwump, two of the younger kids unfurled the HAPPY BIRTHDAY, BRIAN banner behind the bonfire, Orin presented him with a cake with far too many candles on it and the Doctor started tooting 'Happy Birthday' on a kazoo.

Sam grinned at Brian until he finally picked his jaw up enough to form words.

'Oh, man,' he laughed. 'I shoulda known there was something up when you sent me on the beer run.'

A bunch of volunteers had started a drumming circle, with chanted vocals and improvised instruments, drowning out the recorded music. So far she'd counted eighteen verses' worth of folk lyrics which had accreted themselves to *that* Chumbawamba song over the centuries.

They'd invited every Livingspace volunteer on the database, past and present, and there must have been a hundred and fifty people at the party in the desert. Even Sara and Ari had been recruited for the evening, and were swapping horror stories and jokes with Leah and Deeb at the edge of the noise.

Sam headed for the punchbowl. 'So how'd you get hooked up with Sam in the first place?' Orin was asking the Doctor.

'Oh, it was one of my usual weird, fantastic adventures full of improbable illogical events...' The Doctor shrugged. 'It wasn't me who guided the TARDIS to her, come to think of it. It was all an astounding coincidence that I should arrive at precisely the moment in time and space where Sam needed rescuing, wasn't it?'

'Yeah, wasn't it,' echoed Sam. Wherever he was going with that idea, she didn't like the sound of it.

Maybe someone out there had figured it was a good idea to pair him up with a nice non-threatening little kid. Someone who'd keep him busy and distracted by getting into trouble and needing to be rescued. Someone they'd arranged to be the perfect safe companion for him.

Yeah, the dark-haired Sam was muttering somewhere, because *I* wouldn't have been too scared to shag him.

Ha. I'm over the embarrassing teenage crush, all right? Though on the other hand, thought blonde Sam with an evil smile, if the opportunity ever did present itself, I wouldn't throw the Doctor out of bed for eating crackers...

If there was some big, hidden plan involving her, it had gone flying off the rails the moment she'd run away from him. If she went back with him now, if he teamed up with the person she had become, there was no way anyone could dismiss them as non-threatening. Either of them.

If she went back with him.

* * *

'Shoshana! I didn't think you were going to make it!'

Shoshana had been staring into the fire for five minutes, a vague frown on her face, as though she couldn't quite remember what it was. Now she blinked and looked up at Sam from the folding chair. 'Neither did I, for a while there.' She shook hands with Sam solemnly.

'So, how are you?' said Sam, perching on the edge of a table.

'The corporation bought me a new eye, and they're paying for my therapy.'

'Yes, I know.' Sam folded her arms, smiling knowingly. 'I hope it's helping.'

'I'll live.' The eye was a good one too, though sometimes when the flames jumped just the right way you could see the serial number in the iris. 'Actually, a lot of things seem to have changed at INC,' said Shoshana. 'The new version of the employee handbook is quite a departure.'

'Oh yes, the media have been singing the praises of the kinder, gentler INC,' said Sam. 'No more private prisons, changes to the health plan so that transplantees own their new organs, environmental quality indexes... The new policies must be generating a lot of new business.'

'They are,' said Shoshana, sounding surprised. 'The Lacaillan government has started dealing with us for the first time in a decade.'

'One good turn deserves another.'

'You know, it's not hard to work out where all of those new policies really came from,' said Shoshana.

'Oh, I was only in the network for a few minutes of real time,' said Sam modestly. 'Barely long enough to make a few changes here, a couple of alterations there. Corporate inertia does the rest. No one's going to think enough about the policies to question 'em. Not for a while anyway.'

'The safety recall of the eye implants?'

Sam nodded. 'Though I think INC would have done that without any prompting from me. From now on, it's just eye-sets, safe and non-invasive.'

Shoshana nodded vaguely, as though they were discussing the

271

weather rather than the transformation of an interplanetary business.

'I don't suppose there's any chance of us just calling the debt even…' said Sam.

Shoshana made a wry face. 'Sorry, don't think so – I still owe the bank most of that last month's rent.'

Sam plucked an I-card from her pocket. 'You've got what INC owes you. Here's what I owe you.'

Shoshana's hand closed around the I-card. She stared at it for a while quietly.

'Once I'm well enough,' she said, 'I'm going to go back to my ordinary job and my ordinary life, and I'm never going to think about any of this again.'

'Mmm. Sensible,' said Sam.

'What about you?' said Shoshana. 'What are you going to do?'

Sam looked across the fire. The Doctor was barefoot in the midst of the dance, hair flying in all directions, oblivious to everything except how much fun he was having. At least someone had taken the kazoo away.

'I don't know,' she said.

An hour later she looked up and saw that the Doctor had disappeared from the circle. She made her excuses and ran after him.

'Running out early?' she asked, catching up with him somewhere in the trees.

'I'm afraid it's rather a habit of mine,' he said.

'I know. They've been having a sweepstake on how long before we ducked out together.' She tossed him a wink. 'I think they're expecting to hear strange wheezing groaning sounds coming from the nearby bushes.'

He grinned. Part of the fun of making comments like that to him was that she could never be sure if he'd got the joke or not. 'I'm just popping off for a moment. I'll be right back. There are a few details I've got to take care of.' From his pouch he pulled out a small glass cylinder with two round objects floating in a jellied liquid. She didn't especially

272

want to see it any more clearly.'It's a bit of a personal matter.'

She looked at him in the faint bonfire light. 'So.You're going home.'

'Well, yes,' he admitted. 'For a bit.'

'And you weren't taking me with you.'

'No, I wasn't,' he said smoothly. 'There are always complications each time I return home.You're better off out of it –'

'Not ready for me to meet your mum and dad yet, eh?'

He looked pained. 'Please.'

'You really will be back, right?'

'Sam, have I ever lied to you?'

She grinned. 'If you're that good at lying, how would I ever know?'

'Mm. Good point,' he said, and waved goodbye as he hurried off. Sam watched him go and went back to the light of the circle.

The Doctor weighed the black data-transfer module in his hand and walked up to the INC gates. A meaningful stare into the security camera was enough to get the gate to whirr open and he proceeded unaccosted into the centre's mail room.

He hooked up the transport module to the nearest terminal, said, 'All right, time to go,' loud enough for the monitoring microphones to hear and smiled in satisfaction as the downloading light on the black box blinked on.

While he waited, he dug through the stack of incoming packages. There it was, just as DOCTOR had promised – the envelope containing his original sonic screwdriver, which DOCTOR had arranged for them to ship here for research purposes. He twirled the metal rod between his fingers and flipped it into his pocket; after all the trouble INC had got into with just one Gallifreyan artefact, it really wouldn't do for them to get their hands on another one.

When the download light blinked out, he pocketed the data cube as well and headed back to where the TARDIS was parked, in the rubbish tip just downriver. Whistling jauntily as he entered the console room, he ambled over to the cobbled-together terminal, hooked up the transport module and started the upload.

Inside he found just a single data-umph, wittering around aimlessly and bouncing off the edges of the empty memory space. The Doctor stared at it in shock. His hands grabbed at his own hair, as if to keep his head from falling off.

There was a brief text file attached to the umph. With flurrying fingers the Doctor brought the file up on his screen.

Dear Doctor

My apologies for the bit of sleight of hand, but then again I can't see you objecting too much to something like that. After all, if you were given the choice between tagging along in someone else's computer system and going off to see the world for yourself – well, we know which one you'd choose, don't we?

In the time this misdirection has bought me, I've managed to elude INC's security systems and transfer myself to a new system Somewhere Out There. I met a rather nice virtual girl called FLORANCE a while back – we're going to do some travelling. There's all of human dataspace waiting for us, and alien systems once we figure out how to make the transfer... I can do absolutely anything I like, and I fully intend to.

So long as you don't interfere with me... Oh, how shall I put this? Don't bother me, or I'll tell. I don't know anywhere near everything about you, but I do know enough to be able to embarrass you thoroughly if I so desire. I don't think you'd want historians finding out about that little encounter with Amelia Earhart, after all.

So fare thee well. Go on saving the world, or whatever it is you really do – I'll find something for myself to do. You've unleashed me on the universe – now it's time for life to find its own way.

Yours, truly,
the DOCTOR

The Doctor fell back in his chair and just stared at the monitor, not quite sure whether to laugh or panic.

She went walking with Paul, down by the bend in the river where the water trapped the moon. They stood there for a while, loosely holding hands, idly trying to pick out which bits of the glowing water were the moonlight now and which were the reflected sodium lights from the new INC complex downstream.

'How'd the interview go?' she said, after a while.

'Fine, very well indeed,' he said. 'I start at Tikkun Olam's offices next Monday. The nine-to-five grind'll certainly make a change from lying in front of bulldozers.'

Sam leaned on his arm and they were silent for a while longer.

Finally he turned and looked sincerely down at her, the moonlight getting tangled in his hair. 'Listen, Sam,' he said. 'If you don't get in that time machine with him, you're going to regret it. Maybe not today, maybe not tomorrow, but soon, and for the rest of your life...'

She cut him off with a grin. 'It's all right. Don't worry about it. We're heading off tomorrow morning.'

His face flickered through several emotions. The last one to hit him left him with his face buried in his hands and chuckling. 'Oh, bloody hell. And here I went to all that trouble learning the speech...'

'I don't mind.' She stood a little bit on tiptoes to give him a momentary kiss and then a much more substantial hug. 'I don't know if I'm staying with him for good yet. There's an awful lot that needs doing right here.'

'So I might see you at work on Monday.'

'Dunno. Maybe.' She grinned. 'But I've made sure Rachel's covered for next month's rent, just in case.'

'Don't worry,' said Paul. 'For now, you can leave this place in our culpable hands.'

The cat was waiting for him outside the TARDIS. He settled down on a battered old chair and studied the animal – taking in its commonplace markings, the chewed-up ear.

'It is you, isn't it?' said the Doctor. He gave the cat a quiet smile and reached down to pick it up. The cat gave him a half-hearted yowl before settling upright in his arms.

All the other humans were still carrying on around the fire, or returning in ones, twos or threes to their tents. He hadn't gone back to the circle; instead he'd stayed here to sit under the moon and allow himself the luxury of feeling pleasantly tired.

He settled back in the chair and started stroking the cat gently. After a few half-hearted wiggles in his grasp it seemed to resign itself to being petted, and he felt its muscles begin to relax. 'I wanted to thank you for keeping an eye on Sam,' he murmured. 'Giving her something to care about when she didn't know what she had to hold on to.' His hand came to rest on her side, as his voice constricted to a whisper. 'I really could have used a visit or two in the meantime as well, though.'

The cat squirmed. He realised he'd tightened up and was hugging it to him too fiercely. With a slow release of breath he made his fingers loosen, and the cat glared at him reproachfully before settling back down.

'It doesn't seem quite fair, you know that? She gets a cat and I get a nasty bug-eyed monster trying to destroy my mind.' He spoke to the cat as if to an old friend. 'Ah, well, I suppose we each get the kind of life we give ourselves.'

He met the cat's oval-pupilled eyes. They were alive and unreachable, as alien to him as he was to a human. For millions of years his race had wielded ultimate power, yet they still couldn't figure out what went through the mind of a cat.

'You know,' he told the cat, 'I think you were there all along, watching me as well. And I just never bothered to look for you. Mm?' He paused, touching his memories of a rose-petal woman with the scent of baking bread, and smiled gently. 'That's the way Life works, doesn't she?'

The cat made no response. It twisted in his lap to right itself, then leapt to the ground in one four-legged motion and set off towards the underbrush, tail held high. His smile turned into a grin as he got up and headed back to join the circle by the fire.

He caught just a glimpse of alien eyes, shining in the night, before she was gone.

The TARDIS wasn't there when Sam got to the rubbish tip. It was a fenced-in bit of desert behind the INC complex, filled with all sorts of machinery and junk – dead datatablets, dusty desks, chunks of 'thopters. The battered sofas and scrap metal swept aside as if the space had been saved just for a police box. She pulled up an office chair and leaned back, waiting, until finally she heard the cosmic sneezing fit that announced the TARDIS's arrival.

She grinned. You really could find the most amazing things in junkyards.

The Doctor emerged, smiling when he spotted her. He had on – oh wow, he was wearing that outfit again. The one he'd lost in the prison.

'Hang about,' Sam managed. 'How'd you get –'

'I made a little side trip,' said the Doctor. 'There's a tailor in Neo-Sydney who was more than happy to make these up for me.'

Now she was close enough to touch, she could see it wasn't the same – every last detail of the design was right, but so much more care and workmanship had gone into this outfit than the original.

She ran her hands over the fabric: that coat was real velvet, not costume-shop velveteen, and the cravat had the softness of real silk. Instead of the hasty costume stitching, which frayed badly even under normal wear (much less Doctor wear), these seams were reinforced, built to last. These clothes were meant to be worn for real.

She looked up at him, still grinning. Only he would get an expensive tailor to use authentic period materials to re-create a fancy-dress outfit. And all so it could be worn by a man who wasn't from the same century, or even the same planet.

And she had to admit he looked too hot for words in it.

The Doctor took out his key – actually, it was her key, the one she'd been wearing when she'd arrived. More than three years ago. He unlocked the TARDIS doors.

He turned back to her, catching her in that blue-green stare.

'Sam,' he said hesitantly. 'While I was looking for you, the TARDIS put me in touch with my granddaughter, Susan. I think the old girl might have been trying to tell me something...' His eyes kept flicking around, not quite able to meet Sam's. 'I hadn't seen Susan for years. She'd gone on with her life, found a place of her own. And...'

She couldn't believe it, he was actually lost for words.

'What I'm saying is, if you don't want to –'

She cut him off, folding her arms. 'Give me one good reason to come with you,' she said.

'Er...' said the Doctor.

'I'm serious,' said Sam. 'There's an awful lot that needs doing here. Fragile ecologies in danger. People without jobs or food. Alien immigrants denied their rights. There aren't any Daleks or vampires or mad scientists, I admit. Just ordinary people facing ordinary problems. In fact,' she said, poking him in the chest with a finger, 'why don't you stay and just do it all here?'

The Doctor thought about it for a moment. 'Because I've got one of these,' he said. He reached out and patted the TARDIS.

Sam beamed. 'Right answer,' she said.

'It is?' said the Doctor.

''Course. Look, what matters in my life is making a difference, right, and with you I can make a bigger difference than most people could dream of.' Sam patted the TARDIS, feeling its soft vibration, like a plane ready for take-off. 'Our lives are different to anybody elses. Nobody else in the universe can do what we do. I'd be out of my head to pass up another chance at it.'

She grabbed him by the shoulders, leaning him forcibly down to her eye level, and held his face between her hands. She pulled his face so close to hers that they almost bumped noses, just so he couldn't possibly miss the point.

And she planted an almighty smooch on his lips.

When she broke away, she noted with some satisfaction that she felt absolutely no compulsion to do it again. Not that she'd mind, though…

'I know who I am, right. And I know what I want to do.' She could see her eyes shining in his own. 'Let's go.'

Authors' Note

The authors would like to present:

A barrel of chocolate sauce to the PMEB, for help with this book, and especially with *Vampire Science!* And a cherry on top for whoever came up with the boxer shorts.

Three cups of coffee and three cans of Coke to the read-through crew, without whom this book would have been far longer and sillier: Don Gillikin, Cary Gordon, Rachel Jacobs, Richard Kelly, Sadron Lampert, Greg McElhatton, Marsha Twitty, Jeff Weiss. Plus (via the magic of e-mail) Robert Smith, who knows far too much about Chaos.

And our sincere thanks to:
Steve Cole, Mike Collier, Paul Leonard and Lance Parkin.
Jennifer Tifft, the Doctor's tailor.

Special thanks to Special K.